Green River

The Deception Runs Deep

P G Robertson

Copyright © 2024 by P G Robertson

All rights reserved.

No portion of this book may be reproduced in any form without written permission from the publisher or author, except as permitted by U.S. copyright law.

Contents

Dedication	VI
Prologue	VII
1. No Silver Lining	1
2. Ambushed	6
3. Challenging Times	12
4. Deep Waters	16
5. Wise Counsel	21
6. A Change of Plan	28
7. In Country	35
8. On Safari	40
9. Deployment	46
10. Gifted	51
11. A Waiting Game	57
12. Plan of Attack	64
13. Setting the Scene	68
14. The Hearing	73
15. No Victory Dance	79
16. Making Waves	83
17. Making Tracks	88

18.	Whisked Away	93
19.	Providence	98
20.	Not So Clever	107
21.	Gastronomical	111
22.	Shoulder to Shoulder	115
23.	Heaven and Earth	119
24.	Face to Face	125
25.	Half the Job	129
26.	Bouldering	135
27.	Surprise Packet	142
28.	Stranger than Fiction	150
29.	Back in the Saddle	155
30.	Operation Scumbag	161
31.	Moonlighting	170
32.	One Step Sideways	175
33.	Mental Health	182
34.	Power Shifts	188
35.	Distractions	196
36.	Sprung	201
37.	Rules of Life	206
38.	Moving Day	209
39.	Worms	216
40.	Easy Jobs	221
41.	Consequential	226
42.	The Early Bird	234

43.	Carjack	240
44.	Covering All Bases	245
45.	Sick Puppies	252
46.	Flight Risks	257
47.	Jocks Rule	261
48.	Final Push	268
49.	Mopping Up	274
50.	Football	287
	Epilogue	292
	Coming Soon...	296
	Also By	299
	Author's Note	301
	So Many to Thank	302
	Glossary and Surfing Terminology	303

This book is dedicated to my cousin Ian, an institution within our family who was much-loved. He was a kind, intelligent, and insightful man, blessed with a witty and bone-dry sense of humour. Ian also loved a good paperback novel and was a big fan of The Detective Ange Watson thrillers. Sadly, I was unable to publish Green River in time, as I know he would have loved it.

Prologue

The man glanced furtively over his shoulder as he walked towards a car parked on the street. He had faced up to his obsession sometime ago. Like any addict, he had little or no control over the urgings that came to steal his soul away, arriving unbidden and out of nowhere in particular, starting as the tiniest of tiny itches, deep within his core. He would love to say that there was a specific part of his body that was the problem, the source of this itch, but his weakness was a complete surrender of body and mind. Once started, the itch would spread like wildfire, like an insidious infection. However, this disease was different. His illness, far from making him weak and incapacitated, thrilled and energised him like nothing else could, or ever had.

By the time he had slipped behind the wheel of his car and started the engine, he was shaking with excitement and anticipation. He glanced back towards the house he had just left. He still loved his wife and children, having convinced himself long ago that this addiction had no effect on that part of his life, such was his sickness. His wife and family were his rock, the secret to his success, somehow separate, sacrosanct, and enduring. They were the face of who he really was, the guy in the mirror who looked back when he shaved, Mr Dependable, the wonderful family man who everybody warmed to.

Had his fever been less intense, he might have noticed the nondescript silver Toyota Camry parked further back up the street. His leg was shaking as he drove away. It was all he could do to concentrate on his driving, let alone see who might be watching.

He had always loved women. His wife knew that—surely she did. The many secret affairs had kept that part of him alive, the part that she loved as well—his confidence and assuredness, the charm, his sex appeal, the ability to make women love him back. It was all part of the package that he had so carefully curated over time. This skill, to project one image that hid another, had been well harnessed in his career.

His excursion today was borne of something entirely different to his rank-and-file affairs. He had never experienced such lust. To have a woman so completely under his control was intoxicating. Of course, her youthful, almost ethereal beauty was part of the attraction, but it was her complete submissiveness that really turned him on. It didn't matter that the face of this intoxication changed. It was the whole experience that thrilled. His other conquests never treated him this way. Their nagging demands never ended. For the next hour or two, he would get to escape and play king, one with irresistible powers, perhaps a sultan with his own personal harem.

The man on the door let him in without a word. No identification was needed. He was well known. That was lucky, as any words or explanation would have been incoherent, such was the excruciating level of his desire.

Afterwards, when his itch had been thoroughly scratched, he would inevitably experience a brief spasm of guilt. However, soon enough, thoughts of what happened would dispel these fleeting misgivings. Within days, he would feel the first tingle again, something he would suppress as long as he could. That was part of the thrill, keeping his desire bottled up, perhaps distracted by the other women in his life for a while. Letting the itch grow and build pressure made the release even more spectacular—more addictive.

It was the perfect situation, being able to have his cake and eat it too—so to speak. He planned to keep this arrangement going forever.

Chapter 1

No Silver Lining

Detective Ange Watson was not a happy camper. If she was being honest, her last case had turned into a bit of a mess. At the very point where everything had made sense, it suddenly made no sense at all.

While Ange and the people trafficking task force had saved six young women who had been illegally trafficked to Australia, the case had quickly spiralled out of control. The women themselves had gone silent and were refusing to testify against their handlers. Ange had devoted months to studying the intricacies of people trafficking, aware that the perpetrators would likely have a deadly grip on young victims' families. The only way that those women would talk was if they knew the perpetrators had been apprehended and they were safe from persecution. Unless Ange could achieve that feat, it was likely that Australian immigration authorities would soon deport the women back to their homeland, thereby washing their hands of the matter. Sadly, the people who'd lured the young women into servitude would not greet them with gracious and open arms when they returned home. The cold, brutal truth was that Ange was clueless about who the bad guys really were.

The thought of those innocent young women sitting in an immigration detention centre made her blood run cold. In a devastating turn of events, Cua Kwm, the courageous Vietnamese woman who'd sparked Ange's pursuit, had been callously murdered while trapped in immigration detention. Ange was still haunted by the memory of Cua Kwm's death. It had happened on her watch.

Her mind wandered to the dilemma of Henry Chan, a fellow member of her task force who had raised the possibility of Chinese Triad involvement. Chan was a former member of the Cabramatta vice squad. Ange hadn't questioned his expertise about Triads, but she should have, as the tattoos on the captured men that Chan had used to insinuate their involvement had proved to be nothing more than innocuous Chinese symbols. Furthermore, it appeared that their involvement with the people trafficking cell was little more than a shared love for tattoos and mixed martial arts. The nature of Chan's role in Ange's train wreck was both uncertain and unsettling.

To make matters worse, some dreary weather had set in, causing her leg to throb with a dull yet persistent ache, a deep-seated bone-seeking pain that sapped away her sense of well-being. Ange thought she had fully recovered after being shot and seriously wounded by two hitmen from the Ndrangheta Mafia, but she'd been neglecting her rehab routine. That had all been temporarily overshadowed by her obsession with rescuing those young women, but now the ache had resurfaced, a constant reminder of that shooting. The nightmares were also back, and in disturbing detail, stalking her nights and draining away her vitality.

The situation was absurd. After all, not only was she living in Byron Bay, but she was madly in love with the delectable Gus Bell. If you had asked her a year ago what would make her happy, she couldn't have imagined a more perfect existence.

Needing to be rescued from her funk, she rang Billy. If Ange was the inspiration, Constable Billy Bassett was the genius of her investigations. He was also brilliant company.

'How's it going in the big smoke on this dreary Monday, Billy?' Ange asked, trying to sound upbeat. Dragging Billy down into her dark mood would be just plain cruel. 'Has the Dark Web activity you've been tracing stopped?'

'Definitely not, boss. If anything, it's stepped up a level.'

'What sort of activity?'

With almost everyone going online 24/7, Covid-19 had presented a boon for cybercriminals. The department had somehow overlooked Billy's considerable IT talents, and they had posted him as a lowly constable working the beat in Byron Bay. Ange had quickly recognised the value of his expertise, and they had developed into a formidable team. When her boss, Senior Detective Sally Anders, had offered her a job in Major Crimes based in Sydney, Ange had insisted that Billy join her.

'Remember the guy you picked up during the raid on the drug farm in Clearwater? The martial arts dude.'

'How could I forget? What a disaster. It sure didn't help my sinking feeling when I saw the calibre of lawyers who came to his defence. He's also the guy who's been threatening to sue me for racial profiling.'

'Well, he's clearly not feeling threatened. He hardly drew breath before he'd set up shop again.'

'How do you know that? Wasn't his phone somehow remotely wiped clean?'

'Yes, it was. Pretty clever, actually. Lucky for us that Bruce Lee isn't as smart as he thinks he is. He went straight out and signed up with a new phone provider. I arranged a trace on his IEMI.'

Ange sighed in mock exasperation. 'You do this for kicks, don't you Billy? What, pray tell, is an IEMI?'

'International Mobile Equipment Identity. It's like a fingerprint for your phone. He should have dumped his old phone and purchased a new one. I guess a newish Google Pixel is too valuable to throw away,' observed Billy. 'Anyhow, I've gotten access to his phone data through his service provider.'

'You can trace Dark Web browsing activity? I thought the Dark Web was hard to handle unless you knew where you were going.'

'It is. But not if I have a complete feed of his phone traffic. Then I can recreate exactly what he's been up to.'

'Amazing. And exactly what has he been up to, Billy? Surely not more people trafficking?'

'Nothing like people trafficking. A Dark Web shopfront selling a range of performance-enhancing and other illicit substances. As well as under-the-counter medicinal cannabis products, he's selling a bunch of traditional Chinese remedies—it gives his site that whole alternative medicine vibe.'

'Where does he source his products?' asked Ange, desperately seeking some lead she could pursue.

'No idea. I'll probably pass him over to the drug squad soon. Although, those guys are even less technologically minded than us.'

'You mean they don't have you, Billy?' joked Ange.

'Exactly. I'll let you know if I see anything worthwhile in his activities, boss.'

'Before you pass him over, why not get Bree to purchase some of his products using her stash of cryptocurrency? At least then you'll have some physical evidence to hand over.'

'Good idea. I'll work through the logistics with Bree between her hockey practice.'

Constable Breanna White had taken over Billy's position at the Byron Bay station and was also a member of the national field hockey team, with aspirations of becoming an Olympian. Ange had assumed the position of Bree's mentor, and they had devised a scheme to delve into the world of NFTs and Dark Web chat rooms.

'Speaking of shopfronts, what about the Shama website?' Ange asked, referring to the suspicious NFP marketplace that they suspected of being a front for selling trafficked women. It wasn't ideal that Henry Chan had provided the lead to that site.

'It's still live—but sort of dead.'

'What do you mean by that cryptic comment, Billy?'

'Well, the site is still there, but there's been no change to the NFTs on offer. I can't tell if they've forgotten to take it down, or they're waiting for more product.'

Despite the harshness of describing trafficked women as 'product', Ange knew this was precisely how the perpetrators dehumanised them. 'So basically, you've got nothing useful to brighten my day, Billy,' observed Ange with feigned sarcasm.

'Only the sound of my cheery voice. You'll be the first to know when I find something. Have a pleasant day, boss,' said Billy before he ended the call.

She'd just finished with Billy when Senior Detective Sally Anders called her.

'Hi, boss, what's up?' asked Ange, sounding upbeat. Despite yielding nothing, her conversation with Billy had marginally boosted her spirits.

'You need to come to Sydney tomorrow. What time can you be here?'

'I'll need to check the flights. What's happened?'

'Just book your flight and let me know the details. You'll need to drive to Brisbane to catch a plane if necessary.'

Ange noted that her boss had avoided answering her question. 'What's this about and why the rush, boss?'

'I have no idea, but you need to be here as early as possible tomorrow. Pack an overnight bag. Hopefully, you won't need it. And get me those flight details, Detective.'

Whenever Sally Anders addressed her as 'Detective', Ange knew the matter was serious. Wasting no time, she immediately booked a ridiculously expensive seat on the earliest flight out of Ballina for the following morning and promptly shared the flight details with Sally Anders. Since it was still early spring and the weather was warm, she squeezed a few changes of clothes in a small carry-on suitcase. Trips to Sydney had a tendency to stretch out.

She had an ominous feeling that formidable headwinds were bearing down, but from which direction these winds might blow was anybody's guess.

Ange didn't know the half of it.

Chapter 2

Ambushed

The room where Ange and Sally Anders sat was bland and uninviting, a place to pass through as quickly as possible. Its clinical design was also a clue to the fear and apprehension that lay beyond the glass doors, accessed only by a pass-carrying privileged class. Other than the smattering of teal-green reception chairs, the only substantive decorative element was a large embossed sign that revealed all. Police Integrity Command. The department had recently been renamed from the equally predictable Internal Affairs. Sally felt the change was a deodoriser concocted by the commissioner after the Ndrangheta mess. This was a common ploy to cover up a bad smell.

Other than an expensive rebranding exercise, the new name would change nothing. IA becomes IC, and then it was back to the business of being hated. If the axiom about power corrupting ever had a home, it would hang comfortably on the walls of Internal Affairs, Integrity Commands, and Corruption Commissions. Being accountable to nobody was seldom a positive thing.

Ange looked at her boss. With her flight arriving late, they'd had no time to discuss the situation before rushing over. 'It's concerning to be summoned here at such short notice. What do you think this is all about?'

'Nothing good would be my first guess,' stated Anders grimly. 'I called you yesterday as soon as I heard.'

Ange's previous altercation with the then–Internal Affairs had come soon after the shoot-out at Namba Heads. It was only due to Sally Anders' cunning and smart thinking that things ended well on that occasion.

Fear was a key currency used by IC, where the presumption of guilt provided the tool to supercharge their investigations. The recently appointed leader of the Integrity Command made no apology for this draconian Star Chamber approach, and it had garnered vigorous support from several key politicians.

'I guess it might have something to do with the haranguing I received from the commissioner about Clearwater. We'll have to wait and see. Whatever you do, don't react to their taunts. We need to understand where they're coming from before we respond. You don't have a terrific record in this, Detective, so I hope you keep that temper of yours in check. Please do your best to keep your cool,' elaborated Anders. Ange had nothing to say to that.

With Billy's help, Ange had identified a suspected drug farm, nestled in a valley on the outskirts of picturesque Clearwater. Unfortunately, this had turned out to be a medicinal cannabis farm and had not delivered the sensational drug bust that Ange and her drug enforcement mates had hoped for. To say that the raid had fallen flat was a monumental understatement.

After an agonising twenty minutes, a young woman came and led the pair into a small meeting room. Ange's heart sank.

'Hello, Detective Watson. We meet again. And so soon,' said Detective Ben Carruthers, as supercilious as ever.

Ange had unloaded on Carruthers during their last encounter, and her explosion weighed heavily now. She was uncertain whether it was best to be obsequious or outright hostile towards him. After a momentary pause, she chose thinly veiled sarcasm. 'Nice shiny new name that you guys have now. I guess Internal Affairs carried too much baggage. Integrity Command sounds much grander, almost as if you're in control of something important,' she said with a sugar-wouldn't-melt-in-my-mouth smile.

If Carruthers recognised the jibe for what it was, he certainly didn't show it. Ange was almost impressed with the thickness of his hide. 'This is my colleague, Sheena Wadley,' said Carruthers. 'I'm sure you remember her.'

Ange did indeed remember her. A definite arse-wipe.

To make matters even more touchy, Peter Fredericks walked into the room. Fredericks had betrayed his Major Crimes colleagues, his burning desire for a promotion motivating him to leak information on their investigation into the Ndrangheta Mafia.

'You guys remember Senior Detective Peter Fredericks, don't you?' said Carruthers, failing to conceal a self-satisfied smirk. If looks could kill, that smart-arsed rhetorical question would have seen the two Major Crimes detectives despatch

Carruthers to meet his maker.

Anders looked daggers at Fredericks. 'I see you finally got that promotion you coveted so desperately, Peter.' Turning her attention back to Carruthers, she issued a warning born of experience. 'You guys better watch your backs. But I suppose that's an occupational hazard in Internal Affairs—sorry, the Integrity Command.'

Fredericks seemed unfazed by the enmity streaming his way. 'Nice to see you also, Sally.' He nodded towards Ange. 'Ange. I just thought I'd pop my head in to say hello.' He looked back towards his IC colleagues. 'I'll leave you guys to it, then,' he said before he made his way out the door.

Evidently enjoying that exchange to no end, Carruthers turned his attention towards Anders. 'You must be Senior Detective Sally Anders. Ben Carruthers. We've not met, but I think we may have spoken on the phone. Peter has told us so much about you.'

'You know full well that we have spoken, Detective,' spat Anders. 'Enough with the chit-chat. What is this all about?'

'It's just a preliminary meeting,' replied Carruthers. 'We would like to explore what happened in Clearwater, and why you stormed a properly licenced medicinal cannabis facility with such an overt display of force.'

'Please explain your interpretation of properly licenced, Detective Carruthers?' asked Sally Anders in a steely tone.

'You would know that the Clearwater facility was a pilot plant and a key plank in the government's plan to revitalise regional Australia and develop new business activities. I'm sure you can appreciate that the Minister for Regional Business is ropable over this matter.'

Despite her tacit commitment to her boss, Ange couldn't help herself. 'Did the minister know that the Green River Council didn't properly approve the facility in the first place?'

'Where did you get that impression? According to the information provided to me, the CEO had approved the facility under her executive delegation. I guess you might know the Green River Council has recently revoked said approval, but that should play out in the courts in due course. You should have checked your facts before you blundered in with all guns blazing, Detective Watson.'

'I'm certain that the minister's grand regional revival plan didn't extend to selling narcotics under the counter to local residents. Is the minister aware of that?' asked Ange, ignoring the pointed stares from her boss. That the council had revoked the planning approval was fresh news. Whoever had complained to the Integrity Command had access to the latest information.

Sheena Wadley shuffled some papers before finding what she was looking for. 'Oh, that. Apparently, the recipient of those narcotics was a certain Mark Dole. Mr Dole had a legitimate medical prescription for cannabis to help ease the symptoms of Crohn's disease. The facility should never have dispensed cannabis in that way, but they did it out of compassion for Mr Dole's situation. It's barely even a rap over the knuckles situation,' said Wadley, almost gleefully.

The churning in Ange's stomach was becoming increasingly intense with each passing moment. She parried her last thrust. 'And what about the fact one of the workers at the drug farm was engaged in secure communication with the criminals behind the people trafficking operation in Hillburn? Moreover, the phones that were being used by the criminals were wiped clean remotely. Someone had to be behind that.'

'According to our sources, the only communication relevant to this investigation was between two mates. The final fateful transmission, the one I presume you're referring to, was a complete mistake. It's hard to see any greater connection than that of some mates keeping in touch via WhatsApp.' Carruthers paused and let that sink in. A smile glimmered in his eyes, signalling how much he was going to enjoy delivering the next piece of news. 'It's a pity that you haven't emulated the achievements of your Queensland colleagues in locating that cell of illegal immigrants. That was quite a coup—maintaining strong borders being as important as it is.'

Sally Anders' face had gone bright red. 'What do you mean, they located? That was all Detective Watson. Without her efforts, our Queensland colleagues would still be pushing paper around, and those poor women would now work in a brothel at the back of Woop Woop.'

'That's a very different story to the one explained to me. In fact, my boss's counterpart in Queensland was quite specific on that point. Apparently, the head of that operation is in line for a commendation.'

'That would be Senior Detective Wallace, I presume,' sneered Sally Anders. 'A pathetic patronising suck-up if I've ever seen one.'

'You forgot piss-weak, boss. I never told you that Wallace's golfing mate is the head of Internal Affairs in Queensland—they haven't gotten around to changing their name yet. Bernie Peters, if my memory serves me correctly. Wallace dropped that name more than once,' commented Ange. She turned back to address Carruthers. 'I guess you haven't checked your facts with the rest of the task force in Queensland. They have a similar view about Wallace.'

Carruthers' face hardened. 'They might not be so loose with authority and following protocol. Anyway, the task force has been disbanded. As far as I can see, the idea of people being trafficked into Australia was delusional at best. Your precious task force seemed like a waste of resources.'

Ange exploded. 'Surely you cannot be serious. The Hillburn operation was just the tip of the iceberg.'

'As I said, that's not how our Queensland colleagues see things—and Border Force, for that matter,' replied Carruthers before changing gear. 'Now, down to business.'

Wadley had been scribbling furiously in her notepad during the entire conversation, and Carruthers saw Ange glance her way. 'Oh. In case you were wondering, we won't be providing any transcript on this occasion. I got into some trouble the last time I afforded you that courtesy, Detective Watson, and I've no intention of falling for the same trick twice.'

'I was curious as to when you might get to the actual point of this get-together, Detective Carruthers,' said Sally Anders, making no attempt to hide the malice in her voice.

'We're just showing you some professional courtesy. I didn't want to deliver the news by letter. It's more compassionate to do it in person,' said Carruthers, unable to suppress how much he was enjoying being compassionate. 'Detective Watson is to be suspended immediately, ahead of a formal investigation and hearing by the Police Integrity Command about her failures in the Clearwater disaster. This hearing will determine if formal charges are to be brought before the Law Enforcement & Ethics Tribunal.'

A look of abject disgust showed on the face of Sally Anders. 'What a crock. You lot have lost your sense of smell. This stinks to high heaven.'

Carruthers and Wadley seemed unperturbed by those accusations. 'Detective Watson, you need to hand in your badge immediately. We'll be in touch about an expected hearing date,' said Wadley, joining her colleague in the conversation lest Carruthers have all the enjoyment. To add to the theatre of this pantomime, Carruthers held out his hand, as if he expected Ange to hand over her badge, perhaps with the drooped expression of a naughty schoolgirl to add to the effect.

'There is no way that I'm letting you take Detective Watson's badge. You'd probably lose it under all the piles of shit lying around your office. I'll look after it until you get your arse whipped at this supposed hearing,' said Sally Anders.

'So much for keeping our cool,' thought Ange, still in a daze over what Carruthers had just said. She couldn't bear speaking to him again, so she directed her attention to Wadley. 'Will I need legal representation?'

Nothing could eject Carruthers from the driver's seat. 'That seems prudent, Detective Watson. We can supply you with adequate legal representation, or you can supply your own—if you have your own lawyer, that is.'

'Detective Watson will provide her own legal advisor. I wouldn't trust that anyone you suggested could even defend a parking ticket. We've heard enough. I look forward to receiving the full account of your allegations against my lead detective. I prefer to read fiction anyway, so that should be interesting,' said Sally Anders, standing up to signal that the meeting was over.

Carruthers had not finished. 'If I had my way, Senior Detective Anders, you would also face disciplinary action for not properly supervising your officers.'

'Bring it on,' was all Sally Anders would reply, staring defiantly into the face of Carruthers.

'Unfortunately, it seems like you still have one remaining friend in high places, Senior Detective.'

Ange knew that the *friend in high places* was actually Sue Elkington from The Times. Sally had compiled quite a dossier on the dubious political skulduggery of the departmental hierarchy. Said dossier was safely tucked away with her solicitor and to be directed Elkington's way in the event of an emergency. As best as Ange could see, now was one such emergency.

Not wanting to provide Carruthers and Wadley with any more fun, Sally Anders turned and walked towards the door. Ange trailed haplessly behind, still disbelieving about what had just happened. She glanced back to see that Carruthers' face had broken out into a wide smile. Her resolve hardened at that. She planned to wipe that smile from his face, even if it was her last act as a detective.

Chapter 3

Challenging Times

The pair walked out of the office of the Integrity Command in complete silence. Ange speculated that recording any post-meeting conversations in the lift or foyer would be true to form for IC. Evidently, Sally Anders had similar misgivings. It wasn't until they were out on the busy Sydney CBD sidewalk that she spoke. 'Are you OK, Ange?'

'That was not what I was expecting, that's for sure. I don't know what to think, but I guess I need to look for a lawyer. I have some savings, but they won't last long covering legal expenses,' said Ange, the realities of the situation now clear.

'Let's grab a late lunch. I'm sure we'll find something suitable in Chinatown,' suggested Anders, her demeanour having returned to its usual implacable state.

Positively shell-shocked by the events of the past hour, Ange followed meekly behind her boss as they ducked and weaved through the Sydney crowd. Hardly anyone wore a face mask, suggesting that the Covid-19 pandemic was well and truly over. But Ange knew this not to be true, and she reflected on how the pandemic was not unlike her recent cases. Whenever she thought things were under control, they weren't—morphing into some other variant and causing her to start over. She imagined the group that sat behind the people trafficking operation as a type of deadly virus, mutating this way and that, killing people along the way. Just as disease surely walked beside her on the thronging Sydney streets, she was certain those behind the trafficking operation were close by, infecting everyone they touched.

Sally Anders chose a dumpling restaurant, still bustling with a late lunchtime crowd. Once seated, she snapped Ange from her wandering thoughts. 'You must have really struck a nerve, Ange. As badly as this stinks, and as angry as I am, it doesn't change the fact that we will need to take this seriously. Don't worry about the legal expenses. The department would normally cover those. However, I have someone better in mind. Have you ever heard of Owen Fairweather?'

'The QC? The same guy who almost everyone in the department hates with a passion? How could we afford him?' asked Ange in a series of quick-fire questions.

'It's King's Counsel now, Ange. Get with the times. I'm sure that he'll be happy to act pro bono on this occasion.'

'Why on earth would he do that?' asked Ange. She had never been part of a case where Fairweather had acted for the defence, but she knew his fearsome reputation for tearing prosecutors apart. He had destroyed countless cases brought by the police service and had an uncanny ability to sniff out the faintest whiff of inconsistency or sloppiness.

'Owen owes me a couple of favours,' replied Anders offhandedly.

'Out with it, boss. How do you know Owen Fairweather, KC, and how could he possibly owe you any favours?' queried Ange. It considerably buoyed her spirits, knowing that the feared barrister might be on her side.

'Owen and my husband, Max, were colleagues and shared chambers together. Owen was wonderful to me after Max passed away, and we've stayed in contact ever since. Nothing romantic, I might add. Owen is married with four children. How he and Marcia found the time for that, I do not know.'

It was a rare insight into the person who made up the real Sally Anders. 'How did your husband pass away, if you don't mind me asking?'

'Pancreatic cancer. It happened so fast I still can't believe it. We both reasoned that his back pain was caused by being chained to his desk for absurdly long hours. He'd been working on a complex case, and by the time we realised something was wrong, it was too late. It took Max quickly in the end, which was merciful in many ways. It was heart-wrenching to watch such a brilliant, capable, and energetic man wither away and die before my eyes. Without the help of Owen and Marcia, I can't imagine how I would ever have gotten through that horror.'

Sally Anders was a proud and tough woman, but Ange could see the intense pain that still lingered in her eyes. She changed tack to limit any embarrassment. 'Was Max a criminal defence barrister as well? That must have made for some interesting conversations around the dinner table.'

That Sally Anders appreciated the change in direction was clear in the look that blossomed in her eyes. 'Max believed, as I still do, that a strong defence is the foundation of a fair and just legal system. You've seen firsthand what could happen if we let the likes of Carruthers run rampant. Heaven help us if we ever leave those types unchecked. Sure, Max and I would argue hammer and tongs over whether or not someone was guilty, and we came at things from very different perspectives. However, these countless debates helped each of us cement our respective views, and I feel that they helped Max become a better defence barrister and me become a better police officer. Owen and I regularly trade opinions and seek advice from each other. The ledger is firmly in my favour at present, so I'm sure that I can twist his arm to assist. If nothing else, Owen hates bureaucratic overreach with a passion. He can be quite fiery, as I'm sure you've heard.'

'I guess I need to actually hand in my badge. Am I on leave without pay, or something like that?' asked Ange.

'Of course you'll continue to be paid, but can you remain in Sydney for a while longer? As soon as I receive the formal notice from Carruthers and Co, I'll arrange for us to brief Owen. I can't wait to see the look on Carruthers' face when he learns that Owen Fairweather, KC, is representing you,' said Anders, a wide smile lighting up her face.

'I was only expecting to stay one night, so I booked a hotel room. I guess I can extend my stay,' replied Ange before returning to the matter of her suspension. 'What really riles me is that Wallace has taken all the credit for the Hillburn takedown. That's not about me, by the way, but the other members of the task force did all the work. All Wallace ever did was get in the way and play golf with his best mate, Bernie Peters. I'm still shocked by the news that the task force is being disbanded and the women have been labelled as vanilla-style illegal immigrants. Hillburn was probably one of many such facilities, and I'm sure the gang behind the trafficking operations will hardly draw breath before ramping back up to full speed.'

As if on cue, Ange's phone buzzed. It was her Vietnamese-speaking former colleague from the task force. 'Excuse me, boss, this is Judy Ly from Queensland. Do you mind if I see what she's calling about?'

'Sure. Go ahead. I'll order some food while you talk. Interesting timing,' observed Anders, waving to attract the attention of a busy waiter.

'Hi, Judy. I hope that your day is going better than mine.'

'Hardly. I've just been told that the task force has been disbanded. Apparently, people trafficking doesn't exist in Queensland. What a crock. We haven't even scratched the surface. They've reassigned me back to a desk job in crime, and Chris Lambert is dealing with prosecutions of workplace manslaughter.'

'What about Henry?' asked Ange.

'Henry has taken a leave of absence and moved to Singapore. I understand that his wife comes from an extremely wealthy Singaporean family, and they'd been piling on the pressure for Henry and his wife to return home for the birth of their third child.'

With such apparent wealth behind them, Ange wondered why Chan persisted as a detective. 'I guess you know Wallace is getting a commendation for all his fine work,' advised Ange in the most sarcastic voice she could muster.

'You're kidding me. Aren't you?'

'I'm sorry to say that I am not kidding. I've just learned this news myself. The Police Integrity Command has suspended me over the Clearwater operation. I guess we've seriously pissed someone off.'

'What? Suspended? How do you feel?' asked Ly, her voice rising to a near shout.

'Not as badly as I thought I might. Judy, I must go. I'm just with Sally Anders, my boss. I'm sure you remember her from our video meetings. Can you let me know if you hear anything else? I'm probably not supposed to contact anyone from the task force, but I guess I can't stop you calling me for a friendly chat.'

'Will do, Ange. I really enjoyed working with you and your impressive boss. I hope we can do it again sometime soon.'

'Me too, Judy. Stay safe.'

Sally Anders had gotten the gist of the conversation. 'I gather the news of Wallace's upcoming commendation came as a surprise to your colleague.'

'She'd only just learned that they've disbanded the task force and knew nothing about Wallace's slimy commendation.'

'This matter with IC and the timing of the news about the task force seems to have been well coordinated. Interesting.'

Ange then filled her boss in on Billy's latest developments, including the dead end with the Shama NFT site. 'Since our wings have been so thoroughly clipped, I guess it's a moot point,' she commented.

'This is far from over, Detective,' was Sally Anders' last word on the matter before they tucked into lunch.

Chapter 4

Deep Waters

Once back at the Major Crimes offices, Ange handed her badge over to Sally Anders. It was a moment that neither police officer enjoyed. Left at a dead end, Ange wandered back to her hotel room and rang Gus to give him the news.

'Hi, Gus. Remember when you told me how attracted you are to detectives?' asked Ange, trying vainly to make light of her situation.

Even though their relationship was not yet a year old, Gus had the sense to realise this was a loaded question. 'Yeeesss. I may recall that I said something along those lines.'

'Well, I've just been suspended until further notice. I hope you'll still find me attractive.'

'Suspended? What do you mean? How does that even happen?' asked Gus.

'It's all over the Clearwater operation. It seems I touched a nerve.'

'How do you feel about that?'

'I was upset initially, but I'm feeling OK about it. The boss is organising one of Sydney's top barristers to help us out—a King's Counsel no less. I'll need to stay in Sydney a few more days for an initial briefing. Don't worry, the boss assures me that the legal work will be pro bono. I don't mind splurging on some silk occasionally, but not of the barrister kind,' said Ange lightly.

'OK, then. We'll miss you. Buddy seems to enjoy working the floor at the shop, so I reckon we'll cope for a few days. Does that mean you won't be working for a while?'

'Sort of. I'm not sure how long all this will take. It's my first suspension, so this is unfamiliar territory. I expect that I'll have some time on my hands. I should be home by the weekend. Perhaps we can get away for a few days to get my mind off things. Are you busy at the shop?'

'I should be able to get away. Sales will dry up once Buddy departs. Kerrie had a brainwave for Buddy to ink a paw print on his Rusty Bell tee shirts in return for a twenty-dollar donation to the JayTee Foundation. Check your phone. She did a post called *Authentic Rusty*. Those things are flying out the door and we've raised over six hundred dollars for the foundation. I need to place *another* tee shirt order with the manufacturer.'

Ange's best friend, Kerrie, was a bubbly and lovable lifestyle influencer. She seemed determined to make Buddy a star, perhaps even surpassing the popularity of the beloved cartoon character Bluey.

'What does Buddy think of that?' enquired Ange. 'I guess he doesn't know what his real name is anymore. His stage name is better known than his real one.'

'He doesn't seem to mind, although he makes no secret when he doesn't like someone. I feel that it's only fair he gets to choose whose tee shirts he signs. His paw print is like a stamp of approval. The staff love him and find his sense of character intriguing. Don't worry, I still call him Buddy.'

'OK. Give him a hug for me and I'll see you soon. Perhaps we can take a trip down south and stay at your Angourie beach shack?'

'Let's see how things sit when you get home. Good luck with your barrister,' said Gus before hanging up.

Ange went for a walk around the Sydney Harbour to blow off some steam. She was just past the Opera House when her phone buzzed with an incoming call. Since she didn't recognise the number, Ange let it go to voicemail and listened to the message.

'Hello, Detective Watson. It's Alan Campbell, the mayor of Green River Council. We met a few weeks back in our CEO's office about the cannabis farm in Clearwater. I wondered if you could call me when you have a minute. You just missed a call from me, so ring me back on that number.'

It surprised Ange that the mayor of the Green River Council would call her. It was certainly a day of Clearwater revivals. While Ange had taken an instant liking to Alan Campbell during their one and only meeting, she knew little about him.

She found a park bench and sat down to do some research on her phone before she returned the call. What she found came as a big surprise. Alan Campbell, mayor of little old Green River Shire, was also one of Australia's largest cattlemen. His family controlled extensive grazing properties in northern and central Australia, and the media often referred to the man as a cattle baron. He hadn't acted like a baron when they'd met, and Ange found it interesting that he could find the time to serve as mayor of a small regional council like Green River. Intrigued, Ange rang Campbell's number.

'Hello, Detective Watson. Thanks for ringing me back.'

'Call me Ange, please, Mr Campbell. How can I help?'

'Ditto. Call me Alan. I just wanted to thank you for your efforts in uncovering the cannabis farm. We've revoked their planning approval and shut them down. I hear on the grapevine that the operators of the farm are threatening civil proceedings, but we'll be happy to defend that if we must. The townsfolk were apoplectic when they heard what was going on, so I have the support of ratepayers for the action we took.'

'Oh, that. I'm glad it worked out well for you. Unfortunately, whoever's behind that farm is very well connected. There's been some blowback.'

'How so?'

'Well, I've just been suspended from duty, pending a formal hearing by our delightfully titled Police Integrity Command, formally called Internal Affairs. I'm sure you've seen enough TV crime shows to know what they're all about.'

'You're kidding me? That's a disgrace. I'd be happy to provide a character reference if you need one. When is the hearing?'

'I'm not sure. I presume it will take several weeks to play out. I'm due to brief my lawyer in the next few days, so I'll discuss your kind offer with him. By the way, what happened to your CEO, Julia Bennet?'

A bitter tone crept into Campbell's voice. 'Council had resolved to sack her, but Julia sensed the breeze and resigned before I got around to it. Why do you ask?'

'Well, the allegations that the Integrity Command threw at me were quite specific and must have come from an insider. I figured that Julia Bennet would be no friend of mine and a likely source of the complaint. It hasn't helped that I had a run-in with the detective from the Integrity Command in charge of this matter. I was in recovery after being shot in the field, and they tried to take advantage of the situation and stitch me up. What, between Bennet and the Integrity Command, I guess I'm in hostile territory.'

'You got shot? How badly? I've seen a few gunshots in my time, and that cannot have been fun.'

'Pretty badly. My vest stopped a bullet aimed at my chest, although I still suffered a cracked rib. I took another in my left leg that fractured my femur. Besides a few aches and an impressive scar, I'm pretty much back to normal. It could have been much worse. Anyhow, do you know what your former CEO is doing now?'

'No, I haven't been all that interested, but I'll ask around. Leave that with me. By the way, since you now have some spare time, why not come over and visit us in Clearwater? Do you enjoy camping? I have a permanent campsite beside the Green River that I keep for the family. It's a magnificent spot. You're welcome to come for a few days if you're interested. While you're here, perhaps you could cast your eyes over my cattle rustling problem. I'd really appreciate your perspective on what I should do about it.'

'That's very kind of you, Alan. I'll discuss it with my partner and come back to you. Would it be OK to bring my dog? He's a four-year-old red cattle dog that was trained by my father. He wouldn't cause any trouble with the stock. The only reason I have him now is that a bull kicked him and he's wary of cattle. I guess he would have been put down eventually, but Dad's loss was my gain.'

'Sure, your dog would be welcome as well. There are still a few snakes around, but I'm sure your dog has seen plenty of them. Anyhow, I look forward to hearing from you once you speak to your partner. Oh, by the way, I convinced the council to give Brendan Tame his job back and make a cash settlement for his lost wages and inconvenience. We need people like him who are prepared to stand up and do the right thing, even though he probably didn't feel very good about it once Julia Bennet got her claws into him,' replied Campbell.

In order to silence Tame and his suspicions about her role in the cannabis farm development, Julia Bennet had falsely accused him of sexual harassment. Ange harboured a special disdain for people like Bennet, those who exploited their position for personal gain at the expense of others. 'That's terrific, Alan. I'm pleased that your council did the right thing. I'll get back to you about your kind camping offer.'

'Don't forget my cattle rustling problem. It's really bothering me,' said Campbell before hanging up.

Ange mulled over the fact that Campbell was so concerned about some missing cattle when he must own tens of thousands across his properties. She figured it was a case of old habits dying hard. The more she thought about Campbell's proposal, the more it appealed to her. She started hatching a plan.

Chapter 5

Wise Counsel

Just after midday on Wednesday, Sally Anders received the complete statement listing the issues Ange would need to defend. She called Ange before forwarding the email. 'Ange, I've received the documentation from Carruthers. It's as weak as dishwater. I'm about to send it to you, but I don't want you getting upset. We need you to treat this as dispassionately as possible and you can't let them get under your skin. Their plan will be to rattle you and hope you say something that they can use against you.'

'I'll do my best to remain level-headed, but I cannot warrant that I won't get upset, boss,' replied Ange.

'Now, we have an appointment with Owen at his chambers in Elizabeth Street at 10:30 a.m. tomorrow. I'll text you the exact address. How about we catch up beforehand and go through the documentation from IC? I'll meet you in the foyer at 10 a.m.'

Ange checked her inbox to see that her boss's email had arrived. 'I've got the document. See you tomorrow at 10 a.m.'

Ange had been antsy all morning and was happy to have something to occupy her overactive mind. She sat down to study the document provided by the Integrity Command. It was really nothing more than a padded-out version of their discussion with Carruthers and Wadley, fleshing out dates and times and who said what. However, it confirmed Ange's suspicions that Julia Bennet was involved, as it mentioned her and her former position multiple times. It was clear to Ange that the disciplinary action relied on two key points. First, that Ange should not have assumed that anything illegal was going on at the Clearwater property, and she should have checked this with the council before acting. The second was an allegation that she had used unreasonable force when the team raided the property in the early hours of the morning.

As Ange took a long walk around the Sydney harbour, she pondered the approach that Owen Fairweather might take. She was quite looking forward to the experience, although she hoped that briefing a King's Counsel would not become an everyday occurrence.

Ange was already sitting in the foyer of Fairweather's building when Sally Anders arrived. They discussed their thoughts on the Integrity Command's documentation, and Anders agreed with Ange about the key conclusions. At ten minutes before their meeting time, the pair made their way up to Fairweather's floor. The lift opened directly into an elegant waiting area. The chambers evoked a subdued air, with dark walls and tasteful furnishings that sat atop a parquetry oak floor. Dedicated spotlights illuminated some impressive paintings. That one was sitting in expensive and rarefied territory was unmistakable.

Before they had even sat down, an impeccably dressed middle-aged woman came out to greet them. 'Hi, Sally. We haven't seen you for a while. I trust you've been keeping well. Owen is ready for you. Can I get you coffee or tea?'

'If it's not too much trouble, I'd love a flat white. Thanks, Liz. Ange?'

'Same, thank you,' said Ange, pleased to find that proper coffee was on offer.

Liz led the pair down an eerily muted hallway and delivered them into Fairweather's rooms. A forty-something man stood up from a large leather-embossed desk and came around to greet them. Dark hair greying on the fringes set off a tanned and obviously intelligent face. Ange guessed Fairweather to be a shade over six feet tall, and he moved with the confidence and ease of someone who looked after themselves, despite undoubtedly being chained to his desk.

He first gave Sally Anders a hug and a kiss of some tenderness. 'Hi, Sal, it's been too long. When are you coming over to dinner? You realise your goddaughter has just started high school?'

'I know. Life keeps getting in the way. I'll speak to Marcia later today and set something up. Owen, this is Detective Ange Watson.'

The feared barrister turned and warmly shook Ange's hand. 'Owen Fairweather. It's a pleasure to meet you, Detective Watson.'

'Please call me Ange. I'm not sure if you can call me a detective or not at present,' said Ange, disarming Fairweather with her open smile. 'It's so kind of you to represent me. I really don't know how to thank you.'

'Don't give it another thought. I'd do anything for Sally,' said Fairweather, glancing over at a large and beautifully framed graduation photograph on the sideboard. The photo showed a much younger Fairweather, his arm resting on the shoulder of another young man, both sporting the same awkward yet exuberant smiles of youth. Ange saw that Sally Anders' gaze followed, and a look of melancholy and softness came across her face. Ange knew instantly that the other man was Max, Sally's former husband and colleague to Fairweather. Fairweather exchanged a similar look with Anders before returning his attention to Ange. 'If truth be known, I owe Sally many more favours than she owes me.'

Fairweather motioned his visitors towards some comfortable bucket chairs that sat opposite his desk. While he was arranging himself, Ange took the opportunity to look around. Fairweather had a penchant for Australian art, and Ange recognised some artists. Amongst works by Arthur Boyd and Fred Williams, a large painting by Emily Kngwarreye hung on a side wall above an informal seating area. At least a million dollars in artwork hung on the walls. Ange knew the punishing hours that a barrister worked, and she wondered if art was Fairweather's salve for time spent away from family and friends. She hoped not. As impressive as was his art, this would seem a poor trade.

'I love your art. We recently worked on a tricky case that turned on a wonderful painting by Emily.'

'Yes. Art is my chief weakness, one that I shared with Max. Art always provides inspiration when I'm floundering. I somehow seem to gravitate to the piece that best suits my mood. As I lose myself and seek answers to what the artist is trying to tell me, it somehow unpacks and reorders my thoughts. Anyhow, Sally tells me you've recently recovered from being shot. That must have been terrible. I cannot imagine how that felt.'

Liz entered unobtrusively during this chit-chat and delivered the coffees, then turned and exited discreetly without a word. This was evidently a polished move replayed many times each day.

'If I'm honest, Owen, it all happened so fast. I really felt nothing at the time. I fell over, knocked myself unconscious, and then went into shock. The pain came later. Sally might have told you that two Ndrangheta Mafia hitmen were behind that. We seriously underestimated them.'

'Do you think your experiences with the Ndrangheta were behind you raiding the cannabis farm with such force?' asked Fairweather.

That Ange had a fiery temper was a secret that few people understood. It was something that was normally kept safely locked up in a cupboard buried deep within herself. She felt her face blush with the first warning signs that something was about to blow. Anger turned to admiration as she recognised how skilfully Fairweather was interrogating her and getting a sense of how she might react under pressure. She calmed down, knowing that she was being tested by her legal counsellor.

'Not really. Although, if we made one mistake with the Ndrangheta, it was that we came under-prepared and under-gunned. So, yes, perhaps it made me wary and more prudent. However, we only increased our level of preparedness when we learned of the connection between the Hillburn property and the cannabis farm. I don't know if Sally briefed you, but the Hillburn property was a transfer station for a people trafficking operation involving kidnapped young women. Before we knew of the connection, our plan involved a normal daytime raid, not the coordinated midnight operation that we ended up going with.'

'I see the Police Integrity Command allege that the relationship between the two properties was coincidental and a simple matter of two friends communicating via WhatsApp. What do you say about that?'

Now that Ange had a sense of Fairweather's style, she was quite relaxed. She thought for a moment before replying. 'It's possible. However, there were multiple occurrences of synchronous communication between the two locations.'

'Yes, but that doesn't rule out the allegation that this was just two friends. Is there any way that we can deal with this?'

'Possibly. My colleague Billy was tracking all this traffic. Knowing him, he would have kept a log of when such communications occurred. Unfortunately, we got little from the phones themselves, as they suffered a convenient and mysterious factory reset. They were wiped clean,' admitted Ange.

'That is unfortunate, and, as you say, convenient.' Fairweather turned to address Anders. 'I see that Ange is forbidden from contacting anyone involved in the matters at hand. What a terrible perversion of justice that is, but best we follow the rules for the moment. Sally, can you follow that through and get me what you can?'

'Billy has the communication logs, boss, and Judy Ly from Queensland is also annoyed about the situation. Maybe she kept some records, perhaps some screenshots. I'll text you her contact details,' said Ange.

'But that doesn't explain a commando-style incursion in the middle of the night. That seems a rather extreme approach?' probed Fairweather.

'Agreed. It was Henry Chan who raised the alarm when he discovered a potential connection to the Chinese Triads. In fact, I was on my way to Clearwater for the less heavy-handed approach when he called me with the news. Detective Chan was the Chinese expert on the task force, and he advised that people and narcotics trafficking often go hand in hand. When I saw that the farm worker who was selling drugs under the counter in Clearwater town was of Asian descent and had Chinese tattoos, I thought it best that we treat seriously the possibility that Chinese Triads were involved.'

'That sounds like racial profiling, Detective,' observed Fairweather.

'Yes, and no. Ethnic ties and shared backgrounds are almost prerequisites for membership in gangs like the Ndrangheta or the Triads. I can't see how a proper investigation can ignore race in such a situation.'

'Did knowing that another Mafia-style gang could be involved make you trigger-happy?'

'No. Quite the opposite. Being alerted to the possibility that Chinese Triads were involved made me more cautious.'

Fairweather smiled at the calm and comprehensive way Ange had dealt with his series of barbed questions. 'OK. Good. What about the accusation that you should have checked on the status of the property before you barged in with all guns blazing, so to speak?'

'That's interesting. Based on the document that the Integrity Command put together, I reckon the former CEO, Julia Bennet, has provided them with information. What she wouldn't know is that I made some investigations with the council. In fact, I made specific enquiries with a council officer about the subject property—someone who should have known.'

'Why did you do that?'

'There were some anomalies with the way the council serviced the area surrounding the cannabis farm. We were looking for properties that had council refuse collection. A young Vietnamese woman escaped from Hillburn by hiding in a wheelie bin. We had some rough parameters of where she escaped from, and Clearwater was on the list of prospective locations. That's why I paid the Green River Council a visit. In fact, it was the council officer that I spoke to who raised my antenna over the CEO.'

'How so?' asked Fairweather.

'The woman's colleague was sacked after a seemingly bogus sexual harassment claim made by the CEO. I spoke to him—Brendan Tame. Soon after he raised questions about the change to council refuse collection routes, Bennet lumped a sexual harassment claim on him. He had threatened to speak to the mayor. Funnily enough, the mayor rang me yesterday to tell me that the council has given him his job back and made a cash settlement. You can imagine that, in the circumstances, this curious change to refuse collection services put me on high alert about the property. The CEO would know nothing about my enquiries.'

'Do you feel the council officer you spoke with would provide a statement confirming your enquiries about the property you raided?'

'I'm sure she would. Sandy Ellis is her name. She was worried about retribution by the CEO and being sacked. She's a single mum and needs the job. Now that Julia Bennet is no longer the CEO and Brendan Tame has his job back, I'm sure she'll be happy to help,' said Ange. She looked at her boss. 'You can ring her at the Green River Council offices. I'm certain she'll remember me.' Ange looked back towards Fairweather. 'By the way, the mayor of the Green River Council, Alan Campbell, has invited me to go camping on his property. I thought it might be a nice thing to do. Do you see any problem with that?'

'I think that would be fine, just be sensible. The mayor's name isn't mentioned in the documentation provided by the Integrity Command. However, given that we may use a statement from Sandy Ellis, I suggest you don't visit the council offices.'

'That's fine. He has cattle rustling problems and wants me to give him some advice on a way forward. Normally, I wouldn't have the time for such a trifling matter, but it might be a pleasant diversion,' explained Ange.

'OK. I think we've covered the main points. It all looks to be a straightforward case of bureaucratic bullying. I'll contact you or Sally if I have any more questions. I see that they've set the hearing date for the week before Easter. That's another trick of the trade designed to cause the maximum level of angst. The weeks before Easter and Christmas are the two prime times for those sorts of games. Can you make sure that you're in Sydney for the week of the hearing? That way, we can deal with any last-minute issues.'

Owen Fairweather stood, his hands casually resting on his hips, conveying his comfort with the situation. Only thirty minutes had passed since they walked into the chambers, barely time for Ange to finish her coffee. 'Don't give this a second thought, Ange. My job would be a cakewalk if all my cases were as easy as this.'

'Thank you, Owen. I cannot tell you how grateful I am for your help,' said Ange.

'Don't mention that again, please. It will be fun. Nice to see you, Sally. Make sure you come and see your goddaughter. Our Emily looks up to you. I think you're her role model,' said Fairweather.

'Let's hope Emily can do better than yours truly,' replied Anders with a wry smile, one that hinted at her sense of pride at being a role model for her goddaughter. 'I'll contact Marcia today and make a date for dinner,' she added, before Fairweather ushered them out the door.

As they waited for the lift, Ange turned to her boss with a quizzical expression in her eyes. 'You really are a woman of mystery. I guess I'll never truly know the secrets hiding behind that titanium facade.' Her face softened. 'Thanks for this, boss. I feel a lot better knowing that Owen is on my side.'

'All part of the service,' replied Anders glibly.

Ange knew this to be entirely untrue. Many a boss in Anders' situation would have fed Ange to the dogs and then taken the opportunity to join in the fun and further their own reputations.

Chapter 6

A Change of Plan

Ange arrived home early Thursday evening. Gus had picked up some takeaway. The first thing he did was apologise. 'Ange, I really cannot get away this weekend. We're short-staffed and I need to work in the shop. This post-pandemic attitude to work-life balance is sure killing mine. It's infected even my best staff. There seems to be a view that work is something to be taken lightly and not to impede any personal activities. Some even act as if they're doing me a favour by just turning up occasionally. Being stressed and needing some time off for mental health is the latest excuse. The trouble is that Saturdays are always our biggest days in the shop.'

'They work at the planet's coolest surfboard shop, for goodness' sake. How stressful can that be? Now that I'm gainfully unemployed, I can always give you a hand, Gus. Here's a deal for you. If you take a few days off next week and we take Buddy camping in the bush, I'll help you in the shop this weekend. Between you and Kerrie, I'm afraid Buddy's fast becoming an urban lifestyle dog instead of a real one.'

'OK. Sounds like a deal. Anyway, these devil winds are predicted to hang around for the next fortnight, so the surf will be rubbish,' replied Gus, before fixing his partner with a questioning stare. 'I doubt this camping idea is for Buddy's sake, but it sounds fun.'

Ange knew that 'devil winds' was code for swell-killing, mood-altering, depressing north-easterlies. The prospect of being idle in Byron when the surf was rubbish would add to her angst. At least the rain had cleared and her leg had stopped aching. Working in the shop ahead of a camping trip offered the perfect solution. 'The mayor of the Green River Council offered his family camping spot on his property—more correctly, one of his properties. It turns out that he's one of Australia's largest beef producers. A cattle baron, by all accounts. Anyhow, he has a cattle rustling problem, and he had asked my opinion about how he should go about solving it. I thought it might be fun.'

'I gathered that there would be more to this than just a relaxing camping trip. There's some camping gear lying around the garage, but I haven't used it for quite a while,' observed Gus.

'I'll ring him tomorrow and ask what we need to bring along. Alan Campbell is his name. Look him up. He's very impressive.'

Even though Campbell's request for some cattle rustling advice had seemed like an afterthought, Ange sent a text to Billy straight after dinner. She never did things by halves.

Hi, Billy. As you know, I'm not supposed to contact anyone about the Clearwater case. Can you ask Gary Franks from Tweed Heads where to buy those 4G motion detection cameras they used under the bridge? The ones with night vision. I think they might come in handy. Contact card for Franks attached. A

Even though it was late, she hadn't even had time to unpack before Billy replied.

The product ID is BushCamz XT100-4G. You can get them online from www.wildcamz.com.au. He said to use the code '$SERVICE$'. The company offers a nice discount for police service personnel. Their primary use is for tracking wild dogs and foxes. They look cool. Let me know if you need any help with setup. What do you have in mind?

Ange texted Billy straight back.

Just helping a friend with a rodent problem. Yes, I'm sure to need your help with setup!

Billy's reply:

BTW, Gary mentioned that the unit on the mobile phone tower they installed to monitor the cannabis farm was still chugging away. It wasn't

> worth the hassle of retrieving and they're using it as a test to see how long the unit can withstand the elements. He seemed very impressed with how robust the units were. I would stick with his recommendation.

Ange looked online and saw that the units came to just under three hundred dollars each after her service discount. A small solar panel was an extra hundred, and she placed three complete setups in her online shopping cart before going to bed. She would speak to Alan Campbell before finalising her purchase.

The next morning, Ange drove her Prado to the shop, following Gus down the hill to Byron Bay. Buddy took no time in deciding to ride in Gus's Volvo wagon, and Ange noted Gus was driving the Volvo more frequently, choosing it over his Subaru. She knew that this had been Buddy's decision and smiled that Gus would pander to Buddy's preference in that way.

Ange rang Alan Campbell on the drive. After the pair had exchanged pleasantries, Ange got to the point of her call. 'Alan, I've spoken to my partner, and we're keen to take up your kind offer to camp on your property at Clearwater. I'm thinking of coming out next Thursday. Would three nights be OK?'

'Perfect. Unfortunately, I'll be up north then, but that will be fine. I'll text you the contact details of my manager, Fin Templeton. He's a terrific young man. If you text him when you leave Byron, he'll set you up with some meat and provisions at the campsite. Just bring your own breakfast cereal and anything specific that you would like to eat. Everyone uses the camp oven, and I'll make sure Fin organises all the necessities. You can always duck into Clearwater if you need anything else. You'll just need to bring a sleeping bag or some bedclothes, pillows, towels, and any personal items. Have you used a camp oven before?'

'My dad used to take me camping on the farm all the time, and we always used a camp oven. By the way, I'm planning to pick up some video cameras that are specifically designed for outdoor wildlife surveillance. The police service also uses them and they can transmit video over the cell phone network. Do you know how reliable your mobile phone coverage is on the property where the cattle rustling is occurring?'

'It's mostly good, especially on the ridges. Apart from the cattle rustling, I guess they might come in useful for picking up wild dogs. They're a constant challenge, and you wouldn't believe the size of some of those beasts. Wild dogs are indiscriminate killers, and they can sure make a mess of a small calf. Let Fin know how much they cost, and I'll reimburse you.'

'Thanks, Alan. With my police service discount, they come to just under four hundred dollars each. I figure we'll need at least two of the units, but it's hard to know until I get the lay of the land. I'll order three just in case. Once we have them set up, we can always add more down the track. I'll need Fin to organise some SIM cards. We can then arrange for any alerts to be sent to his phone.'

'Wow, are they night vision as well? That seems very high-tech for that price,' asked Campbell.

'Yes, motion-sensing, infrared detection, and night vision. I know what you mean. It seems like only yesterday when this would have been super-expensive military-grade gear.'

'Brilliant. I really appreciate your help with this.'

'One thing that I can't understand, Alan, is why you need me. Isn't this a matter for the local police?'

'We lost the Clearwater police station as part of a consolidation some years back. Our closest station is some sixty kilometres away, and it covers a massive area—mostly highway patrols and traffic accidents. I suspect that they really don't have the resources to look into my problem. Anyway, it was only four cows when I contacted them. You landed in my lap after that cannabis farm incident, so I took the chance to recruit someone from the A-team.'

Ange understood that consolidation was a euphemism for cost-cutting amid inflexible budgets. She briefly pondered if her own efforts and a push for greater digital capability in the department came at the expense of country cops.

'I'm hardly on anyone's A-Team right now, Alan. But just to get something clear, seeing as I am on suspension, I won't be able to do anything other than observe and help Fin. I hope you realise that?' asked Ange, needing to ensure that Campbell maintained realistic expectations.

'I understand. It's more than anyone else has been prepared to do. Being suspended must really annoy you. Are you worried about it?'

'Yes, and no. I always worry that I might have done something wrong in the heat of the moment.'

'I think you'll be fine,' said Campbell in a kindly tone.

'Alan, I know you must have tens of thousands of cattle in your empire. Why are you so concerned about a few head going missing?'

'Excellent question, Detective. Clearwater is where my cattle business started.

When I bought my first property, I'd just finished my apprenticeship as a butcher. I somehow convinced the bank to support me and then got lucky with some prosperous seasons. Whenever the seasons turned bad, I purchased the adjoining properties at rock-bottom prices and assembled quite a substantial holding. As you would know, grazing is an up-and-down business and not every grazier is smart enough to prepare for tough times. The properties up north came much later. My two sons now look after them, but I like to visit when I can. That's where I'm going tomorrow. We now use Emerald Downs for all our prime breeding stock—that's the name of our Clearwater property. Our stock here represents many generations of careful breeding. Whatever I've achieved has come off the back of those genetics.'

'So, you really are the quintessential self-made man?' asked Ange, in awe of this accomplishment. 'How valuable would one of your animals be?'

Campbell laughed at that before dismissing the compliment and getting back to business. 'In the hundreds of thousands of dollars for a top bull. Somewhat less for cow, but not much with modern artificial breeding techniques.'

'Gee. That surprises me. I can't see my dad as one of your customers, Alan.'

'What I cannot understand is how my cattle haven't shown up anywhere. They carry a very distinctive brand. It's like a cowbell with a letter C stamped in the middle—a rather weak play on my surname. Although bushies compete against each other at stud shows, country fairs and the like, there's a strict code of honour about branding. The Campbell brand is very well known, and I doubt any other breeders would touch one of our animals without first checking its provenance.'

'Wow, that's serendipitous. My partner runs his family surfboard business, and his logo is a ship's bell. They're one of the most famous boards in the country. Bell Surfboards. You may have heard of them.'

'I have, which might surprise you for a bushie. We have a holiday house on the Gold Coast. I've heard my sons talking about Bell Surfboards. I hope your partner won't be a fish out of water in the bush.'

Ange laughed at Campbell's clever play on words. 'He'll be fine. Gus has almost taken permanent custody of my cattle dog, so I'm sure Buddy will look after him. I'll contact Fin once I have his details and the specifications of the units, so he can get the SIM cards organised. I'm really looking forward to visiting Emerald Downs. Let's touch base when you get back.'

On the balance of the drive down to Bell Surfboards, Ange mused at what an amazing place Australia was, where a man could start as a butcher's apprentice and end up a cattle baron. Ange knew that Campbell's achievement would not have come without many tough battles. A will fashioned from hardened steel would surely underpin his affable demeanour. Ange surmised that Campbell could be both a powerful ally and a fearsome enemy.

As soon as Ange arrived at the surfboard shop, she made herself a coffee and then went online to complete her purchase of the three surveillance cameras, choosing to pay a little extra for express delivery. If the third unit wasn't needed at Emerald Downs, Ange planned to deploy it on Gus's property. As things stood, he had no security system other than Buddy, and the pair were spending more and more time together at the shop. She figured this trend was unlikely to change, as she barely rated a second glance around the shop once Buddy was in the house.

As a novice in the surfboard sales department, Ange was placed on a steep learning curve. Most people were a joy to deal with, yet some seemed permanently angry at the world and everyone around them. The surfboards sold themselves in the main and Ange realised what an optimistic bunch were surfers. This resonated, as the journey to the beach always filled her with hope and excitement at the prospect of perfect waves, even when she knew this was against the odds. Days filled with perfect waves came rarely, yet those were the images that rolled through the imagination of all surfers. The average days, certainly the miserable days of north-easterly slop, never rated a second thought.

When dealing with a potential customer, she found planting an image of epic waves worked a treat. The customer would unconsciously start imagining themselves riding the coveted board and expertly extracting every ounce of enjoyment from those flawless mind-waves. Once Ange saw the customer drifting away on their imaginary rides, she knew that closing the sale was a mere formality. She fell for the same trick herself, envisioning that a miracle might have happened, and perfect waves sat rolling in across the dunes in Belongil Beach, a mere stone's throw away from the shop. Even though she knew this would be implausible, she felt the need to check out the beach every few hours, ostensibly taking Buddy for a toilet break.

In between dispensing these suggestive images to prospective customers, Ange found time to do some research on branding cattle and how one might go about removing or altering a brand. A properly applied cattle brand remained for the life of the beast. The only viable methods of removal involved either killing the animal for meat or somehow altering the brand. She learned that cattle rustlers had developed ingenious ways to conceal who owned an animal.

Ange doodled and experimented with how she would alter the brand that Alan Campbell had described and turn it into something else. Most ended up looking like a UFO. The best idea that she came up with was to fashion the cowbell logo into a large Western-style cowboy hat and change the letter C to an O, perhaps a brand owned by an Oscar Hatfield or someone similar. She reasoned that, providing a new owner didn't look too closely, it would be a fair enough disguise. With a little imagination, she realised rebranding Campbell's cattle was entirely feasible.

Her mood lifted as she turned her mind's eye away from the ambush tactics of the Integrity Command and onto the cattle rustling dilemmas of Alan Campbell. That his missing animals were potentially worth hundreds of thousands had certainly raised the stakes.

Just like the optimistic surfing customers she'd been serving, Ange started imagining the peaceful respite promised by her upcoming camping excursion.

Chapter 7

In Country

The surf had remained unrideable, and Ange continued working in the surfboard shop. She had grown to enjoy helping customers find their perfect surfboard, but the periods in between sales challenged her patience.

It was with some relief when the happy campers finally got underway and set off from Byron Bay early Thursday morning. Seeing as Ange had made the trip west to Clearwater three times previously, she knew the best places to stop and take a break. Driving in the bush always provided a time for reflection. The first hour was painful, but the combination of a monotonous white line and the soothing and majestic landscape soon saw Ange fall into a trancelike state where she could observe her surroundings yet stay focussed on the road. Since they had left just on daybreak, she remained on the lookout for wayward kangaroos. They were one of the most dangerous aspects of driving in the bush, and not something that Ange took lightly.

She recalled the time when she was driving home from university, running late and overtired after the obligatory post-exam party. Out of nowhere, a large grey kangaroo had leapt out of the bushes. Reflexes had caused her to swerve sharply, and she'd only clipped the animal. Had she connected with the roo head-on, it would have made a mess of her tiny ancient Toyota Corolla and possibly even proven fatal. Her old rust bucket was no sports car and swerving so violently was a dangerous move in itself. Ange had pulled over to check the damage, and the rush of adrenaline had caused her to retch violently on the side of the road—such was the scary reality of what had just happened. She'd imagined phantom roos jumping at her for months afterwards.

They had packed the Prado with a selection of Gus's camping gear and some provisions that Ange had assembled. She'd been forced to probe some cardboard boxes that contained some hitherto unused possessions. As was always the case, her trusty Akubra was in the last box. The hat had been a graduation present from her dad and carried some lovely memories. It was the perfect adornment for a trip to the bush.

Ange broke the rules and allowed Buddy to sit in the comfort of the rear seat. He seemed to enjoy the regular pats and attention he received along the way, and Ange knew Buddy would weasel his way into making this position his own.

The surveillance cams had arrived on Tuesday. With Billy's help, Ange had temporarily installed one at Gus's place and let it run overnight. When she'd reviewed the evening's footage, the level of night-time activity she'd observed was simply amazing. An unexpected bonus was catching the culprit who'd been munching on the jasmine draping the side of the guesthouse. A large grey possum dropped easily from an overhanging tree, crossed over the guesthouse roof, and then attacked the tasty jasmine with gusto. Ange planned to deal with that criminal element another day. A large barn owl flew in for a midnight visit, on the lookout for rodents. The ultimate stealth predator, it sat patiently for a few minutes before flying off in complete silence. Buddy made regular trips around the perimeter during the night, although he had walked straight past the feasting possum without so much as a whimper. This gross dereliction of duty secretly disappointed her.

Ange texted Fin Templeton from one of their comfort stops and gave him an ETA. They agreed to meet at Pam's coffee shop in Clearwater, a place that Ange knew well from her previous trips. After a stress-free five-hour drive, they arrived in Clearwater just after 11 a.m. The Prado had performed brilliantly, and it saddened Ange to realise that she would need to return the vehicle to the Queensland police service one day. She planned to hang on as long as possible, or at least convince Sally Anders that she needed a similar replacement.

Pam recognised Ange immediately, although she only knew Ange as her alter ego, Gloria White. 'Hello, Gloria. You can't stay away from the place, can you?'

Gus looked at Ange sideways, seemingly unaware that he was sleeping with a stranger. He had gotten used to these surprises, though, so he just rolled his eyes and continued patting Buddy.

'You're spot on, Pam. We're going camping this time, so I think we need two of your best flat whites and, if it's not too late, a couple of breakfast wraps. My camp oven cooking is a touch rusty,' replied Ange/Gloria, trying to avoid getting involved in too deep a conversation with the friendly cafe owner, a plan that failed miserably.

'Remember you asked me about drugs last time you were here? Well, you wouldn't believe it, but there was a cannabis farm operating just out of town. None of the residents knew anything about it. How the council gave approval in the first place is beyond me, but I understand they've shut the place down. Thank goodness is all I can say.'

'Wow,' said Gloria White, as if otherwise lost for words. Pam's newsflash supported Ange's view that Alan Campbell had his finger on the pulse of his constituency.

Ange went back to the table and sat with her two male friends and waited for their coffee and food. A dirty mud-splattered Toyota Land Cruiser tray-back 4WD rattled up to the kerb, and a fit young man spilled out. He walked toward where Ange and Gus sat enjoying their breakfast. Ange quickly intercepted him.

'Fin? Gloria White. Pleased to meet you,' said Ange, firmly shaking the hand of the confused man before drawing in close and whispering that he should refer to her as Gloria when in earshot of the all-seeing, all-knowing Pam. Evidently, Alan Campbell had not given him the full story about how Ange had come to town some weeks back. 'I was using this name during an investigation. I think it's best that we keep that story alive,' she whispered.

Ange glanced over her shoulder to see Pam straining to hear what was going on, so she raised her voice for Pam's benefit. 'This is my partner, Gus, and the other handsome boy is Buddy.'

Gus stood up to shake Fin Templeton's hand. At the mention of his name, Buddy had moseyed over to sniff Templeton's mud-splattered jeans. Evidently liking what he smelt, he positioned himself for a proper greeting, rewarded when Templeton bent over and gave him a vigorous scratch. 'Nice dog. Is he a working dog?'

'Not anymore. Buddy was a castoff from my father. He got himself kicked, and he's now cow-shy. He won't cause any trouble with your stock.' Ange then raised her voice marginally to ensure that Pam could hear. 'Alan and my dad go way back and share an addiction to horse racing. They're both smart men, but I can never understand how they get duped by that industry.'

As if he had already read the script, Templeton chimed in perfectly. 'I hear you.

When I'm not dealing with the farms and the cattle, I spend the rest of my time moving horses around and keeping trainers in line. They can be a handful—the trainers, that is. I can't believe how easily they pull the wool over the boss's eyes—although I'm sure he realises the game that's in play. Let me grab a coffee.'

Pam greeted Fin Templeton warmly, obviously a regular customer, before turning to Ange/Gloria. 'I didn't realise that you were camping at the Hilton! The Campbell family campsite is legendary around here. You seem to have found your way around Clearwater, Gloria.'

'Nothing like old family friends,' was all that Ange was prepared to concede.

Pam had already fixed Templeton's preferred poison, and he was back sitting at their table in no time. Ange was intrigued by how young that he seemed. 'How long have you worked in Alan's operation?'

'Around six years now. Before that, I was a commodities trader who got too big for his boots. I had been doing some work for Alan, and he bailed me out when I suffered some personal trading losses. I'd let my ego run amok and thought I knew more than I really did. Anyhow, Alan's bailout came with the proviso that I work off my debt in his operation. He's been very generous to me and my family, and forgave any residual debt a few years back. I live with my wife and two young boys on Box Grove, another Campbell property. Alan and his wife, Billie, live on Emerald Downs, which is their original property. We love it here.'

'Commodities trader. That must have been intense. I presume you're pretty good with IT on that basis?' asked Ange. Her estimation of Alan Campbell had gone up a notch. He was obviously someone who knew talent when he saw it and kept it close.

'I'm OK. Alan filled me in on your plan to establish some surveillance,' said Templeton. He reached into the top left pocket of his shirt and pulled out three SIM cards, handing them to Ange. 'These should work well. They're prepaid for data and text. I went for thirty gigabytes per month, which should be plenty based on what I read online.'

'When do you think you last lost stock?'

'It's hard to say exactly. We've certainly lost at least four cows in the past six months, but those last two really hit Alan hard,' replied Templeton.

'How so?' asked Ange, sensing this might have been the reason that Campbell had gone to the trouble of reaching out for help.

'They were prime breeding cows who would have had calves in tow. Alan is very protective of his breeding stock. We found they were missing when it came time to wean our calves and brand and tag them. I've never seen Alan so upset about anything.'

'Could they have been lost to natural causes?' asked Ange.

'As you would know from your dad, we aren't immune to ticks and gastric worms. We also lose the odd animal to wild dogs, but these latest losses have been too many and too regular. I also scoured the property, but I was more concerned about wild dogs than rustling. What's quite common is for calves to be stolen before they're weaned and branded, but those are normally inside jobs and not what we're seeing here. Anyway, Alan treats his people far too well for that sort of nonsense.'

'Makes sense. I had to ask as we don't want to start our operation only to find it wasn't rustling at all. I did some research and I understand that rustling has become a massive problem with these extraordinary beef prices of late. What's all that about?'

'It's a basic supply and demand problem. Everyone has been stocking up. With this run of good seasons, properties all over the country have been enjoying abnormally high levels of quality feed. To add to that, demand for export beef went through the roof during Covid. It'll all change if we get a dry season or two, and those same properties need to destock.'

They traded small talk over their coffee and food. Buddy sat down beside Templeton, securing as many pats as he could from this wonderfully aromatic stranger. Once their refreshments were complete, Templeton stood up. 'Follow me. I don't think you'll need anything. Emerald Downs is only fifteen minutes north of here, so it's no big deal to whip into town if you require anything special.'

Once on the road, they crossed over the bridge and headed north. Ange briefly wondered if the team from Tweed Heads had retrieved the small camera that they'd mounted under the bridge and used to capture images of the illegal cannabis handover. Driving further north, they passed the intersection with Samsons Road, which led to the former cannabis farm. She pondered what had become of that property and knew that she couldn't resist a reconnoitre at some point. A heavily treed ridge obscured any view of the Telstra Tower, where she knew a more permanent surveillance camera sat chugging away, surveying the now-vacant property.

This restful camping trip would definitely not be boring.

Chapter 8

On Safari

After another ten-odd minutes' drive, the convoy of two swung off the asphalt road, shuddering across a cattle grid and onto Emerald Downs. Ange couldn't recall seeing such a resplendent-looking property. Fin drove them past an elegant homestead surrounded by an extensive rose garden and expansive lawns. A tennis court sat in the distance, conspicuous evidence of the highly social Sunday tennis parties that had been a hallmark of rural life for generations. The crushed granite track wound down to the river, easily identified by the line of trees that snaked across the property.

The vehicles followed the track until it traversed the river at a low-level crossing and then snaked its way through the heavily grassed paddocks until the two vehicles pulled up beside a large waterhole and the permanent camp that was to be Ange's home for a few days. It was like something from an African safari movie and a massive step up from the makeshift affairs that Ange had suffered when her father was in charge. Back then, they had made do with a tarpaulin that was stretched across a rope pulled tightly between two trees. This makeshift affair was highly attractive to the occasional nocturnal visitor who came scurrying in the night looking for an opportune meal. She had adored those camping trips with her dad, even despite those minor inconveniences.

It was hard to imagine a more perfect location for a campsite. The wide emerald-green river flowed slowly to the right and a majestic river gum stood on the water's edge, shading and imbuing a sense of cool serenity in the large waterhole. A thick knotted rope hung from a branch of the overhanging gum tree, a clue to suggest that this was a popular swimming hole during summer holidays. With such a permanent water supply, it was no wonder the homestead looked so lush and green. Alan Campbell was obviously a savvy businessman. Properties like Emerald Downs were usually multigenerational.

The campsite was fenced off from the adjoining paddock and had been recently mowed. It incorporated three large permanent tents, pitched on wooden platforms that sat two steps above ground. A specially mown path led to a small outhouse, positioned some hundred metres away from the campsite to avoid any impact on the waterway. Between the tents and the water sat a large firepit, surrounded by sizeable sandstone blocks, complete with a gantry and large blackened billy for boiling water. Two well-used cast-iron camp/dutch ovens had been placed on the granite blocks, and a large stack of firewood stood beside a long-handled shovel that would manoeuvre the red-hot coals and stoke the camp ovens come mealtime.

Once the cars were parked, Fin ambled over and rolled a laminated satellite map of the property on the bonnet of Ange's Prado. Ange took a moment to pluck her trusty Akubra from the vehicle, and this much-loved hat fell perfectly into place atop her head, making her feel at ease and ready for whatever the country could throw at her.

She joined Templeton in front of the Prado, and he pointed to a spot on the map where the river made a large but gentle curve. 'This is where we are now.' He then turned and gestured towards some distant hills to their right. 'As you can see, Green River diagonally splits the property, roughly sixty percent east of the river, and forty percent between the river and the main road.'

'How do you cope in flood?'

'The river flats flood, and it can cut us off from the western part of the property. We have two crossings, the main one that we just drove over and another ford further to the south. Floods can create difficulties, but they're a part of life and don't really affect us too greatly,' replied Fin before pointing to a heavy treeline on the map. 'The top of that ridge marks the eastern boundary, and Bullock Road makes up the western boundary.' He looked back down at the map and traced out a small creek. 'That's Windy Creek, which is a tributary of the Green River. It's spring-fed from the mountain range and delivers permanent water. Our southern boundary starts where Windy Creek meets Green River, and then crosses under Bullock Road and follows the creek up into the foothills. We don't need to fence all of that boundary on account of the permanent water. We share the northern boundary fence with Tempest Hill, which has been owned by the Gregg family for generations.'

'When did the main road become Bullock Road?' asked Ange. 'I hadn't heard that name before.'

'Back at the turnoff to Fernvale between here and Clearwater.'

'OK. I remember Samsons Road eventually ended up at Fernvale,' said Ange, recalling her previous operation. 'So, going by your description, anyone accessing the property to rustle cattle would need to use the western boundary and the main road. Is that how you see it?'

'Yes, unless they came through Tempest Hill. However, I think that would be unlikely. There might be a way in that I don't know about. Steven Gregg runs the place now. I haven't told them about our stock losses. Maybe they've been a victim as well. However, their road frontage is a fraction of ours and they've cleared it of any timber. Anyone accessing Tempest Hill would be visible from both the road and their homestead. We maintain a line of trees along our road frontage as a windbreak from the crushing westerly winds that rip through midwinter. We have almost three kilometres of road frontage and the place is just over two thousand five hundred hectares. Emerald Downs is the biggest property in the region, as Alan progressively purchased and amalgamated several adjoining properties. He has a standing offer to purchase Tempest Hill if the Gregg family ever sells up.'

Ange knew that this was a substantial holding of prime country. The permanent spring-fed water made Emerald Downs quite a prize. 'Impressive. We'll get ourselves settled and start having a look around in the morning. How about you come down tomorrow for a late-afternoon drink and we can devise a plan to deploy our surveillance?'

'Sounds like a plan. You're free to go anywhere, just keep an eye out for snakes and please shut any gates behind you. I guess I don't need to tell a country girl that rule, but some of our city visitors don't have any clue. We've had a couple of inappropriate breeding incidents over the years,' observed Templeton wryly.

'How do you determine breeding in those cases? I guess you can't be sure what was what?' asked Gus.

'We get all our prime breeding stock DNA tested. Alan takes breeding very seriously. We have two main breeds here, Black Angus and Wagyu. Anything that doesn't measure up genetically gets sold through the sale yard,' replied Templeton. 'Alan saw the opportunity for Wagyu during the Japanese investment splurge in the nineties and was one of the first Australian breeders to jump on board. This was a hugely successful strategy. Asia has an insatiable appetite for Australian Wagyu.'

Wagyu was a Japanese beef breed, and Ange knew that its marbled flesh was highly prized and ultra-expensive, although it was too rich for her taste—and wallet. 'Alan said that a prime stud bull can go for hundreds of thousands of dollars. I sort of get that, but a breeding female can surely only have a dozen progeny at best. I presume that they're not as valuable.'

'Not necessarily. A breeder in top condition can yield up to thirty eggs in a single chemically induced flush—although it's usually more like half a dozen. This process can be repeated every two months or so. The price tag for a high-quality Wagyu embryo has exceeded twenty thousand dollars, so you can imagine how that can soon add up.'

'Incredible. I had no idea about the numbers involved,' commented Ange, her voice filled with genuine surprise. 'What breed were the last lot of animals stolen?'

'Wagyu. All the cattle stolen so far have been Wagyu cows. Whoever is stealing these animals knows their stuff.'

'OK. That's useful to know. So, what are your thoughts about what's going on here, Fin?'

'I'm not sure. It's still possible to see through the treeline in places and observe when we've moved stock into the westernmost paddocks beside the main road. If someone drove slowly past, they could probably see the stock and then come back later. What I can't understand is how they get the stock loaded and away. They would have to do this in the middle of the night. It's not the Newell Highway, but the road is used 24/7. Maybe they're brazen enough to come through one of the access gates.' Templeton pointed out the three main access points along the road frontage. 'The two gates to the south are remnant access points from the properties that were amalgamated into Emerald Downs. You can see the old homesteads from those days. These are both rented to farmworkers, so I find it hard to believe that they wouldn't hear cattle being moved in the night.'

'Surely they wouldn't be so bold as to steal cattle through the main entrance, would they?' asked Ange.

'I doubt it. However, I regularly check the fences and I've seen no evidence that they've been cut and repaired. As you would know, repairing a tensioned barbed wire fence is no small feat, particularly in the dark,' replied Fin.

'Thanks, Fin. We'll have a look around and I'll see you back here late tomorrow afternoon. Hopefully, a fresh set of eyes and a new perspective might see something interesting. At the very least, I'll work out the best locations to deploy our cameras.'

'OK. I'll see you for that drink. By the way, you look quite at home with your Akubra. I reckon you could pass as a jillaroo any day, although I can't see Gus passing for a jackaroo in his surf gear.'

With a laugh, she watched Fin Templeton turn and amble towards his vehicle. After her brothers had moved away, her father would sometimes employ a jackaroo to lend a hand on the farm during a busy season. He had never once employed a jillaroo, the female equivalent. She mused that maybe her father held on to a secret desire for her to return to the farm one day.

Ange was fully immersed in this small but intriguing challenge. For the first time in days, Carruthers and the Integrity Command had ceased to stalk her every thought. Once they had unpacked and set up camp, the trio went for a mid-afternoon walk. More correctly, it was Buddy who took Ange and Gus for a walk, excitedly dashing ahead and then turning to check if they were following. They took a loop back the way they'd arrived and then followed the fence line north. Brandishing makeshift walking sticks for snake protection, selected by trial and error from the detritus left by a large eucalypt tree, Ange studied the fence line for a kilometre or so until they came to the boundary with Tempest Downs. She could see no obvious breaches. Turning east, they traced the shared boundary fence for about five hundred metres, until they came up against Green River. Ange could see nothing that seemed out of place.

Rather than try to cross the river, the trio backtracked south along the Green River and wandered back to their campsite. It had been an early start, so Ange set up their bedding and the couple took a nap, something unusual for them both. The sense of solitude joined the overwhelming silence and sent Ange into a deep sleep, one where she dreamed of cattle rustlers on horseback, rifles ready, their black hats a telltale signal of their nefarious intents. Just before she awoke, Ange had a vivid dream where she came across a dead jackaroo hanging from a large dead tree, an artistic sculpture no doubt imagined after watching too many Western movies with her father as a young girl. She lay awake for a moment and pondered whether the black-hatted castle rustlers were a subliminal allegory for the Integrity Command, and she was the hanging jackaroo—although it would have been a jillaroo in that case. It was all very confusing.

Not wanting thoughts of the Integrity Command to spoil her mood, Ange woke up Gus, and the pair busied themselves getting a fire started and the camp oven loaded full of ingredients for a beef stew. She found a large bone in the icebox that was mostly stripped of meat and realised that this was a present for Buddy. He was most impressed and scuttled off with his prize to sit under the river gum and munch away. Gus pulled some bottles of wine from the Prado, which he plonked in the Green River to cool down before stashing them into the icebox.

As the shadows lengthened under the setting sun, the couple took an invigorating nude swim in the waterhole before changing into some warmer clothes in defence against the cooling air. As Ange sat in her camp chair, glass of wine in hand, gazing across the Green River, admiring the sunset, she could finally cast off her disturbing dream and enjoy the moment and her company.

It promised to be a fun weekend.

Chapter 9

Deployment

The next day, with Buddy at the helm, they traipsed over the property, covering the entire boundary of Emerald Downs. By the time Fin Templeton arrived for drinks, Ange had reached her conclusions.

'Fin, I can't see anything out of place on the western boundary that runs along Bullock Road. They must have come in one of the permanent access points. Are you certain about the farmhands living in the other two houses?'

'As sure as I can be, although they predate me. What about through the Gregg property?'

'No. I really checked that boundary carefully, as I'm sure you have. It's a substantial and well-maintained fence. As you pointed out, it would be quite a business to drop and repair a tensioned fence in the dark without leaving some obvious signs. What about the Windy Creek boundary? That fence seems to have been repaired in several places.'

'That section is often damaged in the event of a big flood. Did you see anything out of place?'

'Perhaps. It looks like the creek flooded recently and covered up any tracks.'

'We had some decent rain in February, but the creek didn't flood badly enough to damage the fence line,' advised Templeton.

'I think we need to install two cameras on your two secondary access points, but we should also monitor the property to the south of Windy Creek. You never mentioned who owns that property.'

'That changed hands two or three years ago. Alan was super annoyed that he missed the place, but it never properly made it onto the market. It seems to have been a related party trade of some sort. What was worse was the value that it changed hands for. That was way over the odds and has raised everyone else's price expectations.'

'OK. I'll need your help tomorrow. We don't need to alert anyone about what we're doing. It will be less obvious if you do the work, Fin.'

'Understand. I'll get everyone to come across and work on Box Grove tomorrow morning. We have a small mob of weaners that need branding, so I'll put them to work doing that. Between the branding and everyone's Saturday shopping duties in Clearwater, we should have time to tackle whatever you have in mind.'

'We shouldn't take long. What we're looking for is a tree with a clear line of sight to each entrance. The trick will be to find somewhere suitable to deploy the small solar charging panels.' She showed him one of the camera units. 'If we're careful, I feel they'll be hard to see with their camo paint job. Make sure you bring an extension ladder and some tools along. A bunch of cable ties might come in handy.'

Once that was settled, they set about enjoying their drinks alongside the Green River and hearing each other's stories. Gus outdid himself and told a couple of surf stories that even Ange had never heard. Templeton opened up about the losses he suffered as a commodity trader. 'I was really good at my job—until I wasn't. I was just lucky that I was working for Alan at the time and he bailed me out. As well as being in charge of Emerald Downs and Box Grove, I also moonlight placing all of Alan's commodity trades and managing his futures contracts. I guess he thought I'd be unlikely to make the same mistake again.'

Once Templeton left, they settled around the campfire and waited for it to furnish enough coals to cook dinner. The rest of the world seemed to fade away.

Ange got the three cameras ready first thing the next morning and was all set to go when Templeton came back and picked her up just after 9 a.m. 'I reckon we've got until lunchtime,' he advised.

As things transpired, installing the two units on Emerald Downs took no time. One camera found a home midway up a stately box tree, and the other on a messy grey gum. The camo colouring allowed the units to blend in perfectly with the trees, and they were almost impossible to see. The third camera, the one that Ange had temporarily installed back home in Byron Bay, was much more difficult. It was impossible to get close to the driveway of the adjoining property without drawing obvious attention. Parking Templeton's 4WD ute down beside the river and under the bridge, the pair bush-bashed their way south until they found a tree suitable for their needs. Without the ladder, Ange needed to give Templeton some help to climb up into the tree. She held her breath as he precariously clung to some large branches to fix the solar panel in a place that would garner some morning sunlight.

Back at the campsite, Ange pulled out her tablet and opened the BushCamz App. Using her phone as a hotspot, they verified that all three cameras were operational. The unit surveying the adjoining property was a minor disappointment, but it gave a decent enough view south along Bullock Road. Ange could configure the three units remotely via the app, setting parameters like target zone and motion activation sensitivity. Alert texts would be sent to Templeton's phone and include a still picture of any incursion. After some discussion, Ange configured the alert parameters to include cars or large animals, and to activate only during the hours of 7 p.m. and 6 a.m. Templeton was most impressed, and Ange emailed him some login details and a web link to the operating instructions. Before Templeton left the campsite, they agreed they would undertake a field test at 7:30 p.m. that night.

The tests did not go exactly to plan, and Ange needed to fiddle with the target zone and increase the sensitivity to be suitable for a human. Apparently, in the world of BushCamz, a human was a medium-sized animal. The alert text function worked perfectly. Gus was also super impressed and pressed Ange to order a fourth unit for his beach shack at Angourie. They completed the order and make payment from their campsite in the country. The ease of making such a transaction while they were 'roughing it' was a juxtaposition that precipitated a spirited campfire discussion on the merits of 'getting away from it all'. They reached no conclusions.

Buddy was especially enamoured with the campfire and plonked himself down as soon as the fire reached that point where it turned from a cooking tool to a conversation magnet. Every so often, he would stand up, stretch himself luxuriously, turn the other cheek and then slump back down. Ange was certain she heard him sigh before he drifted off, although his ears would prick up at the frequent buzzing of Templeton's text alerts. Ange advised Templeton to keep his phone on silent that night if he hoped to sleep. After all, it was implausible to think that the rustlers would arrive while the troops were in camp.

Arriving back at Byron Bay on Sunday night was befuddling. The few days of camping had done a fantastic job of transporting Ange from her troubles. It wasn't as if her worries completely erased her country state of mind, but their return to Byron delivered a sense of otherworldliness. Notwithstanding the deployment of her high-tech motion-detecting and heat-sensitive video cameras, her time on Emerald Downs had distilled some simple pleasures from the complexities of modern life. Sitting around the campfire with a glass of wine, watching the hypnotic flames dance amongst the coals, had become something to savour. Without a television to distract, their fireside conversations had meandered effortlessly from topic to topic. Soon enough, the heat, and the wine would work their magic, and the couple would collapse into bed, fatigued after their busy day of doing nothing.

Stripped of most modern-day conveniences, camping becomes a busy endeavour. Ange concluded four days was the perfect duration. The weather during their sojourn had been superb, warm days followed by cool nights. She had previously experienced camping in the rain, caught in a thunderstorm while cowering under their makeshift tarpaulin with her dad as a young girl. Camping in the cold and wet was a bleak experience, so she knew not to paint too rosy a picture because of their five-star experience on Emerald Downs.

Ange busied herself in Byron for the next few days, struggling to distract herself from what lay ahead. Nothing would stick. There were simply too many memories of her life as a police officer embedded in the streets of Byron to allow her any peace. Even lunch with Kerrie didn't work. Normally these were affairs of fun and laughter, but Ange remained distracted and poor company. Kerrie knew how embarrassed and angry Ange felt about her suspension and tried desperately to veer around and over that topic. Like the best of friends, Kerrie knew when to pull back and let Ange process her own thoughts and insecurities.

Alan Campbell called on Thursday to give her something new to think about.

'Hi, Ange, or should I say Gloria?'

'Hah. Word gets around. Let's stick with Ange. That Gloria White person brings nothing but trouble,' laughed Ange, finding some humour in her situation.

'Fin filled me in on the cameras you installed. He seems most impressed, and it's opened his mind to all manner of possibilities. He's now planning to purchase an expensive drone. I think you might have created a monster. He'll soon be able to watch my every move. Anyhow, I have a present I'd like to give you in person. I have a meeting in Brisbane tomorrow with the Department of Agriculture. Would you have time to pop up? My meeting should finish before midday, so perhaps we can catch up over a late lunch.'

'You didn't need to get me anything, Alan. We really enjoyed ourselves, and your campsite is amazing. I don't feel comfortable taking anything from you,' replied Ange.

'It's not what you think, Ange. It's a joint present we can both enjoy. Is that a yes I hear?'

'Sure, Alan. I need a distraction from my upcoming hearing, and a drive along the Pacific Highway to Brisbane will undoubtedly provide that.'

'Great. Let's meet at 1 p.m. at the Breakfast Creek Hotel for a steak. I'll ring you if I get held up,' said Campbell before he hung up the call.

Ange laughed inwardly at this choice of restaurant. Campbell was one of the country's largest beef producers, yet he would choose steak over the endless culinary options available in town. He would likely poke his head into the kitchen and issue firm instructions to the chef about how to cook his steak. Her father had frequently embarrassed the family in this way, once famously at what was then Sydney's top steakhouse. She recalled how unimpressed the chef had been with her father's cooking advice, especially when he took advantage of the open kitchen layout to make sure that things were done as per instructions. It was an amusing story that was deeply insightful into her father's character. The chef hadn't seen it that way.

Ange was left wondering about Campbell's present, something that must be delivered in person. She pondered over this for the rest of the day. As things transpired, none of her ideas were remotely close to the mark.

Chapter 10

Gifted

Ange waited until the commuter traffic had cleared before tackling the drive north. Brisbane was a newly crowned Future Olympic City, an event that would surely bring significant change. She needed to pass by the Gold Coast and thought briefly about a previous case and the spectacular waterfront home she had enjoyed during her pursuit of the local chapter of the Ndrangheta. They had made Major Crimes look like fools on that occasion.

The Gold Coast and Brisbane cities would likely merge into one gigantic sprawling suburban super-metropolis, such was the unending pace of development. The Pacific Highway connecting these two cities was a perpetual construction site, a critical artery that seemed unable to keep pace with this growth for any decent length of time. It made for a testy drive, and Ange was pleased that she wasn't tackling this as a daily torment. The route to the Breakfast Creek Hotel skirted east and north of the city and flowed easily, providing a painless end to her otherwise tiresome journey and proof that the traffic engineers were at least getting something right.

Although this was Friday, she found a rare car park out the back of the hotel. She had never lived in Brisbane, so this was her first ever visit, and she wandered through the famed waterhole, taking in the institution that was the 'Brekky Creek Hotel'. At the juncture of the Breakfast Creek and the Brisbane River, the beautifully maintained historic building was as impressive as the legend implied. A large embossed sign proudly boasted that the pub had been established in 1889, and the respectful manner in which more recent additions blended with old was impressive and delightful.

Bang on 1 p.m., Ange made her way to the rear of the hotel and the incongruously themed Spanish Garden restaurant, resplendent with a white stucco arched portico. She arrived to see Alan Campbell seated at a table near the entrance. He waved Ange over.

'I know that there are newer and flasher places to eat, but this brings back memories of when I used to show my cattle at the Brisbane Exhibition. We always came here to celebrate our victories. Somehow, after all these years, the Spanish Garden still looks exactly the same. There's something comforting in this place and the memories it rekindles,' said Campbell wistfully. 'My boys boarded at Churchie and I always brought them here for a decent steak whenever I was in town. We used to schedule those lunches so that they missed their least favourite class.' Campbell looked towards the entry to the restaurant as if hoping his teenage boys might traipse in.

'Why did they board in Brisbane? Wouldn't the Armidale School have been closer for you?' asked Ange. 'I boarded at NEGS and my brothers boarded at TAS,' she elaborated. Most every bushie knew of the renowned Armidale schools. Churchie, or the Church of England Grammar School, was also a popular choice among rural families.

'Agree, but we really liked the culture of Churchie, and we especially loved the values and bearing of the young men they produced. Jock, my oldest grandson, has just started in Year 7, so I guess I'll soon need to pull my weight and introduce him to the Spanish Garden. His sister will start boarding at Maggies in two years. Jock's a good lad, but Phoebe is a hard case. I almost feel sorry for the boarding house mistress who gets the job of keeping that girl in check.'

'Don't underestimate a battle-scarred boarding house mistress, Alan. Believe me, I tried every trick in the book to get the better of my old boarding mistress. Miss Anderson was always one step ahead of every move I made. I reckon she had seen it all,' commented Ange as a wistful memory of her own slid by. 'I loved boarding school. It's where I learnt how to shoot a gun—not that it helped me much when I got myself shot. I never even got my gun out of my pocket.'

'Churchie boys must all undertake a year of service—either as an armed service cadet or doing community work. I like that the boys learn how to serve society while also learning about the responsibility of handling a weapon or something similar. You should see Churchie's Anzac Day parade. It's a massive event where the school reads out every Churchie boy who lost his life serving our country. It's quite sobering and a brilliant reminder to the boys that society isn't just here to serve them. Now, let's get some lunch sorted. Have you eaten here before?'

'This is my first time. My dad used to speak about it, but I think he thought it unfit for a *young lady*, as he used to call me back then. And look how that all turned out,' laughed Ange.

'The Brekky Creek certainly had a rough edge back in the day, but it's become well and truly gentrified now. Let me order. What do you want? I'm having a traditional rib fillet with coleslaw and roast potato in the jacket. I couldn't possibly stoop to ordering anything but the original.'

'Sounds perfect. Medium rare, please, Alan,' replied Ange.

In yet another throwback in time, Campbell stood up and joined the line of people standing in front of a massive display of meat cuts, all waiting patiently to choose their steak. While she was waiting, Ange looked around at the lunchtime crowd. Going by the prices, having a steak at 'The Creek' was not a daily treat, and Ange spent some time imagining who was who in the zoo. She rarely saw such an eclectic group of diners at any restaurant. A group of young men at a nearby table looked like lawyers or accountants. She imagined another group as stockbrokers or some other financial wizards. The tradespeople were conspicuous and an obvious sign that construction was booming. A long table of well-dressed women caught Ange's eye, somehow incongruous, although this shouldn't have been the case. Women enjoyed steak as much as men—she was a case in point.

Once Campbell had returned with his number-on-a-stick, he asked Ange about her trip to Emerald Downs.

'It was lovely. What a spectacular property. I can see why you choose to live there. The campsite is amazing and Fin looked after us brilliantly. We set up three cameras to cover the most obvious points where the rustlers might enter your property. However, I find it hard to fathom why rustlers would steal your cattle over others.'

Campbell cast Ange a grave look before commenting. 'I've wondered about that myself. I can only think that this is someone who has a grudge against me. A few toes have been stepped on over the years. The trouble is that none of the people who might have a grudge against me live locally. I believe our family is well-liked in Green River, thanks in part to my position as mayor and our ongoing financial support for local causes. I'm even patron of the Clearwater Sports Hub, and we've donated quite a deal of money to them over the years,' Campbell reflected. He looked positively disturbed by the thought that someone in his own community would feel enmity towards him. 'Either that, or it's just a case of tall poppy syndrome. That's an affliction that Australians seem especially prone to.'

'It would be easier if the culprit is someone with a specific axe to grind, rather than a generic case of the tall poppy syndrome. Presumably, the begrudged will have some connection with you that might give me something to work off. Then again, this could be nothing more than a random person with a profit motive. Hopefully, we've hidden the cameras well enough, and we'll soon discover what is going on. It's also curious that all the cattle stolen have been Wagyu. Any ideas about that?' asked Ange.

'Well, Wagyu has really taken off and is by far the most valuable of my breeding stock. I guess the rustlers know what they're doing—which makes it worse and somehow more personal,' said Campbell sombrely. Ange concluded that the concept of betrayal was more distressing than the loss of his prized cattle.

Campbell's face brightened noticeably as he reached into his leather briefcase and pulled out a large yellow envelope. 'I guess you're wondering what this catch-up is about?'

'Yes, I confess to being perplexed about why we needed to meet in person,' replied Ange.

Campbell handed the folder across the table. 'This is for you. I think you'll find it interesting.'

Ange opened the flap of the envelope and pulled out the contents. A typed report accompanied a series of large glossy photos. A picture was worth a thousand words, so Ange passed over the report and went straight to the photos. They were all high quality, date- and time-stamped on the top left corner, and she instantly recognised Julia Bennet, the ex-CEO of the Green River Shire Council. The first photo caught Bennet crossing a road and was not especially interesting in itself. The second showed her walking into the W Hotel in Woolloomooloo. Ange knew the hotel well. It was on one of her favourite walking routes while she lived in Sydney, midway between her apartment in Edgecliff and the CBD. The third showed the profile of a man walking towards the same hotel. The fourth caught the man looking directly toward the camera, as if he was checking to see who might be watching. Ange wondered if he had seen the photographer. Evidently not, as the next showed him walking through the front door of the hotel. Ange didn't recognise the man, but his face seemed vaguely familiar. She flipped back through the photos and could see that they were all taken on the same day within thirty minutes of each other.'

Ange looked up and spoke to Campbell. 'The man looks familiar, but I can't place who he is.'

'The right honourable Greg Kilroy, Minister for Regional Development,' replied Campbell, keeping the tone of his voice within the matter-of-fact range.

Ange raised her eyebrows at this revelation. Now things were getting interesting. 'I gather this suggests they might have been meeting for some reason. Then again, those series of photos could be purely coincidental.'

'Read on,' was Campbell's simple answer to Ange's implied question.

The next photo blew up any idea of a coincidence. It showed Bennet and Kilroy leaving a restaurant together. Taken at night, the photo was grainy and less clear than the hotel sequence, but it was definitely Kilroy and Bennet. The last and most explosive showed the pair locked in a passionate kiss. Kilroy had pushed Bennet up against a brick wall just around the corner from the restaurant, and the pair were pressed tightly together. Bennet had raised her left knee and wrapped it around her lover, leaving Kilroy's right hand to explore her upper thigh. It was quite a photo, almost art house in the way it so perfectly caught the passion that flowed between the couple.

'Wow. That's some photo. How did you get these, Alan?'

'One doesn't build a business like mine without coming across some underhanded individuals. Over the years, I've enjoyed the services of an exceptional private investigator. Kilroy is not the first politician that we've caught with his pants down. You coming to town and blowing things up made me realise that something wasn't right about our CEO. My PI uncovered more than even I'd expected.'

'How long do you think their affair has been going on?'

'Over three years. It's all there in the report. I'm not exactly sure how Brian secured this information. That's Brian Edwards, my PI. Bennet and Kilroy were regular guests at the W Hotel. What a slime. Kilroy's last election campaign was built on a platform of family values. He even roped his wife and kids into the campaign pictures. Anyhow, I thought you might find them helpful with your current problem. For myself, I'm looking forward to having my day in court against this cabal. Although, I reckon you might get there first. I doubt they'll pursue the Green River Council after these revelations. Now, do you have good legal representation? I'd be happy to help. I know a few quality barristers who I use from time to time.'

'That's very kind, Alan, but I have good legal support. My boss has convinced Owen Fairweather to act pro bono.'

'The QC? Well, Fairweather is definitely top shelf. I think you're in capable hands. How did your boss convince him to assist you?'

'Apparently, it's King's Counsel now, Alan. Don't feel bad—I still can't get comfortable with that change of title either. Apparently Fairweather and my boss's late husband, Max Anders, shared chambers. They went to law school together. We're due to meet next week and go through our strategy. I think Owen will enjoy your present just as much as I have. I reckon he has a wicked sense of humour. Have you found out what Bennet is up to?'

'I heard from a contact in the Department of Agriculture that Julia's been hawking herself around government.'

'That surprises me a little. I presumed that Kilroy would have landed her a flash job somewhere,' observed Ange.

'Maybe Kilroy is worried about being accused of favouritism? Or perhaps he's not happy about his mistress being so close to home?'

'If Kilroy has cooled his heels over Ms Bennet, then she probably won't be too thrilled about it,' speculated Ange. 'I'd sure feel used if I was in her shoes.'

Their meal arrived, bringing the conversation to a halt as they eagerly dug into their steaks. Ange's rib fillet was especially tasty.

Chapter 11

A Waiting Game

Nothing consequential happened during the first half of the week after Ange's surprising visit to Brisbane. She'd opted not to risk the mail but to hand-deliver the explosive envelope to Owen Fairweather in person instead. She took advantage of the marginal improvement in the surf and spent a couple of hours in the ocean each day. Her remaining time was divided among assisting Gus at the surfboard shop, enjoying lunch with Kerrie, and taking Buddy on extended walks. Despite all this activity, a profound sense of boredom was setting in.

She received regular updates from Fin Templeton. No new cattle had been rustled, but Fin reported that some wild dogs were of concern. Ange figured she could leave Emerald Downs to Templeton's eager eye and focus on her own problems.

By Thursday, the waiting had eaten away her resilience, and she acted on an idea that had been forming during her Buddy-time on the walking tracks around Byron. She told Gus about her plan on the weekend before she was due to face the music in Sydney.

'Irrespective of what happens next week, I'm planning to resign from the police service. I can't imagine going back to work after the way they've treated me this past year,' explained Ange in a rush of emotion, so distraught that she was struggling to hold back tears.

'Oh dear. That's a big call,' replied Gus, not able to hide his surprise.

'I know you like me being a detective. I hope this won't affect our relationship,' Ange said, getting to the heart of her worries.

Gus wrapped her in a big hug. 'Of course not. You'll still be you, won't you?' he said, trying some levity to break the tension.

'Maybe. But my job is a big part of me.'

'What will you do with yourself? Remember, we had this discussion once before when you didn't want to return to Sydney after you'd been shot?'

'This situation is way worse. Anyhow, I applied to register a business name this week. Nimble Investigations. I figured that I may as well use my skills while they're still fresh.'

'OK. Sounds serious. Odd name,' Gus commented, not sounding entirely sold on her plan.

A hint of defensiveness crept into Ange's voice. 'I figured it showed that I was agile and flexible. Anyway, the best names were taken.'

'Will this involve spying on people in Byron Bay?' asked Gus in a barbed question.

'Maybe,' replied Ange tentatively. 'Technically, it already does, doesn't it?'

'Only when an actual crime has been committed. Now you'll probably end up following my customers around, checking to see if they're having an affair,' suggested Gus, getting to the source of his hesitancy.

'So, your career is more important than mine. Is that what you're saying?'

'Ange, that's unfair. However, I don't want to become a pariah in Byron because you're sticking your nose in everyone's business. And I think you'll be busy, by the way,' shot back Gus sharply.

It was their first ever genuine disagreement as a couple, and it left Ange feeling hurt and dismayed, not only because she felt that Gus wasn't supportive but also because she knew he was correct. Marital infidelity was likely to be a principal activity for Nimble Investigations.

The pair flounced around the house for the rest of the weekend until Gus broached the subject on Sunday evening. 'I'm sorry that I didn't seem supportive. It shocked me that you planned to resign.' He moved to give Ange a hug. 'I'll support whatever you decide. Just promise that you won't make any rash decisions. OK?'

'I'm sorry as well, Gus. I should have talked to you before getting things rolling with Nimble Investigations. I guess I've become used to making all my own decisions. Let's deal with next week and then we can regroup over Easter.'

She flew to Sydney early Monday morning, ahead of a briefing with Owen Fairweather scheduled for later that day. Despite Owen's assurance when they'd first met, Ange was awash with doubts and fears, her imagination spinning wildly from one disastrous outcome to the next. Ideally, she would have moved into Gus's Sydney apartment, but Bobby Bell, Gus's legendary surfing father, was down staying there for a week with friends.

The Bell boys had amassed an eclectic collection of surfing and travel memorabilia from their adventures around the world. The delightful apartment was part museum and part accommodation. She had stayed there with Gus the previous year when they'd celebrated the wedding of a school friend of Gus, a workaholic who was tying the knot for the second time.

Ange had taken Gus to task over the knowing looks of his friends. 'So, tell me, Gus. Did I pass the high mark set by your former swimsuit model girlfriends?'

Gus had just rolled his eyes and skirted the question, wrapping her in a bear hug, warming her heart with his obvious affection. 'Just don't let yourself go, Ange. That's the best advice that I can give you,' he'd countered with a mischievous grin. They both knew full well that would never happen.

Without the comfort of Gus's homely apartment, Ange was forced to endure the clinical torture that was the department's bland digs in the CBD. Her boss had texted the PIN code to access the place, and it held no pleasant memories. Every time she had stayed there, she was being chased by someone or something. The exception to that was the time she had taken on the role of Lily White, Bree's avatar, the edgy online NFT and crypto trader. That was also a precursor to Ange being shot, a memory that provided little comfort to her overcharged imagination.

After dropping off her bag in the apartment and opening a window or two to relieve stale air, she wandered through the city and picked up some sushi rolls for lunch. With time to kill, she walked across to Hyde Park. Tucked hard up against the CBD, the park was a favourite of the lunchtime crowd, a respite from the frenetic activity of the city. Ange was fortunate to find a vacant park bench and sat admiring the majestic canopy of trees that lined the central spine of the park. This wide and shady avenue was a hive of activity as workers sought a welcome reprieve from their punishing city schedules. Some were like Ange and simply enjoying a peaceful lunch; joggers were enjoying exercise rather than food; another constant stream of walkers buzzed by, perhaps on their way to some important meeting at the other end of the CBD. That such a sanctuary could exist amongst such chaos was delightful, and the beguiling scene helped subdue Ange's worries.

The outcome of the next few days would be very much dependent on her state of mind. She needed to remain calm and considered throughout, no matter what was going on around her or how viciously the Integrity Command attacked. Her actions and her professionalism as a police officer would undoubtedly be targets, but she felt comfortable defending those positions. Attacks on her character would be more troublesome. They would be personal assaults designed to unsettle, hoping for Ange to stumble and say something incriminating. It would not be easy.

At 1:45 p.m., Ange left this peaceful oasis and walked across Elizabeth Street and back into the noisy madness of the CBD. The receptionist ushered Ange straight into Fairweather's chambers, resplendent with its striking paintings. She briefly wondered about the psychology of his remarkable collection. Did it make clients nervous, worried that their troubles might add to Fairweather's expensive trophy collection? Or would they see them as a signal of his abilities, a measure of his success in representing the interest of former clients, hoping this might be repeated in their case? Fortunately, seeing as Fairweather had offered to act pro bono, Ange remained unburdened by such concerns.

'Hello, Detective Watson. Nice to see you again,' said Fairweather, walking around from behind his desk to shake Ange's hand. 'I've been hearing a lot about you.'

'Please call me Ange. People talking about me behind my back makes me nervous. I hope some of this idle gossip was positive.'

'Sally finally came over for dinner on the weekend. She gave me quite the rundown. I hear you grew up on a property near Tamworth. I'm from Orange myself, but not off the land like you. My father was a local solicitor. Fairweather and Associates. The usual stuff of regional towns, conveyancing, wills, border disputes and the like. He hoped for me to take over the practice, but I would have gone stir-crazy. Dad's retired now and driving my mother around the bend. Better her than me,' said Fairweather with an easy and warm smile.

'That seems the trap of family businesses. Believe me, I've seen many a family torn apart by custody battles over the family farm. That's something my father will need to deal with. My vote would be for my parents to sell up and find somewhere nice to enjoy themselves. However, there's also nothing sadder than a retired bushie floundering like a fish out of water in unfamiliar surroundings, their name no longer synonymous with their property. I raised this with them a few times, but it's a can that keeps getting kicked down the road. I think retirement is a vastly overrated concept.' Ange fixed Fairweather in the eye. 'I presume that my country roots weren't the only topic discussed over your dinner with the boss.'

'Sally thinks highly of you. She described you as smart, hardworking, and principled. I think she's a little jealous of your sixth sense—her words—in making connections that move a case forward. Although she said that you were prone to the occasional misstep and misdirection. Would you consider that a fair assessment of yourself?'

'That was nice of the boss to say those kind things about me. And, yes, I am guilty of that last charge.'

'Is that what's going on here, Ange? You going off on some tangent and not following due process?'

Ange looked up sharply. 'Lull me into a false sense of comfort and then thrust at the smallest opening,' she thought to herself before replying. 'Not at all. I did everything by the book.' She looked Fairweather directly in the eye. 'I'm sure Sally told you about all of that.'

Fairweather ignored Ange's implied question, asking another instead. 'Having had time to reflect on the situation we're in, what do you believe it's really about?'

'I reckon that I've trodden on some sensitive toes—probably partly politically motivated, and part vengeance,' replied Ange. She had pondered this question for hours during the previous night, sitting on the veranda in the early hours, overlooking a moonlight sea that sparkled in the distance. Not even Buddy's calming companionship had yielded any definitive conclusions. It comforted her that Fairweather had referred to the situation as if it was a joint problem and not just hers.

'Isn't everything political these days?' responded Fairweather wistfully. Ange wasn't sure by his tone whether this state of affairs was good or bad for business. He pushed on. 'Why do you say vengeance?'

'I clipped the wings of the chief investigator not long ago. Detective Ben Carruthers. He'd taken things too far and put his superiors in a difficult position. I'm sure Carruthers would like to see the back of me for good.'

'OK. Sally didn't go into anything about Carruthers, so you'd best explain.'

'Well, Carruthers and his sidekick, Sheena Wadley, came to stitch me up after the Namba Heads shootings. Surely Sally told me about that incident?'

'Yes, she did. Sally told me you got yourself shot and badly injured and that two criminals were killed. "Ndrangheta Mafia hitman" was the term she used. There was an article in The Times recently about the Ndrangheta. That took chutzpah, tackling them head-on as you did.' He looked at her carefully. 'Are you fully recovered? I guess the mental effects are just as bad as the physical.'

'I'm fine physically, but I still have the odd nightmare. That sorry incident was one of my failures. We should have done more research on how those guys might have reacted when we cornered them. I was convalescing following surgery when Carruthers and Wadley paid me a visit—against Sally's specific request. They tried to take advantage of my weakened position and make me a scapegoat.'

'I don't understand. You dealt with two dangerous criminals. I'm sure shooting and killing them wasn't on page one of the police manual, but why would anyone wish to make a scapegoat out of you?'

'The Ndrangheta had infiltrated the police service at the highest level. Chief Superintendent Gary Bold—Sally's boss, in fact. I'm sure he wasn't the only one, either. Bold had been covering for the Ndrangheta for decades, misdirecting investigations and warning them whenever we got close. It was a massive embarrassment and something the police hierarchy wanted swept under the carpet. And then, little old Angela Watson bumbles in. Blaming an overzealous officer was the perfect solution. They might have gotten away with it, had it not been for the trap that Sally Anders laid. She's one smart and cunning woman, my boss.'

'What, are you saying that Carruthers, the officer we're up against, might be part of the Ndrangheta Mafia?'

'No, no, not at all—he's not smart enough. My guess is that upstairs, the people who were trying to stitch me up, were smarting at being caught out by Sally. I made Carruthers agree to send me a transcript of our interview during my convalescence,' replied Ange, raising air quotes over the word interview. 'According to Sally, that transcript, along with her own recorded conversations, did the trick. They wouldn't have appreciated being humiliated by her, so they likely took it out on Carruthers and Wadley—although Wadley is just his minion. Who else might be a Ndrangheta mole is a mystery, but I'm sure that there are multiple. I'm also certain that Carruthers was dumped on from above, as he rang to apologise. That man would apologise to no one unless he was forced to. He wouldn't know how to spell the word. Anyhow, I couldn't help myself and gave him a dressing down, accusing him of going along with the cover-up and stitching me up when he knew the whole affair stank to high heaven.'

'OK, that's interesting background. But why go again? Surely he knows that you and Sally would revisit the evidence of the Ndrangheta cover-up.'

'I agree. It must be unrelated. Sally told me that her lawyer has a copy of everything and is under strict instructions to send it to Sue Elkington at The Times,' replied Ange. Suddenly, the penny dropped. 'You're that lawyer, aren't you?'

'Very perceptive, Detective. I guess that's why you're paid the big bucks,' said Fairweather with a smile.

'It would be ridiculous in the extreme to think that I've stumbled on another criminal organisation that's infiltrated the police service. They'd probably be more intent on destroying each other than me. I'll wager that politicians and their mates are at the centre of this, playing their dirty little back-slapping games at the expense of us all.'

'You have a rather poor opinion of our political leaders, Detective. Your theory might well be true, but we will have to prove that, and it would be a substantial deviation on our part to head down that route and so late in the day.'

'It's funny you should mention that,' said Ange, reaching into her oversized handbag to retrieve a certain large yellow envelope.

Chapter 12

Plan of Attack

Owen Fairweather opened the yellow envelope and slid out its contents. Like Ange had, he went straight to the large glossy photographs. 'What am I looking at here, Ange?' he asked, obviously not recognising the protagonists.

'The woman is Julia Bennet, former CEO of the Green River Council, and the man is the not-so-honourable Greg Kilroy, the current minister for regional development.'

Fairweather flipped through the photos until he came to the hero shot. 'Oh my. That is quite a photo. Where did you get these?'

'Remember at our last meeting, I mentioned I was planning to visit Clearwater to help the mayor with his cattle rustling problem?' Ange asked, waiting for Fairweather to acknowledge this memory. 'Well, Alan—that's Alan Campbell, the mayor—is covering his bases over compensation being claimed by the owners of the cannabis farm. He knew something wasn't kosher and hired a private investigator. He's very good, Campbell's PI. The report shows a record of Bennet and Kilroy's affair going back over three years, which lines up nicely with when Bennet would have approved the cannabis farm. I've added some media articles about how Kilroy campaigned with his wife and children on a family-values platform during the last election.'

Fairweather sat back in his leather chair, deep in thought. 'If, as you imply, this is all politically motivated, then the party will wish to avoid any scandal, and this will come in very handy. However, the allegations against you will be about failures in due process: that you should have done your research before raiding the cannabis farm, and the like.'

'But doesn't the affair show that Kilroy and Bennet colluded to approve the cannabis farm on the sly? Someone benefited from that decision. This could be all about money—either campaign donations or worse. Nobody will want any attention being drawn to either situation.'

'I appreciate the logic of your theories, but my strong inclination is to focus on the fundamentals of the claims against you and leave the contents of this envelope as the cream on top. As satisfying as it would be, the best outcome would be to avoid using this information. Throwing it into the melee will undoubtedly come with unintended consequences.'

Ange thought this through. It was an insightful observation by Fairweather. Her sense of indignation over the stunt that Bennet and Kilroy had pulled was clouding her judgement. There was no point in showing all their cards unless absolutely necessary. The information Campbell had provided was an ace-in-the-hole to be used in case of emergency and only when it could deliver maximum impact. 'OK, Owen. I hear you.'

'I'm not saying that we won't use it at the hearing, but it's best to plan around it and not base our case on it. You will need to leave that decision in my hands. Now, how about we go through the details of the operation involving the cannabis farm? I have been wondering why Clearwater, and why Hillburn? Can you help me with that?'

'Hillburn is easy. It's located on a major east-west and north-south crossroads and a straightforward drive from Brisbane. I don't think you could pick a better location to service the Queensland mining regions. Clearwater is more difficult. In fact, I was about to cross the town off my list when I witnessed the drug deal.'

Fairweather interrupted Ange's response. 'But why was Clearwater on your list in the first place?'

'From Cua Kwm's interview. She was the young woman who escaped incarceration and alerted us to the trafficking cell. Clearwater fitted the description of her escape.'

'What happened to her?'

'She was murdered while being held in an immigration detention centre up in Brisbane.' Ange's voice trailed off before she sat silent for a second. 'What's really puzzling me is why Clearwater was chosen as the model site for a medical cannabis farm under the minister's new initiative. It's a lovely little town, but it's off the beaten track and not on any major thoroughfare.'

'I presume you have a theory or two.'

Ange gathered her thoughts. 'My preferred theory is that Julia Bennet became aware of the medicinal cannabis initiative and lobbied the minister to consider Clearwater. I get the impression that Bennet is incredibly ambitious and would have been capable of seizing that opportunity. Their affair probably started then or soon after. She certainly didn't appreciate me rolling into town.'

The pair then spent a good two hours going over the troubled Clearwater operation and its link with the Hillburn facility. Fairweather probed Ange at every step, making copious notes along the way. He assumed nothing and called Ange to task on every move she had made. Having to justify herself like that was exhausting, and it pleased her when Fairweather finally put his pen down to rest.

'So, Ange, how prevalent is people trafficking? I'm surprised that this sort of thing even exists in Australia.'

'To be honest, I'm not sure how widespread the problem is in this country, but the operation we uncovered is sophisticated and highly organised. They must surely have government officials in both Australia and Vietnam on their payroll for this to be happening right under our noses.' Ange then gave Fairweather a quick summary of the basics of people trafficking. For once, Fairweather stayed silent as he learned about this insidious trade. His face darkened perceptibly when Ange mentioned the young age of the women commonly trafficked into sex slavery. She wondered if he was imagining his own daughter, Emily, Sally Anders' goddaughter, in another universe and as a victim of such horror. When Ange had completed her synopsis, the pair sat silent for a moment, each lost in their own thoughts on this terrible industry. Fairweather pulled himself from these depths and stood up decisively from his chair.

'OK. I think we're done. This is going to be fun. We need you back on the job and stopping that horrific people trafficking operation,' concluded Fairweather, a succinct summation which lifted Ange's spirits to no end.

She thought it best to avoid mention of Nimble Investigations.

After her session with Fairweather, Ange felt markedly better about where things stood. She filled in Gus before securing a decent night's sleep, notwithstanding her cold and impersonal accommodation. Rising early Tuesday morning, Ange took herself off to make one of her favourite walks, catching the train and bus to Bondi Beach and exploring the coastal cliffs. The northerly wind was already brisk when she arrived in Bondi, but there were still some diehard and desperate surfers trying to eke out some rides from the small insipid northerly slop.

Inspired and uplifted by her walk, Ange then whiled away some time wandering through the Art Gallery of New South Wales before moving on to some shopping. She needed an appropriate outfit for an upcoming function with Gus. This was really a gross exaggeration, as she needed for nothing. However, she wanted to look her best, and it was fun exploring the fashion boutiques of Sydney. Gus had scheduled a cocktail party to raise money for the Bell Jay Tee Foundation, a charity designed to support young regional surfers, those with the talent and the desire to pursue a career as a pro surfer. Gus and his father had formed the foundation in memory of Jake Thompson, a young surfer sponsored by Bell Surfboards before his untimely death. It had been Ange who'd discovered what had happened to Jake, so she had some skin in the game.

Who knew—if the hearing went badly, her only vocation might be as the partner to Gus Bell. She figured that customers wouldn't beat down the door of Nimble Investigations if the principal was a disgraced former detective.

Alone with her thoughts over a late lunch, Ange pondered about her future life. Even though he wasn't beside her in the heat of battle, knowing she had the support of Gus Bell was of great comfort. Despite his stated love of sexy surfing detectives, she hoped he wouldn't care whether she was Detective Angela Watson, Nimble Ange the PI, or just plain old Ange the surfer-girl. Buddy, on the other hand, wouldn't care either way. He seemed happy to tag along on both the surfing and work trips, although Ange suspected he would readily jump ship and move to the Bell Surfboards shop, lapping up all the attention he seemed to garner. Rusty Bell, his online alter ego, had become quite the item around Byron.

After a solo dinner, she settled down to watch a movie. All things considered, she was as ready as she could be for whatever fate threw her way.

Chapter 13

Setting the Scene

Ange's hearing was set down for 2 p.m. and she was desperate to get back home to Byron Bay. Being the Wednesday before Easter, she knew she would miss the last flight of the day between Sydney and Ballina, the nearest airport just south of Byron Bay. She tried flights to Coolangatta, an hour's drive north of Byron, but there were no seats available. Trying to secure a flight on Thursday, the day before the Easter break, one of the busiest days for travel in the year, would be worse still. She privately fumed that Carruthers had scheduled her hearing for this date, knowing full well it would create the maximum inconvenience. After wasting an hour trying to find a flight, she was becoming agitated, so she put her travel plans aside until after the hearing. She needed to focus.

Sally Anders had rung first thing. The pair had agreed to meet outside the foyer of the Major Crimes offices in Bathurst Street at 1:30 p.m. before walking the block to the offices of the Police Integrity Command. Ange had brought along her only formal outfit, a navy pantsuit, mid-range in terms of price but still well cut. She decided on sushi for lunch, strategically placing a series of napkins lest she drip soy sauce all over her crisp white shirt. Her theory was that the rice and fish would calm her stomach. It made a poor job of that.

She paced nervously back and forth along Bathurst Street, a full ten minutes ahead of the time she had arranged to meet her boss. She looked skyward to the eleventh floor and wondered if the tall office building was her current or former head office. Would she be called to face the Law Enforcement and Ethics Tribunal? Being referred to the LEET was a dark day for any police officer and usually a traumatic career-ending event. Even when exonerated, few recovered from being hauled in front of LEET—private investigators included.

Sally Anders walked out of the foyer and rescued Ange from any deeper and darker thoughts. It was the first time she had seen Anders in full uniform, which did nothing for her churning stomach. The pair walked with a measured pace as Sally briefed Ange on the latest developments.

'Carruthers rang yesterday, asking about whether you had legal representation,' advised Anders.

'What did you tell him?'

'That we were still arranging your representation. It's not a complete lie, but I wasn't about to let him know we had Owen on our team, lest he beef up his own side. My guess is that he'll assume you're floundering for decent representation and will be poorly prepared. It will be interesting when Owen introduces himself. That might be fun. Now, other than Carruthers and Wadley, the Law Enforcement and Ethics Tribunal will be represented and oversee proceedings. I understand that person will most likely be a lawyer and will determine if the matter warrants a formal LEET or SACC hearing.'

'I hope LEET doesn't leak as badly as SACC,' observed Ange. She had been called to give evidence before the Standing Anti-Corruption Commission once before and did not hold their ability to keep a secret in high regard.

'LEET has a solid reputation and seems to take their independence seriously. It's our very own Integrity Command that we should be worried about,' observed Anders with a grimace. 'Owen is meeting us outside at 1:45 p.m. Follow his lead at all times, and don't speak unless he directs you to. Carruthers will try to bait you into saying something rash in front of the LEET representative. You need to stay cool, Ange, no matter how Carruthers tries to get under your skin.'

'Got it, boss,' said Ange, sounding more confident than she felt about following that advice.

'Oh. By the way, Owen told me about the dossier on Bennet and Kilroy that landed in your lap. Were you planning on letting me know about that at some stage?' enquired Anders with a penetrating stare.

Ange instantly felt a flash of guilt about failing to bring Sally Anders into her confidence. 'Sorry, boss. I didn't want to burden you with my troubles any further than I already have. I figured Owen would be best to work out how to handle that information.'

Sally Anders' face softened. 'My officers are very much my concern, Ange. But you did the right thing. Owen told me he hopes not to need those photos, and we can save them for future use. That could be a fun hand to play at the appropriate time.'

Owen Fairweather was waiting patiently as the pair walked up to the building in Castlereagh Street where IC had their offices. Well dressed in an impeccably cut yet conservative grey suit, he didn't look particularly intimidating or striking. He carried an oversized leather briefcase, the sort that might carry a thick pile of crucial documents. 'It's a beautiful day, isn't it? This is a lovely time of year, sunny days and crisp cool nights.'

'I hadn't noticed,' said Ange. 'My mind has been elsewhere.' She wondered what might be in Fairweather's briefcase, other than the yellow manilla folder which contained the incriminating photos. Perhaps the briefcase might be empty, brought along for effect, a type of barrister's one-upmanship, a game of sorts.

'Calm down. I'm feeling good about today. Did Sally brief you on how I want you to handle yourself?' asked Fairweather, with a large, relaxed smile.

Fairweather's bearing inspired confidence, and Ange felt her heart rate drop a notch or two. 'Say nothing unless you direct me to. That will be something easier said than done, I expect.'

'You got it. Let's go upstairs, shall we? Oh, I suggest Sally attend to the formalities, but let me do the talking once we're all seated—if you wouldn't mind.'

There was no receptionist to greet them when the lift delivered the trio to the eighth floor. Sally Anders found an intercom and announced their presence, and the trio sat down to wait. The uncomfortable seating had been strategically positioned to face the large imposing sign announcing the Police Integrity Command, just in case one didn't fully appreciate one's predicament.

Time inched past 2 p.m. The trio sat in silence, no doubt having had the same thought about the reception being monitored and any conversation being overheard. It was excruciating. Finally, at twenty minutes past the hour, Carruthers came out to greet them.

'Hello, Detective Carruthers,' said Sally Anders in her coldest voice, glancing at her watch and overtly signalling her displeasure at having been kept waiting. 'We found some legal representation for Detective Watson. Shall we?' She gestured towards the open door.

Without a word of greeting, Carruthers turned and led them into a large meeting room. Sheena Wadley sat opposite the door beside a youngish man. A stern-looking middle-aged woman sat at the head of the table. She looked up briefly before returning her attention to some papers she was reading. Carruthers gestured to three spare boardroom chairs and walked around the table, sitting down beside Wadley. Fairweather sat diagonally next to the still-reading woman. Ange sat beside Fairweather, and Sally Anders sat beside her.

Carruthers finally spoke, gesturing towards the stern woman. 'This is Jane Seaborne from the Law Enforcement and Integrity Commission, and she will chair the proceedings today. This is Ben Frew, a lawyer here at the Police Integrity Command. You already know Detective Wadley.' He looked at Sally Anders. 'First things first, these hearings are confidential. I trust Detective Watson's legal representation is appropriate, Senior Detective Anders.'

'I can assure you that Mr Fairweather is a duly authorised officer of the court and fully appreciates his responsibilities,' replied Anders succinctly.

At the mention of Fairweather's name, Jane Seaborne looked up from her papers for the first time. When she saw it was Owen Fairweather KC who sat beside her, Ange was certain that she glimpsed the faintest hint of a smile creep into the side of her mouth, the one facing Fairweather. Perhaps it might have been a grimace, as discreet as it was, but it was abundantly clear that she knew who the Integrity Command was about to lock horns with. There was no hint of any recognition by the trio from the Integrity Command.

Fairweather reached into the pocket of his suit jacket and extracted four business cards. He slipped one across the table to each of the Integrity Command officers, leaving the fourth for Jane Seaborne. Ben Frew's face turned positively ashen when he saw the letters KC, elegantly written in embossed charcoal type beside Owen Fairweather's name. Wadley looked only mildly surprised, but this revelation didn't impress Carruthers. 'A King's Counsel. You should have paid us the courtesy of informing us you had engaged senior counsel, Anders.'

'You never asked, Detective Carruthers,' replied Anders succinctly.

Carruthers looked at Ange. 'How can a mid-level detective afford the representation of a King's Counsel?' he sneered in a thinly veiled accusation.

Ange kept her mouth shut as instructed as Fairweather calmly answered on her behalf. 'I agreed to represent Detective Watson pro bono. Bureaucratic overreach is a private hobby of mine.'

'Would you mind if I ducked out to the bathroom before we begin?' asked Ben Frew, speaking for the first time and looking most uncomfortable, his bladder having taken a sudden exception to recent developments.

Fairweather's smiling face turned to stone in an instant. 'You should have thought about that earlier—or not kept us waiting for twenty minutes. I may be acting pro bono, but I can't afford to waste any more time on this nonsense than is absolutely necessary. Anyhow, this won't take long.'

Ange grimaced, fighting with all her might to hold back a smile. The scene was set.

Chapter 14

The Hearing

Fairweather didn't give the other side a moment's rest and charged right in. 'So, can we begin? Would you mind reading out the charges against my client again, please, Detective Carruthers?'

'That Detective Watson operated beyond her authority and engaged in reckless and ill-advised behaviour, causing substantial commercial and reputational damage to the public,' said Carruthers, almost proudly, as if he had snared a gotcha moment.

'I presume that the public you're referring to is the cannabis farm operating in Clearwater without the knowledge of the Green River Council,' countered Fairweather.

'The cannabis farm was fully approved and properly licenced, and that is part of the claim against Detective Watson. She should have checked her facts about the property before she waded in with all guns blazing.'

'That's interesting. I have a signed affidavit from one Sandy Ellis. Ms Ellis works at the Green River Council and was the person who my client spoke with before *blazing in*, as you so elegantly put it.' Fairweather reached down and pulled a buff-coloured manila folder from his briefcase. Very deliberately, he slid an A4 sheet of paper across the table to the three people opposite, a fourth to Jane Seaborne. He waited a minute, ample time for everyone to read through Ellis's affidavit. The minute's silence added to the tension in the room. Fairweather looked implacable.

Ben Frew had regained some colour and waded into the fray. 'That was just one person, Mr Fairweather. I hardly think that constitutes proper and diligent enquiries.'

'Well, it wouldn't have made any difference if my client had made enquiries with each and every employee of the council. Nobody knew about the cannabis farm, not even the mayor.' Fairweather slid another sheet of paper across the table. 'This document is a signed affidavit from the mayor, Mr Alan Campbell. It confirms that neither he nor anyone at the Council knew about the existence of a cannabis farm. The exception to that claim, of course, is the former CEO, who I presume is the source of your information.'

Fairweather waited a while longer while Alan Campbell's affidavit sank in. 'Neither of those two key people at the Green River Council reported having any contact with anyone from the Police Integrity Command. If anyone is guilty of sloppy research, may I suggest you look in the mirror?'

One thing Ange knew already was that Carruthers did not enjoy the boot being on the other foot. He dispatched a look of pure malevolence towards Ange.

Ben Frew came in for another crack. 'We can agree to disagree on that point, Mr Fairweather.'

'What on earth is there to disagree on? If nobody in the council knew about the cannabis farm, how could Detective Watson possibly have known? Divine providence, perhaps?'

'There is a register of licenced medicinal cannabis production facilities. Detective Watson made no effort to cross-check the Clearwater property against this register.'

'I spent hours searching for the register that you speak of, Detective. Talk about hiding something in the bottom drawer. I suggest the reason this obscure register is so well hidden is that legalising cannabis, in any form, is a political hot potato. The minister in question has gone to great pains to ensure that nobody reads said register. But we'll get to the minister later. So, I think we've established that my client made all reasonable and proper enquiries before entering the subject property.'

Ben Frew sat silent, while Carruthers and Wadley appeared sullen. The only person to acknowledge Fairweather's declaration was Jane Seaborne. Her telltale nod was lost on nobody.

'Moving on. I presume you have more that you wish to say, Detectives?' prompted Fairweather.

'Yes, that Detective Watson entered the property with undue force, causing distress to innocent members of the public. For goodness' sake, it was a full-blown commando raid.'

'I presume that the innocent member of the public you refer to,' replied Fairweather in his most acerbic tone, and using air quotes over the word *innocent*, 'is the individual who was secretly selling drugs under the bridge late at night in Clearwater. It was this moonlighting operation that brought him to my client's attention.'

'That is a gross exaggeration. Mr Tan, the gentleman's name, was helping a local resident who had a valid prescription for medicinal cannabis. It's hardly cause for Detective Watson to raid the property with an armed SWAT team.'

'So, using your logic, supplying stolen opioids under the counter to addicts, all with valid prescriptions, would also be fine? I must say, I'm gaining an entirely fresh appreciation of the law here today.'

Fairweather handed over a sheaf of papers to Jane Seaborne, the testimony of Ange's colleagues which detailed the sequence of events that led to the raid. 'It seems like a waste of time against this witch-hunt, but this document fully details the events leading up to the raid on the cannabis farm. However, Detective Carruthers knows all of this, or at least he should.'

Jane Seaborne took a moment to scan the document before her barely perceptible nod dropped onto the table with a thud. Owen Fairweather turned to face Carruthers and went in for the kill. 'My theory of what is going on here is threefold. First, you have a personal grudge against Detective Watson after your botched attempt to hobble her over the incident concerning the gun battle with two Ndrangheta Mafia hitmen. I understand that your superiors were less than pleased over your performance on that occasion, Detectives Carruthers and Wadley.' Jane Seaborne raised another eyebrow, suggesting this was fresh information.

'Second, this personal attack on my client is politically motivated. It has nothing to do with justice and is more about covering up an uncomfortable truth. Third, both attacks show a common theme.'

'That's absolute nonsense. What are you talking about?'

'That Ms Julia Bennet, the former CEO of the Green River Council, and Mr Greg Kilroy, Minister for Regional Development, conspired to keep the cannabis farm a secret.' Fairweather let the trio from the Integrity Command stew for a moment before delivering his final accusation. 'Furthermore, it is my belief that Detective Carruthers and the Integrity Command operate under a political overtone that goes contrary to its charter. Be assured that I have read your charter, and I found nothing that infers you should be aiding and abetting political cover-ups, be they internal or external to the police force.'

'Those are big statements, Mr Fairweather. I presume you have evidence to back up those claims?' asked Jane Seaborne, speaking for the first time. Whereas Seaborne had found her voice, Ben Frew seemed to have lost his permanently.

'I do,' said Fairweather simply, as if this was an obvious fact of life. 'Evidence that neither the Minister, the former CEO, nor Detective Carruthers would enjoy seeing. It's your call.' He paused for a moment to fix Carruthers in the eye before speaking again. 'I would call this a career-defining moment, Detective. Do you want me to bring my evidence before this hearing, or would you prefer to drop this nonsense, and we all go our merry ways?'

Carruthers was not yet done. 'I think you're bluffing,' he said insolently.

Fairweather reached back into his briefcase and removed a large yellow envelope, now showing signs of wear and tear from being opened repeatedly. He placed it on the table directly in front of himself. 'I can assure you this envelope represents a ticking bomb.'

Jane Seaborne looked down at the envelope and then up at Fairweather. 'If that envelope contains any evidence of illegal activity, I think you're all duty-bound to disclose it.'

'There is nothing explicitly illegal in this envelope. The only thing illegal is this hearing and the bullying tactics of the Police Integrity Command. It will expose just how politicised the Integrity Command has become. If this behaviour were to become more widely known, it would probably not sit well with the police hierarchy. I can't imagine that this kangaroo court is a one-off, so it might even trigger a review of some of your previous investigations, Detective Carruthers.'

'You need to hand over that folder, Mr Fairweather,' said Carruthers, looking directly at Sally Anders as he spat out those words.

Anders' face hardened, making her conviction clear. 'Not on your life, Carruthers. We will choose when and where this information is disclosed. Let me assure you, it will come to light, but it would be better for you and the Integrity Command if you maintained some distance.'

Owen Fairweather looked at Sally Anders. 'Senior Detective Anders, now that I've witnessed first-hand the recalcitrant nature of the Integrity Command, I'm now wondering why on earth we wouldn't table this report in front of Ms

Seaborne and her tribunal.'

'Because there are bigger issues at play, counsellor. If this plays out in the press now, we may lose whatever opportunity we still have to save a whole lot of lives,' replied Anders forcibly.

Jane Seaborne had been watching this exchange with interest. 'I think I've heard enough. I can see no reason for LEET to take this matter any further.' She looked across at Carruthers and Wadley. 'Of course, I will take further submissions—if I must—but I strongly advise you to drop this action.'

Fairweather took over the thrust of Seaborne's advice. 'One last thing, before the good detectives make their decision. This is as bad a case of bureaucratic overreach as I've ever seen. If the Police Integrity Command ever pulls another stunt like this against my client, or anyone else, for that matter, I will once more offer my services pro bono and launch a very public action, one that you will not slither away from again. That's presuming, of course, that you take my very generous offer to drop the case forthwith.'

To give Carruthers his due, he enjoyed a thick skin and did not cave in so easily. 'What assurance do we have that this isn't one gigantic bluff and your precious envelope contains nothing other than blank sheets of paper?'

Fairweather looked incredulous and turned to Ange. 'I can see why you feel so aggrieved by the behaviour of your *colleagues*,' said Fairweather, spitting out the word colleagues with some disdain as he looked across the table at Carruthers. He then focussed his attention on the battered yellow envelope, opening the flap and pulling the contents, keeping them face down on the table. That this was no sheaf of blank A4 pages was plain to see by everyone sitting in the increasingly stuffy room. It was a beautifully orchestrated and executed move, akin to pulling the pin from a grenade.

'I won't be drawn into making any rash decisions right here and now,' said Carruthers quickly. He turned and addressed the two detectives from Major Crimes. 'You'll be hearing from us in due course.'

Fairweather was having none of that. He looked down at his watch. 'The time is just going on 3 p.m. If I don't hear from you by 4 p.m., I will personally drop this envelope over to Sue Elkington at The Times this afternoon. I will add your contact details before handing it over. We're close friends, Sue and I.'

With that, Fairweather reconstituted the envelope with its contents, stood and heaved his briefcase onto the table, into which he methodically inserted all of his documents.

'Mr Fairweather and Senior Detective Anders, I appreciate your attendance here today,' said Jane Seaborne as she stood. 'Detective Watson, thank you for making the effort to travel to Sydney and attend this hearing.' She then turned her attention towards Carruthers and Wadley. 'The day before the Easter break is clearly one of the most inconvenient times of the year.' Evidently, Seaborne was also unimpressed by Carruthers' puerile ploy.

Fairweather looked down at the business card that lay in front of Carruthers. 'You have my number,' he said in a curt voice, before turning and leading his clients out the door.

Once they were in the foyer, and knowing that they were likely being monitored, Fairweather loudly summed up proceedings. 'That was fun. What a crock of shit.'

Chapter 15

No Victory Dance

Nobody spoke again until the trio had exited the building.

Fairweather looked at the two detectives. 'How about we grab some coffee while we wait for that moron to ring me? I have a long night ahead, so I'll definitely need coffee to get through what needs to be done before Easter.'

'Owen, I hope you have your priorities straight and don't spend all your time at work,' replied Anders.

'That would be a case of the pot calling the kettle black,' admonished Fairweather, looking at Anders sideways as he led them to his usual coffee shop. 'I hear you. This job is a trap for becoming a workaholic. There's always some desperate case or another that can't wait.'

Ange had never properly considered the realities of life at the bar. When barristers and courtrooms came up in conversation around the police station, the chatter usually focussed on the massive hourly rates the top barristers charged, or how the law was on the side of the criminals. That someone would charge five, ten, or even twenty thousand dollars a day seemed a gross miscarriage of justice in itself, especially when compared to their own paltry detective salaries. Ange was gaining a fresh respect for people like Owen Fairweather, sharp minds who were chained to their desks for absurdly long hours. Beautiful chambers and inspiring artwork seemed only modest compensation for the loss of simple pleasures—like having time for a lazy swim in the ocean, for example.

Once they had ordered their coffees, Fairweather looked at Ange. 'So, Ange. Sally tells me that your partner is Gus Bell from Bell Surfboards and that you're a keen surfer? That seems fortuitous. Bell Surfboards are the Ferrari equivalent of the craft.'

Ange looked at Sally Anders with a sarcastic smile. 'Hmm. Sally gave you quite the briefing, didn't she? Yes, I live with Gus in the Byron Bay hinterland. Do you surf, Owen? I can't imagine you have any time for that.'

'To escape Orange, and being cobbled as my dad's unpaid clerk, I always took a summer job at Bega on the south coast of New South Wales. I would surf every day through summer break. It was only when I started working as a lawyer that the sport became a luxury item. My surfing is now reduced to discreet chunks of time during vacation. A group of us take an annual trip to Fiji at a surf resort. It's an expensive way to go about it, but at least I'm guaranteed some quality waves. Marcia comes along for moral support and to soak up some sun and read some books.'

'What do you ride?' asked Ange, realising that this would be the perfect way to repay Fairweather.

'I've got a seven-foot thruster and an eight-foot-ten-inch longboard. I usually end up riding the shortboard in Fiji if there's any size around. I've never totally gotten comfortable with the longboard given how steep and powerful those reef breaks can get.'

'Gus keeps telling me about reef breaks, but I'm yet to experience one,' said Ange. Gus had explained how the swell hitting places like Fiji and Indonesia would travel north from the Southern Ocean, fuelled by violent winter storms. Moving unimpeded through the open ocean, the swell would preserve all its energy until landfall, where its power would slam violently against shallow coral reefs. Unlike surf breaks around Byron, which largely depended on deposits of sand, coral reefs were a permanent structure. Despite their breathtaking power, reef breaks were mechanical in their consistency. So long as you didn't get pushed up onto the razor-sharp shallows, the deeper water alongside the reef provided refuge from the breaking waves. This setup delivered a surfers' paradise.

'You should impose on him to make a trip sometime. Those reef breaks can be confronting, especially on take-off when you're looking down through crystal-clear water onto a sharp coral reef.'

The two surfers traded surf stories as Sally Anders sat watching their obsession play out. After their second cup of coffee, the time was approaching 3:50 p.m.

'I guess Carruthers and Co are chancing their arm over the contents of that envelope,' observed Ange.

'Seeing how they orchestrated this hearing to occur hard up against Easter,

I think it premature to make any assumptions, Ange. My vote is that they're using this as a last opportunity to make life uncomfortable for us,' suggested Fairweather.

The trio sat in silence, finishing their coffee. Sure enough, at two minutes before the hour, Fairweather's phone jangled into action. Ange smiled as she recognised the ringtone used by Sir Kenneth Branagh in his portrayal of Wallander, the tortured protagonist in the Scandi noir detective series. They sat looking at the phone as it rang out. Twenty seconds later, it buzzed with a message. Fairweather replayed the message on speaker.

'Mr Fairweather. It's Detective Carruthers here. Can you call me straight back?' demanded the unmistakable voice.

'Who'd like another cup of coffee?' said Fairweather with a wry smile.

'I think herbal tea this time, please, Owen. Perhaps lemon and ginger?' replied Ange. 'If I have any more coffee, I doubt I'll sleep a wink.'

He made no haste in ordering a fresh round of beverages, and they whittled away another twenty minutes before Fairweather had finished his coffee. He picked up his phone, deliberately pulled up his register of missed calls, and rang Carruthers.

'Sorry I missed your call, Detective. With all the scammers around, I don't answer numbers I don't recognise. You wanted to speak with me?'

Ange could just make out Carruthers' voice over the clatter of the coffee shop. Fairweather sat impassively, his phone to his ear, listening to whatever Carruthers was saying.

'OK, then. A wise choice. Oh, and by the way, if you have any ideas of turning your attention to Senior Detective Sally Anders, I would strongly advise you to reconsider. I understand Sally has an especially explosive device at the ready, one with a hair-trigger fuse that would prove far more embarrassing than our little yellow envelope. Let's hope our paths don't cross again, Detective.'

Once Fairweather had hung up from the call and placed his phone back on the table, he turned towards the two detectives opposite. 'What a tool. You guys are good to go. I don't know how you cope with working alongside the likes of that mob. I imagine it hardly makes for great teamwork, knowing that someone like Carruthers is ready and waiting to knife you in the back.'

Relief flooded through Ange, a deflating sensation as the adrenaline of the past twenty-four hours washed away. Fairweather's insightful comment struck Ange like a bolt of lightning. Fury and anger over the behaviour of Carruthers suddenly turned into feelings of despair. This was his second attempt to hobble her—for nothing more than simply doing her job.

'Excellent,' said Sally Anders. 'It will be good to have you back on the job, Ange. I'll call you Tuesday after Easter and we can get you back in the saddle.'

'I need to process this, boss,' said Ange, the grim look on her face an obvious signal of her despair. 'Can we make it the week after that?'

Sally Anders appraised her star detective with a piercing gaze, making Ange feel as if her boss was reading her innermost thoughts.

'OK, fair enough,' said Anders. 'Let's speak Monday week.' She moved over to Fairweather and gave him a big hug. 'Thanks, Owen. I really appreciate this. Perhaps it's me who owes you now.'

'I think we're square for the time being, although I prefer an imbalanced ledger. That way, we get to see you. Don't be such a stranger,' replied Fairweather. After he had extracted himself from the hug, he turned and shook Ange's hand. 'Have a pleasant Easter, both of you.'

'Thank you, Owen. I'm very grateful for what you did for me,' said Ange.

'My pleasure. Never in doubt,' replied Fairweather, before he turned and walked back to a long night's work in his sanctuary-cum-jail.

Once Fairweather had left the small coffee shop, Sally Anders turned and addressed Ange. 'Congratulations, Ange. Let's speak in ten days.'

'Will do, boss. Thanks for leaning on Owen. I shudder to think what would have happened to me without his help,' replied Ange, confirming the misgivings and despair that Anders had spied.

Despite achieving the outcome they'd hoped for, it all seemed a somewhat hollow victory. Carruthers had irreparably damaged her respect for the police service. Ange now had her old job back but didn't know whether she wanted it. Nimble Investigations was in play, but she wasn't sure that made any sense—especially considering Gus's reaction to that news.

Rather than provide any resolution, her victory had made life abruptly and unexpectedly complicated, perhaps more than any time in her life. Gus's beach shack at Angourie sounded like the perfect place to process these conundrums.

Chapter 16

Making Waves

Ange rang Gus while walking back to her apartment. 'Hi, Gus. Good news. I'm in the clear—well, at least until the next time someone tries to stitch me up.'

'Congratulations, Ange. I'm relieved. You know how attracted I am to sexy surfing detective types. When are you coming home?'

Ange took note that Gus failed to disclose his view on sexy private investigators. 'Yes, well, this supposedly sexy detective is feeling pretty beaten up. I can't get a flight until Easter Sunday, so I thought I'd catch the first train north in the morning. I should arrive in Grafton just before 6 p.m. Any chance you could pick me up and we take a few days at your beach shack in Angourie? I need to talk some things through with you. If that BushCamz unit that we ordered while camping at Emerald Downs has arrived, we can also set that up.'

'Sure. That sounds fun—also ominous. I'll rummage through your wardrobe and put together some clothes. The surf will be small. Do you want me to bring a board down, or will you be happy to pick one out of the garage?'

Her mind automatically retrieved a mental picture of the faded old fibro beach shack, a delightful relic from the fifties that had been in Gus's family forever, and the eclectic collection of not-for-sale boards stacked in the garage. 'I think I need a change of pace, Gus. Let me experiment with one of your garage cast-offs. How's Buddy? Is he missing me?'

'Well, you know dogs don't have the same sense of time. Anyhow, he's been busy down at the shop. We had an attempted break-in the other night. Luckily, Freda from next door happened to be driving by and spooked them. Buddy and I have been sleeping in the shop, thinking that they would come back and have another crack. I really need to up the ante with my security.'

'What about the police? Have you spoken to anyone at the station?'

'Yes, but they're busy with Easter issues and managing the traffic jams. Anyhow, I was fobbed off onto your old mate, Constable Lynch. He seemed to lose interest once he realised who I was.'

'Leave that with me. I'm so looking forward to seeing my two favourite boys. How about I ring you when I'm on the train?'

As soon as she hung up, Ange rang Sergeant Jim Grady. He was Ange's former boss when she worked at the Byron Bay station.

'How did your hearing go? Sally told me about how those mongrels tried to corner you,' asked Grady. His epithet for the Integrity Command didn't calm any of Ange's unsettled thoughts about her recent experience.

'It's all sorted. I caught a lucky break. Also, Sally leaned on a barrister to help me. A King's Counsel, no less. You should have seen the face of the in-house lawyer Carruthers had organised when he saw who was representing me.'

'How did Sally arrange that?'

'Owen Fairweather shared his chambers with Sally's late husband before he passed.'

'Oh, Max, of course. He was a fine man. That would have almost been fun if it hadn't been so serious. Anything you need me to do?'

'Not on that matter, boss. It's settled, hopefully for good. Did you know Gus had an attempted break-in a few nights ago? He and my dog, Buddy, have been sleeping at the shop after my old friend Lynch sidestepped the matter. Would you mind getting the patrol cars to swing by the shop on their rounds? I need a break and we're heading to Gus's beach shack at Angourie for a few days.'

'Will do. I might even bring Lynch back into action over the Easter break. I'm sure he'll enjoy that,' replied Grady sarcastically. 'He fancies himself as a detective. Heavens help with my closure rate, if he was the best I could manage. I'm still on the lookout for your replacement, you know.'

'Thanks, boss. We both know that you could never replace me,' said Ange, finally finding some levity in her day. Jim Grady always helped lift her spirits.

Sally Anders was overcome with a sinking feeling as she left Ange. She thought it a telling omission that her lead detective hadn't asked for her badge to be returned. By the time she arrived back at the office, she had decided her course of action. When she had residual misgivings, her usual way was to sit on things for a few hours, sometimes overnight. Against her better judgement, she picked up the phone and started the wheels in motion. She'd considered making this call weeks ago but judged that it may have made things worse for Ange. After all, arse covering was one discipline that the department had perfected.

'Commissioner's office,' said the stern voice. Sally Anders pictured the speaker easily, a formidable Dolores Umbridge character, an accomplished gatekeeper, and no pushover.

'It's Senior Detective Sally Anders here. Can I speak to the commissioner, please?'

'The commissioner is not in her office. What do you need to speak with her about?'

'I'm not at liberty to say. Just tell her my name and that we need to revisit our agreement. She'll know what that means and I'm sure she will wish to speak with me. It would be best if she could ring me before the close of business today. I'm not in a patient mood.' Despite her assistant's denials, Sally Anders suspected Commissioner Cynthia Phelps was most likely sitting in her office.

'I'll pass the message on. I'm not sure she'll be able to ring you back today.'

'It will save her a lot of time and trouble,' said Anders simply, the determination in her voice obvious.

She barely had time to start work on some administration when her phone rang, an annoying Private Caller. Given the situation, she answered the call.

'Sally Anders.'

'Hello, Detective Anders. It's Cynthia Phelps here. You wanted to speak with me?'

Sally Anders unloaded all the angst that had been building for the past few hours. 'I thought we had an agreement. I can't believe you reneged without even contacting me. At least you had the courtesy of calling me back before I let the dogs out.'

'What on earth are you talking about, Detective? If you're referring to the matter concerning the Ndrangheta, I can assure you, I have not gone back on any agreement—if you could call it that.'

'Well. I've just come from a hearing at the Integrity Command involving Detective Watson. And I use the word *hearing* loosely. It would be better described as a stitch-up. You might recall that she was the lead detective who exposed that your understudy was a Ndrangheta mole. The only reason I agreed to keep that matter under wraps was to protect the reputation of the police service and help with recruitment. Now I find you guys trying to jettison one of our best detectives, presumably to protect yet another sensitive reputation.'

'Hold on, calm down. I know who Detective Watson is, but I had nothing to do with whatever it is you're speaking of. Who was involved from IC?'

'Detective Carruthers and Wadley, but I'm sure this goes well above those two foot-soldiers. If you know nothing about this matter, then you have a bigger issue on your hands,' raged Anders.

'Leave it with me. Do nothing until I get back to you, please.'

Sally wanted to believe that Phelps was being straight with her and knew nothing about the actions of the Integrity Command. She was certain that nasty politics were at play, something which would undoubtedly be the bane of the commissioner's life.

'OK, I'll give you the benefit of the doubt. However, let me say that it's hard enough to do our jobs without this sort of shit. Detective Watson is one of the best officers that I have worked with. She's principled, ethical, hardworking, and a natural investigator. If the department keeps dumping on people like her, then I see no future for any of us. The only ones left will be the snivelling arse-wipes like Carruthers. For goodness' sake, it's just plain depressing.'

That Sally Anders had resorted to gutter talk was a sign of her distress, and this was evidently not lost on the commissioner. 'I understand,' said Phelps simply, before she hung up.

That Ange had been targeted in this way cut Anders to the core. It was disturbing to think she might lose one of her star detectives in such a senseless way, but it was debilitating to realise that her police service colleagues, those who were supposed to stand alongside, would cast Ange aside so readily—purely for the crime of doing a good job.

Sally looked down at the report she had been editing. Unable to find the energy required to lift her pen, she left it sitting diagonally across the sheaf of papers and walked out of her office.

She dearly hoped that the commissioner would get to the bottom of whatever was going on. Should this gaping wound continue to fester, she would even need to reassess her own position.

Chapter 17

Making Tracks

Ange had found a spare seat with a table for her ten-plus-hour train ride. Although it didn't offer the same level of convenience as the fast trains she had enjoyed during her backpacking trip in Europe after university, it was still sufficiently comfortable. An overnight train had been her preferred, but Carruthers had derailed that option with his last-minute capitulation, most likely a calculated ploy on his part to maximise any inconvenience. After the stop-start exit from Sydney, she was finding the clack-clack-clacking of the train quite therapeutic, helping ease away her seething anger at Carruthers and Co.

She had just settled down to binge a Netflix miniseries which she had downloaded onto her tablet when Sally Anders called.

'Hi, Ange. Are you still in Sydney?'

'No, boss. All the flights home were full, so I caught the train. It'll take me all day, but at least I won't miss the whole of Easter with Gus and Buddy.'

'I spoke to the commissioner last night. She assures me she knew nothing about this and is looking into it.'

Ange paused, holding back the despair she was feeling. 'Sally, I really appreciate all that you've done for me, but I'm struggling to come to terms with this. Even though I go off on my own sometimes, I'm a team player at my heart.'

That Ange had referred to her as 'Sally' rather than her usual 'boss' was not lost on Anders. 'Don't let Carruthers get to you, Ange. I made sure that the commissioner knew he was involved.'

'That's the point, Sally. Carruthers was just doing a job that someone higher up had told him to do—and for the second time. He wasn't at all concerned about whether this was right or wrong. He just moved with the tide. The police service seems to have become more about politics than protecting the public. I'm tired of all this nonsense. Despite what you might say about the commissioner wanting to help, the fish rots from the head.'

'I hear you. Don't make any rash decisions. Take as much time as you want. We need you, Ange. I need you,' said Anders in a rare moment of candour.

'Thanks, boss. I appreciate it. Have a nice Easter. I'll be in touch,' replied Ange, unable to shake the weariness from her voice. She made no mention of Nimble Investigations.

Between the distraction of her miniseries, Ange sat staring out the window, thinking through her situation, searching for insights and trying to glean some inspiration from the countryside that flashed by. The train rolled into Coffs Harbour mid-afternoon, and Ange reflected on her past couple of years. She had been a fledgling detective when called to investigate the disappearance of Jake Thompson, the promising young surfer who'd grown up in Coffs Harbour. That investigation had led to her joining Major Crimes, which had proven both a blessing and a curse.

She'd relished getting involved in deeper and complex investigations, pitting herself against sophisticated criminals, but this also made her aware of the realities and the politics at play in the service. The sheer callousness of those scrambling for position had caught her by surprise. Had she stayed at the Byron Bay station, she probably would have been none the wiser to this level of selfish ambition. She would still be happily working away with Jim Grady and Billy, solving minor cases and helping keep her community on an even keel. She wondered if her insights into the soul of the police service had taken away her fire to serve.

Ange was still lost in those thoughts as she rolled into the Grafton train station, an uninspiring stop of pure function. She gathered her things and stood by the door, waiting patiently for the train to come to a complete stop and the hiss of the pneumatic doors to deliver a burst of fresh air. Alighting from her carriage, she looked around to see Gus and Buddy at the far end of the station. Gus smiled, and Buddy strained at his leash. It was hardly the stuff of a romantic movie, but the hug from Gus and the affectionate nuzzle of Buddy's wet nose against her leg warmed her soul.

'Hi, stranger,' said Gus. 'Nice to have you back. How was the train journey?'

'Better than I expected and perfect for the mood I was in.' She knelt and gave Buddy a big tousle, rubbing his ears and massaging his neck. He looked up, his eyes locking with hers and in raptures over such attention.

'How about we grab something to eat in Yamba on the way to Angourie? I have some groceries for the weekend, but I don't wish to cook and I'm sure it's the last thing you feel like doing. I know a place where we can sit outside with Buddy.'

With that, the trio bundled themselves into Gus's vintage Volvo station wagon and took the short drive to Yamba. Ange had spent little time there, but she knew it to be a much-loved coastal town, also the site of the next major lighthouse south of Byron Bay. Their track took them alongside the mighty Clarence River, one of the major watercourses that made up the Northern Rivers region of New South Wales. These rivers had been the source of considerable prosperity for the region, both as a water source and a conduit for transport and travel. It also delivered terrible floods. As always, good and bad were never the black-versus-white situation portrayed in Disney movies.

Once they had settled down at the outdoor table Gus had reserved, Ange could see the stream of people arriving for the Easter weekend. She knew this influx would continue late into the evening as people sought to eke every minute of the precious four-day weekend.

'Are you reinstated as a detective?' asked Gus.

'I'm considering my position, Gus. I've taken leave of absence next week while I process what just happened,' replied Ange.

Over dinner, she gave Gus a full account of the past few days, holding back nothing as she revealed her misgivings and doubts. As Ange wrapped up her conversation of that morning with Sally Anders, she exposed how deeply she was hurting. 'I don't know if I can continue working for the service, Gus. I should never have taken that position with Major Crimes. I think that I've seen too much.'

'Why don't you move back to the Byron Bay station?'

'I can't do that either. That would be like going backwards in life and against the grain of who I am.'

Gus took all this in for a moment before risking any comment. 'Ange, I know you love being a detective. I'll support whatever decision you make, even if it's embarking on a career of spying on my customers,' he said with a wry smile before turning serious again. 'Just don't do anything rash. One of the many things I love about you is your drive and energy. Much of this comes from your job, so be mindful of that. Let's have a nice Easter and put this behind us for a few days.'

Ange loved that Gus seemed supportive but concerned that he was enamoured with Detective Ange and not just plain old Ange Watson. As confused as ever, Ange took a diplomatic position. 'Thanks, Gus. I appreciate your support.'

As if he had read the situation, Buddy whimpered and sought Ange's hand, which moved to stroke his head. She longed to put the past few days behind her and move on.

Once they were ensconced in Gus's beach shack, the Easter weekend diffused into a soporific blur. The surf remained small and insipid, but the water was still relatively warm, and the company was excellent. Some sloppy knee-snappers at Spookies were the best she and Gus could manage. The rest of the time, they wandered along the coastline, taking dinner at the beach shack and falling into bed exhausted, despite having done nothing noteworthy during the day. It was just the respite Ange had needed, and she slowly regained some of her spark, teasing Gus about this and that, taking his good-humoured banter easily in return. Together, they installed the BushCamz unit, deftly placing it in a large native Tuckeroo tree that grew in the front corner of the property.

They were just returning from a walk and mid-morning swim on Monday, about to pack up the Volvo and head back home to Byron Bay, when Ange's phone rang. It was Alan Campbell. 'Hello, Alan. Happy Easter. I hope you've had a pleasant break?'

'Yes, it was lovely, thanks. The whole family came to the house at Currumbin on the Gold Coast. How did the hearing go?'

'The threat of your dossier did the trick. Owen, my barrister, handled it brilliantly, and we didn't even need to disclose any contents. It might come in handy someday,' replied Ange.

'I suppose that means you start back at work tomorrow?'

'Actually, no. I've taken leave of absence for a week.'

'Perfect. How do you feel about a trip to Emerald Downs? There's been a development. Fin caught someone via those surveillance cameras you guys installed. I think you might find it interesting. Sneaky buggers—they knew everyone would likely be away for Easter. Fin was only home on account of one of his kids falling ill. What do you think?'

'Sounds interesting. It might take me a few days to arrange things. I'm down in Angourie with Gus, and my car is stuck at the airport in Ballina. I couldn't get a flight home from Sydney and was forced to take the train.'

'Don't worry about that. I'm flying home from the Gold Coast at lunchtime. How about we swing by and pick you up in Yamba? If we can't land there, I'll text you an alternative. David, my pilot, can work all that out. He can then drop you back at Ballina airport when you're done in Clearwater. I'm happy to pay you for your time, by the way.'

'There's no way I would accept money from you, Alan, especially after how your dossier saved my skin. It sounds intriguing. Let me check with Gus and I'll text you back.'

Before she had time to ask, Gus forced her hand. 'I gather something dropped at Emerald Downs over the cattle rustling problem. Must be interesting if Alan wants your help. He doesn't sound like the type of person who needs any hand-holding. This might be just the tonic you need, Ange.'

Ange looked at him with affection, admiring his level of insight. Without a word in reply, she texted Alan Campbell.

All good. Text me ETA once you are in the air. See you soon. Ange

This was an interesting turn of events and not what she had expected to be doing on her week's leave. It was all about staying nimble.

Chapter 18

Whisked Away

At 1:42 p.m., and within minutes of the ETA that Campbell had texted, Ange watched the sweeping arc of a midsize twin-engine turboprop as it turned to base and commenced approach. It reminded her of the graceful albatross she occasionally communed with in the surf. There was a gentleness about the way the aircraft behaved, as if respectful of the privilege of riding the sky like that. The plane landed without fuss and taxied to where Ange, Gus, and Buddy stood. In his first ever airplane encounter, Buddy looked bemused and interested by this strange object that had fallen from the sky.

The pilot killed the port-side engine as soon as the airplane came to rest. An exit door clicked open and swung down before Alan Campbell climbed down the gangway and walked over. He shook hands with the couple before bending over to give Buddy a scratch on the head. 'Thanks for letting me have Ange for a few days, Gus. I promise to return her safe and sound.' He looked over at the airplane. 'David is an exceptional pilot. He was a senior captain with Singapore Airlines before the pandemic hit and they let him go. Their loss is my gain. I think he enjoys flying the King Air after a computer-controlled jetliner. Are you OK with light planes, Ange?'

'I'd hardly call a King Air a light plane, Alan. But, yes, I've been in plenty of light planes. I feel better that you have a professional pilot. Some of the bushies my dad used to fly with were a worry. I wasn't convinced that their mind was ever fully on the job of flying.'

'Couldn't agree more. I held a pilot's licence when I was young and bullet-proof, but too many people I know suffered mishaps. We use the plane to fly to the properties in North Queensland. It was taking me two days to get up there from Clearwater. I keep David busy,' said Campbell with a mischievous smile. 'Let's get on our way.'

Ange gave Gus a hug and a kiss before giving Buddy an affectionate rub. Heaving a duffle bag over her shoulder, she followed Campbell up the gangway and into the plane. It was more spacious than she had imagined and configured for executives. Pairs of seats faced a small table. Not wishing to risk airsickness, Ange chose a forward-facing seat. After buckling up, she looked out the window as the plane taxied back towards the runway. She caught sight of Gus through a small oval porthole and waved, a move he reciprocated. The plane was airborne within minutes and swooning west towards Clearwater.

As soon as the plane had levelled out, Alan came over and showed Ange where the drinks and amenities were. He had some documents to read, so he left Ange to her own devices. It was easy to enjoy herself, and she marvelled at the countryside beneath. Despite all the concerns about rampant development and overpopulation, Ange could only catch sight of the odd settlement on their track towards Clearwater. As soon as they had left the coast, they covered rugged and dense bushland before crossing over the Great Dividing Range and up onto the central plains. She guessed this fear-mongering about overcrowding was a function of the large percentage of Australians who lived in the cities and pressed up against the coastline, many of whom had never ventured west of the ranges and into the vast expanse of central Australia. As she sat there, alone with her thoughts, she marvelled at the constant nearsightedness of people, thinking that their immediate surroundings reflected the wider world.

Before long, Ange felt the aircraft tilt downwards and begin its approach into Clearwater. The pilot took the craft on a wide loop around the airstrip, giving Ange a magnificent view of the town and the surrounding countryside. Spotting the main road running north-south through the small town, she traced the road north until she came to the junction of Samsons Road, catching sight of the hill where the Telstra phone tower was located. She smiled at the thought of the surveillance camera the team had installed and imagined it plugging away, snapping images that interested nobody. She saw the Green River snaking its way across the landscape, passing through the centre of Clearwater on its way south. The river formed part of the Murray-Darling, one of the world's great river systems. The water flowing through Clearwater would travel thousands of kilometres before discharging into the Tasman Sea at Murray Bridge, between

Adelaide and Melbourne.

By the time the aircraft was on final approach, Ange had assembled a fulsome mental map of the Green River Shire.

The landing was that of an expert, and Ange hardly felt the airplane make landfall. It was an unquestionably civilised way to travel. Ange could understand why Campbell was prepared to pay for the luxury of his own plane over the discomfort and seemingly endless disruption of commercial flights. The plane taxied to a stop, and the pilot killed both engines before coming out of the cockpit to open the door and introduce himself. A man in his early sixties, David Eames exuded an air of calm competence. Ange concluded she would fly with him anytime.

Fin Templeton was waiting for them on the apron and came across to help with the luggage. He looked dishevelled and tired. 'We had an interesting night up here. Let's get settled over at Emerald Downs, and I'll fill you both in.'

Fin had taken Ange to the guesthouse, where she had dropped her duffle bag, before heading to the homestead. They gathered around the kitchen table.

After Sydney and Angourie, her assembled clothes were hardly that of a bushie: more like a fish out of water, or a surfer who'd taken a horribly wrong turn. Alan Campbell summed it up nicely. 'I love your Rusty Bell tee shirt, and I see what you mean about similarities between the Bell Surfboards logo and the brand we use for our cattle. I think I'll buy a bunch of those tee shirts for the grandkids. Probably not ideal for Clearwater,' he observed, looking Ange up and down. 'You look about the same size as my wife, Billie. How about I grab you one of her shirts before we head into town?'

'Thanks, Alan. I certainly would have packed differently if I had any thought of heading bush. So, Fin, what have you got for us?'

The kitchen where they sat was everything Ange had expected. A generous island bench centred the large and well-appointed kitchen. Pots and pans and other cooking utensils hung above the bench on a rack suspended from a high chamferboard-lined ceiling. The cooktop was massive, and Ange figured the room had enjoyed many large and noisy mealtimes over the years. The kitchen table where they sat had been worn and beaten over time, a piece of furniture that was to be used and not fussed over. A scattering of at least a dozen chairs sat around the table, a cornucopia of styles that somehow worked. It was an altogether comforting and calming space. Ange concluded Billie Campbell had style, that special woman's touch to put her men at ease and warm their hearts.

Fin Templeton opened up his laptop and pulled up the BushCamz video app. 'This is the camera that we set up to cover the southern entrance. It pinged me at 2 a.m. Sunday morning. It's a very cool piece of software. The first few nights after you left drove me senseless with pings whenever an animal walked by, so I set the system up to only record vehicles. I was asleep at Box Grove when it happened.' He pressed the play button.

Ange soon saw what looked like a boxy 4WD vehicle drive across the cattle grid guarding the entrance. After only fifty metres, she saw a brief flicker of red from the brake lights as the vehicle swung off to the right and rolled to a halt. Two men got out of the car and walked around to ready the trailer.

'Sneaky. Came in without lights. They must have pulled the plug on the trailer, as those brake lights didn't turn on when they stopped. Did you get a number plate?' commented Ange.

Templeton paused the video and zoomed in on the trailer. The image was grainy and the number plate on the trailer wasn't legible. 'No. But I didn't really need to,' he said obliquely as he pressed play once more.

Over the next thirty minutes, the two men herded two head of cattle into the ute and drove off, still running without lights and seeming to take care not to flare the brake lights as they exited the property.

'Those cattle seemed to move easily into the trailer, Alan. I would have thought they'd be more skittish,' observed Ange.

'We move our breeders around and between the two properties from time to time. It wouldn't have been their first time in a trailer. This heist was well orchestrated,' explained Campbell with a sour look on his face.

'Why do you say that, Alan?'

'First, the cattle were in the road paddock. They probably noticed this from the highway, but that would have required stopping and looking through the trees. Second, they knew which animals to target. There were some heifers in that mob, and they wouldn't have been so easy to handle,' said Campbell, before looking back at Templeton. 'Fin, tell Ange what happened next.'

Templeton let the video play before pausing and pointing to the screen. 'Look here. You get a decent look at the vehicle as it turns around. The decent moonlight was helpful. I guess that was useful for the rustlers as well.'

He restarted the video playback. 'Once they exited the property, I pulled up the southernmost camera, the one looking south along Bullock Road. When I saw that they'd driven north, I jumped in my truck and headed towards Emerald Downs. I hoped to catch them on Bullock Road somewhere, but the vehicle never came by. I kept heading slowly south towards Emerald Downs. Still nothing. In desperation, I figured that the only other option was that they had turned west on Watkins Road before we would have crossed. That turnoff is just north of Emerald Downs, but it's a bit of a goat track and an odd choice. Watkins Road ultimately links up with the main road to Fernvale, the next town almost due west of Clearwater. In a last-ditch effort, I continued south, past Emerald Downs, and turned down Samsons Road. It also comes out in Fernvale, and it's a much better road than Watkins Road. Anyhow, about halfway along, I saw the vehicle pulling out of a property to the left. I could have stopped, but I kept driving, as if I was just passing through. They followed me all the way to Fernvale. I turned off to the south, and they went into town, which was where I lost them. It would have looked weird if I'd started driving around town. I tried to take some photos on my phone while I was driving, but they're totally useless. As Ellie keeps reminding me, photography isn't my strength.'

Ange sensed that Templeton was feeling guilty about not rescuing the cattle. 'You did the right thing, Fin. If you'd spooked them, we probably never would have sorted this out. So, where exactly is the property you saw them exiting from?'

'You know it well,' said Alan Campbell with a large gotcha smile on his face. He saw the look of understanding alight onto Ange's face. 'Yes, I know. It's quite a coincidence, isn't it?'

'I don't believe in coincidences, Alan. I know they do happen, which gets me into trouble from time to time, but they're the exception rather than the rule in my experience.'

'That's why I wanted you to come back out and pay us a visit,' said Campbell, his smile showing no sign of abatement. Despite losing some valuable cattle, he was clearly enjoying himself.

Chapter 19

Providence

'Hang on a minute, Alan,' said Templeton. 'It was the middle of the night, and you know how different things look in the dark. I can't be sure, and I haven't been back again during daylight. I wanted to wait until you guys arrived.'

'There's an easy way to find out. I was only thinking about it as we circled Clearwater before landing,' said Ange. 'Can I use your Wi-Fi, please, Alan?'

'Sure. Log into Emerald Downs. The password is "BillieTea!"' replied Campbell, spelling it out for her.

After all his lessons on internet security, Ange figured that her Billy would have made quick work of that password. She fired up the browser on her tablet and logged in to the Emerald Downs Wi-Fi network, pleased that she had bookmarked the two URLs that linked with the two cameras her team had installed some months back. She felt sure that the first camera, the one under the bridge that had recorded the late-night drug transactions, had been retrieved and was no longer operational. This was of no concern for what she had in mind.

Ange tapped her finger on the second bookmark, the one that linked to the more permanent camera installed on a nearby Telstra tower and focused on the drug farm. She hoped the unit hadn't malfunctioned, or worse, been decommissioned by a technician doing routine maintenance on the tower. Ange held her breath while her tablet worked to establish a connection.

After a tense few seconds, a brilliantly clear image of the drug farm came onto the screen. Ange exhaled, then turned to Templeton. 'What time do you reckon you drove past, Fin?'

Templeton did some maths in his head before replying. 'I reckon between 2:45 a.m. and 3 a.m.'

Ange placed her finger on a slider button and pulled it back in time. Dawn whizzed by and the screen flipped to a grainy night vision mode. The flash of the headlights from Templeton's car was obvious, although Ange went back further in time until the headlights of a vehicle approaching from the west came into view. When she pulled her finger off the slider button, the image paused. Pressing play, she watched the vehicle turn into the drug farm. Once the flare of headlights was gone, they could clearly see a trailer carrying two of Campbell's prize cows. The trailer showed no taillights, confirming that this midnight traveller was no innocent happenstance. Ange paused the video to snip a couple of still images of the car and trailer as it turned into the driveway. Once done, she let the video run at normal speed.

The vehicle drove past the house and the sheds before stopping to the east of the dam. Two men exited the vehicle and then corralled the two animals through a gate that spilled out into a large paddock. Disappointingly, it was impossible to make out the faces of the two men. After closing the gate, the men hopped straight back into the vehicle and drove out towards the road. Templeton's LandCruiser ute came into view, travelling west along Samsons Road. The vehicle containing the cattle rustlers waited as Templeton drove past before it pulled onto the road to follow him.

'Sneaky buggers,' commented Campbell. 'They must have made a loop using the back roads to stay off Bullock Road.'

Ange let the video play until both vehicles disappeared from view, then pressed pause and turned to the two men. 'Does anyone recognise the vehicle?'

'Few people around these parts drive a Land Rover Defender. Especially one kitted out like that,' suggested Campbell, Templeton's nodding head confirming this statement. 'No bushie would run on such aggressive tyres. The noise on the highway alone would drive them crazy—not to mention the unnecessary expense.'

Ange had a flashback to her childhood, when she had 'solved' the case of the illegal shooting on her parents' property. She had observed some unusual tyre tracks along the farm boundary and spied a 4WD shod with tyres of the same distinctive tread in town one day. Her father had been most impressed. 'Come on, you guys. Out with it,' she demanded with a wide smile.

'A rooster by the name of Tony Daicos. Owns a gastropub in Edenview just south of Clearwater,' replied Campbell with a grimace, as if he had a nasty taste in his mouth. 'Billie and I eat there often. The food is excellent. I've seen that vehicle parked out the back dozens of times.'

Ange held herself in check, her detective training coming to the fore. 'No offence, Alan. But we can't just rely on that. I'm done with charging in half-cocked around these parts. I'll get my colleague to review the images. Let's see if he comes to the same conclusion.' Ange turned to Templeton. 'Do you think they might have recognised you, Fin? Whoever was driving the vehicle must be locals. Would there be any reason you might travel this way so late at night?'

'Ellie's parents live just south of Fernvale,' replied Templeton. 'Sorry, Ellie is my wife. I married a local girl, although we met at university. We do sometimes travel this way to visit Ellie's parents. It's much of a muchness which route we take from Box Grove. Most of the locals would know that. Ellie was quite the catch and is well known around the region, at least by most local men. It would be unusual, but it's conceivable that I might have been driving that way to visit them for an emergency.'

'OK. Whenever you get the opportunity, drop a few clues that you had to make a late-night visit to your wife's parents. That can't hurt,' concluded Ange.

'Do you have a decent satellite image of the property?' asked Campbell.

Ange opened her email app and then searched for emails from Billy, scrolling down to the date when she'd first become interested in the drug farm. Billy had sent her a high-res satellite image of the property. Once she found it, she clicked on the attachment and the image popped onto her screen.

Campbell studied it carefully. He pointed to the massive Colorbond shed. 'This was the shed used for cannabis production, am I right?'

'Correct,' said Ange. She suddenly remembered a curiosity from the raid and pointed to a smaller shed. It was located midway between the shed and the dam that had served as the water source for growing cannabis hydroponically. 'The forensic guys collected some blood samples from this shed which turned out to be bovine. I remember the guys commenting that the shed was either a home abattoir or a sadistic torture chamber, as it contained a small gantry and meat hooks. After the lab confirmed the blood samples weren't human, I didn't think it was relevant and forgot about it.'

Campbell pointed to a small silo and what looked like a row of feed bins. 'I never worried about this until now, but they must be feeding the cattle grain to finish them before slaughter. Daicos must be using the beef in his restaurant.

What a waste of top breeders,' he observed with a look of disgust.

Ange knew that grass-fed beef was the tastiest, but grain-fed beef contained a higher fat content and was also the most tender. Grass-fed beef that was finished off with grain was the best of both worlds.

'Where would they purchase the grain from, Alan?' asked Ange.

'Fernvale Agricultural Supplies. I'm almost certain about that. A feed truck would deliver the grain as needed,' replied Campbell. 'The truck drivers wouldn't know that any cattle on the property have been stolen. Provided the bills were being paid, they wouldn't look twice.'

'I'll get my colleague onto identifying that vehicle as a priority,' said Ange before sitting back in her chair. She needed a moment to think. 'I don't suppose there's any chance of scoring a cup of tea, Alan?'

'I'm sorry. What a poor host I am. If Billie was here, she would have scolded me silly.' Campbell fussed around making tea while Ange sat deep in thought. The silence was broken when her phone pinged with the images sent by Templeton. Ange had just a moment to skim through them before Campbell returned with a tray laden with tea-making paraphernalia, along with a bowl of plain old rich tea biscuits. The trio sat silently, the only sound being the odd slurp of tea and the crunch of a biscuit. Ange was amused to see that Campbell was old-school and dunked his biscuit before each bite. With the correct tools for contemplation now in place, Campbell and Templeton seemed to understand that Ange needed to be left to her own devices. After a full ten minutes of silence, the unmistakable clang of a grandfather clock in the next room broke the spell. Ange counted out the four loud chimes, signalling that the time was 4 p.m., as good a time as any to get a move on.

'OK. Fin, how about you take a run out to the agricultural supplies company first thing tomorrow and make some enquiries about getting some feed delivered? See what you can find out. Perhaps ask plausible stuff like how often they make deliveries along Samsons Road, maybe ask for a name or two as a reference if the conversation goes well. Will they know who you are?'

'They'll know me for certain. What excuse should I use?'

Ange had already thought this through and answered Templeton's question immediately. 'How about you say that you're looking at acquiring another property in the area? Tell them you're thinking of using it to finish some steers and saw the feed bins on a neighbouring property. Would you likely know when a property might be for sale off-market, Alan?'

Campbell looked up at that idea. 'I guess. Everyone knows I buy the odd property. It would raise eyebrows but not be especially alarming or out of the ordinary.'

'Good. Hopefully, Billy, my colleague, can use his software box of tricks to confirm the identity of the 4WD vehicle. I'll also ask him to analyse the video feed and see who's been visiting the property,' added Ange. She looked across at Campbell. 'Alan, if we take this cautious approach, we might place your cattle at risk. What are your thoughts?'

'I'm OK with that risk. We need to sort this out. I'm still the mayor, remember? I can't be the only person who's had their cattle stolen,' replied Campbell.

'Fin, you look dead on your feet. Go home and get some rest. I'll get Billy on the case this afternoon. Perhaps we can regroup tomorrow morning once you've made your enquiries over at Fernvale.'

Campbell thanked Templeton and suggested that Ange meet back in the main house at 6:30 p.m. for a steak. 'It's the one thing I can cook well,' he commented, once again reminding Ange of her father.

She wandered back to the guesthouse. Once she was comfortable, she rang Billy. He answered quickly.

'I'm pleased that you sorted out your problem with the Integrity Command, boss. I can't believe that mob. It's sometimes hard to work out who the real enemy is—the criminals we investigate or your friends at the Integrity Command. What's up? It's not like you to call on Easter Monday.'

'Thanks, Billy, but it's been a bit of a hollow victory. Sorry to bother you, but I need a favour—one that needs to remain between us. Don't worry, it's nothing untoward, but I've officially taken some leave of absence,' replied Ange.

'Sure, boss. It's nothing that I won't have done before,' he replied, a not-so-oblique reference to the many weird and wonderful requests he had shouldered during their association.

'Great. I'm about to send you some links to two video feeds and some time slots. There's a vehicle that shows up in both and I wondered if you could make out a number plate and hopefully confirm who owns the vehicle? You might need to use some of your software wizardry, as the images aren't particularly clear.'

'Sure, boss. I'll be ready,' replied Billy, his cheerful tone of voice a timely reminder that not all her colleagues were mongrels looking to take her down.

'Great. You might recognise one of the video feeds.'

'Sounds ominous. Continue,' urged Billy.

'The property at Clearwater with the cannabis farm that we raided. You know the saying—birds of a feather flock together. And you also know my rule about coincidences. However, I see no need to poke the bear, so keep this on the low-down between us, please.'

'You just cannot stay out of trouble, can you, boss?' observed Billy.

Ange ignored Billy's jibe and spent a moment to fire off a sequence of messages containing the video links. 'You remember that video camera we installed on the Telstra Tower at Clearwater? As you know from your conversation with Gary Franks from Tweed Heads, it's been plugging away ever since. Can your software map out a specific field of vision and identify when something passes through that window?'

'Sure can,' he replied confidently.

'Brilliant. You should have the images and the URL for the camera feed by now. What I'm looking for is a complete log of every vehicle which drives through the main entrance. If you could compile a log showing images, dates, and times, that would be perfect.'

'Easy. I'll download the video file straight away. The system will operate on a continuous loop, replacing the oldest video with current stuff. I'll run that through my software when I get to work tomorrow. Are you in Byron Bay?'

'No, I'm back in Clearwater. I've been privately helping the local mayor with his cattle rustling problem. Not for money, just a personal favour that I owed him. I wouldn't normally bother you, but this is far too weird of a coincidence.'

'No problem, boss. No need to explain. I'm on it,' replied Billy. 'As always, your coincidence is my coincidence.'

That evening, over dinner, Campbell explained some of his journey to becoming a cattle baron. 'It was touch and go in those early days. The bank was itching to foreclose during my first poor season. It was only Billie and her teaching job that kept us afloat. I had to stay butchering, and we were dead on our feet. I'm not sure how we found the time or the energy, but when Billie fell pregnant with our first,

I knew things needed to change. My epiphany came when I realised how difficult a poor season was for anyone ill-prepared or without their finances in good shape. So, I went on the offensive. I pitched my idea to the bank down in Sydney, and they agreed to support my countercyclical plan. I guess they were more used to people with their hand out in bad times, so my longer-term approach struck a chord. From that point, I saw tough seasons as a golden opportunity, and it completely changed my perspective—and the fortunes of our family. Unfortunately, with all the environmental activism going on, being a grazier is not the respected vocation that it once was. Now we're akin to environmental vandals in the eyes of some in our society—a highly vocal part at that. It makes my blood boil. Not only do we care deeply about the well-being of our animals, but it's also in our own best interest to look after our land. Believe me, I've seen what happens to properties which have been resumed for national park. With no one looking after the land, invasive species soon take over and ruin the place. It takes a lot of effort to maintain a property,' explained Campbell wistfully.

'My dad has said the same thing often enough. He blames the fact that the bush and the city have grown further apart, and city dwellers have lost all perspective about where the food on their plate comes from,' commented Ange. 'I think some tension between environmentalists and progress is a positive thing, but someone always goes too far. It's the zealots who cause the problems. To your point, the activists are certainly making better use of new media than the agricultural sector. It was tensions between activists and property developers that saw me hauled in front of the state's anti-corruption commission.'

'I'll bet that was fun. I read about that incident when I was doing my research on you. It seemed like you were roached by that activist from Byron Bay.'

It interested Ange that Campbell had undertaken some background checks on her before they'd started their rustling project. 'You don't know the half of it. Strangely, in the end, I came to respect the motives of that activist—just not all of his methods. His son was killed by the Ndrangheta Mafia to silence him. He was harmless in reality, and his murder was an unfortunate and unintended consequence of our investigation. Losing a child would be a terrible thing. The activist and I eventually formed some level of rapport.'

'I like the sound of your father. He seems like my type of guy. Perhaps we should set up a social media campaign just for bushies. We could call it the *country crusaders*, or the *bushie brigade*, or something similarly banal. Tell me about your mother. Being so isolated in the bush can be a tough life for a woman.'

'Mum is a typical salt-of-the-earth type. I categorise her as someone who will always stand by her man but will give him plenty of prods and kicks up the backside along the way. It's all about the grandchildren for her now, despite my failures to add to her growing brood. Mum's very level-headed and keeps in check the many conspiracy theories that Dad concocts when he's out in the paddock. She just rolls her eyes whenever Dad goes on one of his rants. Her solution to the woes of the world is to let the Country Women's Association take a shot at running the country. Going by what I see in my job, I suspect we could do a lot worse,' she added with a smile of deep affection.

'Billie was never the CWA type, but she's all about community and is always off doing something around town to help out. I get the credit, but I put all our achievements down to her. Billie effortlessly made the move from schoolteacher to mother, and then to CFO as we built our empire. Life is all about the grandchildren for her as well, which is just lovely. It's her seventieth coming up on June twenty-nine this year, and I plan to throw her a big surprise party here at Emerald Downs with all her friends and family. She'll hate being the centre of attention, but she'll have to live with it. You two would get on like a house on fire. By the way, you never told me how you became a detective at Major Crimes?'

Ange explained to Campbell how she had been working away as a junior detective in Byron Bay when the case of Jake Thompson, the missing young surfer from Namba Heads, came across her desk. That case led to a job offer at Major Crimes, the role which eventually saw her being shot in the coastal scrub.

Campbell was incredulous. 'So, are you telling me that a simple missing person's case ended up with you being shot by two Ndrangheta Mafia hitmen?'

'I know. It's hard to believe. I had no clue who I was pursuing until the last minute. By then, I was totally committed to the chase. If I am honest, getting shot didn't hurt as much as being pursued by Internal Affairs—as they were known before they changed their name to camouflage their incompetence. I was about to toss in the towel when my boss, Senior Detective Sally Anders, put me on the trail of people traffickers. Now that those mongrels at the Integrity Command have had another crack over our raid on the cannabis farm, I'm considering my options. It's a tough enough job as it is without knowing the people you work with are so desperate to stitch you up.'

'Is people trafficking really a problem in Australia? It seems fanciful and more something for Texas, USA—not Texas, Queensland.'

'Alan, I can assure you that it's happening, and probably right under our noses. People trafficking is the second-most-profitable form of organised crime. Once the traffickers work through the logistics around immigration and borders, it's open slather. High profits and low scrutiny create the perfect environment for criminals to prosper. A trafficked prostitute can make up to a quarter of a million dollars a year for her handler. Plus, with such a public focus on strong borders, and lots of other more visible crime to worry about, people trafficking is simply not high on the public's agenda. When the public doesn't seem to care, neither do the politicians nor the authorities that work under them.'

Campbell fixed her with a penetrating stare. 'You don't sound like someone about to toss in the towel. If people like you don't care about those poor young women, who will? What happened to the women you rescued up north?'

'Our very own immigration officials are trying to ship them back home as illegal immigrants. The women are too scared to speak up and it doesn't bear to think what will happen when they arrive back home. You can imagine that silencing them might be a priority for whoever captured or lured them to Australia. The whole thing is deeply depressing.'

Campbell sat back in his chair and seemed in deep contemplation of Ange's story. The pair sipped their red wine in silence for some minutes until Campbell broke the somewhat gloomy mood that had descended on the pair. 'I'd be happy to help sponsor some of the women you rescued. There's always some job to be done around here or up north. Now, getting back to your situation, I think those women, and the ones after those, need you, Ange.'

Ange just sat and sipped her wine. She knew that Gus held the same opinion as Campbell, as would Jim Grady, and her dad, for that matter. Her own minor challenges seemed trivial when measured against the plight of those women. In her heart of hearts, she knew that Campbell was right. Nimble Investigations took on a puerile light.

As she lay in bed later that night, cocooned in the deathly silence of Emerald Downs, a silence where even her innermost thoughts screamed out loud, she was transported back to her childhood, when she would lie awake late into the night, awash with the dreams and aspirations of her life ahead. All things considered, saving young trafficked women seemed like a reasonable calling. Whether she had the stomach to brave the stench wafting her way was another matter.

Chapter 20

Not So Clever

Ange had just returned from an early-morning walk down by the river when her Billy rang.

'What's up, Billy?'

'I worked out who owns that vehicle. It wasn't as easy as I thought it might be, as I could only make out four letters and numbers with any confidence. The other two were totally obscured by dust or mud,' replied Billy.

'OK. Fill me in. What brilliant scheme did you come up with to work out the puzzle?' Ange knew how Billy relished his work being appreciated. She could almost hear his beaming smile over the phone.

'When I cross-referenced the four letters with the colour, make, and model of the vehicle, I was still left with eleven possibilities, none of which lived near Green River. So, I ran the same details through the traffic infringements that have been handed out in and around Green River, and as luck would have it, there was only one that ticked all the boxes. It's owned by a company called Tasty Hat Pty Ltd, which is based out of a postbox in Sydney. I ran that name through the New South Wales business registers, and I got a hit. Tasty Hats is the holder of a liquor licence for a pub in Edenview. I checked, and that's just over twenty kilometres south of Clearwater. The licensee is a guy called Tony Daicos. I looked him up, and he was a former top restaurateur and celebrity chef in Sydney before he went bust and left town in 2014.'

'It's referred to as a gastropub. Your old boss, Jim Grady, has even lunched there. He said it served exceptional food. Your conclusion confirms what Alan Campbell thought. He was certain that he recognised the vehicle, but I needed your expert opinion before I fronted Daicos. Don't panic about your analysis of the video feed off the Telstra tower, but it will be good to be thorough, if only to stamp out the cattle rustling problem,' concluded Ange, before she ended the call.

After a shower and a change of clothes, she wandered over to the homestead, where she found Campbell sitting at the kitchen table on the phone. He pointed her to the coffee machine, and Ange busied herself dealing with her addiction, her ear catching the odd order from Campbell about cattle and feed.

'Good morning, Ange,' he said, after finishing the business of being a cattleman. 'I hope you had a decent night's sleep. Some of our guests can't deal with the peace and quiet. It still blows my mind that they would prefer noise and chaos over solitude.'

'It took me back to my childhood, Alan,' commented Ange. 'Good news. My colleague confirmed your suspicions that the mystery vehicle is owned by Tony Daicos. How well do you know him?'

'Reasonably well. We eat there often enough,' replied Campbell, before sitting back in his chair and thinking through the implications of this latest news. 'I've probably been paying for steak butchered from our own cattle.'

'I'd like to pay him a visit today. Not as Detective Ange Watson—well, not yet at least. Remember that seventieth birthday party you plan to throw your wife? Well, Alan, meet Ms Gloria White, your new event planner.' Ange playfully extended her arms in a dramatic gesture. 'How many people do you expect will attend your birthday party? I reckon we spare no expense,' she proposed with a mischievous smile. 'Putting him to the effort of preparing an estimate is the least we can do in the circumstances.'

'I like your style, Ms White. Let's make the party a humdinger and shoot for one hundred and twenty guests. Will you head off now or wait for Fin to report in?'

'Let's wait for Fin. I looked online. Daicos's pub is open for lunch today, so I reckon I should turn up around 11 a.m. Seeing as we're in the middle of school holidays, they should be as busy as anything.'

That settled, Ange finished making her coffee, enjoyed with some toast and homemade marmalade that Campbell had laid out on the bench. At just after 9:30 a.m., Ange heard a vehicle pull up outside, followed soon after by Fin Templeton. He was buzzing with energy.

'You'll never believe what I found out.'

Ange could tell that he was feeling like a master sleuth. 'Sounds interesting, Fin. What happened?'

'Well, I went to Fernvale Ag Supplies as we agreed and started asking them about feed bins and delivery schedules. I also dropped a story about my phantom late-night visit to Ellie's parents to help with a calving. They run a few head on their hobby farm. Anyway, Ken, the owner, took me outside to show me the different-sized feed bins they use. Blow me down. There was the trailer that the rustlers used for their heist. I couldn't believe my eyes when I saw it. He has several trailers that they hire out, but that's the largest one. It was still dirty, and Ken mentioned that he planned to clean it up later today. I made a song and dance about how I urgently needed a similar trailer to get me out of a fix. I concocted a story that ours had broken an axle and agreed to hire it as is. It's hitched to the back of my ute.'

'That was quick thinking, Fin. We can take some samples from the trailer that might prove that it was on Emerald Downs,' suggested Ange.

'That's the sort of story that I'd expect a former commodities trader to come up with to keep a deal in play,' observed Campbell.

'My colleague confirmed that the Land Rover Defender is owned by Tony Daicos,' added Ange.

'Ms White here is planning to visit Daicos later this morning,' advised Campbell, gesturing towards Ange in case Templeton might be confused about who was who in this zoo.

'Brilliant. Your visit sounds interesting. Ms White gets around, doesn't she?' replied Templeton, still beaming over his discovery.

'I suggest we regroup this afternoon and get around to documenting what we find on the trailer. I'll ring some contacts in forensics on the drive back from Edenview and get the low-down on what we need to do. At the very least, we'll need some surgical gloves, a bunch of Ziplock bags, and some permanent markers. Can you get that organised, Fin?' asked Ange, before switching her attention to Campbell. 'Alan, between the car and the trailer, I'm confident that we have enough to move on Daicos. It's a matter for yourself, but if I was in your shoes, I would watch and wait to see who's been helping him. Doesn't it seem odd that your cattle seem to have been targeted?'

'I agree. I've been pondering that. What are your thoughts, Ange?' replied Campbell.

'Well, we have surveillance on the property where the cattle are being held, but it would be good if we had eyes on the comings and goings of Daicos and his pub. I'm still offline, remember? I'd prefer not to involve any more of my colleagues just yet. What about your PI?'

'He's just about to wrap up something else he's been doing for me in Sydney. I reckon I could have him over by tomorrow. I'll get David to pick him up in the King Air.'

'Alan, are you telling me that not only do you have your own pilot, you have your own PI as well?' exclaimed Ange with an equal measure of jest and surprise in her voice.

'No. No, of course not. However, I've kept my PI hopping of late—well, ever since I met you, that is,' ribbed Campbell, evidently no slouch in the jesting department himself.

'OK. Seems like we have a plan. I'm off to lunch. Wish me luck,' said Ange decisively before breaking into laughter. 'Oh, I forgot. I'll need a car. That might come in handy.'

'You can use Billie's Mercedes,' offered Campbell, before reaching into a large bowl sitting on the kitchen bench and fishing out a set of car keys. 'Her car is pretty well known around these parts and should confirm your charade of the surprise party.'

He threw the jangling bunch of keys across to Ange. 'Go do your stuff. I can see why you enjoy being a detective. If it wasn't always so serious, it would almost be fun.'

Chapter 21

Gastronomical

Once Ange had found her way around Billie Campbell's Mercedes, she settled in for the forty-odd-minute drive south to Edenview. The trip took her back through Clearwater and then across some beautiful countryside, rolling over ridges swathed in olive-green eucalypt trees, then down into river flats dominated by the massive emerald canopies of the camphor laurel. As elegant as the tree was, Ange knew well of its invasive nature. Although native to Asia, it had been imported from England as a source of camphor wood, used for chests to keep moths and vermin away from precious woollen clothes. It had seemed a good idea at the time, but they were now a major pest. Their bountiful annual crop of small black fruit was much enjoyed by birds, who then deposited their seedy by-product while sitting on fences and the like. If property owners weren't diligent with pest control, they would soon find their fence lines destroyed and the property overrun with rapacious saplings.

With autumn well underway, the bushfire season had now mercifully passed. After successive years of above-average rainfall, the countryside was loaded full of fuel ready to ignite. As she drove up the narrow valley towards Edenview, she pondered the devastation that a bushfire would wreak on the charming vista. Topography would funnel and concentrate the fire as it rushed up the valley, most likely fanned by unruly hot and dry northerly winds, leaving only the southernmost end as the only avenue for escape. It was a deadly setup.

Ange had been called to assist firefighters during the frequent summer bushfires which overtook the coastal scrub in Northern New South Wales. Sometimes she had been asked to investigate a fire that had been lit either deliberately or negligently, although electrical storms were the most common culprit. A fire in coastal bushland was bad, but a fire fuelled by eucalypt or camphor laurel trees was terrifying. Both species contained highly volatile oils in their leaves. When the fire reached a certain heat intensity, a vapour trail would form above the tree canopy. This would provide the perfect conduit for the fire to leap ahead, sometimes hundreds of metres at a time. Fire breaks were all but useless during such an event.

A firefighter who she'd worked alongside during a particularly dangerous bushfire had told her that fires fuelled on vapour produced heat so intense that the trees below would literally explode. It was not possible to stay ahead of such a beast, even in a fully equipped fire truck. Ange had thought her firefighting colleague was exaggerating and had undertaken her own research. He wasn't. The precious lives of firefighters, often volunteers, were lost almost every summer as they were overcome by smoke or consumed by flames. She shivered at the thought of an out-of-control bushfire racing up the valley towards Edenview, something even Billie's flash car could not outrun. She couldn't help but see the similarities between that scenario and her recent encounter with the Police Integrity Command. That bushfire would have likely gotten out of control if not for the help of Owen Fairweather and Sally Anders.

The Mercedes approached the outskirts of the delightful little town some ten minutes before 11 a.m. The Edenview pub was easy to find, a two-storeyed bookend to a cluster of historic buildings that were pushed hard up against a sidewalk, remnants from an era where people walked or rode their horse to the shops. Ange drove past the pub and turned down a small side street, finding a substantial car park tucked discreetly behind, a modern appendage that had most likely consumed one of the stilted wooden houses that fronted the quaint side street. Ange recalled a favourite axiom of a friend of hers, who asserted that, should someone smart ever invent a drive-through toilet, they would be a smashing success in modern Australia.

Once parked, she took in the other vehicles and spied the troublesome Land Rover Defender with its large and aggressive tyres. 'Good, Daicos is here,' she thought to herself as she wandered around to the main street. A generous awning wrapped around the corner and extended down the street, protecting the historic storefronts from the elements. The scene roused an old-world charisma, evoking images of pioneers and time-rich locals eager to slake their thirst and enjoy some companionship in the gracious watering hole, a focal point of their little community. A street-facing espresso bar, strategically positioned in one corner of the pub, was just shutting down for the day. That was a pity, as the thought of a professionally made coffee caused Ange's stomach to emit a sharp rumble of desire. It was no drive-through, but the espresso nook was definitely convenient for passers-by, whether travelling by car or on foot.

Continuing along the street, Ange discovered a delightful clothes store that had opened alongside the pub. She wandered into the boutique and browsed through the tasteful collection of country lifestyle clothing and stylish accessories on offer. Next door to that was an antique-cum-giftware store, showing off an eclectic mixture of old and new goods, all obviously curated with considerable care. Ange stopped and browsed for a moment, seeing things that reminded her of the stuff at her parents' house. She detected an air of authenticity to the wares on display, perhaps collected from surrounding properties as they changed hands, or maybe as tastes morphed with progressive generations. She had a relaxed chat with the proprietor, a woman Ange guessed to be in her late forties, and the woman explained that the pub next door exerted quite a pull and that her small venture was built around their well-heeled patrons.

It was just past 11 a.m. when Ange ventured into the pub. She was immediately blown away by the standard of the decor. The art déco styling was a stark contrast to the building's late 19th-century red-brick exterior. Considerable care and attention had gone into the transformation of the building from a rough-and-ready public bar to high-end restaurant. It was spectacular.

An elegant bar served a smattering of patrons, enjoying a pre-lunch drink. Ange wandered past the bar and into the dining room, searching for the maître d'hôtel. The room was a hive of activity. Ange recognised the bearing of the staff and picked them as local folk of various ages. A bustling, middle-aged woman approached Ange. 'I'm sorry, but I'm just letting you know that we're fully booked.'

Ange's 11 a.m. appearance was evidently not uncommon, perhaps yet another blow-in hoping to score a cancellation or muscle their way onto a table. 'That's a pity. I would have enjoyed sampling some lunch. I've heard wonderful things. As it happens, I'm here to speak with Mr Daicos. Is he in today?'

'Do you have an appointment? We're very busy. It's school holidays, you know,' replied Suzanne—as identified by her black-enamel-and-gold name badge.

'No, I'm sorry. I don't have an appointment. Would you mind asking if he had a spare fifteen minutes? I'm sure he'll want to see me. My name is Gloria White. I'm an event planner and I have a once-in-a-decade opportunity for your restaurant. It's all very exciting,' replied Ange confidently, channelling her friend Kerrie to assume the guise of a gushy event professional.

The women eyed Ange suspiciously before relenting. 'OK. Let me check. Please wait here.'

Ange took in her surroundings, noticing a wide carpet-covered stairway that led upstairs. A sign warned that the upper level was reserved for house guests only. Ange walked someway upstairs and spied a glass door that was protected by a proximity card reader. It was all top shelf, and renovating the Edenview pub would have come with a substantial price tag.

The woman returned. 'Mr Daicos can spare you ten minutes. As I said, we're very busy today. Can you follow me, please?'

'Ten minutes will be more than enough,' replied Ms White.

Chapter 22

Shoulder to Shoulder

Suzanne led Ange back around the staircase. She stood and knocked outside a partially open door. 'Come in,' said a gruff voice from the bowels of the room. Suzanne pushed the door wide open and Ange stepped into a softly lit room. Her eyes took a second to adjust before she could properly take in the generous space. Although the room was fully internal and enjoying no windows or outlook, the combination of artistic lighting and tasteful decor made it immensely appealing. The furnishings seemed comfortable and comforting, a tranquil place where someone might escape for extended periods. A large couch stood against one wall, where a crumpled navy pillow suggested that catnaps were commonplace. Ange briefly wondered what her psychiatrist might say about a CEO's office that was so secret and hidden.

She had assumed that the famed restaurateur would be ruddy and slightly overweight, so she was surprised by the thin, hawkish man who stood up to greet her. Her eyes quickly scanned his features. Despite a completely shaven head and a notable proboscis, his most striking feature was undoubtedly two piercing dark grey eyes, hinting at the intelligence that sat within.

'Tony Daicos. Please take a seat. How can I help you?'

'Gloria White. Pleased to meet you. I have a wonderful opportunity that I'm hoping you can help me with. Mr Alan Campbell from Emerald Downs asked me to come and see you. Do you know Mr Campbell?'

Daicos's eyes narrowed imperceptibly. 'Everyone around here knows Alan Campbell. Alan and his wife are regulars at our pub. I'm curious as to what Mr Campbell wanted you to see me about.'

'Well,' replied Ange, conjuring up her most bubbly tone of voice. 'Alan wishes to throw a monster birthday bash for his wife, Billie. It's her seventieth coming up at the end of June. We share some mutual friends and Alan asked me to help organise the event. He was most insistent that I approach you about catering for the party. Alan is extremely complimentary about your restaurant.'

Daicos's expression instantly assumed a more relaxed appearance. 'How many people are we talking about? We can only seat eighty people in our restaurant.'

'Oh, no. Alan wants to spare no expense and expects at least one hundred and twenty guests. Going by my experience, that number will probably grow to one hundred and fifty when the invitations go out. Seeing how integral Emerald Downs has been in their lives, Alan wants Billie's party to be held on the property.' She glanced upstairs. 'Although, I expect some will wish to stay here, given your amazing reputation. Do you know Emerald Downs?'

Daicos narrowed his eyes again. 'I've driven past the property on my way north, but I'm not overly familiar with it.'

Although Ange was already convinced of the restaurateur's guilt, she pressed on with her pantomime. 'Well, I've picked out a few potential sites. There's the tennis court, of course, but that seems a touch obvious. Then there's the lawn beside the homestead—however, I'm a little concerned about the slope. My preference, and Alan agrees, is to hold the party on the flat by the river. This would give vehicles easy access and provide ample room for a marquee and for guests to mingle by the river. We'd have to bring in a generator and toilet facilities. What do you think?'

'Sounds interesting. We'd need a reheat kitchen and facilities for staff to plate up. It could look amazing, for sure.' He paused for a moment. 'I'd want to promote our participation in the event, perhaps even get some coverage in the lifestyle magazines,' added Daicos, his initially wary stance having changed position to one of thinking through logistics and imagining the opportunities presented by such a gala affair.

Just as Ange was about to ramp up the pressure, Suzanne walked to the door and made herself obvious. 'I'm sorry to interrupt, Tony, but we have a problem with a double booking. They insist that they're close personal friends of yours. Can you come and help sort it out?'

Daicos gave his maître d'hôtel an exasperated look. 'If they are close personal friends, I think I might know that they'd made a booking.' He stood up and addressed Ange. 'Sorry, can you give me a minute to sort this out?'

'Sure, Mr Daicos, take your time. These things can quickly get out of hand,' she answered with the knowing voice of someone supposedly in the trade.

Once Daicos had left his office, Ange stood and took in the room. With no windows to get in the way, the walls were plastered with framed awards and magazine articles. Daicos was clearly proud of his achievements. A caricature caught Daicos perfectly, despite the grossly exaggerated depiction of the man. The sketch had been signed by the artist. One wall had been reserved for photos of Daicos with VIPs and celebrities, some of which were signed.

Her breath caught as she studied one large glossy black-and-white photograph. Daicos beamed as he rubbed shoulders with an iconic NRL star—although Ange failed to recall that star's name. However, it was the man standing on the other side of the rugby league legend that had grabbed her attention. It was none other than the honourable Greg Kilroy. The group of men were several years younger than the present day, well before Kilroy had assumed the role of minister for regional affairs, but it was unmistakably Kilroy.

This was the missing link. Ange whipped out her phone and snapped off a series of photos before moving through the others on the wall. When she heard the steps of Daicos, she quickly stashed her phone.

Daicos returned with an irritated look on his face. 'They were close personal friends of a vague friend. We're going to set them up at the bar. It happens.'

Ange turned from studying the photos, all wide-eyed. 'Wow. You've certainly amassed some awards, and also had the ear, or should I say stomach, of some impressive celebrities, Mr Daicos.'

'Call me Tony, please. Most of those date back to my restaurant in Sydney. That was before I moved out here and renovated the Edenview pub. There were some heady days in Sydney,' commented Daicos, failing to mention the effect that a cocaine addiction might have had on his own head.

'So, where were we?' asked Ange innocently.

'We were talking through some logistics and the possibility of gaining some coverage in the lifestyle magazines,' replied Daicos.

'No fuzzy head today,' thought Ange to herself. 'I'll speak to Alan about that, but I think it should be fine. He really wants it to be a lavish affair. I know how these things work. In fact, I have some contacts in the media that might help.' She was so deep in the role that she almost blurted out the details of Kerrie's lifestyle blog, a potential disaster given the Superhero Detective Ange Watson posts which

Kerrie had made after the shooting incident. She regathered herself and pushed on. 'It would be towards the end of June or early July this year, so there's plenty of time for all that. I convinced Alan that you would want to select and supply the wines that best suited your menu,' she said with a conspiratorial grin. 'That should help make it worthwhile.'

'Sounds good. It's very hard to make any margin on food alone,' commented Daicos gravely, as if to drive home the point that being a restaurateur was a tough game. 'What sort of latitude would I have on the menu?'

'Good point. Seeing as their lives were built on the quality of their herd, Alan would like you to use cattle from Emerald Downs. Alan runs Wagyu and Black Angus, and he plans to select some prime steers and finish them on grain. That is, of course, once you let him know what cuts you plan to use. You might not know, but Alan started life as a butcher. He sure knows his beef cattle.'

Daicos shifted his gaze downwards for a second, appearing uncomfortable again, before the strength of the opportunity brought him back to life. 'OK. How about I prepare a fee estimate and send it over? You said to include beverages?'

'You provide everything you can, right down to crockery and cutlery, if that suits. I'll fill in the gaps for anything that's problematic for you. The fewer parties involved, the better—at least that's my experience.'

'The saying about too many cooks spoiling the broth is not by accident,' added Daicos, seemingly now convinced that he had a live one on the hook.

Ange had been using Gloria White so frequently that she'd taken the time to order some simple but elegant business cards online. She always kept a few in her wallet for emergencies and slipped one to Daicos. 'Thanks, Tony. Send me your fee estimate and any qualification or questions. There's no desperate hurry. As I said, I'm getting ahead of the game. Alan is a stickler for things being organised, and celebrating his wife's seventieth is very important to him. Deal with it once you get through the school holidays.'

With that, Ange left Daicos cocooned in his office and walked back to the Mercedes. She spied a security camera facing the car park. It took all her will to keep her phone pocketed and not skim through the pictures she had just taken. Finding that missing link was exhilarating.

Once clear of Edenview, Ange pulled over and flipped through the images. Many of the subjects were familiar, but she could only recall the names of a couple. The prime shot of Daicos and Kilroy was unmistakable.

Chapter 23

Heaven and Earth

Ange had made the drive back to Clearwater in a daze and failed to notice the darkening sky and clouds that were sweeping down the valley from behind her. She stopped in at Pam's coffee shop, but it was already closed for the day. The best she could do for a meal was some fruit and a muesli bar, a far cry from the gastronomic feast that patrons of the Edenview pub would be tucking into.

She was still munching the last crumbs of her lunch as she drove through the front gate of Emerald Downs. Alan Campbell and Fin Templeton were off to the right of the homestead, grading some steers in the cattle yards. They saw Ange driving down the gravel entry road and immediately started walking back to the homestead. Ange stood on the veranda and waited for the two men to walk up the steps.

'Well?' asked Alan Campbell. 'How did you go?'

'Better than I could have hoped,' answered Ange obliquely. 'I need a coffee and a few of your rich tea biscuits, Alan. I missed lunch.'

Alan led her into the kitchen and rustled up some tea and biscuits for himself and Templeton. Ange already knew her way around the espresso machine, so she got to work fashioning her poison. She waited until they were all settled around the kitchen table, sipping and munching their smoko before she began.

'Tony Daicos is as guilty as hell, but he's also clever. However, his big weakness is greed, and he's keen to cater for your lavish birthday bash, Alan. We're going to have it down by the river and it all sounds spectacular. I hope I can make it,' explained Ange with a wicked smile.

'So, what did you find out?' asked Templeton. A loud rumble followed his question, adding some theatre to the moment.

'Is that thunder?' asked Ange.

'Yep,' replied Cambell, looking up at the heavens. 'We're expecting a storm front to move through any minute. We could sure use the rain,' he added wistfully.

'Fin, did you organise those Ziplock bags and marker pen? Quick, let's get some samples off the trailer before it rains.'

'Sorry, I never got around to it,' admitted Templeton. 'I hadn't thought about the storm.'

Campbell quickly rummaged around in the kitchen drawers and dug out some bags and a pen. 'Here you go. Billie is a stickler about having an organised fridge.'

Ange handed Campbell her phone. 'Excellent. You can act as official photographer, Alan.'

With that, Ange picked up some kitchen knives, and the trio rushed outside and crawled over the trailer, taking several samples and labelling them accordingly. Once Ange felt that they had sufficient, she took the labelled bags inside and put them in a container in the fridge. 'This isn't ideal, but it's also not the assassination of JFK,' she concluded, putting some perspective on their endeavours. 'Hopefully, we won't need these, but one never knows where this investigation might lead us.'

Ange then gave Campbell and Templeton a fulsome description of the nuts and bolts of her visit with Tony Daicos. Just as she was about to deliver the coup de grâce, a lightning bolt cracked nearby, causing everyone to start. They all waited silently for the thunderclap and some sense of the proximity of the storm front. Almost by reflex, Ange had started mentally counting the seconds between the lightning and the thunder. Sixteen seconds. It was still over five kilometres away. 'Can we go back out to the veranda, guys? I just love watching thunderstorms roll in.'

'Great idea,' replied Campbell. 'My father used to drag me out of bed in the middle of the night to stand on our veranda and watch the sky light up.'

'It will provide an appropriate backdrop for the bolt of lightning that I'm about to deliver,' commented Ange, her voice now filled with excitement.

The three traipsed back out to the veranda. Just as they arrived, the heavens opened up with a torrential downpour. Massive raindrops slammed into the ground in a ferocious assault. Wild sheets of water washed over the property, punctuated by flashes of purple light. It was a spectacular sight. The ground shook with each successive roll of thunder, like a gigantic bass drum beating high in the sky.

Seeing as the Australian Christmas arrives in the middle of summer, the oppressive heat and humidity produce the perfect environment for violent thunderstorms. When Ange was a little girl, her father explained that the rumbling thunder was actually caused by Santa Claus, rolling his boxes of presents around and preparing for his midnight deliveries. It never occurred to Ange to question the impracticality of Santa's thick woolly red suit, completely incongruous in the brutal Aussie summer—such was her anticipation for the treasures within those imagined boxes. She pulled herself from those delightful childhood memories.

'Daicos has a trophy wall showing him shoulder to shoulder with a gallery of stars. There were sports stars, singers, TV and movie personalities, even the odd politician. Funny, but one of those politicians was the honourable Greg Kilroy, our very own minister for regional affairs.'

'Hah,' replied Campbell thoughtfully. 'I knew that guy was into more than our CEO.' He paused and looked out across his property as if deep in thought. The trio stood in silence for some minutes as nature's spectacular show reached its crescendo. Then, as if at the behest of some conductor up on high, the rain suddenly moderated, easing into a steady stream of soaking rain: calming, life-giving, relieving, restorative.

'This is the good stuff. I hope it lasts. Unfortunately, it's a narrow storm front,' mused Templeton.

Ange followed his gaze across the paddock. She was almost certain that the grass pastures were already greener as they soaked up the deluge.

'What does this tell you, Ange?' asked Campbell.

'I'm not entirely sure, but it provides us with the missing link between the cannabis farm and your stolen cattle. Thanks to your PI, we've already established the steamy relationship between Kilroy the minister and Bennet the CEO. Maybe Daicos is a silent partner in the cannabis farm and slipping Kilroy a backhander? Then again, Daicos could be dancing to the tune of a bigger puppet master. Perhaps he leaned on Kilroy to get the farm approved, and Kilroy let his dick do the talking with Bennet? There are quite a few possibilities,' observed Ange.

The rain gradually eased until it was reduced to a mist, almost like the gentle post-coital caress of a lover, a stark contrast to the frantic intensity of moments before. Ange felt her mind slowing and gathering perspective. 'There is one thing that doesn't fit for me. If Daicos is involved in the cannabis farm, it also suggests he might be involved in the people trafficking. I'm still convinced that the Clearwater and Hillburn operations are joined at the hip. I figure Daicos for someone who would be involved in drugs. That's a given. But trafficking young women? That doesn't gel with the guy I just met and the type of business he runs as his day job.'

She turned to Campbell. 'Alan, I think we need to hold off from moving in on Daicos for a while—at least until I've worked out what all this means. Anyway, you need to watch and learn who he might be connected to locally. It seems implausible that he just decided by chance to take your cattle, and yours alone. When is your PI coming out here?'

'I understand, Ange, and I agree with your conclusions. It's also nice to see that you're thinking of jumping back into the main game,' observed Campbell insightfully. 'David is taking a run to Sydney in the King Air to pick up Brian, my PI, sometime tomorrow. When are you wanting to head back east, Ange?'

'Well, I would have said today, but this storm has put an end to that. Could David swing north to Byron Bay or Yamba before turning south to Sydney tomorrow morning?' Ange remembered her car still sitting at the Ballina airport. 'Actually, I'll need to be dropped to Ballina. I'd forgotten that my car has been there for over a week. I'll need to take out a mortgage to pay my parking fee.'

'Of course. I put David on standby. How does 8 a.m. suit you? If Fin is correct, this weather will have cleared by morning, but let's say 9 a.m. Best be on the safe side to burn off any mist or fog.'

'I could get used to having my own plane, Alan. I'll need to win the lottery, but a girl can only dream,' replied Ange with a laugh.

'Now, about dinner,' said Campbell decisively. 'I think we should take a run to Edenview and have a celebratory dinner at the pub. What do you think? Fin can bring Ellie. You'll like her. She used to be a lawyer before becoming a full-time mum. Comes in handy.'

'Is that wise, Alan? Are you sure you can stay cool?' queried Ange, trying to dampen this idea, determining that it was fraught with unnecessary risk. 'Anyway, Suzanne, the maître d'hôtel, said that they were super busy. I doubt we'll get a table.'

'Oh, we'll get a table—that I can assure you. Even if they have to serve us on the sidewalk. It's one advantage of being the mayor. Everybody wants to stay on the good side of the council. Anyway, according to my event planner, I'm about to be their biggest customer. Let me get it organised. Fin, you go home and pick up Ellie and we can all go together from here. How does 5 p.m. sound?'

'Brilliant. Ellie has been at me for a night out for ages. I'll get her cracking on finding a babysitter. It shouldn't be hard, seeing as it's school holidays,' answered Templeton.

'So, it's Alan at work and Ellie at home. Who's the most demanding?' asked Ange mischievously.

'Hmmm, that's a tough one.' Templeton paused theatrically. 'Definitely Ellie at home. She can be relentless once she has her mind set on something. I reckon you two will get on like a house on fire.'

Campbell smiled at that small exchange before directing his attention to Ange. 'Don't worry about me losing my temper. I've played much higher staked games than this.' The jovial expression on his face hardened. 'I need to look that slimy bugger in the eyes and watch him squirm.' His face brightened again. 'It'll be fun. Trust me, Ange.'

'Not for Daicos,' she observed, reducing the trio to the merry laughter of comrades-in-arms.

The group went their separate ways and Ange walked to the guestroom to shower and change. She rang Gus once she was dressed for the evening. 'Hi, Gus. How are things in Byron?'

'Busy beyond belief. Have you found who's responsible for the missing cattle yet?'

'Yes. It's been an illuminating trip. I'll fill you in when I see you. Alan's pilot is dropping me off in Ballina tomorrow. I'll pick up my car and come straight to the shop.'

'Fantastic. Buddy and I will be waiting. Why don't you text me when you're twenty minutes out?'

'Sounds good. I'm looking forward to seeing you guys. I'm also in terrible need of some saltwater therapy.'

'Well, you sure are in luck. There's a serious swell building. It should be pumping tomorrow. It'll depend on how the wind behaves overnight, but we're certain to get some waves. Some of our sponsored surfers are champing at the bit. They reckon Lennox Heads is about to go off, but we'll have to wait and see. How about I pick up some gear for you and we head straight to the surf? I'll get the low-down from the guys first up.'

'Sounds exciting. Don't expect me to be seen anywhere near your sponsored surfers, Gus. That would be embarrassing for both of us,' Ange concluded with a self-deprecating laugh.

'Hah. We'll see,' replied Gus. 'See you tomorrow, then. Safe travels.'

'I could get used to this private plane thing. Are you sure Bell Surfboards doesn't need one?'

'Not on your life. You know the saying—planes and boats are great fun, so long as they belong to someone else.'

Chapter 24

Face to Face

Ange's return drive to Edenview presented a very different perspective than earlier in the day. A parched land had been softened by the rain and a willowy mist hung in the valley. The dark green groves of camphor laurel trees evoked images of a soft English dale, a stark contrast to the glaringly Australian landscape of that very same morning. Ange had read somewhere that early English artists had considerable difficulty catching the brutal Australian light in their paintings, accustomed to soft northern hues as they were. In fact, it took many years before Arthur Streeton finally got it right. Since her investigation into the forged painting by Emily Kngwarreye, Ange had made a habit of spending time in art galleries when the opportunity presented itself. Depicting the Australian light properly was essential in any landscape. She figured that early English artists would have felt quite at home that evening.

Alan Campbell had not been exaggerating when he'd suggested that the Edenview gastropub would make room for its mayor. Suzanne was almost sickening in her gushy greeting, assuring the mayor that the best table in the house had been reserved for the foursome. Ange wondered who had been bumped—perhaps another of Daicos's supposed close personal friends. As the party enjoyed a pre-dinner drink, Ange observed how extraordinarily popular Campbell seemed, confidently holding court to legions of fellow diners. He seemed to know at least half the patrons, suggesting to Ange that the Edenview pub was a place for locals, not just a place to be ticked off by celebrities and gastronomical tourists.

Their table was splendid, but she failed to grasp the weight that was put on *the best table in the house*. Kerrie would undoubtedly disagree, but surely the object of the exercise was to enjoy a good meal, not to be seen and heard, the best seat in the house a trophy that was worth spending time and effort aspiring to. That sort of thing seemed childish to Ange, something for those of shallow and insecure character.

In typical cattleman form, Campbell had ordered the porterhouse steak, going to extreme lengths to ensure that it would be cooked according to his liking—'medium rare, on the rare side, but make sure the fat is cooked until it's all crispy and caramelly—actually, make it rare, not blue, we can always slap it on the grill again if required.'

Ange could not resist a knowing smile as Campbell issued his orders to the chef. He caught Ange's look. 'I'll bet your father does the same when he eats out,' he surmised. Ange had rarely met someone so perceptive, and she was developing quite an affection for this surprising man.

As soon as Suzanne had taken orders and departed, Campbell had posed an obvious question. 'I'm a little surprised that there isn't any Wagyu on the menu. Maybe he hasn't gotten around to butchering his last haul.'

'I reckon that he might be taking time to finish them with grain, Alan,' suggested Templeton.

'You're probably correct, Fin,' agreed Campbell. 'That may have stuck in my craw,' he added sombrely before letting the conversation naturally drift this way and that.

The meals were unbelievably and undeniably good, no matter what opinion one might hold of the proprietor. In fact, it was one of the best meals that Ange had ever eaten.

Ellie Templeton was a delight, reminding Ange of the surprising depth of country folk. She had made the plight of modern-day bushies a pet project, railing against a society that sought to turn them into villains and impugn their lifestyle and their livelihood. 'It really pisses me off that nobody acknowledges the role that pastoralists have played in building the wealth of our nation. And what about the immense part the Chinese played, coming out here in droves during the gold rush? It's almost as if those early Chinese never existed.'

'I agree,' said Ange in between mouthfuls of delicious food. 'There's not a multigenerational Chinese restaurant in every country town in Australia by chance.'

'And then there's this ridiculous attitude towards mining,' added Ellie. Fin Templeton rolled his eyes as his wife raged against wokeism, a look of intense affection sitting deep within his eyes.

'Where on earth do they think their iPhones and electric vehicles come from—let alone the energy to charge them each night? Not from solar panels, that's for sure.'

'I hear you, Ellie. However, I'm not against maintaining some tension to keep each side of the fence honest. Believe me, I've seen what can happen when woke takes control, and also when the developers rule the roost. Neither situation is ideal.'

Ellie looked at Ange with a measure of respect, evidently enjoying the repartee. 'So, tell me about your job, Ange—sorry, Gloria,' she asked, dropping her voice conspiratorially. 'It's so cool what you do. Fin tells me you got yourself shot in a gun battle. How was that experience? By the way, I really want you to meet our eldest. She aspires to become an environmental scientist. Honestly, I don't know who her real parents are,' she implored, rolling her eyes dramatically.

'Getting shot was not a highlight of my career. Honestly, I don't remember much about the shooting itself. It's been the aftermath that's been a bit of a struggle: the nightmares and imaginary bogeymen in the bushes. The mind is an amazing thing, how it deals with that sort of trauma. Anyway, I think you exaggerate how cool it is being a detective. To be honest, I'm considering my future at the moment. I'm on leave and only in Clearwater as a favour to Alan. Actually, I've applied to register a business name. Nimble Investigations. What do you guys think?'

'Oh no, that wouldn't do. You simply can't stop being a detective. We need people like you to stop the bad guys from taking over,' Ellie demanded, her serious expression suggesting her statement was not to be taken lightly. Ange noticed Campbell's concerned gaze, reminiscent of her father's disapproving look whenever she concocted some hare-brained scheme to escape her share of farm duties.

As if on cue, the bad guy of the moment came over to their table. 'Alan, lovely to see you back. Gloria filled me in on your plans for a birthday surprise for Billie. I hope we can be a part of that. How was the meal, by the way?' asked Tony Daicos, exuding the confident ease of a popular and successful restaurateur.

'That porterhouse was exceptional, Tony. The best that I've ever had. I presume that was Black Angus? I hope so,' demanded Campbell.

'Spot on. I mostly serve Black Angus—and some Wagyu that I put on for the snobs.'

'There's nothing like a steak from an animal that's been loved and looked after,' said Campbell, fixing his host with a piercing stare. 'Did Gloria tell you how insistent I am that we use our own steers for the party? We're not one of the top studs in the country for nothing, you know.'

If Daicos could have crawled into a hole, he surely would have. Campbell let him stew for a moment before he relieved the tension. 'We're so lucky to have your restaurant in our region, Tony. I couldn't imagine anyone else being part of this special surprise we've got planned.'

Daicos squirmed until that very last suggestion, when relief flushed through his demeanour. 'I'm just as excited as you are, Alan. By the way, your meal is on the house. After all you do for our region, it's the least that we can do.'

'Thank you, Tony. That's very generous. I'll look forward to receiving your proposal for our little celebration.'

As Daicos made his leave, Campbell muttered under his breath, 'Snake in the grass. He's sure going to be surprised.'

Suzanne came over to clear the last of the plates and offer tea and coffee. 'Did Mr Daicos mention that the meal is on the house, Mr Campbell?'

'He did. Thanks, Suzanne,' replied Campbell, stopping to fish a fifty-dollar note from his wallet. 'I don't want you to miss out on account of Tony's generosity. Please take this tip. I know how hard you guys work.'

Suzanne positively beamed with delight. Evidently, patrons at the Edenview gastropub were not habitually generous tippers. Perhaps they thought the convention stopped at the Great Dividing Range.

'Remember, Mr Campbell, if ever you need to dine here, just let me know. We'll always make room for you and your family.' She glanced at Ange. 'And your guests.'

After coffee and tea had been consumed, the diners made their way to Campbell's Toyota LandCruiser to make the forty-minute drive home.

'How very disappointing,' was all Campbell had to say.

Chapter 25

Half the Job

The next morning while Ange was enjoying coffee and breakfast, she confronted the reality of their progress thus far. 'Alan, despite our strongest possible feelings, we really have nothing concrete to rely on. We know that Greg Kilroy was enjoying the company of Julia Bennet, and that some men associated with Tony Daicos rustled two of your cattle the other night and took them to the drug farm. We also know that Daicos knows Kilroy, but have no idea if they're besties or just onetime acquaintances caught together in a lucky celebrity photo. Your PI is going to play a crucial role in working out who may be connected to who. That and the analysis of the surveillance video of the drug farm.'

'I see how easy it is to jump to conclusions. Knowing when you've got enough evidence to act must drive you crazy,' observed Campbell.

'Or need a King's Counsel,' commented Ange drily. 'I admit that I'm prone to great leaps in logic. Sometimes that races me forward, sometimes sending me back to retrace wasted steps and start over. I'm pretty sure of one thing. If Daicos is the rustler of your cattle, our little ploy with the birthday party will put a temporary hold on his activities. I'm guessing his fee estimate will run to thirty or forty thousand, plus what he'll make from the grog. He'll have no wish to put that sort of profit in jeopardy.'

'It's good that we had this chat, as I may have been goaded into doing something rash. The front of that man—makes my blood boil,' replied Campbell in a stern voice.

'And don't forget the bigger picture here, Alan. I'm as sure as I can be that your cattle will be safe for the moment, but I can't say the same for those poor young women about to be deported. I really don't know how all this is connected, but my radar is pinging loudly. Anyhow, back to your problem. I'll chase up the video analysis later this week. I don't want to lean too hard on Billy. His skills are hot property in the department and the work I've asked him to do is really a favour. Remember, I still haven't picked up my badge.'

Campbell fixed Ange in a lengthy stare. 'I'm sure that you'll make the right decision. Now, if I need to send you anything, what address should I use?'

Ange thought for a moment before replying. 'Send it to Bell Surfboards at their outlet in the Byron Bay Industrial Estate. Best check the address on the internet before you send anything over. The outlet is so well known that just writing "Bell Surfboards care of Byron Bay" would likely do the trick.'

'OK. Seeing as we almost share a logo, I'm pretty sure I'll remember those instructions. Now, let's get you to the airport. Your pilot awaits. Before I forget, you never sent me the bill for those webcams.'

'Oh, that. I was about to, but got cold feet during the whole attack on my character. I didn't want to muddy the waters with money changing hands between us. If I resign, then it'll be a moot point, and I can bill you through Nimble Investigations.'

'That's ridiculous—on both counts. I could give you cash, but I guess that might appear like a backhander if either of us were taken to task by another overzealous prosecutor. I'll leave this in your hands, but know that I absolutely detest owing money. It's not a way to go through life. Promptly paying my debts is a personal fixation of mine, one that has served me well over the years.'

'OK. I hear you loud and clear, Alan. I'll get to it when the time is right,' promised Ange, avoiding any further discussion.

They walked to Campbell's LandCruiser. Ange threw her duffle bag on the rear seat and Campbell drove slowly out to the main road. There was still the odd puddle around, and the countryside had taken on a markedly greener hue, but evidence of the previous night's histrionics had all but disappeared. Campbell summed up the situation nicely. 'The ground was desperately thirsty and sure gulped down that unseasonal rain last night. It's a big help and relieved some of the pressure that was building. We'll need some more early-winter rain if we're to make it through spring and early summer.'

Ange smiled inwardly at Campbell's assessment. Most farmers and graziers were in awe of Mother Nature and all that she could provide, yet they were convinced that she held a personal grudge. Even in the most favourable seasons, the assumption was that they would be punished for such good fortune, and their ongoing struggles with the weather would soon resume in earnest.

Campbell looked across his property. 'I don't really know what's normal anymore. The climate seems to have become more changeable in the past few years, at least from where I sit. What's caused that is beyond my expertise, but it's certainly not the result of a few farting cows that some would have you believe,' he stated forcibly, the predictable conviction of a cattleman.

'You're sounding like my dad again, Alan,' laughed Ange. 'I'm not sure either, but I am certain that Mother Nature is far more complicated and more connected than we give her credit for.'

They drove towards the Clearwater airstrip in silence, ruminating over that discussion. Campbell briefly looked away from the road and fixed Ange with a penetrating stare, the type of stare given when an assessment of character was afoot. 'What do you think about all this environmental activism, Ange?'

Ange paused and thought through her answer carefully before speaking. 'A consistent and balanced debate would be ideal. That might keep pressure on everyone to do the right thing. I often think back to the way we used to approach many things in our society: rubbish, smoking, air pollution, adding lead to fuel, not using seat belts, as examples. Pushback on those accepted norms caused us all to take stock and do something positive. The difference today is that everything is so easily polarised, and dissenting points of view are cancelled before any proper debate can be held. Perhaps this has always been the case, and the cancel culture was reserved for those with the money and power—such as the tobacco companies, for example. I've seen the best and the worst of both sides. I just hope the middle ground is willing and able to stand up and fight for balance.'

'Good answer. Have you ever thought of entering politics?' laughed Campbell, returning his attention to the road and making the turn into the Clearwater airstrip.

He parked the LandCruiser beside a small hangar, and the pair walked onto the tarmac and approached a waiting David Eames. Campbell shook hands warmly with Eames, signalling that mutual respect sat between the pair. Eames then shook Ange's hand. 'That was quick, Detective. I expected you to be here for a week at least.'

'It's Ange, David. Sometimes surprising things fall from the trees when you've given them a vigorous shake.'

'OK. We're all fuelled and ready to go. Alan, I'll text you my ETA in Sydney when I'm about to take off from Ballina. Can you let whoever I'm picking up know where and when?'

'Sure. Your next passenger is Brian Edwards. He's helping me with a vermin problem,' replied Campbell obliquely. 'Thanks again, Ange. I expect that we'll be in touch sooner rather than later. Good luck with your career deliberations. I'm sure that you'll make the right decision in the end. For the record, I'm not a huge fan of Nimble Investigations, either as a business name or a vocation, but feel free to ignore my opinion on the matter.'

Ange made no reply to this career advice, and the pair shook hands, the firm country-type of handshake that said so much. Ange ascended into the plane and threw her duffle bag into the spacious cabin. A King Air is quite a large plane when you're the only passenger. She looked around, assessing where she might wish to sit.

Eames decided for her. 'Would you like to sit up front, Ange? It can get lonely up here sometimes. Alan always keeps me company when it's just the two of us.'

'That would be wonderful. I've never sat up front before.' Ange manoeuvred herself into the co-pilot's seat. Eames helped Ange fasten her more-complicated-than-usual seat belt and handed her a set of headphones. 'Here, put these on and we can chat. Just keep off the air during take-off and landing. You'll get the hang of it. Let's go.'

With that, Eames opened a small window and yelled out 'All clear' before successively kicking the two engines into life, waiting until each was whining happily, harmonics joining them into a wavering drone. This reminded Ange of the pulsing song of the cicada, where the tune of each individual insect would combine to create a different melody—that summer bushland chorus she loved so deeply.

With a minimum of fuss, Eames had them in the air in no time. They had taken off to the east, and the aircraft only needed a gentle turn to find their east-north-easterly track to Ballina. Ange saw the spinning dial of the altimeter reach ten thousand when Eames levelled out at their cruising altitude. 'It should mostly be a smooth flight, but I expect some turbulence as we pass over the range,' he said, looking over at Ange. 'You've made quite an impression with Alan. *Precious cargo* was the term he used. Is everything OK with Alan and the business?'

Ange realised that having a detective hovering around the Campbells had caused Eames some angst. Perhaps he was worried about his job, or perhaps it was genuine concern for his boss. She quickly doused any fears. 'Everything is fine. Alan wanted my advice on how best to deal with a problem he has, something important to him but otherwise insignificant in the scheme of things. I can see why you might enjoy working for Alan. He's quite a man.'

With that concern put to rest, Ange settled into enjoying the flight. She could see a cloud bank perched above the escarpment to the Great Dividing Range. As Eames descended towards the coast, he swooped gracefully around the gigantic pillows of white. Ange wanted to reach out and trail her arm against the fluffy clouds, just as she might on the face of a steepening wave. Sitting up front like that, she then imagined that this was the view of the albatross or petrel as they swooned across large swells, far out to sea. The experience was exhilarating, and Ange could understand the pilots' addiction.

Soon enough, Eames was looping gracefully around the Ballina airport before making his approach. His chatter with air traffic control was like another language. Ange was surprised at how quickly they seemed to fall from the sky before Eames eased the aircraft into a gentle landing.

'Well done, David. That was a wonderful flight,' concluded Ange.

'That was easy with these light conditions. Coastal landings can be a handful if the sea breeze gets up and I'm forced to deal with a stiff crosswind.'

The plane taxied slowly over towards the clutch of small buildings that formed the terminal of sorts. Eames shut down the port-side engine and left the starboard engine running. Once it had stopped, he opened the passenger door and gestured for Ange to disembark. 'I'll make a quick turnaround. Just walk straight to the small gate over there. Once you're clear, I'll start the engine again and be on my way. Nice to meet you, and best of luck with Alan's problem, Ange.'

Ange hesitantly descended the stairs amidst the whine of the starboard engine and hastened off the apron. After turning to wave goodbye to Eames, she skirted the airstrip and walked towards her waiting Prado. She felt like a movie star.

The parking fee came to two hundred and fifty dollars. Ange briefly wondered if she should claim the expense from the police service or whether Nimble Investigations was now responsible. There was a lot to think about.

Gus gave Ange a big hug when she arrived at the Bell Surfboards shop. Buddy broke up their embrace, demanding his share of the attention. 'Sorry I forgot to message you, Gus. I was distracted by sitting in the co-pilot's seat. It was a magnificent flight.'

'It's all good. I've packed you some things for today,' replied Gus, pointing to a small sports bag. 'Why don't you get changed, and then let's go surfing. I hope that you're feeling fit,' he advised with a big smile, a strong clue to what the rest of the day held in store.

Chapter 26

Bouldering

Once the trio had said goodbye to Buddy and were tucked in the Volvo and on their way, Gus filled Ange in on what he had planned. 'One of the guys phoned me this morning and said that Lennox is on fire. Have you ever surfed Lennox Heads, Ange?'

'No, I haven't. I've been meaning to, but the stars have never fully aligned.'

'Well, you're in for an experience. When it's firing like today, Lennox is a big wave that's not for the fainthearted,' explained Gus. He glanced over into the back of the Volvo, which was stacked with a quiver of four surfboards. 'I packed your midsize and your city surfboard that you call Franky. One of the hardest things about Lennox is getting in and out of the water. There's no real jump-off point, so you'll be forced to clamber over a series of large slippery boulders, and then make a dash for it once a wave washes over. Getting back out of the water is even worse. The waves continuously pound you from behind and up onto those bloody rocks. It's almost impossible to have a decent surf at Lennox without losing some skin. I gave wetsuit booties a try, but the loss of feeling in my feet made them a poor compromise.'

'Wow, Gus. You're not selling this session very well.'

'Oh, believe me. If it's half as good as the guys are saying, then the inconvenience of the boulders will be a small price to pay. It's an amazing break that holds a large swell brilliantly.'

'We'll see,' was Ange's tentative reply.

The car park that serviced the surf break was perched on top of the headland, sitting approximately one hundred metres above sea level. Deep swell lines extended to the horizon. Ange watched for a moment and counted the time between the waves rolling in, calculating it to be around fourteen seconds. A long swell interval means deeper troughs and higher peaks, confirming that this was a significant groundswell.

Waves viewed from above normally looked bigger than they were, but these swells were undeniably huge. Ange watched as a surfer who had been patiently sitting out wide catch the last and biggest wave in a set of three monsters. Slightly missing his take-off, he careened down the face, only partially in control. It seemed to take forever for the surfer to race down the long, sloping wave face. He recovered some balance and attempted a hard turn right, desperately seeking to make up for ground lost during his sketchy take-off. Speed bleeding away during the change of direction, a wall of whitewater enveloped him in a confronting wipeout. Ange held her breath and waited for board and surfer to reappear. Fortunately, he had chosen the last wave in the set, and clear water was in sight. She watched the surfer scramble onto his board and paddle furiously back into the fray, wondering whether he was smiling or grimacing.

Gus pulled her from concerns over that surfer to her own plight. 'By the way, Ange, there was one thing I forgot to mention,' he said with a sneaky smile. 'Seeing as we have three of our sponsored surfers in the water today, I organised some photographers. Maybe we can get a couple of photos of you today. I've already let them know that you'll be joining us.'

'I'm not sure that I'm up to this, Gus,' Ange replied with a pensive look on her face.

'Every surfer faces these fears, Ange. I'm also a touch apprehensive. Sometimes I worry that I may have forgotten how to surf at all. Let's take it slowly and stick together. It'll be an exhilarating experience, even if you don't catch a single wave. I threw in your 2mm steamer. While you might get a little hot, I think the extra protection on your legs and arms is worth any slight discomfort. We don't need any more scars on those sexy legs of yours.'

Ange touched her scarred gunshot wound in reflex, reminding herself that she had experienced worse traumas than a little old wave, no matter how humongous it might be. 'OK, Gus. I'll hold you to the sticking together part. I thought being a police officer was dangerous enough without falling into your clutches.'

'Good stuff. Now, I picked up an extra-long leg rope for you at the shop. This will help keep distance between you and your board in this bigger surf. Plus, not only will this leg rope have extra stretch and be unlikely to break, you'll also be able to dive deeper if a wall of whitewater is bearing down on you.'

'Wow, Gus, you need to brush up on the concept of buyer's remorse. Your explanation of why I might need an extra-long leg rope certainly hasn't helped with my confidence,' replied Ange, her tone of voice thick with a blend of fear and irony.

Once the pair were kitted out, Gus led Ange down a dirt track, which led to the rocky foreshore. The descent to sea level made the waves seem more intimidating. Ange followed Gus as he picked his way around the boulders and headed further out along the headland, examining how the waves were breaking as they went. Even though the waves broke on an unchanging rocky sea floor, swell size and angle were variables that needed careful consideration.

Gus finally made his choice. 'OK, Ange. Let's try here. The trick is to pick your way carefully over the boulders and then wait for a surge of whitewater to leap onto your board. If you can clear the rocks, the backwash will then give you a helping hand on the paddle out.' He pointed to a wave that was curling over. 'We need to time our run so that we can clear the spot where that wave is about to break. Once you're on your board, I suggest you go like the clappers.'

Ange said nothing, but her grim expression showed what she thought of this plan. She followed Gus's lead and picked her way over the boulders, looping up her extra-long leg rope and pinching it against Franky so as not to trip up. Things became increasingly difficult as slimy, seaweed-covered boulders, slick with seawater, became treacherous obstacles. Whitewater surged across and around the boulders, destroying any visibility of what lay below. Ange painstakingly crab-walked her way further out, using whatever appendage necessary to feel her way. A larger wave successfully pushed her off balance, and she tumbled over a large barnacle-covered boulder in an indelicate capitulation to the elements. Fortunately, thanks to her wetsuit, her only injury was pride.

Regaining her composure, Ange saw Gus a couple of boulders further out to sea, waiting patiently, his eyes fixed on the incoming waves. Mercifully, he seemed to have missed her rolling misadventure. She scrambled over beside him, one large boulder between them, and waited in an ungainly stalemate against the relentless sea.

After surviving three successive swells, Gus turned to Ange and gave his opinion of where things stood. 'OK, this is the last wave of the set. Follow my lead and then paddle like hell. Good luck.'

As the wave surged around them, Ange leapt forward and jumped atop her board, thrashing her way out to sea, channelling her inner Energiser Bunny. She judged that things were going well until she saw an enormous wall of blue water rearing up in front, intent on cleaning her up. Her heart jumped in fear, and she paddled with even more conviction, if that were possible. Knowing that a failure to make it through that wave would signal the end of her surfing session, she stroked with all her might up that immense face, finally punching through the curling lip of the wave. A spray of seawater streamed off the wave top as it crashed behind her. Ange closed her eyes until the deluge had stopped, then quickly wiped her eyes clear, only to see another even larger wave bearing down.

A surfer further along the line-up paddled for the wave. Jumping to his feet in an elegant take-off, he was soon racing down the face in total control. Ange was still paddling furiously and was pleased to see that the surfer had her in his sights. He changed course ever so slightly and, as Ange strained to make her way through and over the wall of water, he turned close behind her. If she hadn't been so focussed on survival, she would have lifted her feet, so precise was the surfer's track. He had his own job to do.

No time to look back. A third wave rolled in. This time, Ange was far enough out to paddle gracefully over with no further histrionics. Severely out of breath, her heart beating madly, she propped herself up to a sitting position and took stock. Adrenaline coursed through her body, causing her legs to twitch and flutter. She could feel the effects of lactic acid building in her arms, further weakening those tortured muscles. She sat like that for a couple of minutes until the next set of waves loomed large. Not wanting to undo all her hard work, she paddled further out and watched them roll by. Now she was too far out, with no prospect of catching anything at all. This was turning into a nightmare.

A much stronger paddler, she could see Gus well ahead of her. He paddled back down the line, turned, and sat beside Ange. 'What do you reckon, Ange?'

'I reckon this is crazy. I don't know how I'm even going to get back in, let alone surf any waves.'

'Oh, that. I did mention that getting back to dry land is the tough part,' he said with a wicked smile.

'Angus Bell. If I hadn't handed in my service revolver, I would probably use it later to repay your kindness,' she replied with no hint of a smile, making sure Gus knew the full extent of her angst.

'Just watch for a while and I'll pick out a wave for you. Look, here's Johnny K, one of our guys.'

Ange could see the bobbing head of a surf photographer. She wondered how he'd managed to carry his enormous camera over those treacherous rocks. Johnny K was deep inside, and Ange could see him being crunched by the breaking wave. The epitome of grace under pressure, he slipped to his feet and streamed down the face, barely escaping the thick collapsing lip. Seemingly unfazed by his narrow escape, Johnny K carved a hard bottom turn, turning one-eighty degrees and heading back up the face, before snapping a ridiculous re-entry in total defiance of that crushing lip. A drone zoomed by and followed Johnny K down the line. Ange turned and watched as he disappeared and reappeared, making turn after turn as he sped away.

'See how easy that was, Ange?' said Gus, sticking the knife in even further. 'Come on, let's get you onto the last wave of this set.'

In her heart of hearts, Ange knew that the longer she stayed still, the less likely it was that she would catch a wave. The final set wave came into view, one only three-quarters as big as the one Johnny K had just shredded to bits. She took a deep breath and, without a word, lay on her board and paddled back toward the impact zone and into position. No point in thinking further. She stroked into the wave, feeling its immense power as they joined forces. Judging that she was on the wave, Ange jumped to her feet and raced down into the fray.

Still in relatively deep water, the first thing she noticed was how incredibly fast the wave was travelling. The second thing she noticed was how much time she had to make her take-off and negotiate the face. Smaller waves required lightning-fast movements. This was almost slow motion by comparison. The third surprise was how much speed she had collected during the drop, and she took extra-special care of that first bottom turn, pushing with all her might to ensure Franky's tail bit the water. As she made the long carving turn, she looked up and saw the wave building ahead. She pulled halfway up the face and then turned back down the line, picking up as much speed as possible to make the next section. Once through, she turned downwards and made a second bottom turn, repeating her moves of moments earlier, carefully matching her speed over the water with the pace of the breaking wave. Four such moves later, the wave finally petered out and Ange rolled over the back and into the trough, collapsing on her board. Her heart was singing.

She looked toward where Gus had been sitting, but he was nowhere to be seen.

Glancing back towards the shoreline, she realised that her ride had been hundreds of metres long. Another dose of adrenaline surged through her veins. No time to sit stationary. She immediately started her long methodical paddle back towards her take-off point.

Ange only caught eight or nine waves that day, surviving one awkward wipeout when her hand slipped on take-off and she tumbled uneasily down the wave together with Franky. Waiting for the crunch of board against body, she was relieved that the extra-long leg rope did its job perfectly. Her strategy of waiting for the larger set waves to pass also worked a treat on that occasion, and she extracted herself from the impact zone with a minimum of fuss.

Gus had moved further out along the line-up to be with his sponsored surfers. She saw him catch a bunch of waves and admired his form. She found him so very sexy all the time, but even more so when he was carving down a massive wave face.

The rides were quad-burning monsters and the paddle back out to her take-off zone was simply punishing. After her first successful ride, Ange had used two pandanus palms growing on the headland as markers. The swell and incoming tide created a sizeable sweep, so even maintaining that position was exhausting. She hardly ever had time to sit still on her board and catch a decent breather.

After one especially long ride, just as she was gathering her strength to make the paddle back out, she saw another surfer making his way to the shore. She followed his lead and paddled across some deeper swirling water towards the rocky shoreline. Gus wasn't kidding about the difficulties of making dry land. Each incoming swell slammed her from behind, causing her to lose balance on almost every occasion. She felt her left foot scrape across a barnacle, then Franky took a knock against a boulder. It was a nightmare. By the time she had made landfall, she felt completely and utterly beaten into submission.

Her fellow surfer kindly waited until she was safe and sound. 'I'm not sure whether to love or hate this break. On one hand, dealing with those boulders is just plain brutal, but on the other, it keeps loads of people away. How amazing were those waves today? Did you get many?'

'As many as I could manage. I saw you earlier taking one of the set waves. You crushed it.'

The surfer beamed with pride. The solo nature of surfing made the recognition even more special. 'I reckon there was only one other woman out there today. Well done in braving that. Lennox can be confronting when it's this big.'

It was Ange's turn to beam. She glanced downwards to see that her left foot was bleeding. 'Thanks, catch you later. Best attend to this war wound.'

She walked carefully back to the car and, after retrieving the key from the surfer's lockbox that hung from the tow bar, she removed her wetsuit and changed into some dry clothes. She rummaged around in the glove box and was pleased to find a small motorist's first aid kit. Fortunately, the wound was minor, although she had no intention of admitting that to Gus. There was some serious credibility to be earned from the session she had just enjoyed.

Gus must have seen her beside the Volvo and came in just over thirty minutes later. Ange watched intently as he scrambled up the boulders and out of the ocean. It was oddly comforting to see that his clamber was no less difficult.

'How amazing was that?' he said once he reached the car. 'I saw you catch quite a few. What did you think?'

'Incredible waves, certainly the biggest that I've surfed by quite a margin. I couldn't believe how powerful they were. Your guys were crushing it. I saw Johnny K pull off some ridiculous moves.'

'He was on fire today. We should get some spectacular shots for our social pages. I'm going to push for a spread in *Surfing Life*. This has been an epic session by any standards.'

Ange was still buzzing with the wonderful combination of fatigue and excitement, still coming off the high of her spectacular, if daunting, session. It was a poignant reminder that she could so very easily have given in to her fear and stayed on the shore. Seeing the ocean like that in all its power and glory, up close and personal, was an experience that she was unlikely to forget.

By the time they had retrieved Buddy from his home away from home, and Gus had attended to some of the unending demands of being a business owner, they arrived home just on dark, too tired to make any effort with dinner. Pre-made ravioli, bottled pesto, some parmesan cheese, and chilli sauce were the best they could manage. They washed down their meal with a glass of Shiraz from the Barossa Valley.

Ange didn't last past 8 p.m. before she collapsed into bed, filled with the happy exhaustion that comes with hard-earned accomplishment. She was fast asleep when Gus joined her, and he later swore that she slept with a smile on her face.

Chapter 27

Surprise Packet

Ange woke early and tested out her foot. It was sore, but not enough to stop her enjoying this self-enforced leave of absence. She checked the surf report and saw that the swell had dropped considerably overnight. The wind was mild and coming from the south-south-east, but this was predicted to swing violently to the east late afternoon and continue in that direction right through the weekend. If Ange was to enjoy another surf, it needed to be that morning. Once she had coffee and toast prepared, she roused Gus from his slumber and told him of her plans to take a run down to Namba Heads and Sliders, her favourite break on the planet. Gus declined to join her, as he wanted to review the photos taken at Lennox Heads and start beating the bushes with the surfing magazines and online blogs. They agreed that Buddy could spend the day at the shop until Ange returned to pick him up.

Soon enough, she was zipping south along the Pacific Highway towards Namba Heads. She was in a wonderful mood, and the Prado buzzed along to the eclectic beat of Vampire Weekend, Ange singing loudly when she could keep up. An incoming phone call rudely interrupted her private concert. It was Alan Campbell. 'Hi, Ange. I hear that you had a smooth flight back to Ballina.'

'It was a beautiful flight. I loved scooting around the fluffy clouds as we dropped over the escarpment. Gus and I then enjoyed an amazing surf session. Even though I was scared out of my wits the whole time, it was an incredible experience. Today I'm planning a far more relaxed session at Namba Heads. Your old mate Terry Scott is the local councillor, so I might check in and say hello once I've finished my surf. Anyway, what's up? Have there been some developments with our mate Tony Daicos?' asked Ange.

'No, nothing on that front yet. Brian has only just begun, but he won't let go until he's run Daicos well and truly to ground. The patience of that man is astonishing. Anyhow, I've sent you a present as a small sign of thanks for all your work. The courier company promised me it would arrive at Bell Surfboards by Monday morning at the latest.'

'There was no need to send me anything. I've really enjoyed delving into your little problem. It's been a welcome diversion.'

'I understand, but it's probably not what you think. I wanted to alert you to keep an eye out for it, and not make any rash decisions about your career until you've received it. That's all I'll say. Will you promise me to do as I ask?'

'Now I'm really intrigued, Alan. OK. I'll do as you ask and keep my cards close to my chest until then.'

'Excellent. Now forget about it until Monday morning and have a lovely surf. Say hello to Terry for me, please,' concluded Campbell before he hung up the call.

Ange hardly noticed when the music restarted, deep in thought as to how on earth Campbell's present had anything to do with her career. She had fashioned no viable theories by the time she had reached the car park for Bushies Beach and the jump-off point for her walk around to Sliders.

The sea transported her from thoughts of cattle rustling, people trafficking, integrity commands, and all things untoward. The sun was well above the horizon, transforming the sea into a medley of soft blues and deep greens. Large swaths of glassed-off water blotted the ocean, and she could see her favourite pod of dolphins wallowing out wide. She hoped that they would swing by for a visit, perhaps dishing up a few surfing lessons on their way past.

As she arrived at Sliders, she looked back along the sweeping bay that led to Bushies Beach and the headlands to the north, imagining the small picturesque sandy coves that lay hidden between the rocks. The stunning vista both calmed and inspired her. Nature had a habit of imbuing that state of mind in Ange, something for which she was ever grateful.

Some locals acknowledged her as she paddled into the line-up. It was nice not to be hassling for waves, and everyone took their turn. Her injured foot softened up in the seawater and was soon forgotten. It proved to be a wonderful and therapeutic session, a totally different experience from just twenty-four hours before. The sea was like that: one moment light and transparent, the next dark and mysterious; sometimes menacing and malevolent, other times calming and benevolent; giving and taking life at will; instantly changeable, yet always absolute. It was no wonder that the ocean was a source of boundless fascination.

Ange was sitting on the deck enjoying coffee with Terry Scott when the predicted wind change rolled in. She remembered the first time she'd met Scott during the Namba Heads investigation, and how Terry had torn strips off the lazy and inept Sergeant Darren Billings. That memory always made her smile. It wasn't until later that she'd realised Billings was being paid off by the Ndrangheta Mafia.

Terry had just been filling her in on some lesser-known facts about their mutual friend. According to Terry, nobody knew half the stuff Alan Campbell did for his community. One story he told involved the building of a grandstand for the local rugby league club. Volunteers had been slaving away for years, holding cake stalls in the main street, raffling off frozen chickens and meat trays at local pubs, and sweating their way through annual fun runs and walkathons. After five years, the trickle of funds had barely shifted the needle on the large sundial-cum-cashometer, now a faded source of frustration and certainly no longer any call to action. It hung from the rusty tin shed that served as the toilet block and change room for visiting teams. Home-team players were expected to arrive already dressed for battle. At the rate they had been going, the fundraising committee was not even keeping pace with inflation.

Alan Campbell quietly offered to pay the balance of the new stand, much to the delight and relief of the tired and almost defeated committee. According to Terry, the new grandstand, complete with change rooms, showers, and a small canteen, would have costs hundreds of thousands of dollars. Once word got out that construction was about to start, a local tyre seller had jumped on the bandwagon, offering a further donation of some ten thousand dollars. This last-minute donation came with the catch that the stand be named in honour of the tyre merchant's family. This put the committee in a tough place. They had always secretly intended to name the new grandstand in honour of their major benefactor, but new building regulations meant that they desperately needed the extra money.

Campbell heard about the tyre merchant's offer and the condition placed on the new funds. According to Terry, Campbell insisted that the committee do whatever it took to get their hands on the extra money. He insisted that they remain silent about his donation and was happy to let the tyre merchant puff his chest out with pride. But of course, Clearwater being a small town, everyone knew the truth of the matter. However, this gracious gesture proved to be a shrewd move by Campbell, as the tyre merchant felt compelled to commit to a substantial annual sponsorship, one that was still in place to this day. Over the years, the entire sponsorship had probably grown to match Campbell's initial contribution.

Terry reckoned that Campbell had been a shoo-in when he'd stood for mayor, becoming even more popular when his mayor's salary was donated into a special fund to support local kids as they left to study at university. Terry couldn't say a bad word about Campbell, other than to warn that he was known to be merciless if ever his trust was betrayed or his generosity abused.

Ange saw the wind change in the trees just as Terry was wrapping up his tribute to Campbell. The sharp gust of wind came just at the right time, as if on cue, somewhat symbolic of what a traitor to Campbell's goodwill might experience. Within just thirty minutes, the pair were forced to retreat off the deck and seek shelter inside. She knew that the ocean was the source of this howling wind, yet another sign of its uncompromising power.

As she drove home, she mulled over Terry's expose about the real Alan Campbell. Terry himself was a tireless worker for his local community, so this tribute to his friend carried considerable weight, his potent warning even more impactful. She reflected on the times when she had been too soft over betrayals of trust, and how it almost always came back to bite her. A mongrel was a mongrel, no matter how they dressed themselves up. She made a resolution never to fall for the same trick again.

With the surf a complete mess and no pressure of work to intrude, Friday fused into a weekend devoted to relaxation and reflection. Ange and Gus had a long boozy Sunday lunch with some friends, sampling the fare at a new gin distillery that had opened in the hinterland behind Byron Bay. The Subaru was left to spend the night at the distillery, and Ange and Gus went home to a night of passionate, almost frantic, lovemaking. As they drifted off to sleep, Ange thanked the gods, those of earth and/or heaven, for delivering Gus into her life. It wasn't lost on her that this wondrous gift had come from the darkest of tragedies. Inevitably, as was so often the case, her mind drifted across the ocean, nature's ultimate giver and taker. These opposing notes of yin and yang formed the soft melody that accompanied her slumber, helping her push aside the pivotal decisions that would come with morning.

After helping Gus retrieve his Subaru, Ange dropped off Buddy at the shop, leaving him in the capable hands of his adoring fans. Still in limbo-land, and with the easterly wind already on the fresh side, Ange decided to catch a Monday morning Pilates class with her friend Kerrie. She checked to see that no parcels had been delivered before driving into the town.

Her phone buzzed, and she saw that Sally Anders was calling her. Although it went against her grain, she ignored the call and let it slide through to voicemail. Once she was parked and walking to her class, she shot off a text.

> *Hi, boss. Tied up this morning. Will give you a call sometime this afternoon. A*

Her boss texted straight back.

> *OK. You won't be able to avoid me forever. Ring me when you get out of the surf.*

Ange smiled at her boss's response. It was pretty close to the mark, although she had incorrectly guessed the true nature of her diversionary tactic. After the strenuous class, muscles tensed, relaxed, stretched, and then tensed some more, she and Kerrie enjoyed an early lunch together.

'So, tell me, what on earth is going on with you? You've normally got to rush off to one battle or another on Monday mornings,' asked Kerrie, no slouch at reading the tea leaves.

'I'm stuck at a crossroads in my career. I never really filled you in, but my so-called colleagues tried to make me a scapegoat over my last operation. It was a case involving trafficked young Asian women. I realised that I was more interested in solving the case than my superiors were. Anyway, I'm deciding whether to toss in the towel. What do you think of Nimble Investigations as a business name? Be honest. It's not getting rave reviews so far,' Ange replied wistfully.

'I'll need to divorce you as a friend if you become a private investigator in Byron Bay. As for the name, it sounds like a sporting physio practice,' was Kerrie's quick-fire response. She fixed Ange with a penetrating stare. 'I know that you'll do the right thing.'

Ange was left in no doubt about Kerrie's opinion of her business idea and arrived back at the shop to find an express courier satchel waiting for her at the front counter. She made a complete hash of ripping open the unrippable, forced to borrow some scissors to complete the task. Inside was a large yellow envelope. Her heart rate doubled in a second. The last time she'd received an envelope like that from Alan Campbell, it had contained the equivalent of dynamite.

Ange walked upstairs to the mezzanine level and found Gus's office empty. She figured he was probably roaming around the factory somewhere. Quietly closing the office door behind herself, she sat down behind his desk, carefully opened the envelope, and slid out its contents. As before, the first few pages contained a table of dates, times, and descriptions. An inveterate skipper-ahead, she quickly flipped through these pages of text, not bothering to study any details. She knew that the thick sheaf of glossy photographs was where the interesting stuff would be found.

The first glossy page was a photomontage showing a sequence of shots of a man and a woman standing on the side of a sporting field in progressive stages of cheering and supporting their team. The photo had been taken from a considerable distance away, but it looked like a school sporting event in Ange's eyes.

A second photomontage showed what Ange assumed to be the same man, leaving his house and getting into a silver Toyota Camry. This series of photos was taken from a much closer range and Ange immediately recognised the right honourable Greg Kilroy.

The third photomontage showed Kilroy hooking up with Julia Bennet to enjoy some light relief from their busy days. It looked as if the amorous couple may have availed themselves of Bennet's apartment, although that was conjecture on Ange's part. She paid these images scant attention, as Kilroy's affair with Bennet was old news.

The next sequence of photos had been taken from elevation and showed Kilroy walking across the street towards an older-style two-storey building of brick construction, painted in tones of dark grey or charcoal. Going by the glass shopfronts, some sort of retail or commercial outlet sat at street level, with offices or flats on the second level. A large awning shaded the entire main road frontage. Painted timber windows adorned the upper level, protected by older-style security grilles. It was a quality building that would have been developed in an era when merchants lived above their shops, something old that was new again with modern town planning theory. It looked as if the photos had been taken from just across the street and were of amazing quality. She could easily make out the words 'The Pulse' embossed on the awning in classy silver lettering. Ange paused briefly to search that name on her phone and found it to be a stylish bar and restaurant at Surrey Hills in inner Sydney.

Turning back to her sheaf of photographs, she followed the sequence and saw that Kilroy had walked down the side street and then pressed a buzzer of some sort, suggestive of a hidden door concealed in the side wall of the charcoal-coloured building. He looked up, as if identifying himself in a security camera, before a door opened and Kilroy walked straight inside, the door closing immediately behind him. It was all very mysterious, and an odd place for a government minister to be hanging out, but hardly a smoking gun.

Her first impression of the next photograph was similarly unimpressive, one that showed the upper level of the building in close-up and in greater detail. She quickly flipped it over to reveal another facsimile. Ange caught herself from blithely skipping through this sequence of photos before retracing her steps and studying them more closely. Her heart skipped a beat when she realised that the subject of these photos was not the building, but rather who was inside. As Ange leant forward and peered through the windows, haunting doll-like faces leapt from the page. She took stock and carefully stepped back through the portraits that were staring out through the windows. She was left in no doubt that the faces were of different women taken at different times. They were all unmistakably youthful and of Asian descent.

Edwards was obviously prone to theatre, and the last of those images was the most chilling. He had caught the perfect moment, zooming in to capture a stunning young woman gazing out a window. With the afternoon light casting an otherworldly glow on her flawless face, she stared out into the world with a baleful expression. It was impossible to ignore the security bars, evoking a sense of confinement for the young woman. Ange remained transfixed by that image for ages before progressing to the last section of Edwards' dossier.

The third-to-last was a montage of four snaps showing Kilroy leaving the side door. A small date-and-time stamp on the bottom of each image confirmed that Kilroy was a regular visitor to the establishment.

The second-to-last photo caught two men in the process of leaving the building by the same door. A shortish, well-dressed Asian man was accompanied by a tall and heavyset Caucasian, an absolute brute wearing a poorly cut black suit and with heavy tattoos visible down the right side of his neck. Ange had seen this combination before—the bossman and his muscle.

The last image showed a close-up of the Asian man, suggesting that the photographer had made the same conclusion about who was the important figure of the two. The fact that this was the last in the impressive series of photographs hinted that Ange was expected to know the subject. While there was something oddly familiar about the guy, she just couldn't put a finger on why.

Chapter 28

Stranger than Fiction

Deep in thought, she wandered downstairs to get some coffee, hoping that a caffeine hit would extract the clue that was lurking somewhere in her mind. It was always annoying when that happened, a memory that simply refused to reveal itself. The harder one tried, the more elusive the quarry, almost recalcitrant in its evasiveness. Ange knew from prior experience that distraction was the best strategy. Then, just as one's consciousness was caught unawares, she could leap in and snatch that memory from the depths.

With coffee in hand, Ange wandered around the shop, looking at the latest boards. Buddy was 'helping' some potential customers as they browsed, grifting regular pats and scratches. He glanced over at Ange, as if considering his chances, before turning back to his marks, evidently considering them more fertile ground. Ange almost laughed aloud at her fair-weather friend before turning to walk back upstairs. On her way, she passed by the wall that Gus had reserved for photographs of his sponsored surfers. She saw that some shots from last week had already been posted and was pleased to find that she hadn't made the grade.

Gus's surfing gallery reminded her of her visit to Tony Daicos's gastropub in Edenview. The elusive memory came like an express train. She quickly drained her coffee and then pulled up the collection of photos on her phone, flipping through them until she had found the sequence of shots of Daicos's VIP trophy wall. Ange carefully studied each image in turn. It was the fifth photo that had inspired her recollection, one showing Daicos, Kilroy, and her mystery Asian man all together. She studied the faces that made up the rest of the troupe, some of which were vaguely familiar celebrities having now slipped from prominence. Going by the stupid party hats, they all formed part of a larger group of New Year's Eve revellers, and Ange guessed that the shot must have been taken some time ago.

She leaped back up the stairs to Gus's office and compared the photos in Campbell's dossier with the one on her phone. She was left in no doubt that one was an older version of the other. Flipping back through Campbell's photographs, keeping them in order, she studied the tables of text that had prefaced the photos. It made for interesting reading. Kilroy was a busy boy, and it took some heavy mental gymnastics to grasp the full extent of his activities. In just one week alone; he had attended school sport on Saturday morning with his wife and children; paid The Pulse a visit that same afternoon; gone to dinner with his wife on Sunday; visited Bennet for a booty call on Tuesday at lunchtime; been back at The Pulse by Thursday; hooked up with Bennet again on Friday for a lunchtime liaison, although he hadn't looked his usual smug self after that; then attended a black tie fundraiser that night, playing the part of a doting husband to his glammed-up wife. By the next Saturday morning, Kilroy was back at school sport, pressing the flesh with his constituents, once more the supreme family man.

Where Kilroy ever found time to work was a mystery. Ange felt a twinge of sorrow for his wife and spent a moment studying her amongst the various photographs. Chief cheerleader to her children's sporting exploits, she had a softness about her smile, an enthusiasm for her family that appeared both genuine and deeply attractive. Why Kilroy would stray towards the likes of Bennet made absolutely no sense. Ange reluctantly admitted that Kilroy possessed a certain calculated attractiveness.

The entries in Kilroy's ledger that corresponded to photos had been highlighted, but the period covered some three weeks in total. It was an immense body of work that had entailed impressive patience and attention to detail. However, it was the last highlighted entry that astounded Ange.

> *'Harry' Linh, emigrated from Vietnam to Australia in 1997 to study pharmacy. Now a successful business identity with a chain of restaurants and nightclubs in Brisbane, Sydney, Canberra, and Melbourne. Be careful with Linh. He seems to know all the wrong people.*

Ange mulled this over for a few moments before ringing Campbell. 'Thanks for the gift, Alan. As you suggested, it wasn't what I was expecting. It's an impressive body of work. I hope that you didn't do all this on my account.'

'Not entirely. Kilroy is as dodgy as all heck, and I needed to do my research thoroughly. I'm pleased that you found it interesting,' replied Campbell.

'Who on earth is your private investigator? That's the work of a real professional.'

'Oh, Brian. He's an interesting character alright. I met him when my boys were at boarding school. He was their rowing coach. Earned himself an Oxford Blue for rowing back in the day. Oh, and also ex-MI5.'

'Whoa. That explains a lot. How on earth does someone from MI5 end up in Australia as your PI?'

'Extracting information from Brian has been like pulling teeth. The short version is that he was working for MI5, acting out the part of a rowing coach at Oxford, when he fell in love with an Australian student. She was studying molecular biology, and when she had finished her studies, Brian followed her back to Australia. Eleanor now heads up a successful biotech company. He tried to get a job in Australia, but his former employer wasn't interested, and our mob, ASIO, didn't want a bar of him. Brian comes from old money and, with no kids to worry about, was going stir-crazy with boredom. I suggested that he would be the perfect person for a job I needed doing, and the rest is history. When you come across someone like Brian, you don't let them out of your sights, even if his posh English accent makes him sound like a tosser,' explained Campbell with a subtle chuckle, a sign that he didn't consider Brian any type of tosser at all.

'A bit like Fin Templeton, heh? You know that I'm learning a lot from you, Alan. What do you think is going on?'

'It seems obvious to me that Kilroy, Daicos, and Linh are connected somehow, which probably explains how a secret drug farm ends up in my shire and how Bennet fits into the picture. I reckon Kilroy is a sex addict, and I'll bet that Linh has both Kilroy and Daicos in his pocket. How all this fits into my cattle rustling problem still has me beat, but I feel confident that Brian will run that conundrum to ground. The full extent of what Linh and Kilroy are into, and whether this involves your people trafficking investigation, is, I guess, where you come in. Brian reached out to some old colleagues to get a heads-up on Linh, but it's not much to go on.' Campbell paused for a moment before finishing his train of thought. 'Imagining what's happening to those women haunts my nights, Ange.'

Even though Campbell's offhand comment could have been a perfect opening, Ange remained mute and an uncomfortable silence fell upon the call, lasting a full ten seconds, until Campbell broke the spell. 'I'll keep you posted about Daicos. I'm not bound by any confidentiality clauses, but I guess you might not have that same luxury. That is, of course, assuming that you plan to stop Kilroy and Linh and rescue those women.'

'You sure know how to sweet-talk a girl, Alan,' replied Ange as a dry smile crept across her face, plucking the conversation from the deepening shadows.

'I knew that you'd do the right thing, Ange. All I can say is good luck and godspeed,' said Campbell, a mixture of affection and respect clear in his tone of voice. 'Speak sooner rather than later, I hope.'

Ange walked downstairs in a daze. Even though the decision had already been made, she needed to take stock and think through the implications of the task she was about to embark upon. She picked Buddy's dog lead from where it hung on a hat rack. He was deeply enraptured by the attention that two customers were lavishing on him but instantly recognised the jangle of his lead, spinning away from their clutches and racing over to where Ange stood. Properly harnessed, Buddy fell into place by her side as Ange walked out the door. With no direction in mind, she wandered around the industrial estate, checking out the eclectic collection of shops and factories. She was always so intent on the Bell Surfboard shop that she had forgotten how much talent and imagination beavered away in the depths of that small industrial hub. She stumbled upon a sculptor's studio and spent some time admiring his work. The artist fashioned curious objects and figures out of old rusty pieces of metal and roofing iron. Unravelling the meaning behind each piece somehow allowed her subconscious to form some order to her thoughts.

She admitted to herself that Campbell had her pegged. It went against her grain to leave those poor women in the hands of callous people traffickers. However, as things stood, she had nothing to go by—other than her strong suspicion that Linh was up to his eyeballs in this horrific enterprise. While she had strong evidence of Kilroy's connections to Linh, that could be easily explained away by a clever lawyer. Sure, his affair with Bennet might spell the end of his career as a politician, but that was no given. Many a politician had successfully steered themselves around accusations of adultery. The fact that Kilroy habitually fed his addiction while playing the part of a dedicated family man and loving husband showed that he was skilled in the art of deception. As much as she loathed the man, he was certainly handsome and obviously charismatic. He would probably be fine, a successful minister likely protected by a party machine that wished to avoid embarrassment.

Ange could not believe that his wife wasn't suspicious about his activities. Perhaps love really was blind, although she didn't come across as a complete fool in the photos Ange had studied. Instead of the architect, Ange considered the possibility that Bennet had been used as a pawn, but she shed no tears for the former CEO of the Green River Shire Council.

Suddenly, as if a switch had been thrown, her decision was made. Holding Buddy's lead awkwardly in the crook of her arm, she called her boss.

Chapter 29

Back in the Saddle

Anders picked up the call after just two rings. 'If I didn't know better, I might think that you'd been avoiding me,' she answered, making clear where her thoughts had been travelling.

'It wasn't personal, boss. I made a promise to myself not to do anything rash.' Ange then filled Sally Anders in on the dossier that Campbell had sent her, pausing often to answer the many questions posed by her boss.

Anders summarised matters succinctly. 'I agree that all of this is suspicious and I'm sure that you're onto something. However, as I see things, there's nothing concrete in all of that, certainly nothing that we can lean on. I haven't seen the photos, but I gather you've made the same conclusion. Am I correct about that?'

'Yes. I agree. What Alan Campbell sent me is nothing more than a solid lead,' replied Ange. 'The only link we have between Clearwater and Hillburn is the WhatsApp communications between the two locations—and those have been all fortuitously wiped clean. I've never believed that this was all happenstance—and now we find out that Kilroy is thick with the mysterious Harry Linh.'

'I hear you. Hillburn was wrapped up way too quickly and conveniently for my liking. So, what are you proposing, Ange?'

'I'd like to probe this relationship a little further. It might not help us with Cua Kwm and people trafficking, but the relationship between Kilroy and Linh looks dodgy and something we should be interested in. However, I have a few prerequisites. Call them demands if you like.'

Sally Anders was as cool as could be. 'Fill me in, Detective.'

'Well, it shouldn't surprise you to learn that, other than Billy and Bree, I don't trust any of my so-called colleagues anymore. I'd like both of them to work with me on this.'

Anders was quick to answer. 'Agreed, but you'll need to clear Bree's secondment with Jim Grady. Is that all?'

'Not quite all, and here's the crunch. This thing with Kilroy and Linh is a powder keg. A shady underworld figure connected to the political inner circle through a corrupt, philandering government minister. One doesn't need to be Einstein to figure out that it's going to blow up at some point. I don't plan to be hung out to dry again. You've been the only person in the hierarchy who's supported me, but, as I see it, your ability to help has been based on blackmail—and I say that in the nicest possible way, boss.'

The pair laughed at this, both knowing that Ange was referring to the evidence that Anders had assembled on the politicisation of the service and their preference to cover up any rotting wood rather than fix the problem. Ange continued. 'I know you think you have the commissioner under control, but I'm not at all comfortable that she would have my back. If this blows up and politics comes back to bite us, then you'll have my letter of resignation on your desk before you can blink. However, I need you to promise me that, in that event, you'll unleash the dossier that Owen Fairweather has safely tucked away. I couldn't live with myself if I left knowing that the service was rotting so badly from the head.'

Sally Anders paused, as if weighing up her options. Ange knew that it was a big ask. Her boss's career would be under threat the moment she threw the hand grenade that Fairweather was keeping safe. 'I'll staple my letter of resignation to yours, and then I promise that Owen will send my dossier to Sue Elkington at The Times. You have my word, Ange. That, of course, comes with a proviso that you don't do anything stupid.'

Ange laughed. 'You know that I can't possibly guarantee that, boss.'

'What about Daicos, the restaurateur? He seems to be the person who links Kilroy to Linh,' asked Anders.

'Alan Campbell has him under surveillance. His PI is top-shelf. Which brings me to the last of my demands.'

'There's more? I thought we were done with those.'

'We were, but I just thought of it. Seeing as I don't trust any of our colleagues, I'd like to use Brian Edwards, Campbell's PI, for any additional surveillance work we need done. I presume that he would need to be officially working for us to allow any evidence to stand up in court. Do you have any budget for that? I'm certain that we won't find anyone better. Did I tell you he's ex-MI5?'

'MI5? Really? You'll have to fill me in sometime on how that's even possible. OK, I'll find some budget, but there's a limit to how far that will stretch,' replied Anders before pausing, as if doing some math in her head. 'Let's give it a month. I'll divert Billy in your direction. You'll need to speak with Jim Grady about seconding Bree. I'll also need some sort of documentation for the arrangements with Campbell's PI. You'll need to organise all of that.'

'Done. I'm pleased. Thanks for humouring me, boss. I really enjoyed the chat.'

'Sure,' chuckled Anders. 'You got everything you wanted—and hoisted me on the gallows beside yours. I knew from the moment we first met that you'd be trouble.'

'You know that I'm not coming back out of any sense of loyalty to the service, present company excluded,' added Ange, a serious tone ringing in her voice. 'At the heart of this is a group of poor young women, lured or taken from their homes, abandoned by everyone—including us—and forced to live a life of prostitution or slavery. I can't get past the fact that Cua Kwm was murdered to cover up the trail, and that I could have done more to prevent her death.'

'Ange. We've been over this. You did more than anyone else to protect that woman. But I understand how you might feel this way. The best thing you can do is take down this mob and make her death count for something.'

Ange made no reply to that logic. However, she could not shake a feeling of responsibility. Sure, there had been other deaths which happened on her watch, but they were either objects of her investigations, or in some way complicit in their own deaths. Cua Kwm was innocent on all counts—innocent in an absolute sense.

In her heart of hearts, Ange understood the truth of her boss's assessment. The best way to assuage her guilt was to avenge Kwm's death. There were other young women who were currently in the servitude of traffickers and their network—not to mention the next shipment, and the shipment after that.

Sally Anders broke the gloomy pall that had descended on the call. 'By the way, I think Bree is a keeper. Not only has she made a profit on her crypto trading activities, but she identified who was behind a crooked initial coin offering. We referred the matter to Interpol, and they seem pretty chuffed. It turned out to be a money laundering operation for a Russian outfit that they'd been chasing. We earned some serious brownie points with Interpol over that. Seeing as you and

Bree are based in Byron, it might make sense for Billy to come up your way. We could rent an office somewhere if you needed it.'

'Leave that with me. Let's plan to kick off next Monday. That will give Billy time to tidy up his desk and make his way up here. Also, it allows me time to square things away with Jim Grady and sort out some digs.'

'OK. Speak later, Detective. Nice to have you back on the team, Ange,' concluded Anders, her softer-than-usual tone a telling sign of her sincerity.

As if on cue, Gus walked into his office. Ange quickly reassembled her dossier and slid it back into the envelope. 'Hi, Gus. I've just got off the phone with the boss. I've decided to give the service one last chance.'

'I'm pleased for you, Ange. Walking away from that people trafficking case would have haunted you forever. Now you can put it to bed.'

'That's essentially what the boss said. Now, speaking of beds, would you mind if I turned your guesthouse into our nerve centre to bring those mongrels down? Billy is coming up from Sydney to join us. I figured he could sleep in the bedroom, and we could set up shop in the living room. Bree will be joining our operation. It should be fun. I'll lean on Billy and Bree to provide free crypto and NFT advice over dinners,' said Ange with a smile.

Gus walked around the desk and gave her a big hug. 'It's nice to have you back, Detective Watson. I was missing your spark. Do you realise just how boring my life would be without you in it?'

Ange took a leaf from Buddy's book and fell into Gus's embrace, lapping up his affection. Sure, it was nice to solve the odd case, but it was the people around her that made her sink or swim. It was nice to be swimming again.

Gus pulled back from the embrace. 'I was saving this for the right moment, but now seems like as good a time as any. Remember how you nearly didn't join us for the epic day at Lennox last week?'

He reached down and picked up a picture frame that was leaning against the wall. Holding the frame in front of his chest, he then dramatically turned it around in a ta-da moment, revealing an amazing photograph of Ange navigating a massive deep blue wave face, one that stood well above her head. The photographer had perfectly captured the instant when she was leaning into a deep bottom turn. Her right hand trailed almost casually against the wave face, and the move looked so stylish that she took a moment to register that it was actually her.

'Oh, Gus,' was all that Ange could say for the moment, savouring this stunning memory, now recorded forever. 'This is just incredible. Thank you so much. My first surf photo—and what a cracker.'

Gus arranged the photo on his desk, and they both stood back to admire it some more. After a moment, Ange turned to face Gus and fixed him with a knowing smile. 'Point taken. What doesn't kill you makes you stronger, and all that. There seems to be a lot of it going around.'

That night, as if a chilling omen, Ange suffered a terrifying nightmare. This tale was a departure from her typical nocturnal diet of Ndrangheta hitmen jumping out from behind bushes and opening fire in her direction.

Ange had been feeling her way along a series of darkened corridors, a grungy and foreboding maze of sorts. She saw a violet glow in the distance and made her way cautiously toward what she hoped was a way out. The source of that light was distressing.

The hallway opened into a large domed circular room. An open-sided walkway circled the space and in the centre of the chamber stood a macabre super-sized birdcage. It was lit with a series of stark spotlights; the type used to highlight actors on a darkened stage. This actor was the young woman featured in Brian Edwards' photo album, but she was no willing participant in this performance. Gripping the bars that held her captive, the woman gazed at Ange with a face full of sorrow.

Ange cautiously approached the edge of the walkway and stared down. All that she could see was darkness, an abyss that stretched to eternity. She assessed whether she could leap across the chasm, but even with a runup, she knew that she wouldn't even make it halfway. Ange stared at the young woman, her eyes pleading helplessness.

Ange scanned the area, desperately searching for an alternative route across the chasm. Suddenly, her eyes fell upon a sniper's rifle, discreetly protruding from another dimly lit corridor on the far side of the room. The rifle swivelled mechanically until it was pointed directly at the captive woman. The weapon's menacing intent was obvious.

Ange yelled out. 'No. Stop.'

Her strident yelp, sharp and piercing, shook her from the dream and jolted Gus out of his slumber.

'It's OK, Gus,' said Ange in a shaky voice. 'It was just a nightmare.'

'Do you want to talk it over?' asked Gus, his voice drowsy and laborious. He had played this midnight role many times in the past year.

'No. I understand where this came from. You go back to sleep.'

Gus rolled over and readily complied with her suggestion, while Ange stared up at the ceiling for hours. She didn't need any psychiatrist to understand the source of her torment.

Chapter 30

Operation Scumbag

Despite Jim Grady's feigned annoyance at losing a constable for a month, Ange knew he was secretly pleased that she was back working with Bree.

'Bloody hell,' he exclaimed when Ange rang to pitch him the idea on Wednesday morning. 'Between playing for the Hockeyroos and doing your dirty work on the Dark Web, she doesn't have any time left to work for me—and I'm her actual boss.'

'Perhaps you can keep our old friends Walton and Lynch busy in Bree's absence. Don't worry, boss, if I can't sort this out in a month, then Sally is going to shut me down. Who knows, I might come looking for a job. Then you'd have your hands full,' Ange shot back, enjoying the repartee with Grady. Try as she might, she couldn't break the habit of calling him boss.

'OK. You win. I'll send her your way on Monday morning. Is there any other pound of flesh that you need from me, Detective?'

'No, that will be all—for the moment. Thanks, boss. I do appreciate it,' replied Ange, her tone dripping with sweetness. She knew Grady would be grinning, despite having lost his constable for a month.

She then rang Alan Campbell. 'Hi, Alan. How are things going with the surveillance of Daicos?'

'Pretty well. Brian thinks he has it all figured out, but wants to double down on his evidence before he tells me his theory. He can be a touch secretive at times, is our Brian. I guess they teach that sort of behaviour at MI5 school.'

'That's excellent news. Speaking of Brian, I wanted to ask a favour.'

'Tell me,' replied Campbell, without hesitation.

Ange then filled him in on what she had in mind for Brian Edwards.

'Of course. I'll tell him to wrap things up here as quickly as possible and fly him wherever you need him. I know cattle rustling gets under my skin, but that's nothing when compared to what you're working on. I'm happy to pay Brian for his services. That way, he can't say no.'

'No, that's unnecessary, Alan. We don't kick off until next week, so let him finish his job on Daicos. I'll need him in Sydney. Hopefully that works for him. Also, I've secured some funding from the boss. We need to make it all official to ensure that any evidence Brian collects can be used in court—assuming we get to that. Can you ask Brian to call me after you've spoken to him?'

'Will do. Brian lives on the northern beaches in Sydney, so that should work out rather well. I reckon he'll have Daicos and company sorted by the end of the week. We'll need to reel this in soon—otherwise the suspense will kill me.'

Barely two hours had elapsed before she received a call from an unknown mobile phone number. She answered with an insipid 'Hello,' ready to drop the call in an instant should it be a robocaller.

'Detective Watson? It's Brian Edwards speaking. Alan Campbell said that you wished to speak with me.'

Even though Ange knew some of his backstory, Edwards' posh public school accent still came as a shock, incongruous against the broad Australian drawl of his mate Alan Campbell. 'Oh yes, Brian. Thanks for calling. Call me Ange, by the way. Remember those interesting photos that you took of our beloved minister of many affairs, Greg Kilroy? Well, I'm curious about his relationship with the other man that you identified, Harry Linh. How would you feel about doing a surveillance job for us?'

'That sounds most interesting, but you'll first need to tell me what this is about. Most importantly—why me? Surely you have your own people for that sort of work.'

Ange spent the next hour briefing Edwards on her people trafficking investigations, also explaining how politics had a habit of crash-tackling her. 'My boss and I are concerned that Kilroy will have loads of political mates to call on, probably even the police minister himself. The current New South Wales Government is a bit of a boys' club, and we have no idea about who knows who.'

'I'm intrigued. Count me in. Alan probably told you I worked for MI5. Now, that's an old boys' club if there ever was one. While I understand from my former colleagues that things are finally changing, the one thing that remains immutable is politics. When do you want me to start?'

'Great. Thanks, Brian. We kick off next week. The boss has only given me a month to sort out this puzzle, so we'll need to get on our bikes. Can you text me your email address, please? I'll need to send you some paperwork so that this is all official.'

'Understood. Will do. That should give me ample time to wrap up Alan's problem. I'd best go. I'm on the job as we speak.'

'Brilliant. I'm also quite invested in what happened to Alan's cattle. I'll be keen to hear your conclusions at the appropriate time.'

Within seconds of ending the call, Ange's phone buzzed with a text containing Edwards' email address. Ange had a good feeling about him, although she should have expected nothing less from someone in Campbell's inner circle.

Ange spent the rest of the week teeing things up with Billy and Bree and making sure that they had any loose ends tidied up. She also worked with Anders and the legal department to settle a contract with Brian Edwards, something which proved considerably more difficult than Ange had imagined it should. While her legal department was usually the annoying stickler for detail, it was Edwards who proved obstinate in this case. She didn't understand what the fuss was about, but the dispute revolved around documenting his job description. Ange wanted this to be defined broadly and loosely, while Edwards insisted on clear and narrowly defined parameters. In the end, they settled on *photographic and video surveillance of suspects as directed by Major Crimes*. Perhaps it was his Oxford and MI5 background that made him so pedantic, but she was pleased to finalise his terms of engagement. Ange could already hear the clock ticking in the background.

Billy commandeered a van from Sally Anders and drove up from Sydney with his computers. He arrived Sunday evening, and after enjoying a drink on the balcony overlooking the ocean and the lights of Byron Bay, Ange showed him to the guesthouse that would serve as his digs for the next four weeks.

Ange slept restlessly, eager to embark on their project. Despite waking early, she let Billy sleep in, and walked over to the guesthouse just on 8 a.m. bearing gifts of coffee and toast, only to find that Billy was fully set up and raring to go. He had even brought along his own computer desk, which was now supporting four monitors.

'That was quick, Billy. And here I was thinking how kind I was letting you sleep in.'

'I couldn't sleep, boss. This should be fun. I'll need your Wi-Fi code to run some tests and check that you have enough bandwidth. I brought a satellite link with me as a backup option, in case we need it. What type of firewall do you have?'

Ange's blank stare suggested that she had no clue. 'Honestly, boss, how you haven't had all your money stolen defies belief. Luckily, I assumed the worst and brought along some kit that I'll install between the Wi-Fi router and the internet service. We don't want to pick up any fleas when we roll around on the Dark Web. Some of the new kit that's coming out to thwart digital intruders is pretty cool.'

'OK, Billy. I hope I'll still be able to watch Netflix once you've done your thing,' she joked.

Bree arrived twenty minutes later. She had brought a laptop and a single monitor, which she plonked on the kitchen table. 'Wow, Billy. Anyone would think that you're trying to impress a girl. Either that or compensating for some feelings of inadequacy.'

'Hilarious, Bree. Do you learn this stuff on the hockey field, or do you make it up as you go?' taunted Billy, his beaming smile a telltale sign that he was genuinely pleased to see her.

'Which brings me to our first item of business—which would be you two. We can't have any relationship issues getting in the way,' remarked Ange. The fact that Billy and Bree had hooked up just as Ange was getting herself shot had been of some concern. Even though she trusted them both implicitly, love is often blind, and lovers are easily distracted.

Bree answered quickly and confidently. 'Don't worry, Ange. Billy and I have cooled our heels. Long-distance relationships really aren't all they're cracked up to be, so we've downgraded ourselves to good friends,' she said, adding air quotes over the *good friends* part. 'We'll keep our eyes on the ball.'

'Excellent. I didn't want to put you on the spot like that, but I know first-hand how hard it is to juggle work and a relationship. Bree, why don't you get yourself set up while I grab my laptop? There are coffee pods on the bench and milk in the fridge. Make yourself at home and we'll get started in ten.'

The first hour involved Ange bringing her colleagues up to speed with the latest developments. She tabled the sheaf of photos and the documentation on Kilroy's extracurricular activities.

'Busy boy,' commented Bree drily.

Billy succinctly summed up the position. 'Those are terrific photos, but they don't really tell us anything other than deepen our suspicions. I reckon that they could all easily be explained away if push came to shove.'

'I agree, Billy. I have no intention of falling for that two-card trick again. We also need to assume that Linh's political connections extend well beyond Kilroy. I think we can expect some serious blowback the moment we rattle his cage. We need to be totally buttoned up before we make that move.'

'So, boss, what's your plan, then? We can't go knocking innocently on the front door like we did with Ethan Tedesco—and remember how well that went.'

Ange winced at that memory, reliving her fury when she found that Tedesco and his Ndrangheta Mafia mates had been one step ahead all along. Their impromptu visit to his palatial apartment had achieved nothing other than alerting him to their interest.

'Bree, what are your thoughts on the Shama website, the one we suspect was used as an auction site for the trafficked women?' asked Ange.

'Billy and I have discussed this, and it's hard to say if the site is still in use. We have no way in without some login credentials. I've tried the previous login details we'd commandeered from Merv the Miner, but I lost interest when it became clear the authorisation had been revoked. It's a dead end until we can get access. Even then, the site may well have been moved or abandoned on account of all my failed login attempts,' explained Bree with a dejected look on her face.

'I understand. It was a long shot. So, the only link we have between Clearwater and Hillburn is the now-deleted WhatsApp communications. I don't think any of us buy the notion that this link is entirely innocent. Billy, you said that you had access to the phone traffic of the former drug dealer from Clearwater, and you'd discussed with Bree about buying some stuff from his drug-dealing Dark Web site.'

Bree looked sheepish. 'I never acted on that idea, Ange.'

'Why not? That should be easy for someone with your Dark Web expertise.'

'It's not that. I baulked at buying performance-enhancing substances on the Dark Web. If anyone found out about this, I'd be dumped off the Hockeyroos in an instant. It's a case of guilty until proven innocent with that stuff. Even if I cleared my name, I'd never get back on the team. Mud sticks. Anyway, you were busy, and I didn't want to bother you. It didn't seem important compared to what you were dealing with.'

Ange admonished herself. She hadn't given Bree's position as an elite sportsperson a second thought. 'I'm sorry, Bree. I wasn't thinking straight. Can you help Billy purchase some of that stuff?'

'Well, that's the thing. It would look more legitimate if I purchased it using my usual credentials. How about you write a letter authorising me to make the purchases and I'll clear it in advance with my coach? I can easily explain it away as being part of an investigation into illegal PEDs. Think of it like a parental note to the teacher,' explained Bree.

'You'll have the letter within the hour. Can you make the purchases today? Get the products sent here, which should put your involvement beyond question, Bree. I guess it wouldn't look totally out of place if a surfboard manufacturer was buying this stuff.'

'What's the rush, boss?' asked Billy.

'I'd like you guys to trace the crypto transactions and see what else the Clearwater drug dealer is up to. Once you have a line on his wallet, you can see what else he's been up to—can't you, Billy?'

'Sort of,' replied Billy with a hesitant expression on his face. 'I can see what's coming in and out, but not necessarily who they are or what the transactions represent.'

'I hear you, Billy. Unfortunately, he's our best lead. I'll sort out the letter of authorisation right now, and you two sort out what you plan to purchase,' said Ange as she turned and walked back towards the main house.

She'd barely got done with emailing Bree her 'teacher's letter' when Alan Campbell called.

'I have some news, Ange.'

'I sure hope it's good news.'

'More like a mixed bag. C2Z Pharma filed its claim in the federal court of New South Wales last Friday afternoon. I guess that's positive news for your investigation, as I don't reckon they would push on with this case if they thought anyone was breathing over their shoulder.'

'Perhaps, Alan. It might also mean that they're not implicated in my investigation. How much are they claiming?'

'Sixteen point two million dollars,' answered Campbell casually, as if he was informing Ange about the price of milk.

'Wow. Are you concerned?'

'Not yet. Although, in my experience, nobody wins in court. It would be better if you brought these mongrels down before we ever got to that point.'

'So, no pressure, then,' replied Ange, her voice dripping with irony. 'If it *does* go to court, when would the hearing take place?'

'A directions hearing is set down in five weeks. That's where the judge will consider the merits and the complexity of the matter before setting aside time for the actual court case, which could be months away. Best case is that you bring down Linh, Kilroy, and Julia Bennet before the directions hearing and the other side withdraws the action. It seems that our interests are tightly aligned.'

'What about Daicos?'

'I'll keep a watchful eye on him. There's something weird about this situation. It seems like a terrible waste to steal such valuable cattle and just butcher them for a few steaks. If I didn't know better, I'd say it was personal.'

'OK. Thanks for the update, Alan. Let's stay in touch,' said Ange as she ended the call.

As she walked back to the guesthouse, Ange noticed that she had a missed call from an unknown caller. The number didn't ring any bells, so she just assumed it was another annoying spam call. There was no message on her voicemail when she checked.

Her workaround to thwart the burgeoning spam industry was to not answer unknown calls and then call straight back if they left a message. No message equals no return call. Her strategy had been working well.

Bree looked up as Ange walked in the door. 'I've already cleared that with my coach. She seemed pleased to hear that we're investigating performance-enhancing drugs, so I didn't burst her bubble. Billy and I are just about to make our purchase.'

'How much do we know about Linh?' asked Billy.

'Not much. I reckon that needs to be the first task. Once you've completed your purchases, let's spend the rest of today finding out as much as we can about Harry Linh: where he came from, who he hangs out with, who might owe him a favour, the full extent of his business activities. Billy, how about you start by reaching out to your mate Nelson at the tax office and see what information he might have on the guy, then run any leads to ground. We need to pull apart his commercial empire as best we can. I recall reading somewhere that C2Z Pharma had a long-term lease for a portion of the Clearwater property, the part where the sheds and the house were located. See if you can find out something about the owner of that property.' Billy nodded his agreement to that plan.

'Bree, a fancy bar owner like Harry Linh, must have a huge social media presence. See what you can dig up, maybe check out the Dark Web as well. Billy, surely you have some facial recognition software to help with that?'

'Yep. Now that we have some decent images of Linh, I can set Bree up to trawl through the internet for something interesting.'

'Excellent. I must be learning about your world of tech.' Ange smiled. 'I'm going to look into the relationship between Linh and Kilroy—and Daicos, I suppose. Although Brian Edwards has been monitoring Daicos for the past ten days.'

'Who's Brian Edwards?' asked Billy.

'Oh, I forgot to mention. Brian is the fourth member of our team. He took these pictures. I've never actually met him, but he acts as Alan Campbell's PI. Alan is my cattle baron mate and paid for Edwards to follow Kilroy and take those photos. Edwards is also ex-MI5.'

'Whoa,' exclaimed Billy. 'So, we've got two junior constables and a lame detective joining forces with an ex-MI5 operative. This boat could be a bit of a lopsided paddle.'

'Interesting analogy, Billy. Brian Edwards is also a rowing coach. Don't underestimate yourselves. Remember, you helped collapse Ethan Tedesco's digital empire and flush out the Ndrangheta.'

'Yeah—just after Tedesco got away with some seven hundred million dollars in crypto and you got shot,' observed Billy drily.

'Funny. OK, let's get to it. I'll continue to work over in the main house, and we can regroup for lunch.'

Just as the trio were about to go their separate ways, Ange's phone pinged with an incoming text from Alan Campbell.

> *Brian has finished up here in Clearwater. David just dropped him back to Sydney. He's all yours. Good luck, Alan*

Ange considered texting back, but her curiosity got the best of her. She rang him instead. 'Did Brian find out anything interesting?' she asked as soon as Campbell answered the call.

'Very. I'll need to sit on it for a while before I take any action,' replied Campbell in a somewhat sombre tone.

'Out with it, Alan. You can't keep a girl hanging like that after all we've been through,' probed Ange, keeping her tone of voice light in contrast.

'It seems like I have a rat in the ranks. It's all very disappointing. I'll ring you in a couple of days when I've come to terms with everything.'

'It's not Fin, is it?'

'No, no, not at all. In some ways, it's even worse. Anyway, you've got far more pressing matters on your plate. Oh, by the way, Brian said he was going to email you something this afternoon. Your briefing seems to have caught his interest.'

'OK, Alan. It's probably best that you don't make any moves on Daicos until we're sure how it all fits together. Are you OK with that?'

'Yes, I agree. It will be hard not to act on what I know, but it's more annoying and disappointing than anything else.'

'Thanks, Alan. Let's speak in a few days when you're ready.'

'Roger that. Fingers crossed with your investigations, Ange. I'll be thinking of you.'

Chapter 31

Moonlighting

Their regrouping over lunch proved to be a fizzer, as nobody had made any significant progress. The reality of their task was sinking in. The only winner of the morning was Buddy, who moseyed around the property, stealing affection from the susceptible or distracted. Just after 5 p.m., Ange wandered over to the guesthouse to call a halt to the day's work. She spied Buddy sitting underneath Billy's desk, pressed up against his leg as a constant reminder that he was ready for some affection. Ange shook her head and muttered beneath her breath, 'So much for being an outdoor dog.'

It was a lovely afternoon, and the trio assembled on the patio to discuss their progress. Buddy trailed behind and plopped himself down within reach of Ange's right hand, well aware of who buttered his bread.

'Billy, you go first. What have you found out?' asked Ange.

Billy did not seem happy. 'Linh presents a clean slate as far as the tax office is concerned. All his businesses seem to make a consistently modest profit and all fit well within the parameters that the tax office uses for data-matching. According to Nelson, the only red flag that he could see was that the businesses were so reliable and consistent in their financial results. In terms of his business interests, Linh is the sole proprietor of bars in Brisbane, Sydney, and Melbourne, all under the same umbrella and trading as The Pulse. He's also an investor in a series of gyms called Mind over Matter MMA. As well as Brisbane, Sydney, and Melbourne, their gyms are also located in some of the larger regional cities: Newcastle, Wollongong, Toowoomba, Townsville, and Albury-Wodonga, by memory. And then there's his investment in C2Z Pharma, the company that was behind the medical cannabis operation. C2Z was the only entity racking up trading losses, no doubt assisted by our efforts. A blind trust is the ultimate beneficial owner of the property where the cannabis operation was located. The trustee of that entity is called the Large Island Pastoral Company, where Linh is the sole director.'

'Clever name,' observed Ange, seeing as Australia is both the largest island and the smallest continent on the globe.

'That same entity owns a second property in Singleton. I pushed Nelson to disclose who's behind the blind trust, but he wasn't comfortable with that idea. In his words, *there's just nothing to see here, Billy.*'

'Great,' was Ange's exaggerated reply. 'What about you, Bree?'

Bree's expression turned to one of frustration. 'No luck here either, Ange. I spent the day trawling the media for recent photos of Harry Linh. He's not very conspicuous for somebody with his hands in so many pies.'

'Don't feel bad, both of you. I didn't do any better. I went through all the photographs that I took in Daicos's office, but nothing new leapt out as being useful. The press had a bit to say about Daicos and the failure of his Sydney restaurant, but we already knew the essence of that. Kilroy is a darling of his party. I guess it doesn't hurt when you're handsome and enjoy an attractive wife and adoring family. He's very good in front of a camera and certainly looks to be the complete package—at least until the truth comes out.' Ange paused briefly, as if in a state of total disillusionment. Her face brightened, catching her colleagues by surprise. 'I did, however, receive a fascinating email from our very own spy.'

Waiting until she had the full attention of her colleagues, she distributed a single A4 sheet of paper. 'Apparently, Brian Edwards was moonlighting while working for Alan Campbell. You can read it later, but let me summarise the key points. First, Linh moved to Australia from Vietnam to study pharmacy at Sydney Uni—second-class honours no less. After working for one of the pharmacy chains for just on four years, he was granted permanent residency status in Australia. He then purchased his own pharmacy. Those aren't cheap, so he must have had some financial support behind him. This move obviously went well for him. Before long, Linh had assembled a chain of five pharmacies, which he sold to his former employer. He then took an early retirement and travelled extensively for a few years, visiting Vietnam several times. In a change of vocation, Linh opened his first bar and restaurant in Sydney under the name "The Pulse," the same establishment where Brian photographed Kilroy. When I look back over the dates, this would coincide with the period when Daicos enjoyed being a high-profile Sydney restaurateur. My guess is that Daicos and Linh might have crossed paths through the Sydney social scene, but that's conjecture on my part.'

'That doesn't get us far, Ange,' observed Billy.

'I agree, but that isn't the interesting part. I must say that I'm very impressed with our spy. He must have kept some worthwhile connections from his time in MI5. Anyway, while both of Linh's parents have passed, he remains close to his only sibling, a younger sister who still lives in Hanoi. And...guess what she does for a living?'

After being met with the blank stares of her two younger colleagues, Ange continued. 'She runs a successful employment agency, specialising in overseas placements. It's called EZ Jobs. Does that name strike a chord with either of you?'

More blank looks forced Ange to elaborate after she realised that Bree and Billy didn't know of her interview with Cua Kwm. 'Remember that this all started when a young Vietnamese woman escaped from being held captive in Hillburn? Well, she was lured to Australia by the prospect of a well-paid job in hospitality, all organised through an agency in Hanoi.'

Understanding spread across her colleagues' faces. 'I presume that you think this is the same agency that Linh's sister owns?' asked Billy.

'I'll need to go back over my notes, as Kwm's interview was all in Vietnamese, but I think this is too much of a coincidence to be random. You know my thoughts on coincidences, Billy.'

'What name does she go by? Linh's sister, that is,' asked Billy.

'I can't pronounce her name, but it's spelled N-G-O-C. I think, for this exercise, I'll be referring to her as Madam Linh.'

'Perfect. Madam Linh even sounds shadowy and mysterious, perhaps a Medusa-like character with writhing black snakes for hair.'

'That image works for me, Billy,' added Bree with a grin.

Ange stared out across the ocean as the trio sat in silence for a minute or two. 'Despite our slow start, I think we've made solid progress. Let's sit on this information overnight. I'll try to dial in Brian Edwards to our morning meeting and we can plot the next steps. Now, how about we head down to the pub for something to eat? If Bree drives us down to Byron, Gus can ferry us home. I'll let him know we'll collect him on the way past. Are you ready to leave now?'

Buddy was unimpressed with being left at home. Ange watched him wander dejectedly back to his bed on the veranda. Initially worried that he would be a wanderer, she was pleased that he seemed to know his place and understood that one of his core responsibilities was to watch over his home and its occupants. His other job, being Rusty the social media tart, was juxtaposed against Buddy the homebody. Ange often wondered if human celebrities dealt with their stardom so effortlessly.

Being a Monday night, the Byron Bay pub was quieter than usual, and the group easily found a table. Once they had ordered their meal and settled into their drinks, Ange noticed a group of four twenty-something men staring daggers in her direction. One of them looked vaguely familiar, and Ange endured their vengeful glares for a full ten minutes before she remembered the incident. She had been called in to lend a hand on New Year's Eve celebrations. As was often the case, things got out of hand in the early hours of the morning.

As she patrolled the streets, Ange had come across a posse of half a dozen young vigilantes making a nuisance of themselves. Full of alcohol, drugs, and strong opinions, the gang had appointed themselves defenders of all things local and were hassling tourists walking on the foreshore. Ange had called in reinforcements and had them carted off to the watchhouse for the night. No charges had been laid, but evidently grudges were still being held. Toxic localism was something that made Ange's blood boil, and she would dearly have loved to pursue the matter further, but her boss had doused her flames with a dose of reality. Nobody had been hurt, and it had been New Year's Eve after all. Nothing would have been achieved other than to waste valuable police resources and the court's time. Regretfully, she had let the matter slide, and the vitriolic troupe had been released the next day, suffering nothing more than a self-induced hangover.

Persistent malevolent stares suggested their brief incarceration hadn't worked. This cast a pall over Ange's evening, reducing it to a darkened state that even the lively and spirited conversation of her radiant dinner guests could not shift.

The nightmares came back to haunt her that night, this time following a more familiar theme and quite unlike the very specific birdcage affair of a week earlier.

As her psychiatrist had suggested, she woke Gus and verbalised her fears. 'Gus, everywhere I went, someone was watching me. In one case, I was being watched through a sniper's scope. I guess this was all triggered by seeing some guys in the pub who I'd arrested one New Year's Eve. That, and our own surveillance activities, I guess. It was just like that song by the Police.' She paused and fixed Gus with a determined stare. 'With Buddy spending so much time down at the shop, I think we should get some security installed around the house. I could get Billy to do the research while he's here. What do you think?'

Gus muttered his agreement. Ange wasn't sure if he liked the idea or just wanted to go back to sleep, but she resolved to implement her plan in the morning. Three sleepcasts later, and after realising that her wounds were not yet fully healed, she drifted back into a fitful sleep.

The noise in the kitchen plucked the woman from a deep sleep. Once she was half awake, she slowly rolled over and sat unsteadily on the edge of the bed until she had her bearings. She'd not long moved in and was still adjusting to her new surroundings.

'Bloody cat,' she muttered to herself as she slid on her slippers. 'I must have left the bathroom window open again.'

It was the third time since she moved in that the sneaky thing had gotten into her apartment.

She reached down to her bedside table, plucked her phone off her wireless charger, and opened up the camera setting. If she could get a picture of the cat, she could shove that up the nose of the neighbour who owned the scrawny mongrel. She'd been so pissed off when she'd confronted the man, but he refused to accept his beloved could cause any trouble. 'Cat people,' the woman thought derisively.

Using just the glow off the screen on her phone, she made her way down the small hallway toward the kitchen.

Caught completely by surprise, she felt muscular hands grab her from behind. A cloth was swiftly pressed against her mouth, silencing any attempt to call out.

The shock rendered her helpless, causing her phone to fall loose and clatter on the tiles, a discordant noise among the deathly silence. The woman briefly worried that the screen on her phone had most likely shattered. Despite this absurdity, it was her last lucid thought.

A sharp pain traced across her neck. Within seconds, her life started draining away. She was no longer conscious when finally discarded on the kitchen floor.

There was no cat in sight.

Chapter 32

One Step Sideways

As soon as Ange could see Billy moving around the next morning, she popped over to the guesthouse with a gift of coffee. After years of working together, she knew Billy's poison was a flat white with one sugar. 'Don't get used to this, Billy. I wanted to ask your opinion about something.'

'Beware of boss bearing coffee. If there isn't a proverb about that, there should be. Out with it,' replied Billy as he took possession of his bribe and took a sip. 'Wow, that's good. I'm such a pushover,' he added jokingly.

'I think we should get a security system installed here. With Buddy spending so much time at the shop and the sensitive nature of what we're doing, it seems like the prudent thing to do. I wondered if you could do some research on what system might suit us best.'

'That's easy. I just installed a similar system for my parents. The package included three cameras, all solar-powered and connected through your Wi-Fi network. The only downside is when your Wi-Fi goes down, but you can get an option for a SIM card as backup. It's amazing. Motion-sensing, infrared, facial, pet recognition, with motion alerts sent to your phone. You can even hold a conversation from your phone through the cameras. My mum used that feature to scare off some kids poking around in their garage the other night. The area where they live has been suffering lots of break-ins and carjackings lately. All underage kids. I spoke to the local sergeant, who sounded frustrated and powerless. Apparently, organised crime has recruited these kids to do their dirty work. The criminals know that, if the kids are caught, they'll only receive a warning. He even told me about one gang where the kids carry a stack of prepaid envelopes, already pre-addressed to burner locations. As they make their way from house to house, they simply stuff the envelopes with loot. Then, after stealing a car for their getaway, they stop off at a series of postboxes and get rid of any evidence. The car gets thrashed and trashed before they abandon it somewhere and hey presto, it's a clean heist. It's pretty clever, actually.'

'Incredible. That's a modern-day version of *Oliver Twist*,' commented Ange. She noticed a vacant look on Billy's face. 'Please tell me you've heard about *Oliver Twist*. For goodness' sake, you're not much younger than I am.' His lack of reply was all the answer Ange needed. 'Truly, Billy? *Oliver Twist* is a story set in London in the mid-nineteenth century about a young orphan who's enticed into serving as a pickpocket alongside the gloriously named Artful Dodger. This latest incarnation is even smarter. I can see why the sergeant you spoke with is frustrated.'

'I thought Artful Dodger was a band?'

'Actually, I think they're a band as well. How did we end up discussing your literary education?' jested Ange.

'You were bribing me to do your homework and organise a security system. By memory, the setup that I organised for my parents cost a little over two thousand dollars. Would that sort of price be OK?'

'Actually, I was expecting to pay more than that. Sounds good. Can I leave this in your hands? What happened with your mum's eye-in-the-sky moment?'

'She reckoned the kids didn't seem all that worried, even when she put on her angry mum's voice. The only reason that they didn't steal Dad's classic BMW M3 is because it's a manual. Nobody under thirty can drive a manual anymore, so that's probably your best protection.'

'Huh, I'd never thought about that. Gus will be pleased to hear that his Volvo wagon is safe. He'd be devastated if anyone stole that car. Probably Buddy as well, seeing as it's become his vehicle of choice after he abandoned me and the Prado.'

'The M3 is such a cool car, even better in canary yellow. The correct name for that colour is Dakar Yellow—as my dad keeps reminding me. You need to be a confident guy to be seen in yellow,' commented Billy.

While Ange said nothing to Billy's observation, she agreed with him on all counts. Gus's Volvo was also yellow. 'I'll see you back here once Bree arrives and we can begin our conference call.'

Ange texted Edwards on her way back to the house to check that he was available to take a call at 9 a.m. She was pleased to get a thumbs-up emoji in reply.

After seeing off Gus and taking her breakfast, she walked back over to the guesthouse as soon as she heard Bree's car scrunching up the driveway, just on 8:45 a.m.

Once they were settled, Bree provided some insight into what she had been contemplating overnight. 'I think we should focus on the relationship between Kilroy and Linh. There's something very dubious about those two. Given the breadth of Linh's empire, his record is far too clean for my liking. As far as I can determine, he's never gotten so much as a speeding fine. And then there's Kilroy—Mr Wholesome Family Man who screws around like nobody's business.'

Ange looked at her watch and saw it was showing just on 9 a.m. 'Let me get Brian Edwards on the line.' She paused and rang his number.

He answered almost immediately. 'Hello, Detective Watson.'

'Call me Ange, please, and I'll call you Brian—if you don't mind. I've got two of my colleagues with me. Billy Bassett, a workmate of many years and our IT guru, and Breanna White, our expert on cryptocurrency, NFTs, and lurking on the Dark Web.'

'That's a small team. Is that it?' asked Edwards immediately.

'Yes, along with our boss, Senior Detective Sally Anders. This case leaks like a sieve, and I totally trust Billy and Bree—and Sally, of course. It's just us working on this problem.'

'OK, so why the focus on digital?'

'Good question, Brian,' replied Ange. 'The trafficked women rescued in Hillburn were being sold through a Dark Web site that posed as a marketplace for NFTs. Bree stole the login credentials from some scumbag and accessed the site one time, but she's been locked out ever since.'

'What exactly are NFTs? I've heard the term bandied around, but I haven't bothered to understand them,' asked Edwards.

'Non-Fungible Tokens. It's a crypto thing that basically ascribes value to sketchy digital images and icons,' answered Ange. She visualised Edwards screwing up his face. 'Don't worry, I still don't understand how that's possible, Brian. But Bree here sold one of her NFTs for the crypto equivalent of some forty thousand dollars.'

Billy stepped in to help Ange out. 'She's a dinosaur, Brian. NFTs are also a brilliant way to launder money.'

'I'll give you a lesson in the new world one day, Brian,' offered Bree with a wide smile.

Ange got the conversation back on track. 'We figure breaking into their network in a digital sense is our best option—especially given our tiny team. If we get wind of a new shipment of women, and I hate using the term *shipment*, we can mobilise some additional foot soldiers.'

'I gather you've read my dossier on Harry Linh. However, to make sure that we're all on the same page here, can you step through the reasons you consider him a person of serious interest? It would be a pity to waste our valuable and limited time on the wrong target,' surmised Edwards.

'Excellent suggestion, Brian. There are several reasons that I can think of. First, Harry Linh controls the drug farm through the Large Island Pastoral Company, although we don't know who the ultimate beneficial owners are,' started Ange before being distracted by a thought. 'Which reminds me—Billy, did you get around to analysing the video from the drug farm and identifying any comings and goings?'

'Not yet. You've kept me busy moving towns, remember?' shot back Billy. 'I'll get onto that as soon as everything is under control here.'

'You forgot, didn't you, Billy?' teased Bree.

The sheepish look on Billy's face confirmed Bree's allegation, but Ange let this go through to the keeper—as did Brian Edwards.

'Moving on, the second reason is we know that the protagonists at Clearwater and Hillburn were communicating via WhatsApp.'

'Do you still have a record of those communications?' asked Edwards.

Billy answered. 'No. Those phones were all wiped clean remotely.'

'Clever. Whoever is pulling the strings knows their stuff,' observed Edwards. 'Sorry to interrupt again.'

'That's fine, Brian. You struck a raw nerve with that observation,' admitted Ange. 'Fortunately, the drug dealer from Clearwater is not so clever and kept his old phone. Billy has been monitoring his activities, which at this point are limited to dealing in illicit drugs and PEDs on the Dark Web. Billy, any luck with the trace on the crypto transactions for the drugs you purchased?'

'There's just been a series of small inflows at the moment, boss. I'm waiting for when he pays his supplier. That should be more interesting.'

'I detest PEDs,' revealed Edwards. 'They haven't been such a problem in rowing, but that's only because there's no real money involved in the sport.'

'Or hockey,' added Bree.

'Oh, Brian. I forgot to mention that Bree is a member of the Hockeyroos, our national women's hockey team.'

'Impressive,' commented Edwards. 'That must be demanding. Sounds like you're holding down two jobs, Bree.'

'This is my third job. My real one is back at the Byron Bay station,' joked Bree.

Ange loved how this banter had developed so naturally. It was a sign that her team was already gelling together. She'd always felt that humour was hugely underrated in the workplace. 'Now, getting back to job number three. However, we've just been discussing reasons for our Linh obsession. With his pharmaceutical background, I'm sure he can readily source the type of substances our Clearwater mate is selling.'

'And MMA gyms would be a fertile marketplace. I doubt that the mixed martial arts fraternity is as tough on PEDs as the mainstream sports. Bringing that shopfront down would seem a worthwhile side benefit of your investigation,' noted Edwards.

Ange then gave Edwards a rundown of Cua Kwm's tragedy and her potential link with EZ Jobs and Madam Linh.

'Oh, and there's one more reason I'm so obsessed with Harry Linh. My intuition,' she stated, somewhat sheepishly.

She was surprised when Edwards didn't dismiss this out of hand. 'Never discount intuition. It stems from a myriad of clues and inputs, some of them subconscious. My experience is to always remain circumspect, but never dismiss your intuition.'

Ange summarised the position. 'Intuition aside, guys, even with the links between Linh and Kilroy, Kilroy's apparent sex addiction, Linh's involvement with the Clearwater drug farm, the drug dealer and his links to Linh and Hillburn, and Madam Linh's employment agency in Hanoi, we actually have nothing concrete to go on.'

'I think that's a decent summary of where we stand, Ange. However, I also agree that there's enough smoke curling off Linh's empire to make him our focus for the time being,' added Edwards.

'So, we all agree that we're up the creek looking for a paddle,' stated Ange with a wry grin. 'Harry Linh and his links to the Clearwater cannabis farm are our only viable leads. So, on that cheery note, let's brainstorm some ideas. Billy, what are your thoughts?'

Billy looked up and to the right, a sure sign that the cogs in his brain were spinning rapidly. 'It would seem that they, whoever exactly they are, are quite careful about who's let into the Shama website. If Linh is involved somehow, he'll have some login credentials. If we could glean his username and password, then we might have some decent access. Of course, they could have moved the site, but Linh would know that if he's involved.'

'Makes sense, Billy. How could we achieve that?' asked Ange.

Bree piped up. 'Well, the most obvious way is to monitor his phone or computer, either by camera or using someone inside his operation who's cooperating with us.'

'I'm concerned about how much time that might take. Brian, what are your thoughts on getting some video of Linh at his desk working on his computer?'

'I'm on site now and I can't see any way of doing that from the outside. Perhaps I could launch a drone and buzz around to find a suitable viewing angle, but that would be perilous. I also agree that turning someone inside his operation will probably take months—not the few weeks that we have available.'

'Since you're the only spy on this team, Brian, let's scrap that idea. What are you doing on-site now?' Ange inquired sharply.

'I'm trying to gain a full picture of who's coming and going through that side door. Going by *my* intuition, I reckon something shady is happening behind that door. Knowing who visits and when could be helpful.'

'Seen anyone interesting?' piped in Bree.

'I've only just arrived, but I'll keep you guys posted on the comings and goings.'

'I know this is probably a stupid question, Brian, but is there any risk that you could be seen?'

'Not a chance. I rented an apartment through Airbnb. It's on the second level, diagonally across the street. I use the fire escape to get in and out, so I'm quite confident that my presence will remain undetected by Linh and his cronies.'

'OK. With the video idea off the table, are there any other suggestions?' asked Ange.

'The next idea would be to install a keylogger on his laptop. That would tell us exactly what keys he pressed and when,' offered Billy.

'That would be perfect, Billy,' commented Bree. 'It's the same idea that skimmers use when they fit some hardware on the front of an ATM.'

'It's not that easy. We could install something via a scam email, like the phishing ploy that we used once before. If we knew his email address, then I guess we could try that. Like the rest of us, he'd be getting spam emails all the time, so it wouldn't come with any extreme risk.'

'That seems worthwhile running to ground. Bree, how about you focus on finding an email address for Linh?' said Ange. 'Any other ideas, Billy?'

'I'll reach out to my hacker community and get some options together. We can go through the merits and practicalities of each,' replied Billy.

'I'd like to make this 9 a.m. meeting a regular event. We can go through your options tomorrow, Billy. We need to chase down the Hanoi connection that Brian identified. Interpol owes Bree a favour, but any ideas on that, Brian?'

'I wouldn't get Interpol involved. We'd never know who they might deploy and who they might have connections with. Interpol is too much of an unknown quantity for my liking. My contact, the one I sourced that basic information from, is no longer in the field. For what it's worth, my preference would be to get someone local who we can trust. Nobody immediately springs to mind, but let me keep pondering that.'

'OK, I understand. I have an idea as well. Between us, we should be able to solve that problem. Is that all, guys?'

Edwards had more to say. 'What about Linh's grazing interests? He might show up in the rural press, maybe country lifestyle magazines. Perhaps Bree could scan these to see if something interesting shows up. It might not be any use with the people trafficking, but it could help us understand what's been happening at Emerald Downs—along with Billy's video analysis, of course,' he said diplomatically, reminding Ange that Edwards had two bosses.

'Worth a shot,' conceded Ange. 'See what you can dig up, Bree.'

This was no massive concession, as Ange knew that leads often came from the most surprising places. 'Let's get on with it.'

Chapter 33

Mental Health

As soon as she was back at her makeshift desk, Ange rang Judy Ly, her former colleague from the now-defunct people trafficking task force.

'You're a welcome relief, Ange. I'm dying of boredom here,' Ly answered immediately.

'Hi, Judy. Why would you be bored? Haven't you moved up the pecking order after your task force coup de grâce?'

'Wallace took all the credit for that. I've been sequestered away in the equivalent of a basement filing room. They've stuck me on a desk working this juvenile crime epidemic that's out of control here in Queensland.'

'Wow, that sure is a coincidence. I was just speaking to my colleague Billy about that very issue this morning. He reckons that the best protection is to swap your automatic car for a manual.'

'There's probably some truth in that. However, the issue is a mess. My fellow officers are sick and tired of catching these kids, only to have the courts let them off with barely a slap on the wrist. Within a heartbeat, those same offenders are back on the streets and back in the game. The politicians keep talking tough, but they don't really want to touch the idea of incarcerating kids for stealing stuff from rich people. The few times they've tried, the press dug up a grim-faced mother who claimed her darling disadvantaged son was being victimised and harassed by heartless police.'

Ange could imagine the hapless mother staring balefully into the camera, pleading that 'Johnny's a good kid. He's the real victim here. My gorgeous boy just made a couple of silly mistakes and got himself involved with the wrong crowd. It's those police bullies who should be ashamed of themselves, picking on kids like my darling son. It's yet another case of the haves versus the have-nots.'

'I have some sympathy for the court's position. Sadly, placing a juvenile offender into detention will all but ensure that he becomes a fully blown criminal by the time he's an adult,' Ange commented, visualising her own imaginary darling son.

'I agree. The whole situation is a giant game of pass the parcel. Hence why they gave the job to the junior Vietnamese shitkicker.'

The pair shared a laugh over that reality before Ange got to the point of her call. 'I wondered if you might need a holiday in Vietnam. Perhaps connect with your roots and all that?'

'Sounds intriguing. Fill me in,' asked Ly in an enthusiastic tone of voice.

Ange spent the next twenty minutes bringing Ly up to speed, stopping several times to answer questions posed by her former colleague. 'Judy, I don't suppose you remember the name of that employment agency that Cua Kwm's brother used to arrange her job in Australia. I know it'll be on record somewhere, but you guys were speaking Vietnamese, and nothing sank in from our interview with Kwm.'

'Sure do. It was called EZ Jobs. I recall thinking that it was a clever name. Easy to remember and came with the promise of a cushy job.'

'That's it,' exclaimed Ange. 'It has to be the same outfit.'

'So, out with it, Ange. What do you want me to do?'

'Can you take some leave to visit Hanoi and do some digging around for us? We could ask Interpol, but we figure that might be taking too many chances. What do you think?'

'I'm definitely in. Anything to drag me out from under this pile of excrement. I have some holidays owing, and I'll pull on the mental health argument. Those are the magic words at the moment. Who knows, I might even keep my holiday leave intact. Also, nobody will bat an eyelid over me going to Vietnam to visit my cousins.'

'Brilliant. How soon can you get away? My boss has only given me a month to bring this to a head. You remember Sally Anders, don't you?'

'Of course I do. Tell you what. If I do a decent job, I want you to put in a positive word for me. I'd love to come and work for your boss and say goodbye to Wallace and his cronies. Regarding timing, if I pull the mental health card, I reckon I can get away by the weekend. I'll need to get an air ticket, but let me have a look online and get back to you.'

'Of course I'll speak to Sally, irrespective of how this goes. If you can't get a ticket, let me know and I'll see what I can do. We can normally get preferential ticketing when we need to. But it'll be quicker and easier if you sort out the ticket yourself and then we can reimburse you.'

'Terrific. I'll come back to you once I have things sorted from my end,' replied Ly, sounding far more upbeat than when speaking about juvenile crime waves.

'Oh, one more thing. Did you ever sort out who owns the property in Hillburn?'

'Not really. The farmhouse and buildings were leased to a Singaporean company and the rest of the property was leased on agistment to a local farmer. We never learned who was behind the Singaporean company. Wallace lost interest once he'd secured his commendation. I could try to reach out to Henry Chan if you wanted?'

'Let's leave Chan be. I don't trust him after his theories almost got me fired. Anyhow, we've plenty else to do. Thanks for coming on board, Judy. I hope it's not another leaky boat,' said Ange wryly. The pair laughed at Ange's expense before ending the call.

She returned to her work looking for connections between Linh, Kilroy, and Daicos, but this was proving heavy going. Kilroy was everywhere, whereas Linh had become increasingly reclusive over the years. Daicos had all but dropped off the radar since opening his gastropub, which seemed incongruous with the trophy wall of VIPs proudly displayed in his office. Her complete lack of progress was mercifully interrupted just after 4 p.m. by a call from Brian Edwards.

'Hi, Brian. What's up?' answered Ange, her breezy voice providing some insights into her delight at being interrupted.

'Kilroy just paid a visit to his Palace of Pleasures. That's the nickname that I've given to The Pulse. Linh was also there, so I can't be certain whether Kilroy's visit was business or pleasure—or both. Anyhow, I overheard a conversation that I thought you should know about.'

Ange's ears pricked up. 'How on earth did you overhear a conversation? I thought you were stationed across the street from The Pulse and on the second floor.'

'I am, but we caught a lucky break.'

'How so? It doesn't sound like luck to me.'

'I have this high-tech directional microphone that I find comes in handy in situations like this. I don't know how these things work, but they really are incredible. Anyhow, I saw Kilroy exiting the side door and was taking a few photos when I saw him reach for his mobile phone. He was facing the wrong way, and I couldn't see the screen on his phone, so I stopped with the camera and switched to the directional mic. My interest was piqued when your name came up.'

'My name came up? You're kidding me. Don't tell me our cover is already blown,' exclaimed Ange, her tone of voice suggesting that she wasn't kidding at all.

'No. In fact, I think the conversation would suggest the opposite. I recorded what I could, and I'll send a copy to your mobile phone. However, I would be careful who you share this with. It would not be ideal for you to be seen spying on a government minister. The time will come for you to use it, but I caution you that the time is not now.'

Ange's phone pinged with an incoming message. She pulled the phone from her ear to see that Edwards had sent her an audio file. 'I'm intrigued, Brian. And, yes, I will heed your advice. I hear the voice of experience talking. Thanks for the heads-up. Speak tomorrow at our meeting.'

After laying her phone on the table, Ange clicked on the file and started listening.

[Kilroy] Hi, Nathan. It's Greg here. We may have a situation that needs some monitoring.

[Nathan] What sort of situation?

[Kilroy] Remember the name Harry Linh?

[Nathan] Yes. He's been a generous donor to the party, if I recall correctly.

[Kilroy] Absolutely. *Very* generous. Anyhow, he's suing a redneck council who backflipped on their planning approval for a medical cannabis farm. It formed part of my regional jobs' initiative.

[Nathan] Hah, you can't help some people, can you?

[Laughter]

[Kilroy] All these do-gooders are driving me nuts.

[More laughter]

[Kilroy] I don't want any political flack to come our way, so I think we should keep an eye on things.

[Nathan] OK. Makes sense. Why are you calling me?

[Kilroy] Remember that detective I told you about who had a major bee in her bonnet over the matter? A woman by the name of Watson.

[Nathan] I made sure that the commissioner clipped her wings after that. She was hauled in front of Internal Affairs, or whatever they call themselves now.

[Kilroy] She still might have an axe to grind. It wouldn't help if she started spruiking conspiracy theories in court.

[Nathan] But why would she be involved? Wouldn't the matter be between your mate Linh and the council?

[Kilroy] Yes. That's my understanding, but you can never tell who the council might call to give evidence. If I was in their shoes, I would definitely be calling Detective Watson as a witness. I think it's best we stay ahead of the fire.

[Nathan] OK. I hear you. What do you want me to do?

[Kilroy] Just make some enquiries and make sure she's tucked safely under a rock somewhere. Hopefully, she's already been sacked.

[Nathan] I'll make some calls. Now, while I've got you, we need to make a decision about this upcoming by-election. The premier's got someone in mind, but I'm not so sure. We need to identify a...

Only bits and pieces of the conversation were intelligible after that. However, going by what she heard, it appeared as if party politics were on their minds. She instinctively knew that Nathan could only be the venerable Nathan Bradley, the current police minister. The recording was dynamite. She wasted no time in forwarding it to Sally Anders with some covering words.

> URGENT. Boss, you need to listen to this and call me straight back. The contents are explosive, so best you find somewhere private before pressing play.

Ange paced around the house while she waited for Sally Anders to call her back. When the call came, she answered on the first ring.

Anders started the conversation. 'Where on earth did you get this, Ange?'

'Brian Edwards. He got lucky while he was watching The Pulse, the bar that Linh owns. He saw Kilroy make a call on his mobile phone as he exited the premises and thought it worthwhile listening in. Brian has some fancy directional microphone that he uses. Don't worry, he's totally confident that our cover isn't blown.'

'It sure clears a few things up. Of course, we can't use it—at least not until we catch them red-handed.'

'I know. I think it's best that we keep this between us. Oh, and Owen Fairweather if you think it appropriate. I wanted to get to you urgently, as I think you might be getting a call from the commissioner enquiring about my well-being. We need to get our story straight.'

'Agree. Taking a call from the commissioner about this will confirm every bad thought that I've ever had about her. What do you have in mind?'

'I haven't had time to fully think it through, but my feeling is that we should make sure everyone feels confident that I'm out of the picture. You could start by divulging your concerns about my mental state and that I'm on the edge of resigning—both of which are true.'

'Go on,' demanded Anders in a reserved tone of voice, suggesting that she wasn't entirely on board with those declarations.

'Tell her you've given me the job of looking through a recent spate of juvenile crime incidents in Northern New South Wales. Perhaps you could say that you've chained me to a desk looking for some patterns. We all know what a stinking mess juvenile crime is, and that job would be the equivalent of cleaning the departmental toilets. By the way, that's the same job our Queensland colleagues have given Judy Ly. She was the Vietnamese officer who worked on the task force with me.'

'OK. Sounds good. I remember Detective Ly. Even the politicians will realise that job is a monumental hospital pass,' replied Anders. 'I'll keep you posted.'

Chapter 34

Power Shifts

After Sally Anders had hung up from the call with Ange, she had time to think through the implications of the past hour. She became more and more agitated, incensed to the point of seething. How dare they all play their dirty political games at her expense, even worse when something genuinely sordid lay at the core of the matter?

Equally disturbing was the part that the commissioner had played in hobbling Ange with the Integrity Command. Phelps had lied outright when she pretended to know nothing of IC's pursuit.

She craved a glass of wine at home in front of her paintings, but waited pensively in her office. Even though she dearly wanted to avenge how Ange had been targeted, part of her hoped that the commissioner would never call. At least then she could dispel some of her fears that the service had lost all self-respect and was nothing more than a political plaything.

Sally busied herself with some administration as two more hours inched by. She would prefer not to be caught driving when and if the commissioner called. While she could have made a recording using her phone app, she needed to take notes and create a record which could be used in court if necessary.

She was just about to call it quits and head for home when her phone buzzed with an incoming call. Her heart rate jumped a notch when she saw it was the commissioner.

'Hello, Commissioner. To what do I owe the pleasure?' answered Anders, acting out the part of a faithful servant.

'It's Cynthia to you, Sally. How have you been?' queried the commissioner, her voice dripping honey and sweetness.

'Pretty good, all things considered. There's nothing especially interesting on my plate, so I guess that's a good thing.'

'I couldn't agree more, Sally. I'm praying that we don't have any repeats of that disastrous raid on a licenced medicinal cannabis farm up north.'

'Nice transition. She didn't take long to get to the point of her call,' thought Anders, not trusting herself to reply in the face of such obsequiousness.

The commissioner pushed on. 'Out of interest, what happened to that detective of yours who precipitated that shocker? Detective Watson, if I recall.'

'She's quite a talented investigator. Sadly, trouble seems to have a way of following her around. Last I checked, she was thinking of resigning. Personally, I think that might be the best outcome. She has a habit of upsetting the culture that we've worked so hard to create in the service,' replied Anders, keeping an even tone to ensure that her sarcastic observation remained hidden.

'What's she doing now? I presume she's yet to resign.'

'I've put her behind a desk and in a small box, as much for her protection as ours. She's looking at a spate of juvenile crime incidents up north. I doubt she's finding that job deeply rewarding,' Anders answered easily. Having rehearsed her spiel beforehand made lying all the easier.

'I hear you. What a minefield that issue is. Everyone is ducking for cover on that one, including me,' replied Phelps, with a chuckle. 'I hear on the grapevine that the proponent of the cannabis facility has filed a civil claim against the local council. I guess there's a chance that we'll be roped into that. It would be best if the Watson situation was resolved before any court case starts.'

'I'm doing my best, Cynthia,' replied Anders, now back to speaking the truth.

'That's great. Nice to chat, Sally. We must catch up for a drink sometime.'

'Love to. Let me know when you have a slot in your busy diary and I'll make sure to find time,' offered Anders, just before she heard the click of the commissioner dropping off the call.

Even though the commissioner's call had been expected, it still came as a punch to her stomach. She recalled when Phelps had acted as if she was clueless about the Integrity Command's pursuit of Ange. Anders now understood that the commissioner was as accomplished a liar as her political masters. Before she focussed on cleaning up her notes, she sent Ange a text.

Just took the expected call. It played out exactly as we planned. Keep up the pressure.

The sheer temerity of the commissioner to act so innocent made Sally Anders madder than she could remember, especially knowing that Phelps had been busy loading the bullets designed to kill Ange off.

It was times like this when she missed Max the most. She readied herself for some deep soul-searching that evening as she paced around the house, debating the disturbing turn of events with her dear departed husband.

Ange was having dinner with Gus while her boss was speaking with the commissioner.

'You seem more distracted than usual, Ange. Anything you want to talk about?'

'I'm OK,' lied Ange. 'I'm on a treadmill at the moment and I need to run as fast as I can. Sorry if I seem distant. It's definitely not you, Gus.'

'Subject to how it goes this week, why don't we plan to spend the night down at Angourie? It's not healthy mixing your work and home life like this. You'll need to draw the line occasionally to keep your perspective intact.'

Ange looked at him quizzically. 'That sounds like the voice of experience talking.'

'Sort of. I think that this work-from-home movement will end in tears. It's no wonder mental health is such a big issue right now. Knowing when to switch on and off is difficult. I know that it sounds good in theory, but I feel that both work and home lives are suffering for lots of people in our society.'

'I get it, Gus. Let's plan for the weekend. But isn't working from home the new normal?'

Gus seemed to take his cue to move the conversation on. 'From where I sit, the situation has become an insidious problem. Even the staff who need to work in our factory feel as if they're being punished by having to come in to work each day. One of my shapers asked me if he could work from home. It would have been an absurdity three years ago—now it almost seems a right. A mate of mine runs a PR consulting firm, and he reckons productivity has dropped twenty percent since work from home became a thing—not to mention quality control. He's so exasperated that he's planning to pull the pin and demand a complete return to the office for all his staff. He knows that he's going to lose a bunch of them, but he reckons he'll need to fire them anyway at the rate he's going.'

Ange's phone buzzed with the text from her boss. She drifted away from her conversation to read it. She wasn't smiling when she returned from that distraction.

'I rest my case, Ange,' observed Gus, also not smiling.

'Point taken,' replied Ange, forcing a smile to put an end to the conversation. She stood up and cleared the plates from the table, already deep in thought about exactly how she could keep up the pressure on Linh and Kilroy. Hopefully, their combination of digital and physical surveillance would provide the evidence that they so desperately needed.

After another restless night, Sally Anders called just as Ange was getting out of the shower.

'Hi, Ange. There's been a development.'

Ange immediately stopped what she was doing. 'I know to be worried whenever you start a conversation like that. What's up?'

'Julia Bennet was found dead in her townhouse this morning.'

Ange felt the universe tilt. 'How?' It was the only word she could summon.

'It's been reported as a break-and-enter that turned violent. According to the officer I spoke to, Bennet's wallet, phone, laptop, car keys, passport, and some jewellery were stolen.'

'When did this happen?'

'Sunday night. I'd logged her as a person of interest in our system but was only notified this morning. I rang you straight away.'

'How was she killed?' asked Ange, still dazed and capable of only short and obvious questions.

'One of her own kitchen knives. It happens more than you think. The intruders seem to have entered through the door from the courtyard and Bennet was found dead in her kitchen.'

'Did any of the neighbours see anything? Any prints?' asked Ange, her mind functioning again.

'Nothing at all. They must have worn gloves, and they left the place spotless—except for Bennet's body lying in a pool of her own blood.'

'That doesn't sound like juvenile criminals: more like an expert. I simply don't buy the whole home invasion theory. The timing is way off for that.'

'I agree. It's way too much of a coincidence. I already asked to see if we could track her computer or phone, but no luck,' replied Anders.

'But why would someone kill Bennet?'

'I leave you to work that out, Ange. One thing's for sure, it won't hurt Linh and his prospects in court.'

'What do you mean?'

'I imagine that the defence would have called Bennet to give evidence, which would likely have caused the prosecution some problems. Now the case will be about the word of the big bad council against the actions of some poor attractive woman who's met a terrible tragedy. I'm sure the prosecution will conjure up all sorts of grandiose statements to support their argument. The council won't stand a chance,' added Anders.

That Anders had been the wife of a criminal defence barrister was obvious, and Ange instantly recognised the truth in her statement. 'Are we going to get involved in investigating Bennet's murder?' she asked.

'It's being handled by homicide, and they have absolutely no reason to hand it over to us. I could lobby the commissioner to get involved, but we both now know whose side she's on—and it's not ours,' stated Anders emphatically. 'Does Bennet's murder impact your investigation, Ange?'

Ange realised that the only role Bennet had been playing was that of Kilroy's ambitious mistress. She had all but put Bennet out of her mind. 'No. I'd discounted her completely. Looks like I'll need to investigate her background and connections more thoroughly.'

'OK, Ange. I'll leave you to it. The commissioner's personal interest in your well-being has me feeling uneasy. I can hear the clock ticking, but I can't tell if it's a stopwatch or a bomb,' Sally Anders remarked bitterly.

Ange caught Sally Anders just before she hung up the call. 'Boss, can you speak to homicide and impose on them to go the extra mile with the crime scene? You could insist that Bennet was a person of interest in a major case, and we need every stone unturned. I just don't believe that this was an unfortunate accident. Every crook leaves some trace, no matter how good they are.'

'I'll do what I can. You need to get on your bike and start pedalling, Detective. Otherwise, this *major case*, as you put it, will turn into a fizzer.'

'I assume someone has already contacted her next of kin, but when you talk to homicide, can you ask them not to make any public statements or release her name? It would also be helpful to keep watch over her apartment.'

'You're asking for too much now, Detective. Who would you hope to see visiting her that would be of any use to you? Apparently, you are well acquainted with the movements of Greg Kilroy,' commented Anders acerbically. 'After all, the killers are unlikely to pay the crime scene a visit and reveal themselves. And why not publicly release her name?'

'I'm thinking that we should orchestrate that somehow. That way, we can be ready to gauge any reaction,' replied Ange, sounding a little unsure of herself and her reasoning.

Sally Anders remained silent for a few seconds before replying. 'I'll see what I can do, Detective.' Evidently she was also unsure of the sense of Ange's last request.

Ange got dressed on autopilot and sat on the edge of the bed, her mind in fibrillation. Bennet's death rattled her confidence and conviction about the underpinnings of her investigation. She had concluded that Bennet was the ambitious aggressor, the type of woman who used her charm to get ahead by screwing Kilroy. Turned out, she was actually the one who got screwed over.

Bennet must have been expendable. If they would kill her so readily, a few anonymous trafficked girls would be quickly disposed of should push come to shove. This raised the stakes of Ange's wider investigation and the need to stay under the radar. There was someone she needed to inform about this latest development.

Alan Campbell answered the call on the second ring. 'Hi, Ange. Any news?'

'Yes, but not good news. Julia Bennet was found dead in her townhouse yesterday. It's being viewed as an unfortunate break-and-enter situation, but I'm not buying that for a moment.'

Campbell remained silent for a few seconds. 'That's a shock. I disliked the woman, but she didn't deserve this.'

'It's too much of a coincidence, Alan. I had Bennet pegged as the poster girl for ambitious corporate climbers, but now it seems as if she's been used and discarded like trash. Someone needed to silence her. Perhaps she was threatening Kilroy over their affair. I'll need to look deeper into her.'

'I'll save you some time and shoot you the dossier that the recruiter prepared when we employed Julia in Green River,' offered Campbell. He went silent again. 'This sure won't hurt Linh's civil claim.'

'That's exactly what the boss said,' said Ange.

'I would have called her as a witness and taken my chances that my testimony would trump hers. Now it will be my word against a poor dead woman. The ruthless cattle-baron-cum-environmental-vandal. Bloody hell, they might even suggest that I arranged her death. I won't stand a chance,' commented Campbell, sounding dejected.

'You're even more pessimistic than the boss, and she's the wife of a defence barrister,' observed Ange.

Campbell's voice took on a determined tone. 'If Linh is responsible for her death, then he must be desperate for money.'

'Or Bennet's affair with Kilroy was causing him trouble,' countered Ange. 'Kilroy didn't sound like someone who was ready to murder his lover in his conversation with the police minister. Although, he'd hardly go around crowing about his involvement.'

'When were you speaking to him?'

'I wasn't. Brian overheard a conversation between them.'

'Oh, that. Brian mentioned that Kilroy is most interested in your well-being.'

'Brian shouldn't really be speaking to you about that,' advised Ange sharply, somewhat miffed that Edwards had betrayed confidences.

'His contract with you only covers photo and video surveillance. I thought he made that quite clear,' replied Campbell assuredly.

Why Edwards had been so pedantic when negotiating his contract was now obvious to Ange. 'OK. Nicely played, Alan. I'm pleased that I can trust you—otherwise I'd need to give Brian his marching orders.'

'It's the best of both worlds. I'm not bound by the same ethical standards that you are. However, I promise not to abuse your trust or embarrass you in any way—at least not before coming to you first.'

'Now you've really got me worried,' laughed Ange. 'How will you approach the civil case against the council now that this has happened?'

'Council has already agreed to let me recruit the legal team and essentially run the case. The quid pro quo is that I've offered to foot the bill if it all goes pear-shaped. Bennet's death raises the stakes a touch higher than I expected. Frankly, I'm hoping that you'll bring down this cabal well before anything gets to court.'

'I can feel the screws being tightened as we speak. Thanks, Alan,' replied Ange, her laughter now a touch more strained. 'How much time do we have?'

'With the legal team I have in mind, I can string them out indefinitely. There's nothing urgent about the matter and Bennet's death doesn't change that. It's just an argument over whether any compensation is due. I'll need to step up with lodging my counterclaim.'

'What counterclaim? Aren't they the ones claiming compensation?'

'They might think so, but council can always counterclaim. Perversion of council business over the changes to refuse collection and the development approval, mental health impacts on the community, loss of ratepayer trust in the council itself. Those are just a few thoughts off the top of my head,' replied Campbell, having found a spring in his voice. Ange mused that having Campbell's financial capacity was a distinct advantage and a rare luxury. As she had learned, there were lawyers and there were lawyers, just as there were cattlemen and there was Alan Campbell.

'OK. I'll do my best. By the way, did you know that Linh controls a second grazing property near Singleton? The Large Island Grazing Company—same outfit that owns the cannabis farm in Clearwater.'

Campbell went suddenly silent, pausing the conversation for a full five seconds. 'No, I didn't. That's very interesting.'

'Anyhow, Alan. I'd best go. I have my 9 a.m. conference call starting soon. Your mole will be joining us,' said Ange, finding some levity to end what had been an otherwise depressing conversation.

'I've got some stuff I need to run to ground as well. Thanks for the call, Ange,' said Campbell as he signed off.

Ange's 9 a.m. team meeting was a wake-up call for everyone. There was now no hiding the fact that whoever they were up against was ruthless and dangerous. Ange was still putting her money on Harry Linh, but she forced the team to explore alternative targets. After running through and dismissing the other key players, no viable options were presented, at least none that they knew about.

Chapter 35

Distractions

After such an explosive start, the rest of that week moved along steadily. The 9 a.m. meetings became more about routine and keeping the pressure on than anything else.

Bree's Dark Web order arrived, and she recognised some of the products. She explained that potential Olympians receive training on prohibited substances and performance-enhancing drugs. The bottles of tablets looked like any other pharmaceutical and were professionally packaged and labelled. Bree had added some traditional Chinese medicines to her order, but despite their exotic appearance, nobody could decipher the underlying ingredients. Ange bundled them all into a courier bag and despatched it to some forensic colleagues for analysis. She'd worked with the same guys on the Namba Heads case and they knew their stuff.

Billy was still monitoring the dealer's cryptocurrency movements. His only observation was that the guy had developed quite a tidy business. Going by the number of apparent sales that were passing through the account, Billy hoped that the guy would soon need to make a purchase to top up his inventory.

Jim Grady rang after lunchtime on Thursday to check in. 'How are the high and mighty going up at the Ponderosa? Your old boyfriends are missing the female touch around the office.'

'Those tools. I can't say that we feel the same way, boss. Truth be known, we're not exactly hitting it out of the park,' she said despondently. 'By the way, it wouldn't hurt to drop the hint that Bree is helping me look into the juvenile crime epidemic. There's been a surprising amount of interest in my general well-being of late and that's the story Sally Anders and I are using as a smokescreen to our activities.'

'Will do. Those snakes from the Integrity Command aren't slithering around again, are they?'

'No. It's worse than that, but I can't say any more, boss. I promise to return Bree safe and sound. She'll be back at her desk before you know it.'

'Famous last words, Ange. I'll believe that when I see it. You've already stolen Billy, so why not Bree? Tell you what, I'll let you have Walton *and* Lynch if you give me Bree back.'

'Boss, you're not helping yourself,' laughed Ange, enjoying the light-hearted banter to relieve her frustration.

At least Ange received a WhatsApp message from Judy Ly on Thursday evening to say that she would be arriving in Hanoi on Saturday. Ange was delighted with this news, as she hadn't heard from Ly since their chat earlier in the week. While it wasn't exactly progress, everyone who mattered would soon be in place.

The only other worthwhile achievement was the installation of their new security setup. Ange simply could not believe the capabilities of a modern home security system, something that would have been science fiction only a few years ago. Billy had configured app alerts to pop up on both her phone and Gus's phone, trained the system to recognise Buddy and the regular faces that visited the property, and shown them both how to access the cameras offline. They messed around, confusing Buddy with the voice-over-camera feature, although he soon worked out what was happening and spoiled their fun.

Friday was equally uneventful, and with frustration stalking her every move, she decided to take Gus up on his offer for a night at the beach shack in Angourie. With winter around the corner and the water already cooling off, she pulled out her wetsuits and added them to a change of clothes. She had everything she needed already packed in the Volvo by the time Gus came home.

'Gus, let's head down to Angourie tonight. We can stop off in Yamba for dinner on the way. It might be our best chance, as we're stuck in the doldrums right now. Things will probably become intense once we catch a break on the case.'

Gus needed no further encouragement. 'Sounds good. Let me have a shower and throw a few things together. Give me fifteen minutes.'

'Perfect. I assume you'll want to take the Volvo. I've already packed my gear and Buddy is raring to go. He's no fool, that dog. Ever since he saw me packing, he's been clinging to me like a limpet.'

Soon enough, the trio were zipping south down the highway, humming along to the tunes of Fleetwood Mac. Gus seemed to do that whenever he was driving the Volvo, choosing classic music that somehow seemed appropriate for their classic ride. It was a step back in time, also appropriate for the timeless beach shack that was their ultimate destination. After a pleasant dinner in Yamba, enjoyed in the outdoor dining area of the aptly named Pacific Hotel, perched on the cliff beside the lighthouse, the troupe arrived at the beach shack just after 9:30 p.m. As soon as they opened the house, Ange could feel the sea breeze carrying her worries and cares away. Suddenly irrefutably tired, Ange brushed her teeth and collapsed into bed while Gus busied himself around the shack.

Buddy loved the beach shack as much as Ange did, finding the raw wooden floorboard very much to his liking. He could also sleep inside, a rare treat that he savoured intensely. Ange considered the veranda a much more agreeable spot, but she guessed the thrill of being let into the inner sanctum was the principal attraction. He'd been like that ever since leaving the farm, inching himself ever more deeply into their lives.

Swamplands dotted the scrub that separated Angourie from Yamba. Bulbous cane toads would hop from the wetlands to feast on the insects which swarmed around streetlights and glowing houses. As well as being deadly for insects, cane toads have poisonous glands under their tough and gnarly skin. The toxin was deadly for most animals, including dogs. Only the wily crow had figured out how to roll cane toads over and peck at their underside, the sole part of the toad that was unprotected. Ange had no desire to see whether Buddy could resist such a seemingly easy snack.

With all that going on, it seemed incredible that someone of authority had determined that importing such a rapacious and deadly pest into Australia was a sensible idea. The beetle which the cane toads were tasked with eradicating seemed innocuous by comparison. A terrible idea for wildlife, but a godsend for Buddy and the thrill of sleeping inside.

Whether it was exhaustion, the sea air, or the humming waves that crashed onto the headland, Ange slept like a baby. She awoke later than usual feeling refreshed and rejuvenated. A light easterly greeted her morning, the worst possible wind for finding a clean wave to surf. Instead of racing down to the beach, she took a leisurely breakfast on the veranda with Gus before selecting a board from the garage that would be her ride for the day. She chose a twin-fin fish design with plenty of width to help slide across the predictably sloppy waves. Gus picked out an old single-fin longboard, a class of board that he rode with style. Planning to spend a sizeable chunk of the day at the beach, they wandered to the back-beach laden with towels, wetsuits, snacks, drinks, books, and the essential sunscreen that would extend their day. Upon reaching the beach, the trio trudged south until they found a shady tree under which to drop their gear. The surf was pathetic, but the water was nice. Buddy kept them amused, chasing any inquisitive ghost crabs that sidestepped their way towards him as he lay on the sand. It was a game that tired neither Buddy nor the crabs.

After lunch, the pair pushed some sand around until it made the perfect bed, complete with a custom-made pillow, and dozed off for an afternoon nap, comfortably shaded under nature's umbrella. When they awoke, the light easterly breeze had sharpened its teeth and swung to the north, whistling through the needles of their casuarina tree. Suddenly chilled, they loaded up and drifted their way back to the shack. Ravenous after their calorie-starved day, they made an early dinner, classic tuna pesto pasta fashioned out of cupboard love.

Still early, the pair opened a bottle of white wine and drank it on the veranda. Buddy sat down beside them, seemingly also touched by the soothing and rejuvenating effects of the salt air as it washed over them. Before they knew it, the bottle was empty, and it was time for bed.

It had been weeks since Ange had made love to Gus, and desire came with an intensity that took her by surprise. As soon as they reached the bedroom, Ange urgently tore Gus's clothes off. She took a moment to admire his physique, drinking in his powerful energy and vitality. She loved the feel of Gus's skin and let her hands roam over his body. It was such a turn-on as he responded to her touch, sensing his desire grow.

The intensity of their lovemaking ebbed and flowed as they lost themselves in another world, one where time had no meaning and every sense was heightened. When they were done, the pair lay in each other's arms and drifted off to sleep, the type of sleep that came after one's desire was quenched, the comfortable contentment that sat between lovers who had nowhere to go and nothing to do other than enjoy each other and relish the afterglow.

It was sometime around 2 a.m. when Ange's phone buzzed. Force of habit pulled her reluctantly from a deep slumber. She interrogated her phone with bleary eyes, forcing them to focus on the source of this annoyance. Her eyes widened when she spied the notification from their new security system. Not especially alarmed, she clicked on the notification, expecting to see a scrub turkey, perhaps a cat or a possum enjoying the fact that Buddy wasn't on patrol.

It wasn't anything like that.

Chapter 36

Sprung

Now wide awake, Ange clicked through the sequence of three cameras. She could see two people hiding under darkened hoodies and keeping their heads down. Ange gauged them to be young males, at least going by the coarseness of their gait and how they leaped up the stairs onto the veranda, looking like a pigeon pair. The only difference that Ange could spot was that one was wearing white sneakers, the other shod in black. While Black Shoes peered into the guesthouse, White Shoes scoped out the house.

She held her breath as White Shoes walked along the veranda towards the camera which covered the front of the main house. White Shoes seemed totally at ease, pausing at the camera to flip it the finger. Ange caught her breath. They not only knew that they were under surveillance, but they also obviously didn't care.

The thought of what had just happened to Julia Bennet sent a shiver down Ange's spine. She put down her phone and dialled Billy's number, waiting patiently while it rang out. She immediately pressed redial, eventually rousing Billy from his slumber.

'Billy. It's Ange. There are two intruders scoping out Gus's place. They're both wearing hoodies. Can you get a look at their faces?' asked Ange, trying to imbue a sense of urgency to help Billy fully wake up.

'Boss, I'm not there. Bree and I had a few drinks at the pub. I've crashed at her apartment. I reckon that I'd still be over the limit,' replied Billy, his slurry voice revealing a cocktail of fatigue and the lingering effects of alcohol.

Ange put the call on speakerphone and pulled up the camera that covered the garage and driveway. She could see that Billy's van was nowhere to be seen. The only car parked in the garage forecourt was her Prado. She'd been too lazy to bother shuffling the cars around after they drove off in the Volvo.

'OK, Billy. Don't worry. I reckon they'll be long gone by the time you made it up there. Could you ask Bree to see if there's a patrol car nearby? Perhaps they can swing by and scare them off.'

'Will do what I can, boss. Sorry about this.'

'Don't be sorry, Billy. It's not your fault. You're entitled to the occasional Saturday night off work,' replied Ange.

Gus was awake by this time. 'What's up, Ange?' he asked in a croaky voice.

'There's two intruders scoping out the house, Gus.' Ange turned the face of her phone so that Gus could see the goings-on. The app was still showing the garage camera, and they watched as the hooded intruders disappeared behind the Prado. A loud hissing sound was soon picked up by the microphone.

'The bastards,' exclaimed Ange. 'They're spiking my tires.' She could hold herself back no longer. She picked out the microphone icon on the security cam app and yelled into her phone. 'Get off our property. I've got you on security camera.'

So much for her angry voice. The only response she received was an arm that extended over the bonnet to flip her another finger. Ange was shaking with rage. 'I'll going to let the dog out,' she yelled. This time she was flipped a double bird.

Realisation came in a flash. They knew that nobody was home. Whoever it was had obviously been watching and waiting for them to leave. Abruptly, as if they had gotten what they came for, the intruders turned their backs on the camera and casually wandered down the driveway and off into the darkness.

Ange was so amped up that sleep was an impossibility, so she went into the kitchen to make herself some tea, while a sleepy Gus went back to bed. Buddy seemed none the wiser about the drama, dragging himself up off his bed and trundling over to keep her company. Transfixed by several replays of the video footage, she thought through the implications as she waited for the kettle to come to a boil. Cup of tea in hand, she grabbed a pen and paper off the sideboard. Ange found that writing stuff down provided some order to her thoughts, especially when those thoughts came in the middle of the night.

1. *They knew that nobody was home. Watching us.*

2. *Made no attempt to break in. Not interested in burglary.*

3. *Vandalised Prado. Why that and not something else around the house?*

4. *Why not steal the Prado as a getaway? Automatic transmission.*

5. *Has our cover been blown? Are Linh and Co onto us?*

Halfway through her mug of black tea, she was still mulling over these points when her phone buzzed with a fresh alert. Ange clicked on the alert and was taken back to the garage camera, where a patrol car was easing up the driveway. She watched as two officers exited the car. In the grainy infrared image, she couldn't make out the identities of either officer. Their torches came on, flaring her vision and making identification even more difficult.

Ange suddenly remembered that the cameras came with a floodlight feature. She found the correct icon on her phone app and clicked on the light. Then, speaking into her phone, she briefed the officers through the speaker on the camera. 'It's Detective Ange Watson here. The two intruders have gone. They left on foot about twenty minutes ago. They don't seem to have broken in or taken anything, but I'd appreciate if you guys could have a look around.'

'Will do,' replied a male voice before making their way further into the property.

Ange progressively clicked on the floodlights for the other two cameras. She made a note to ask Billy to configure the lights to come on automatically in the future. She watched as the two officers strolled around the property, checking doors and windows as they went. After a thorough inspection, they came back into the garage and walked around the Prado. One of them walked up towards the camera and spoke.

'The place is secure, and there's no sign of forced entry. The only damage that I can see is to the Prado out behind me.'

'That's my work vehicle,' replied Ange.

'OK, then. They've vandalised your car. You're not going to like it.'

Ange didn't recognise the officer, even though she could clearly see his face. She guessed it to be one of the station's new recruits. 'Don't worry about the car. They had to come up the road from the east. Can you drive around and see if you can pick them up? You can ring me on my mobile,' said Ange. She reeled off the ten digits of her phone number and watched as the officer wrote them down in a small notebook pulled from his shirt pocket.

'Will do,' replied the officer, before the pair jumped back into their patrol car. Ange watched the car's taillights disappear down the driveway. Not wanting to waste battery power, she turned off the camera's spotlights, returning a grainy infrared scene to her phone.

In between drinking multiple cups of tea, Ange paced up and down the small kitchen. Buddy kept her company for a while until he realised that she wasn't going anywhere and the whole exercise was fruitless. He eventually slunk off back to his bed, performing his obligatory pirouette before plopping himself down and promptly falling asleep, leaving Ange alone with her out-of-control imagination.

It took over two hours for the expected phone call to come in, one showing an unknown number. Knowing that this could only be the police officer, she answered the call.

'Detective Watson, it's Constable Mathers here. I was just over at your property. We've driven around the entire area, and there's been a wild party at one of the big houses nearby. That's a mess and there's been a lot of damage. That's why we took so long.'

'Was there anyone suspicious at the party? Anyone wearing a hoodie?' asked Ange.

'There were lots of suspicious people and loads of hoodies. Some of them scattered when we drove up. We're trying to contact the owner. As I said, there's been a lot of damage. We'll get someone up to dust your car for prints, but I wouldn't hold my breath that it will yield anything useful.'

'OK. Thanks so much. Keep me posted if you find something interesting,' replied Ange, before hanging up the call.

With sleep an impossibility, she picked up Buddy's leash. The jangle of the chain roused him instantly from his dog dreams, and the pair wandered towards the ocean. Once they found the right spot, they sat down and waited for the sunrise. It gave her some time to think, but the sun, when it came, provided no fresh inspiration. Ange always considered sunrise to be grossly overrated. East coast surfers commonly surfed at dawn, taking advantage of lighter offshore breezes that were precipitated by the cooling early-morning landmass. In summer, the dawn line-up was almost painful as surfers peered out towards the horizon with squinted eyes, trying to dodge the piercing summer sun as they scanned the ocean in search of the perfect wave.

This sunrise was more painful than most. There was something decidedly off-cue about what had just happened. At least it looked like the intruders weren't there to murder anyone.

Chapter 37

Rules of Life

Seeing as the night had been so fractured, Ange let Gus sleep in. By the time he stumbled out of the bedroom, she had probed the evening's events from every angle. 'It's weird, Gus. The intruders had absolutely no interest in breaking into either the house or the guesthouse. Then there was my car, an automatic no less, sitting out in the open just asking to be taken for a joyride. They would have easily broken into the house and found my car keys in the drawer of my bedside table. It wasn't their first raid, and I seriously doubt that the site will yield any fingerprints. It's annoying, and I'm pissed off about them spiking a tyre, but it's pretty innocuous—at least as far as midnight intruders go. They also must have been watching the place. I'm certain they knew nobody was home, including Buddy. You saw how they flipped me the bird when I threatened to sic Buddy onto them. It makes no sense.'

Billy rang while she was making coffee. 'Hi, boss. The guys dusted the car, but they didn't seem too enthusiastic about what they found. Sorry I wasn't there.'

'Billy, don't worry. They were waiting until the coast was clear. If not last night, it would have been another time. How many tires did they spike on my Prado?'

'None. That part of your car is fine. However, you won't like what they did do.'

'You're the second person to tell me that. What's happened?'

Billy remained silent for a second. Her phone pinged with a message containing a single photo. Ange held the phone away from her ear and clicked on the image. If it wasn't so serious, she almost would have laughed. There, on the driver's door, spray-painted in big black letters, was a message of sorts.

FUCK OFF BITCH

'Thanks, Billy. It's almost a relief. Going by what we know so far, something so petty and obvious would hardly be the work of Linh and Co—or the Ndrangheta,' replied Ange.

'I can't believe that you're so cool about it, boss,' commented Billy.

'It's just a car. I'll get it fixed. Who knows, it just might stop some of those crazy mums from gazumping me in the car park at the supermarket,' said Ange, her sense of humour having returned. 'We should be back at the house mid-afternoon. See you then.'

After a pleasant swim, an early lunch, and an even earlier nap, they left on the drive back to Byron around 3 p.m.

Jim Grady called Ange on the drive. 'I hear you had some unwelcome visitors last night, Ange. The guys just let me know that there weren't any fingerprints of interest. What are your thoughts?'

'I've given this a lot of thought, and I'm now certain that it has nothing to do with my case. It's more likely something else. By the way, what happened with the party Constable Mathers broke up last night? Do you know where it was?'

'Oh, that. It was close by Gus's house, further up the hill and a bit to the north. These kids nowadays are completely brazened. They must have known that the house was rarely used and organised a rave party over social media. Kids came from all over. What parent lets their teenage kid out to attend such a party on a Saturday night? Either the parents knew about it, or they didn't know about it. Both scenarios are bad. Some people around here do my head in. Then they'll be the first to blame us when something goes awry.'

A light bulb went off in Ange's mind. 'Boss, did you spread the rumour around the office about me looking into juvenile crime?'

'Yes. I did. Let me ask a few questions around the station,' he replied, a grave tone creeping into Grady's voice, suggesting that he correctly guessed where Ange was going with her train of thought.

'I'll check with Sally, but I'd be surprised if she spoke to anyone. We only recently came up with the idea as a ruse. I reckon that the kids had me in their sights, which conveniently coincided with that rave party. I'll bet we can even see the party house from Gus's place.'

'Possibly. I gather that you won't have much trouble identifying it. The kids trashed the place. There should be tradies coming and going for weeks based on what Constable Mathers told me. I'll keep you posted. Keep your eyes open,

Ange,' warned Grady.

Ange briefly pondered the implications of the commissioner being in the pockets of any organised crime figures who ran the juvenile networks. 'Surely not,' she thought to herself, although stranger things have happened.

As soon as they arrived home and let Buddy loose, he immediately knew something was amiss. All business, he prowled left and right, using his superpower to sniff out the source of the disturbance in the ether. Ange marvelled at this amazing skill and briefly imagined the tangle of iridescent scent lines that made up Buddy's world. Once comfortable that the hooded intruders were no longer there, Buddy loped over and sat beside Ange and Gus as they assessed the damage. Seeing the state of her Prado was a shock.

Gus broke the sombre mood as they surveyed the artwork. 'Well, the artists won't be the next Banksy or win any literary wards. I'll take the Bitch Buggy to work tomorrow. I know the owner of that paint and body shop a few doors along from the factory. He owes me. I cut him a deal on a his-and-hers surfboard package last Christmas.'

It was amazing how laughter could rebalance one's perspective.

Chapter 38

Moving Day

Mondays had always been moving days in Ange's opinion, and she was determined to make this Monday count. She saw the matter with the Prado as a dangerous distraction from the major task at hand. She felt compelled to tell Sally Anders about the incident, if for no other purpose than to put to bed her ridiculous notion that the commissioner had somehow instigated the incursion. Ange rang her first thing on Monday morning.

'There's no way, Ange,' replied Anders immediately on hearing Ange's thought-bubble. 'Not after that whole thing with Bold and the Ndrangheta. She might be a political tart, but I don't see her as another mole for organised crime, especially over something so small-time. Do you need another car?'

'I'm not sure. It might make people take me more seriously,' she jested. 'Gus has taken the Prado to a paint shop near his work. Hopefully, they can simply buff out the damage. I'll send you the bill, though. Remember, it's still technically a Queensland police vehicle. You will need to replace my car when they realise. I'm thinking a new Prado will do nicely.'

'I'd forgotten that your car isn't on our books. I guess Wallace might find it a rather appropriate piece of sign writing. Let's wait until the Queenslanders ask for it back. Keep me posted, Ange. I hope you're realising that you're seriously messing with my head with that absurd allegation against the commissioner,' commented Anders.

'Did you get anywhere with homicide over Bennet's murder site?' asked Ange.

'Sort of. I asked them to take another look, and it seems as if they gave the place a thorough going-over. The only item of note was a cigarette butt found in the laneway on the other side of the wall to her courtyard. The laneway is only used for garages and rubbish bins. I pressed the guys at homicide for an urgent DNA test, but it didn't ping anyone in the system. All we know is that the smoker was a Caucasian male. Honestly, it could simply be someone taking their dog for a walk, or someone having a secret fag away from their wife's prying eyes.'

Despite feeling deflated, Ange concealed her disappointment. 'Thanks, boss. It was a long shot. I'd best jump to our daily meeting. Speak soon.'

Her parents had drummed into her that punctuality was fundamental to showing respect for those around her. The time set for their morning meeting was 9 a.m., so 9 a.m. it was. After an update from Ange on the events of the weekend and some humorous banter at Ange's expense over her new paint job, Edwards dropped a bombshell to kick-start the week.

'Your boy has remained active over the weekend. He paid a visit to his electoral office on Friday, followed by dinner with his wife and some friends at a restaurant, then he enjoyed his Saturday ritual—sport with his children in the morning before visiting The Pulse for some afternoon delight. The good news is that Kilroy is convinced you're out of the picture, Ange.'

'That's great, Brian. But how do you know all of this? Aren't you watching Linh and The Pulse? I can't believe you picked up all that information with your directional mic, as impressive as it is.'

'I have been watching The Pulse. It's quite busy, that side door. I'll have a report to you later today about the comings and goings. It would be best if you turned a blind eye to this, but I have access to Kilroy's phone.'

Billy's ears pricked up. 'How did you achieve that?'

'I took advantage of Kilroy's social-climbing personality. My wife, Eleanor, is a committed foodie. She has this friend who's a successful restaurateur, Kevin Allwood.'

'I've heard of him. He has quite the following,' commented Ange.

'He knows of Tony Daicos, by the way. Anyhow, Kevin's business model is to buy struggling restaurants, smarten up the décor and menu, and then leverage his reputation to make them a raging success. Once his new restaurant is doing a roaring trade, he flips it and takes a long holiday on the proceeds. As soon as any restraint of trade clause in his sale contract has elapsed, he then repeats the performance. His latest venture opens next month. I'll get you an invitation. The Campbells will be there.'

Ange interrupted. 'That's all very interesting, but what has this to do with

Kilroy?'

'I sent him a text with a personalised invitation to the opening. I knew he wouldn't be able to resist checking it out.'

'And that text contained some spyware,' proposed Billy. 'Clever. Where did you get that from?'

'My old mates back home. I'll share it with you sometime when we get together,' replied Edwards.

'Won't he be suspicious?' asked Ange.

'Not a chance. The text invite sent him to the official site handling the RSVPs. There's no way he'll be suspicious. It's a legitimate invitation and a legitimate event. The social pages have been talking about it for weeks. Kevin is a master of making his latest venture an instant success, even before it opens.'

'OK, Brian. I have some reservations about this. Let me think it over,' replied Ange. 'Any mention of Julia Bennet in what you've heard so far?'

'Nothing. Given what I observed a couple of weeks back, I would have expected him to organise a rendezvous with Bennet and round out his usual weekly diet. It's possible that he has another phone, but that would seem uncharacteristic of Kilroy and his risky approach to life and love.'

Ange had seen lots of guys like Kilroy—she'd even dated a few. 'Male fails', she called them. 'Interesting. Billy, where are you at with getting access to Linh's empire?'

'The only way that I can see is to get some spyware onto Linh's computer, something that logs keystrokes as a minimum.'

'What are the options, Billy?' asked Ange. The similarities of this undertaking to what Edwards had just achieved were not lost on her.

'The best bit of malware that I've found is something called Wormraider. What I like about this one is the way it completely erases itself and leaves no trace. It hides from basic virus and malware scans but deletes itself as soon as it detects a full system scan has been activated. The only problem is that it also deletes itself after one week of being installed. The hacker community is highly protective of Wormraider. They're trying to keep it secret as long as possible.'

Bree chimed in. 'Have you been stalking the Dark Web, Billy? I hope we haven't come across each other in some sordid chat room.'

'No. That's your domain, Bree,' laughed Billy, before returning to his serious self. 'I have some major dirt on a super-hacker. He's one of those curious types who loves the challenge of breaking in, as opposed to someone causing damage or theft. He knows that I'll bust his balls if he ever causes any actual harm. But in a roundabout way, he's doing a community service by exposing vulnerabilities in the organisations he targets.'

'OK. I get it. We need to be careful about the timing of when we deploy Tombraider.'

'It's Wormraider, boss. That's the other problem—getting it onto Linh's computer.'

'Another problem? That's two. I thought that there was only one, Billy. Fill us in about this fresh problem,' insisted Ange.

'To guarantee Wormraider goes undetected by malware detection software, it needs to be installed directly onto his computer.'

'How so?' probed Ange.

'Like using a thumb drive or some other USB device,' explained Billy.

'Any ideas on how we can achieve that?'

Billy's dejected tone of voice almost said it all. 'None that makes any sense right now. We could risk sending it via email, but our chances of success will plummet.'

'OK. Let's call the meeting for today. I'll leave it to our very own IT brains-trust to come up with a way into Linh's computer by this time tomorrow. We need to make some solid progress this week—otherwise we'll be out of time.'

Alan Campbell rang Monday afternoon with some interesting news. 'I think I've solved the riddle of my cattle.'

'Don't keep me in suspense, Alan.'

'Linh is breeding Wagyu. That's why Daicos was stealing my cattle specifically. It makes sense, as they're the most profitable cattle to breed right now.'

'How did you find this out?' asked Ange, thrilled that at least one mystery might have been solved.

'I reached out to all the major Wagyu studs I know and asked if they'd sold any semen to the Long Island Pastoral Company. I said that the company wanted to buy some eggs from me, and I needed to check that they paid their bills. We might be competitors, but the beef breeding community is tight. Anyhow, I struck pay dirt.'

'That was clever thinking, Alan.'

'It gets better. I asked Fin to go back through the ribbon winners at the Royal Easter Show for the past few years. He came across Harry Linh standing proudly beside a blue-ribbon Wagyu heifer. I just sent you the picture.'

Ange's phone blipped, and she opened the image that Campbell had just sent. It was definitely Harry Linh standing beside his Wagyu heifer, although he seemed smaller than she had imagined. Though he looked like a fish out of water, his beaming smile was genuine. Ange pondered the powerful role of ego as a motivator. While Linh had largely disappeared from public view, the lure of standing proud at the Royal Easter Show was impossible to resist. 'That doesn't conclusively prove that Linh is behind the theft of your cattle, Alan. It could be a side hustle for Tony Daicos.'

'Agree. That's why I'm calling you. Can you speed up your analysis of the video of the cannabis farm in Clearwater? This is totally killing me, and I'll need to deal with Daicos and friends before long—otherwise I might go mad. I just don't get it. Billie and I have continued to eat at Daicos's pub every other week, as per usual, just to keep up appearances. It's a thriving business and I simply cannot see why he needed to get involved in this sort of caper.'

'Alan, let *me* give *you* some advice for a change. In my experience, it's usually greed, revenge, love, or money that provides the clue in situations like this. That and peer pressure and the company one keeps. I'll remind my colleague about the video analysis.' Ange sheepishly realised that she hadn't pushed Billy over that matter. Other events had taken control of her thoughts.

'Interesting. Thanks, Ange. I know that you're busy, but try to get me that analysis when you can.'

'Will do, Alan. Thanks for the call. Let me process your news. Hopefully, it will help me make some sense of this mess.'

'By the way, I've just asked Sandy Ellis at the council to email you the information I have about Julia Bennet. I'm inclined to appoint Sandy as our new CEO. We don't need any more high-powered executive types. I reckon that someone who values their job and understands the local region will serve us much better.'

Ange pondered her call with Campbell and shivered at the thought of Linh. Maybe they could lure him into the open through his passion for Wagyu? It seemed ironic that one hand was stealing cows to harvest their eggs and, if her intuition was correct, the other hand was stealing young women and selling them as sex-slaves or brides.

One thing she was now sure of was that Harry Linh was not a nice man.

The last big Monday move came early that evening when Judy Ly called via WhatsApp. 'Hi, Ange, I've checked out EZ Jobs. They seem legitimate. There were loads of people who came and went from their offices during the time I was watching them—way too many people for it to be an outright scam or false front.'

'That's a pity,' said Ange in a dejected voice. 'Did you see anyone interesting?'

'No, just lots of Vietnamese faces who I didn't recognise,' replied Ly.

The day had been going so well to that point. 'I'm sorry to send you to Hanoi on a wild-goose chase, Judy.'

'Oh, don't worry, I'm a long way from giving up. I have a plan, one that involves me taking the overnight train to Sapa this evening. Remember Cua Kwm told us she came from the hill tribes in that area and that her brother had responded to a flyer he found lying around? I reckon it's worth a trip. If I could get my hands on a flyer that directly links EZ Jobs to what happened to Cua Kwm, then we'd have something concrete to push on with. Sapa has an enormous market where people from the region converge to sell their wares. Scouring that market for information is worth a shot. I was just a child when I first visited Sapa, and I've always wanted to go back. Plus, the overnight train should be fun.'

Ange was relieved. 'Fantastic. Fingers crossed that you find something. Failing that, make sure you have fun so that all isn't lost. When do you return to Hanoi?'

'I'll train it up there tonight, leaving tomorrow for digging around the markets. I've booked a place to stay tomorrow night, and I catch the train back Wednesday evening. That leaves me two full days. If I can't find what I need in that time, then I guess it's not there and we'll need to try some other angle.'

'I'll be thinking of you. Good luck, Judy,' said Ange, before ending the call.

Gus returned home just before darkness set in. Ange went out to greet him and see how the repairs had gone.

'Eddy removed all the paint, but it's not perfect. If you look at the door carefully, you can still make out the words.'

Ange moved around the car and could easily see the shadow of the words from certain angles.

'Eddy reckons that the paint they used has etched into the clear coat, leaving that shadow outline that you can see. The only solution is to repaint the whole door.'

'It's not too bad, Gus. I guess the Bitch Buggy moniker might stick. I really don't have time to get it repainted. Perhaps I can think about that once we've finished with this case. How much do I owe Eddy?'

'Nothing. He was happy to help. The boys found it quite amusing. They've seen you around the shop and consider that you're anything but a bitch. Eddy reckons they think you're hot—their words,' replied Gus, before he caught the look in Ange's eyes. 'Of course, I agree with them—about you being hot and all that.'

Ange laughed. 'You almost tripped up there, Angus Bell.'

Chapter 39

Worms

The first thing Ange did on Tuesday was to ring Sally Anders and fill her in on Campbell's latest news. 'Alan Campbell has had approximately one million dollars' worth of cattle stolen. Do you think that's enough to get a search warrant in place for Linh? Surely there are enough fingers pointing in his direction to get something sorted.'

'Truly? That's significant,' observed Anders. 'Don't tell me you're planning to raid Linh's premises, Ange? It seems way too early for that.'

'Not literally—well, not yet, at least. Hopefully that can come later. We're hoping to design a plan for a digital raid. But now you mention it, having a search warrant that extended to a physical raid would be prudent. We can never be sure when that might be needed, and having it in place would save time and effort.'

'I hear you. With the commissioner looking over my shoulder, I'll need to be careful which magistrate I choose. Leave it with me. When will you need this by?'

'I can't say, but not for a day or two. We don't yet have a viable plan to break in without alerting Linh that we're breathing down his neck. I've got a call at 9 a.m. to work through the options.'

'OK, Ange. I'll do what I can. Shoot me over a summary of your suspicions about Linh as soon as you can.'

'I'll do it now. It'll be just an email summarising all the main points. Will that be sufficient?' asked Ange.

'Sure. I'll contact you if I need anything further. Speak later today.'

Ange spent the next thirty minutes compiling an email to her boss. She knew that documenting thoughts and ideas was a useful way to test one's logic. Once she'd finished typing and reviewed her work, she realised her theories weren't as solid as she would have liked. She dispatched the email with crossed fingers.

The Tuesday morning meeting was interesting to say the least. Ange opened the discussion with the latest news. 'We now have another reason for breaking into Harry Linh's empire.' She spent the next few minutes updating her team about Linh's obsession with Wagyu beef cattle.

Bree expressed her thoughts. 'Huh. Other than a brief notation about the purchase of Linh's Singleton property, I've found virtually nothing on Linh on social media or in the rural press. I would never have thought to look through the ribbon winners at the Royal Easter Show. Ego really is a powerful force.'

'Billy, you need to get onto that video analysis of the Clearwater drug farm. Even if it yields nothing to help our investigation, it might help Alan Campbell out with his dilemma about Tony Daicos, not to mention his looming court case.'

'I started, but then you keep distracting me,' pleaded Billy. 'I'll finish it as soon as I get a free moment.'

'I'd appreciate that, Billy. Now, you guys, the clock is ticking. Any ideas? What about Tombraider?' asked Ange.

Billy shot her a sarcastic look. 'You'll tire of that joke before long, boss—and I rest my case about being distracted. Regarding our *Wormraider* challenge, I'm wondering if we need to revisit the idea of turning someone on the inside. Maybe we go through Brian's photographs and see if they yield someone who we can lean on.'

'That sounds like a lot of work and I just don't see we have the time for that approach. What about you, Bree?' asked Ange.

'My idea is to lure Linh into a Dark Web chat room and coax him into clicking on something or other. Just like I did once before with an NFT.'

'You'll first need to lure him into the chat room. Then, won't he be unlikely to click on a random file if he's on the Dark Web? It seems difficult to pull off,' queried Billy.

Bree seemed annoyed. 'It's no worse than your idea, Billy.'

'Settle down. What's gotten into you two? Any idea is a good idea,' Ange stated forcefully, trying to bring the meeting back onto an even keel.

'Why don't we rattle Kilroy's cage and see where that gets us?' proposed Edwards calmly, as if an idea had just occurred to him, his calm English public-school accent bringing everyone to attention. 'Do you think he might have played a part in Julia Bennet's murder?'

Ange thought for a moment. 'It doesn't make sense after the call you recorded. But I guess it's conceivable that he is a wolf dressed in sheep's clothing and a callous killer. Stranger things have happened. Brian, you have ears on Kilroy's phone. Does he have an alibi for the Sunday night before last?'

The team waited patiently for Edwards to check his mystery phone spying app. 'He was at home all evening. I assume he's heard about her death, but it's surprising he hasn't reached out to anyone. He might be spooked already.'

'For the sake of the exercise, how would you propose to rattle his cage?' asked Ange.

'Why don't we send Kilroy an anonymous letter, one containing a USB thumb drive with some juicy images of his affair with Julia Bennet? Ange, could you get your hands on a photo from Bennet's crime scene?' asked Edwards.

'Should be doable. Anyway, I'll need to get the OK from the boss for this plan. I'll check.'

'We could add some photos of Linh with Kilroy,' continued Edwards.

'And Wormraider,' added Billy.

Ange went silent as she thought through the fundamentals of this plan. 'That's brilliant, Brian—and Billy. The more I think about it, the more I like it.'

Billy was on board. 'By infecting Kilroy's computer with Wormraider, we'll be able to see what he's up to. If he is involved in Bennet's death and has an accomplice, he might show them the photos as well, maybe even Linh himself. It's a cracking idea. I'll need to check with my super-hacker contact that the USB will be good for multiple downloads, but I can't see why not.'

Bree was the surprising voice of reason, showing that she had an old head on her young shoulders. 'We can't assume any of that will happen. We need to keep plodding away on all fronts. Assuming Ange gets the OK from the boss for Brian's plan, then anything that comes our way concerning Linh or anyone else will be a bonus.'

Ange gave Bree a nod of respect before moving on. 'Looks like you win the prize for our next step, Brian. I also agree with your take on how Kilroy will react. There are two things that we need to be careful about. First, we need to be judicious in our selection of images to put on the thumb drive. We wouldn't want to give away our surveillance activities, so selecting the perfect images isn't as easy as it sounds. Second, we only have one week before Billy's malware evaporates. I doubt Brian's idea will work more than once. So, we need to time our run perfectly, which doesn't leave us much leeway before Sally Anders pulls the plug on the operation.'

These two realities of life caused a halt to the discussion. After a long and pregnant pause, Brian Edwards got the show back on the road. 'How about I make a first cut and put together some images, and then you and I can go over them together, Ange?'

'Sounds good, Brian. I'll speak with the boss and get my hands on Bennet's crime scene photo. Bree, you stay active in the Dark Web chat rooms in case something's heating up. Perhaps a new shipment of women in the wind, maybe some unhappy customers, even someone looking to trade up? Anything that would even remotely suggest increased activity in that area.'

'Will do,' replied Bree.

'Billy, you need to get your hands on that malware and execute some trial runs. It's a high-stakes play and we can't afford any failures. Use me as a dummy if you need to. As you've already said, Wormraider needs to be good for multiple downloads.'

'Agree with all that, boss. Oh, and good to see you've got the name locked down,' replied Billy. 'What about Clearwater?'

'What do you mean, what about Clearwater?'

'The video analysis of the cannabis farm, plus monitoring the crypto transactions for the drug dealer,' answered Billy.

'I know how to use BCExplore, so I can look after the crypto transactions. Pass that over to me, Billy,' offered Bree without hesitation.

'Leave the video surveillance to one side for the moment, Billy. You can slot that in for when you're bored,' suggested Ange, before she realised that Alan Campbell's PI was on the call. 'Brian, Alan agreed that our investigation needs to take precedence over his cattle.'

'Don't worry, Ange. Alan told me the same thing before he trafficked me to you,' jested Edwards.

'I'll try to buy us some more time when I brief the boss. Anything else that we need to discuss?' asked Ange, pausing for a moment to take stock. 'OK, then.

Excellent meeting and well done, everyone. Seeing as we each have a lot to get on with, let's skip tomorrow's meeting unless someone has something important to report or has made a significant breakthrough. On that note, let's all get to it.'

Ange rang Sally Anders straight away, but the call went straight to voicemail. She checked her emails and saw that Bennet's CV had arrived from Sandy Ellis at the Green River Council. Given that Bennet had been a topic of conversation at their meeting, Ange took a moment to skim through it.

Bennet's career trajectory was exactly as Ange would have expected, rapidly leapfrogging upwards from one job to another. Nothing particularly interesting caught Ange's attention, but it made her reflect on her own career, wondering if she'd been in the same job for too long.

The memory jumped from her subconscious while she was staring at Bennet's photo in the top-right corner. She pulled up her phone and compared Bennet's mobile phone number with the missed call. They were identical.

Her mind spinning, she pressed redial. The call went straight to voicemail.

'Hi. It's Jules. Leave a message and I'll get back to you,' came the upbeat greeting.

Ange quickly hung up. She saw no point in leaving a message for a dead person.

Chapter 40

Easy Jobs

Ange rang Sally Anders to brief her on the latest developments. She worked backwards. 'Why would Julia Bennet try to call me?'

'It might have been a pocket call?' suggested Anders.

'Agreed, but I wouldn't be atop her list of favourite numbers. I can only think that I gave her a business card when Jim Grady and I fronted her in Clearwater. She called me the week before she died. It's just way too close for comfort, boss.'

'Are you thinking Kilroy?'

'Unlikely. Brian has been snooping around Kilroy and is reasonably confident that he was home the night Bennet was killed. Then again, he's unlikely to kill her himself, so I guess he needs to remain on the list of suspects. I think it's more likely to be Linh over the court case—but that's a stretch as well.' Ange chose not to disclose the complete extent of Brian's snooping around Kilroy, justifying it as Edwards' allegiance to Alan Campbell.

'What's your plan, Detective?'

Ange then summarised her team's brainstorming session before getting to the crunch. 'I'll need a photo from Bennet's crime scene. Can you organise that?'

'Hang on. I'm not yet on board with your plan,' stated Anders before grilling Ange about the ins and outs of rattling Kilroy's cage.

'So, in summary, you're asking me to approve your plan to send incriminating photos to a serving government minister, and then infect his computer with a virus so you can see what he's up to. That's a big ask, Detective.'

'Not if Kilroy is included alongside Linh in the search warrant. He's a viable suspect in the murder of Bennet,' shot back Ange, knowing that she was being tested by her boss. 'I promise Billy will only snoop around Kilroy's computer to search for evidence related to his relationship with Linh and Bennet. We already know that they're connected, but not how deeply. If nothing useful turns up, I'll have Billy erase the virus, and nobody will be any the wiser.'

'Except me,' observed Anders drily. 'OK. Send me some notes justifying this idea. I'll need to find a magistrate who's as suspicious of politicians as I am. Should be doable. Anything else?'

Ange was on a roll and pressed on. 'Boss, we need more time, and Bennet's murder raises the stakes. Could you cut us some slack?'

'One step at a time. You'll be the death of me, Ange.'

'I hope not. Thanks, boss. Remember to send me the photo of Bennet,' pressed Ange.

'Goodbye, Detective. You sure know how to ruin someone's day.'

Ange was sure that Sally Anders' expression would betray a faint, barely discernible smile.

Brian Edwards sent through a dozen or more photographs featuring Greg Kilroy and friends late Tuesday afternoon. Ange sat on these overnight and rang Edwards Wednesday morning to workshop the most appropriate photos. After some debate, they settled on four.

The first selection was a straightforward choice that they both agreed on—the hero shot from weeks ago, where Julia Bennet had her leg wrapped around Kilroy in the alley after their romantic dinner date. For the second and third, they chose before and after shots of Bennet and Kilroy coming and going from Bennet's townhouse. Kilroy was wearing a tie on the way in, but no tie on the way out, and Bennet had changed her top. One needed little imagination to discern what had happened in between the two photos. The fourth was reserved for Bennet's crime scene photo.

Selection of the fifth and final photo triggered some spirited debate. The trick was to catch Kilroy and Linh together, but in a manner which didn't jeopardise the team's surveillance activities. Every option they considered was ultimately discarded after they thought through the implications. They were about to go back to the drawing board when Ange remembered the shot which she had snapped off Tony Daicos's trophy wall. There was a moderate risk that this image would put the Daicos project at risk, but Edwards seemed comfortable with that possibility. He would use some of his image manipulation software to create a fresh black-and-white reproduction, one that looked like a press photo from the social pages. They debated whether to leave Daicos in the image. Ange had reservations, but Edwards seemed relaxed. 'Tony Daicos is already toast. Even if Kilroy or Linh recognised where the image came from, I can't see that it changes anything where Daicos is concerned. Honestly, by the time I'm finished with that photo, it will barely resemble the original—except for the players involved. I'll send the photos around to everyone once I'm finished with my photoshopping.'

'OK, Brian. I'm on board with that logic. I'm also curious to see your completed image,' Ange agreed, before signing off.

As things transpired, it was mid-afternoon on Wednesday before Sally Anders finally got back to Ange. Anders was brief and to the point.

'I'm sending you an email with the search warrant, plus a photo of Bennet that doesn't leave much to the imagination. Now, Detective, I need something from you.'

'Fantastic. How can I say no to you after that?' said Ange, thrilled that her boss had come through.

'I ran into the commissioner at an executive planning session this morning. You can imagine how hard that was for me. However, your brilliant idea might have backfired somewhat, as she wants a briefing on the work that you've been doing on juvenile crime.'

'Great,' replied Ange in an overly exaggerated voice. 'Well, it seemed like a sensible idea at the time.'

'Perhaps you could use AI to generate something? I hear that's all the rage right now.'

'Let me speak to Judy Ly. She's been doing something for me. Given the tight timeline that you're holding me to, I really don't want any distractions. That being said, it would be helpful if the commissioner and her political mates fully believed our story. Leave it with me.'

Ange wasted an hour registering for ChatGPT and asking it to provide a summary report about the juvenile crime epidemic sweeping across Australia. She had to admit that it did a terrific job, one that hit the highlights but offered nothing substantive. The report was filled with grand motherhood statements about needing better prevention and rehab programs, improving government collaboration, and better data and analytics. She cut and copied the output and saved it in a Word document. It was the first time that Ange had used generative AI, and the results blew her away. She was still thinking through the possibilities and consequences of this amazing technology when her co-conspirator called on WhatsApp.

'Hi, Judy. I was just thinking about you. Any luck?' asked Ange.

'My visit was definitely worth the effort. I've organised an interview with EZ Jobs tomorrow. There were quite a few organisations touting similar services, so I ran up a few dry gullies. I made a point of mentioning Australia, which weeded some agencies out. However, I'm pleased that I scoped out EZ Jobs beforehand, as it matches the address of my appointment.'

Ange was slightly alarmed at this news. 'What are you planning to do at the interview? Isn't that too soon? We don't want to spook Linh and his sister.'

'I rang from Sapa using a Vietnamese SIM card that I purchased. It was really noisy, and I made a point of apologising for the background noise of the markets. My cousin's daughter is going to come to the interview with me and pose as our version of Cua Kwm. Let's face it, we have Kwm's complete storyline.'

'OK, I guess. Is your niece up to this? We don't want to put her in any danger—or you, for that matter.'

'Sammy is seventeen and drop-dead gorgeous. She wants to become an actress, in Hollywood no less. Sammy is her Western stage name. Her real name is Dung Ly. Dung means beautiful in Vietnamese, but the name is a shocker for any English speaker. She thinks Sammy Ly sounds better, and I must agree with her. Anyway, we'll need to make up some fresh alter egos for our interview.'

'That is so funny. OK. Give it a crack. If either of you feel uncomfortable or threatened, abandon ship and get out of there. Are you already back in Hanoi?'

'No. I'm booked on the night train back to Hanoi. I just have time for an early dinner before it leaves from Lao Cai around 8:30 p.m.'

'Where is Lao Cai? I thought you were in Sapa.'

'The town of Lao Cai is hard up against the Chinese border on the train line.

Sapa is only a thirty-minute taxi ride away. You can actually see China from the Lao Cai station, and Cua Kwm's story about her sister's abduction by a Chinese gang has been haunting me. Sapa was wonderful, by the way. You should visit sometime.'

'This is brilliant, Judy. Well done. Maybe I'll pay Vietnam a visit when all this is over. I don't suppose that I could ask another favour?' enquired Ange, feeling guilty about having Judy do so much of her dirty work.

'Sure. Tell me.'

'The commissioner made some enquiries about what I was up to. We have eyes and ears on Greg Kilroy, the minister who can't keep his dick in his pants. We know he got in contact with his political mate, the police minister. Using you for inspiration, Sally Anders and I concocted a story that I was working on juvenile crime. Going by your experience, that seems to be the equivalent of being put in the bottom drawer and out of sight. Anyhow, it's backfired. The commissioner is expecting a briefing report on my findings so far, and I think it's in our best interests that she wholeheartedly buys into our story.'

'I agree with that logic. Bloody hell. I thought our police service was too political. Yours takes that to an entirely different level.'

'I know. It's depressing. So, I asked ChatGPT to write me a report, and it did an amazing job—without saying much. If I send you that report, I wondered if you could flesh it out with some of your actual research? Where you can, of course.'

'No problems. I've got my tablet with me, so I'll do it on the train tonight. Writing this from memory will make it less clear where the information came from. You'll have something credible in the morning. I'm intrigued to see what sort of job ChatGPT did.'

Ange went to her laptop and attached the report to a WhatsApp message and shot it off to Ly. 'It should come through any second.'

'Got it. I'll speak tomorrow after our interview, if not before.'

'Thanks, Judy. I really owe you for this. Safe travels, and I hope you catch a decent night's sleep.'

'I think that's a given. Who could resist the lullaby of a night train journey?'

Chapter 41

Consequential

Ange woke up the next morning to find that Judy Ly had completed her report. She took a moment to marvel at the connectedness of the world and the speed at which things could be done. She imagined all the connections and packets of information that were zipping around the globe on the internet superhighway, visualising a giant ever-expanding ball, one fashioned from iridescent multicoloured strands of wool.

Like most things, there was good and bad in this hyper-connected world. For the good, she could harness artificial intelligence to draft a report, send it to Judy Ly, who was on some train halfway around the world, and have it edited and returned—all within twelve hours.

On the not-so-good side, there seemed absolutely no escape from this bombardment of information and demands on one's time. Ange's great escape was, of course, surfing and the ocean. It had only been a few days, but she could already feel the pangs of that addiction.

As she read through Judy's document, Ange made a bunch of minor editing and formatting corrections, a process that she found helped her read the contents thoroughly and not skip ahead. Judy had done an amazing job of bringing the bland AI draft to life, expanding its scope to cover the involvement of organised criminal gangs. There was a section on the strategies that these gangs were using, and she even suggested some future focus areas for both apprehension and prevention. Once Ange was happy with how the report read, she emailed it to Sally Anders.

Ange then messaged her team to see if they had anything substantial to report at the planned daily meeting. She received a thumbs-down response from Brian, although nothing from Billy or Bree. She figured that they were busy, so she opted to cancel their 9 a.m. get-together. It was pointless to have a meeting just for the sake of it and waste people's time.

Jim Grady called mid-morning with some interesting and weirdly comforting news. 'Hi, Ange. I may have figured out what happened with your car. A couple of kids were caught acting suspiciously and pulled into the station for questioning. I listened to the recording of their interview, and they were incredibly belligerent and obnoxious. The interviewing officer lost his cool, which seems likely the cause of your incident.'

'Boss, you're sounding a touch evasive. You'll need to elaborate.'

'Well, the interviewing officer was your old mate Gerry Walton,' explained Grady.

'What did he say?' asked Ange in a resigned tone of voice. Walton was the gift that kept on giving, his mouth always one step ahead of his brain.

'That the kids better watch out, as the female dream team of Detective Ange Watson and Constable Breanna White were on their case—or words to that effect,' explained a sheepish Jim Grady. He was Gerry Walton's boss, after all.

'OK. That news is bizarrely comforting for a couple of reasons. First, it's not related to our investigations into people trafficking. And second, my opinion that Gerry Walton is a moron remains intact.' Ange paused, thinking further about this news. 'I wonder how they found out where I live. It's not exactly my official residence, as I haven't wanted to jinx myself by going through the motions of updating all my records. I think my current status would be more accurately described as *a person of no fixed abode*.'

'I know, I wondered the same thing. Perhaps either you or Bree have a tracker on your car.'

'I'll check with Billy. Maybe he can do a scan of our vehicles. Thanks for the update, boss.'

Ange rang Billy and then added Bree to the call. She filled them in on Jim Grady's explanation before asking Billy if he had any pieces of kit that could detect trackers. Bree gave that line of thought short shrift. 'I just had a look through your socials. You've been tagged in a bunch of photos that were taken at Gus's place. It wouldn't be hard to work out. There's even a couple of me at your birthday party last year.'

'Let me guess. Kerrie?'

'She's certainly the most prolific,' answered Bree diplomatically.

'OK. That seems the most likely. Billy, I know it's probably overkill, but I'd sleep more soundly if you did a sweep of all our vehicles occasionally.'

'Sure, boss. I'll get some kit couriered up from Sydney. By the way, those new tracking tags which use phone pings to transmit location are amazing. No wonder criminals are using them to track shipments of drugs. An alert would have sounded on your phone if someone had planted one of those on you. It's cool stuff.'

'Thanks, guys. I'll need to have a chat with Kerrie about her posting habits, but that genie's probably well and truly out of the bottle.'

The day turned crazy just after lunch. Bree came over to the house and literally dragged Ange across to the guesthouse. Billy was totally engrossed in his computer screens and Ange could see they were filled with information.

Bree was buzzing with excitement, and it was most definitely the contagious type. 'Ange, we've hit the jackpot. Billy, why don't you run the boss through what's up on your screens?'

'You should recognise these dashboards, boss,' suggested Billy.

Ange nodded in feigned agreement, although the dashboards were vaguely familiar at best.

Billy evidently sensed Ange's confusion. 'They're outputs from BCExplore, the crypto tracing software we use.' Billy pointed to the left-hand monitor. 'This is the dashboard of the drug dealer's wallet—the one you busted in Clearwater. You can see all the inflows from his customers.' He pointed to the top line of a ledger of sorts. 'This is Bree's transaction and where we started. You can see how active he's been since then.'

Ange nodded her head in agreement. 'Got it, Billy.'

Billy pointed to the last transaction in the ledger. 'And this is where he's made the payment to his supplier yesterday. I did the calculations, and I reckon his markup is somewhere around two hundred percent. He's doing extremely well.'

Billy then pointed to the dashboard on the right-hand screen. 'And this is the wallet for the recipient of his payment—presumably the wholesaler.' He pointed to the transaction on the top line of the right-hand ledger and then to the corresponding transaction on the left-hand ledger. 'You can see that these two are for the same amount.' Billy turned his attention to the right-hand screen and pointed to a transaction further down the ledger. 'This came in this morning.'

Ange could see that this transaction was for a substantially larger amount than all others. 'Wow. How much is that, Billy?'

'I worked it out to be the equivalent of one hundred and twenty-five thousand Australian dollars—give or take.'

'Any ideas what it's for?'

'No idea. It could be a master dealer, but that doesn't gel with the other transactions coming through.'

'Or it could be a payment for a trafficked woman, or women,' suggested Bree.

'Guys, can we tell who owns the wallet on the right-hand screen?' asked Ange.

'No idea,' replied Billy once more. 'The person would need to buy something from a vendor that BCExplore recognises.'

'Or if he cashes in his crypto using one of the normal crypto exchanges linked to a bank account,' added Bree.

'Can we go back over past transactions?' asked Ange.

'We can, but this software application works best when we look forward and not backwards. I actually don't know how it works, but assembling past transactions seems to take forever and chew up a lot of computing power. There might be other software apps out there that do a better job of that, but working out what to use and becoming proficient would take me more time than we have.'

'OK. So we really have nothing.' observed Ange. She saw the look of disappointment creep onto the faces of her two younger colleagues. 'Other than some very suspicious transactions. Let's keep monitoring this and hope for the best.' A memory of a conversation with Brian Edwards sprang to mind. 'Brian made the comment that Harry Linh must be desperate for money to risk dragging the Green River Council into court. If his theory is correct and what we're seeing on your right-hand screen is Harry Linh, then he may need to cash in some of his crypto sooner rather than later.'

'He won't do it to any Australian domiciled bank,' said Billy smartly. 'As you know, Aussie financial institutions must report any unusual transaction as part of money laundering legislation—and that includes crypto exchanges. He'd run it through somewhere without the same strict rules as us.'

'Like Vietnam, perhaps?' asked Ange.

'Bree, how about you take over my computer for the rest of today to monitor the crypto wallets?' suggested Billy. 'Maybe you can also do some research on offshore crypto exchanges? The extra screens will help. I'll work on my laptop instead. I've got a spare monitor in the van. Anyway, my laptop is probably a more typical system for testing Wormraider. I might need to borrow yours as well, boss.'

'So you can infect me and spy on my emails, Billy?' replied Ange with a smile.

'You're already an open book. If I'd wanted to spy on your emails, boss, I would have done that ages ago,' joked back Billy.

'OK. Let me brief Brian. We need to throw as many ideas as we can at this and hope one sticks. Brilliant work, guys,' said Ange, rewarded by the pleased look on the faces of her two colleagues. She reminded herself that everyone occasionally needed encouragement.

As soon as Ange was back at the house, she sat on the veranda and rang Brian Edwards. 'Brian, we really need to get a video camera into Linh's office.'

'I just can't see that's viable without a lot of planning and some more resources. I've had the same thought and I've been looking to see some way in, but The Pulse pretty much runs 24/7. A video cam would need to be carefully positioned and expertly installed.'

'I hear you. What about a microphone? Your phone app is amazing, but it doesn't catch casual conversations.'

'I know. I've made that suggestion to the people who designed that app. I'll reach out to them to see if they have an upgrade, even if it's a beta version. If Google or Apple can do that through your phone, I don't understand why the app can't do the same,' commented Edwards. 'We could smuggle in a microphone. Perhaps in a package addressed to Linh. Maybe we could send him something? I've used that ploy before.'

'OK. There are a few options there. Let's take this offline and we can regroup at 3 p.m. to review our options. Billy and Bree can update you with their news. Speak then, Brian.'

She occupied herself until 3 p.m., searching for innovative ways to install a spy camera. After confirming that this was unworkable in their situation, she concluded that Brian's microphone idea was definitely a better option.

Ange started the meeting by asking Billy and Bree to outline their recent development. Edwards asked lots of questions which helped sense-check their progress. Once done, Ange turned their attention towards Edwards. 'Brian, can you outline your ideas for getting some additional surveillance in Linh's office?'

'The second-best idea is a later version of the phone app that transmits permanently. We'd need to get the app onto Linh's phone, and then we'd need to log in to his Wi-Fi to access the mic. There are far too many variables for my liking.'

Billy evidently agreed. 'Who knows what sort of security he has on his Wi-Fi system? I doubt that he'll be like you and fly around the internet naked, boss.'

'Thanks for pointing out my technical incompetence, Billy,' said Ange as she rolled her eyes. 'Moving on. What's your best idea, Brian?'

'Smuggling something into his office that has a microphone already deployed. I've done that before.'

'Give us some examples, Brian?' asked Bree.

'My favourite was an expensive bottle of scotch whiskey where we'd installed a mic in the wooden box it was presented in. Another was when we intercepted a mattress that the subject had bought online. That was interesting.'

'The mind boggles, Brian,' mused Ange.

Bree piped up. 'I think I've got the answer. The owner of that wallet just purchased something from an online store. Ange, what do you think any aspiring pastoralist might need for next year's Royal Easter Show?'

Ange thought back to the picture Alan Campbell had sent her. The reason Linh had looked like a fish out of water leaped from her subconscious. 'An Akubra hat.'

'Bingo,' replied Bree.

'How long ago?' asked Edwards.

Bree looked back at the screen. 'I guess within the last hour. The name of the vendor didn't show up immediately. I just noticed it now.'

'Brian, Bree will send you the address. Drop what you're doing, pick up whatever kit you need, and get over there. I'll contact the vendor and make sure they hold the item until you get there. OK, guys, let's jump to it.'

The rest of the day was a blur. Ange successfully contacted the vendor of the mystery Akubra and put a halt on any plans for despatch until Edwards had done his thing. It was just before 5 p.m. when Edwards called.

'Ange, I got the mic installed on the top of the hatbox. It looks just like one of the security tags that retailers use. I also slipped a second smaller mic under the hatband in case the box gets discarded. It's a big hat.'

'What model?' asked Ange, pulling up the Akubra model range on her laptop.

'It's called the Golden Spur.'

Ange scrolled down the page until she saw the hat in question. 'I see it. That's an enormous hat for a small man. I can see where you would have hidden the mic.'

'I ordered a same-day courier and waited until they collected the hat. By the way, it's definitely Harry Linh who owns that crypto wallet. As you can probably guess, I'm well acquainted with his address. The hat should be delivered to his office at any moment. I'm heading back to my home-away-from home to check if the mics are working.'

Ange was impressed. 'That was well done, Brian. Let me know how it goes.'

Edwards sent a WhatsApp message to the team just after 6 p.m.

> *We now have ears in Linh's office. All quiet on the western front.*

Billy and Bree both responded with congratulatory emojis.

It wasn't until early evening that Ange received a WhatsApp call from Judy Ly. Ange answered immediately. 'How did the interview go, Judy? It's been a little crazy here, but I've been worrying about you all day.'

'It went really well. Sammy was amazing. I actually think that she might have a future as an actor. I'd briefed her about Cua Kwm and she played that part beautifully. Once the receptionist saw Sammy, she ushered us in to speak with none other than Madam Linh herself. As I might have said, Sammy is absolutely gorgeous and Linh couldn't have been any more enthusiastic about recruiting her.'

'That was fortunate. Where did you leave things?' asked Ange.

'Linh explained that she had one job left in Brisbane for someone like Sammy, but Sammy would need to leave next Wednesday. I quizzed her about passports and air tickets, and Linh said that they would handle everything. She wanted to take Sammy's photo there and then, but I resisted. I said that the family had no clue about this idea, and that I would need to come clean with them before we could move forward. We agreed to come back once all that was done. Linh pulled back and said that this wasn't a problem. According to her, they had regular groups going to Australia.'

'Judy, this is amazing. It's the break we needed. We now have some indication of timing. I've had Breanna White looking for information on the Dark Web, but she's had no luck.'

'What do you want me to do now?' asked Judy Ly.

'Have a holiday' was Ange's first thought until realisation dawned. 'Actually, Judy, what would be good is to build up an ironclad chain of provenance for any evidence we collect.'

'What do you mean by that?'

'Well, let's assume that we rescue some trafficked women once they arrive in Australia. It would be helpful to link them directly with Madam Linh and EZ Jobs. Going by what you know of the premises, how easy would it be to get eyes on any comings and goings?'

'Like most of Hanoi, the EZ Jobs office is on a very busy street. It should be doable. Leave it with me. It's not exactly my thing. Do you have anyone who could help set up a camera and the like?'

'I have a few ideas. Be careful when you scope out the offices the second time around. We don't want to be too obvious,' warned Ange.

'I'll whizz by on my cousin's moped. With a face mask and helmet, I'll blend into the scenery like you wouldn't believe. There are simply millions of mopeds in Hanoi. I'll get back to you tomorrow.'

'Terrific. I can't tell how impressed I am with this work, Judy.'

'My pleasure. Just make sure that you tell your boss,' jested Ly, before hanging up the call.

Ange almost called her crew together for a late-night meeting, but opted to wait until morning and think through her options.

It proved another restless night, although this time one borne of excitement rather than fear.

Chapter 42

The Early Bird

Ange was champing at the bit by the time their 9 a.m. meeting rolled around.

Brian Edwards delivered some startling news. 'I hear that you've prepared an excellent report on juvenile crime. The commissioner is impressed, and you've even won over Kilroy and his mate the police minister. There's been no mention of people trafficking in any of the conversations that I've heard. Linh left his office shortly after his new Akubra was delivered and hasn't been back.'

'Have you learned anything from Kilroy and his infected phone which suggests he's involved in Bennet's murder?'

'Nothing whatsoever. Either he doesn't know, doesn't care, or he's a callous assassin. Based on my assessment of the man, I would go with my first option.'

'That's excellent news. I have some progress as well. As best we can determine, the next shipment, and I detest using that word, of women out of Hanoi looks like it will arrive in the middle of next week.' Ange then filled the group in on Judy Ly's achievements. 'We have two things to decide. First, I think we need eyes on Madam Linh's employment agency shopfront so that we can cross-reference the comings and goings and tie them to whoever gets shipped to Brisbane. Any ideas on that before I move on to the second issue?'

'How official does this need to be, Ange?' asked Edwards.

Ange paused and thought this through. 'Seeing as this is happening outside our borders, and considering how we might use any information, I can't see that it makes much difference either way. It might be a different story for the Vietnamese authorities, but I don't know enough about how their system works—or if they'd even be interested.'

'Before you sent Detective Ly on her mission, I remembered someone who *retired* to Vietnam. More like *escaped* from some dubious relationships back home, but he owes me,' suggested Edwards. 'I'm not sure where he lives anymore, so it could take a day or two to track him down. How long will Detective Ly remain in Vietnam?'

'Judy's achieved all this since arriving last Saturday. She's way ahead of where I thought she'd be. I reckon at least another week if we need her.'

'OK. I'll come back to you. You should think about a backup plan. I agree that having some evidential link with Hanoi is crucial.'

'If push comes to shove, I'll need to let Judy install a camera herself. I know some old friends who can lead her through this. The less she's seen hanging around Madam Linh's office, the better. Let's hope you can bring home the bacon, Brian,' replied Ange. 'Now, about our second decision. Knowing that we only have a week, when do we deploy Wormraider?'

After a lengthy silence, it was Billy who spoke first. 'We need to know more about the shipment, as you called it, so the sooner we shake up Kilroy, the better.'

'I agree, Billy,' chimed in Bree. 'I suppose the million-dollar question is how should we get the goods to Kilroy? We can't just put it in the post. Who knows when that might be delivered? Also, a courier seems too obvious.'

'Putting a blank envelope in his mailbox would risk getting his wife involved, which may come with unexpected consequences. It worked for the Ndrangheta with me, but I lived alone back then,' added Ange. 'Any other ideas? Brian, you have a sense of his daily movements.'

Edwards took no time in considering his reply. 'I reckon he'll almost certainly attend school sport on Saturday. It's rugby season, which makes it the place to be seen by the who's who amongst the parent community. Kilroy normally leaves his wife to do the ferrying duties and drives himself. His wife leaves early and commonly picks up other kids on the way, whereas Kilroy arrives just before the games begin. Perhaps I could drop an envelope in his car while he's off watching a game? This might also confuse him about who's been watching.'

'That sounds brilliant. How on earth would you pull that off—getting into his car, that is?' asked Billy.

'I've already harvested the signal from his remote locking transponder. I wouldn't need to start the car. All I need to do is unlock it, slip an envelope on the seat, and lock it back up. Three seconds should get me in and out while all the spectators remain focussed on the game.'

'Brian, I sort of wish that you hadn't told me about your harvesting adventures,' laughed Ange. 'You certainly are full of surprises. What does everyone think about Brian's plan?'

'It's perfect, boss,' answered Billy.

'Ticks all the boxes that I can see,' offered Bree.

'OK. Project Early Bird is a go,' said Ange, with a lively spring in her voice.

'Why Early Bird?' asked Bree.

"You know, the early bird catches the worm, right?'

Billy endorsed the name in a roundabout manner. 'Do you lie awake at night dreaming this stuff up, boss? I like it.'

'I thought it was brilliant, even if I say so myself. Given that we've pulled this trigger, we need to meet daily from now on. I'll also add Judy Ly into our WhatsApp group. Is everyone OK with that?'

'Can we make tomorrow's meeting mid-afternoon?' asked Edwards. 'I'll be busy breaking into Kilroy's car all morning.'

'Good point. Let's shoot for 3 p.m.,' agreed Ange. 'You're the centre of attention at the moment, Brian. If something happens, let me know and we can reschedule. Billy, you need to get ready your end to receive any feed from Linh's computer. Bree, now that we know a shipment of women is imminent, you need to step up your surveillance on the Dark Web and see if you can validate our assumptions.'

'Will do, boss,' replied Billy and Bree, almost in unison.

Sally Anders rang around lunchtime. 'Well, Ange. You may have found your calling.'

'Is this in relation to the report I emailed you yesterday? I understand that the commissioner is most impressed.'

'How did you know that? She only rang me twenty minutes ago.'

'Through Kilroy via the police minister. We discussed it at our 9 a.m. meeting,' replied Ange nonchalantly, as if this was just another routine development.

'The commissioner is genuinely impressed. You may have made a rod for your own back. She's planning to make juvenile crime your baby—assuming you don't resign first,' mocked Anders.

Ange avoided discussing her future employment prospects and carried on. 'Brian Edwards also believes that Kilroy is unaware of Julia Bennet's murder. Either that or he's a brilliant actor. I suppose he is a politician after all,' said Ange, her voice trailing off, implying a close connection between the two professions. 'Anyway, he's about to see the grisly details of her death—if all goes to plan. The image you sent me will be dropped off tomorrow.'

'He is good, that PI of yours,' observed Anders.

'You don't know the half of it. In fact, you probably don't *want* to know the half of it. If this backfires, there are some things that you might prefer to remain in the dark about.'

'I'm not sure that I like the sound of that, Detective. You are, after all, my employee.'

Ange took on a serious tone of voice. 'Boss, you know I'm at the point where I don't really care about my status in the department anymore. What I do care about is protecting those women and bringing down Kilroy and Linh. I don't wish to drag you down with me. It is a high-risk strategy that we've put in play but, given the time pressures, it's our last chance. My only request is that you protect Billy and Bree. I'm already on the record as a rogue officer, so make that legend true before anyone dumps on them. If it all goes well, you can be the hero.'

'You're not helping yourself here, Ange. Naturally, I will protect your colleagues, and I do understand your feelings about the department. I've got similar reservations,' replied Anders ahead of a long pause. 'However, I also trust your instincts and judgement. If you think that this is the only way, then get on with it. If it turns to custard, then I think you have a future as the face of juvenile crime. In all seriousness, that really seems like something we should be involved in.'

'Thanks, boss. I appreciate that. After my own recent experience, I also agree with the juvenile crime situation. If we don't get involved because of the political risks, then we're no better than the politicians. There is one thing that I wanted to discuss with you.'

'Out with it. Is this another of those things I shouldn't know about?'

'Yes, and no. We need someone to pick up the trail of any women arriving in Brisbane. Where did you leave it with the feds? I'm thinking about the guys that we've used before. I trust those guys with my life—obviously.'

'I haven't leaned on the brass, but I reached out to the guys who handled the

Hillburn takedown. They're seriously pissed off about what happened. Frankly, I reckon that they'd crawl over hot coals for you.'

'That's perfect. Do you want me to reach out, or should you do it?'

'I think you reach out first. If they can't get involved without something official to back them up, then I'll come through the correct channels. I'll dream up some highly confidential operation that needs localised support,' suggested Anders. 'I still don't trust my compatriots in the feds after all that's happened.' Sally Anders went silent for quite some time before continuing. 'Ange, this stuff that you don't want me to know about, I think you need to fill me in on what you're planning. It's not just your career that's on the line.'

'Fair point, boss.'

Ange spent the next ten minutes enlightening her boss about spyware and their upcoming plans.

'I share your concern, Detective. This strategy definitely seems high-risk. All I can say is break a leg—and preferably not the one with stainless steel screws in it.'

Ange rang Andy Barnett on WhatsApp. His own team had chosen him as the leader of the Hillburn operation, so she figured he would be the best person to approach.

'Well, well,' said Andy Barnett expressively, as he answered the call. 'Look who the cat dragged in. I thought that you'd been covered over in kitty litter?'

'More than once, Andy,' laughed Ange. 'I'm developing quite a taste for the stuff.'

'Hah, funny. What's up? I assume that this isn't a social call.'

Before she popped the question, Ange filled him in on her plan and explained how he might fit in. 'What do you reckon? Can you guys help me out? We'd love it to stay under the radar, but my boss can speak to your boss if necessary. If I'm being honest, we don't trust your bosses.'

'Neither do we after what happened to you. Also, what went down after the Hillburn operation was a disgrace. It's a complete joke to think that people trafficking into Australia was solved with one single takedown.'

'And to make matters worse, people trafficking isn't just a one-way street.

Since Australia's borders reopened after Covid, the number of Australians being trafficked out of the country is on the rise. They almost never return,' added Ange sombrely.

'I think we can do this off-grid. It feels like we're all in need of some time off for mental health reasons. I'm suddenly feeling deeply traumatised by what we've seen recently,' remarked Barnett, his voice dripping with irony. 'How long are we talking about here, Ange?'

'Three to five days, tops. If we can't nail this down within that time frame, then other events will swamp our little rowboat. By the way, Andy, if it all goes sour, this is all on me. Agreed?' asked Ange in what was more a statement than any question.

'Your boss filled us in on what happened to you. The guys were super pissed when they heard. We'll look after ourselves, thanks. We've been planning for that eventuality ourselves since your boss reached out, and it won't be pretty.'

'Oh dear. I feel like a virus that keeps infecting anyone who works with me.'

'You're our type of virus, Ange. Although we might need to move to Sydney. Tell your boss to expect a call,' laughed Barnett.

'At the rate I'm going, I'll have single-handedly filled Major Crimes with misfits,' joked Ange in return. 'Thanks, Andy. I appreciate it. I'll set up a WhatsApp group that includes the whole team. It's called Operation Early Bird. Subject to how the deployment of our Wormraider goes, our next meeting is tomorrow at 3 p.m.'

'The boys will be raring to go. Speak then,' said Barnett as he signed off.

Ange took a moment to appreciate the wonderful people she had surrounded herself with. Alan Campbell preached this same philosophy on life. It was, without a doubt, a sound philosophy to follow.

Chapter 43

Carjack

As soon as Ange could see movement over at the guesthouse, she made herself some coffee and wandered over to check in with Billy. He was already hard at work on his multiscreen universe. 'Hi, Billy. Do you want me to fix you a coffee?'

'No more coffee for me for a while. I've already had two. I couldn't sleep knowing what's in play today, so I've been up for hours running tests and double-checking my configuration of Wormraider. Actually, I've just sent our man from MI5 some detailed instructions on how to configure his USB thumb drive. As you can imagine, it's tricky.'

'How so? And what did you tell Brian to do?'

'I've set the files up in a folder in a cloud drive and then given Brian instructions on how to image the folder directly onto his thumb drive. The normal process would be to download, save, and then transfer the files from computer to thumb drive, by which time he would be infected. You see what I mean?'

'Billy, I really don't know what I would do without you. Without getting too technical, how does Wormraider do its stuff?'

'It's a work of art, boss. Essentially, Wormraider sits in the background collecting data, which it encrypts and sends to a remote server that I've set up. To avoid detection by virus and spyware protection software, Wormraider sends the data in small packets and at discreet intervals.'

'What sort of data? I assume it will be the useful type,' asked Ange.

'As well as logging keystrokes, it keeps track of any websites visited. It even takes screenshots periodically. What's really amazing is that I can configure when and how often those screenshots are taken depending on the situation. It's probably

Wormraider's superpower, as it doesn't waste valuable resources keeping swathes of screenshots of online newspapers, for example. I mean, it will still take those screenshots, just not as frequently. Given that the ultimate prize would be for Wormraider to find a password for the Shama website, or whatever it's called now, I've configured Wormraider to take screenshots every five seconds whenever TOR is being used.'

'TOR. That's the browser used to access the Dark Web, isn't it?' asked Ange.

'Correct, boss. It's good to see that some things technical are making it into that twisted brain of yours.'

'Funny, Billy,' replied Ange dramatically. 'So, does this mean that we can watch any infected computer in real time?'

'I take back my last compliment,' commented Billy drily. 'The data collected is cut and diced into small bundles before being sent to the server. I can see whenever new data is arriving. However, the more data we collect, the longer the lag time before it provides us with a complete picture of what's been going on.'

'I see. That's tricky.'

'I know. What's worse is that once we release Wormraider, I can't alter the operating parameters. Learning how to use it has been a crash course. Being the latest weapon of the hacker community, there's no easy-to-read user manual to download. I owe a bunch of favours that I hope won't come back to bite me.'

'So, if it doesn't work properly, then we'd have to go through the rigmarole for a second time. I don't think it would work twice. This seems way riskier than I'd hoped for, Billy.'

'That's what I've been doing since the early hours of this morning. As risky as it seems, we need to assume that Wormraider makes its way to the perfect host. I've infected my laptop and I've been accessing some Dark Websites and the like. I'm pretty confident that I've finally got the balance right. Key logs and websites will be sent first, so there won't be much lag there. Screenshots contain a lot more data, so they'll take a while to filter through. Most people don't fully shut down their computers after every session and normally leave them in sleep mode. If that happens, then Wormraider can keep dispatching packets of data 24/7.'

'OK. I trust your judgement, of course,' responded Ange, her concerns only partly mollified.

'Oh, I forgot to mention that Wormraider is designed for multiple targets, so any data harvested from unique IP addresses is kept separately. Fingers crossed we need that feature and we have eyes on Kilroy, Linh, and whoever else may be involved,' added Billy.

'So, how do you read the data that's sent over?'

'That's straightforward. I have another piece of kit that decrypts the data and reassembles it all. Think of it as an antidote. It's an app called Drench.'

'Hah. Of course it is. I can't tell you how many sheep I've drenched growing up. That's why counting them doesn't work for me in the middle of the night. It's too much like work for me. Where does this stuff come from, Billy?'

'Who knows? Cybercriminals, enquiring minds, state spy agencies, the military, industrial espionage, to name just a few. Once someone gets their hands on any new malware, they can pull it apart, improve it, change it to suit their specific purpose. That's why Wormraider is such a closely guarded item. It will be useless once it makes itself onto the hit list of the malware protection industry.'

That concept caught Ange off guard, plunging her deep in thought for a moment. 'That poses a conundrum for us, doesn't it, Billy? Our job is to stop crime in its tracks. However, here we are, using some piece of illicit malware whose efficacy relies on the fact that authorities don't know of its existence. If we spill the beans, like we probably should, then it won't be useful to us anymore.'

'And I will have burnt all my connections in the hacker industry, which would plunge us back into the Dark Ages. Don't think this through too deeply, boss. It will do your head in. It's something that I've been grappling with for some time. I think of it like sending someone undercover and allowing criminal activity to continue for years before acting.'

'I clearly haven't given this enough thought. When exactly does the end justify the means?' posed Ange.

'I reckon saving a bunch of young innocent women from slavery and prostitution should be sufficient justification, boss. I know that I'll be able to sleep at night if we can pull off this heist.'

Ange gave him her most benevolent smile. 'Thanks, Billy. You're not just a pretty face, are you?'

'Not even, boss,' replied a beaming Billy. 'I'll let you know when our stolen data starts rolling in.'

'You had to spoil our moment by using the word *stolen*, didn't you? I'm hoping to hear from Brian shortly. Hopefully, everything goes according to plan and we toast your success later today. Fingers crossed that we survive this slippery slope we're on,' replied Ange, her smiling face in contradiction to the concerns rumbling around in her gut.

Her discussion had amplified the importance of their project and the consequences of failure. Unable to quell her churning stomach, she took Buddy for a walk along the lane. She could see the party house off in the distance where a couple of tradies were already at work. Ange led Buddy up the driveway to say hello, whereupon the tradies dropped whatever they were doing and lavished some attention on Buddy. Surfers themselves, they recognised the now famous Rusty Bell, and they chatted openly for a minute or two. Nobody could believe the damage that those kids had foisted on the property.

The view to Gus's house was expansive. She could clearly see her Prado parked in the garage forecourt but was relieved to discover that she couldn't see inside either the main house or the guest quarters.

After dragging a reluctant Buddy away from his newfound admirers, she was just arriving back at Gus's house when a phone pinged with a WhatsApp message from Brian Edwards.

Mum is piling kids into her car. Looks like they're off to sport. Kilroy should be on the move inside the hour.

Ange heard a car coming up the driveway and saw that it was Bree. She was waiting for Bree to park when Gus walked out of the house.

'Ange, I need to head down to the shop to see Kerrie. She's scheming something and wants me to bring Buddy along. Is that OK?'

'That's fine, Gus—except for the bit about Kerrie and her scheming. The mind boggles about what that woman has in mind for our dog. I guess it's better that she does her stuff down at the shop, seeing how my living arrangements have been broadcast over social media. Anyhow, today is going to be a busy one—actually, it will probably be the same for the entire next week. I hope you won't feel neglected.'

'I understand. At least I'll have Buddy to keep me company—and Kerrie, it seems. Catch you guys later,' replied Gus as he headed for the Volvo with Buddy in hot pursuit.

Bree was brimming with excitement. 'Linh just received another payment. Same amount as the last,' she explained with a grimace. Ange said nothing. Her look of disgust was an adequate response.

The two women walked into the guesthouse and checked in with Billy. They had barely exchanged pleasantries when Brian Edwards sent another message.

> *Kilroy on the move. Hold tight. BTW, no luck with my contact in Vietnam. My hands are full. I'll need to leave that matter to you, Ange.*

Chapter 44

Covering All Bases

In what was patently a case of buyer's remorse, Billy remained focussed on relentlessly testing Wormraider. Bree dived straight into her Dark Web chat rooms while Ange took Brian's advice and started thinking about Hanoi.

She planned to discuss the situation with Andy Barnett, but first rang Judy Ly on WhatsApp for an update. Despite being early morning, Ly answered immediately.

'Judy, how would you feel about setting up the surveillance cam yourself? I can organise some help and guidance from here, but I think you doing it might be our only shot,' asked Ange.

'It's already underway, Ange. I was going to fill you in at our meeting this afternoon. I went to one of the big technology outlets in Hanoi and picked up everything I need. It was a colossal store with an incredible range, mostly Chinese stuff. Evidently, the Chinese are the gurus of covert surveillance. The unit is being installed this morning by my cousin—the one whose moped I've been using,' advised Ly.

'Aren't you worried that he might blow our cover?'

'Not at all. This is Vietnam, Ange. For one, I'm sure you've seen photos of the spiderweb of cables that wrap around Vietnamese cities. That mess isn't held together by people in smart uniforms and driving official-looking vehicles. My cousin won't stand out at all. He came with me on our drive-by yesterday to check out the situation. There's a pole right outside EZ Jobs. The unit is fully charged and is topped up with some solar cells on top. I went for the unit with a SIM card so that we didn't need to tap into any cables or Wi-Fi networks. It was expensive, as I didn't want to risk choosing a cheap and nasty unit,' explained Ly.

'This is impressive work, Judy. Well done. We'll obviously cover any costs. Let me know how the installation goes, please?'

'I have to go, Ange. My cousin is just about to head off. I'll be in touch.'

After she had finished with Judy Ly, and with nothing to do but wait, Ange walked back to the house to fix herself some more coffee and brunch. The butterflies in her stomach were fluttering wildly, and she hoped that some food might help calm the developing tornado. She was just finishing her toast when Edwards sent a WhatsApp message to Team Early Bird.

> *Kilroy has seen the package and is on his way home. The rest of the family won't leave school sport for a while. Let me know if he's appropriately infected by our virus. Over to you, Billy.*

That seemed like the perfect cue to head over to the guesthouse nerve centre and wait it out.

It was almost a case of a watched screen never delivers. Ange's phone eventually provided a much-awaited distraction. 'Hi, Brian. What's up?' she asked.

'Our photo album has put the willies up Kilroy. He's just organised to meet Linh at 1:30 p.m. over at The Pulse.'

'That's terrific news, Brian,' replied Ange. She was about to mention Judy Ly when a loud yelp came from Billy's direction.

'It's working. The first packet of data off Kilroy's computer just rolled into the server,' yelled Billy.

'I guess you heard that, Brian. Well done. Let's see what drops when Kilroy visits Linh this afternoon. Will you be still watching The Pulse when we have our 3 p.m. meeting?'

'Sure will. My microphone works perfectly, as I've heard Linh speaking on his phone about his cattle. He is quite obsessed. Speak later, Ange,' replied Edwards, before dropping off the call.

Ange turned to Billy. 'Well done, Billy. Does the data make any sense?'

'Not yet. It's like a slowly dripping tap. It will take a while to fill up the bucket.'

'Understood, Billy. Stop hassling you. Now that we know when Kilroy is visiting The Pulse, keep us posted if our stars align and we infect Linh.'

As she walked back to the house, Ange looked longingly across at the ocean. It could be quite some time before she could scratch that itch again. The waiting game was never her strong suit, so she busied herself around the house. Her phone started pinging around midday with incoming Instagram posts tagging Buddy, aka Rusty Bell. She had set up an alert whenever Rusty made it to the small screen, more to keep track of Kerrie than anything else. Kerrie had commandeered Buddy as the face of an upcoming longboard surfing carnival. It was no wonder Kerrie was such a success. She had an uncanny sense of the zeitgeist, and dogs were still all the rage, an obsession that had persisted long after the initial Covid pet explosion. Buddy looked so adorable.

She heard a yell of success from the guesthouse before she received the message. While Ange might be a surfer out of water, Billy was in his element.

We've got both fish on the hook. Just received some data from Linh's computer.

Edwards sent Ange an audio file just before 2 p.m. His brief accompanying message was intriguing.

Just recorded this conversation. It will do your head in, Ange.

She sat on her balcony, put her phone on speaker, and started replaying the recording Edwards had sent. The early chatter was not particularly noteworthy, but it allowed Ange to make out the slightly accented Linh. She heard a knock and then a door open and close.

[Kilroy in angry voice] Why on earth did you murder Julia Bennet?

[Linh] What are you talking about?

[Kilroy] Someone just sent me some photos. There's a couple of me with Julia, another of you and me together. It also included a truly horrific photo of Julia's dead body.

[Linh, in a strident voice] I can assure you that I had nothing to do with that. What was the photo of you and me together?

[Kilroy] I'll show you. I hope you haven't got a weak stomach.

[Long Pause]

[Linh] That is awful.

[Kilroy] And here's the photo of you and me together.

[Linh] I don't remember that photo being taken. It could be CGI. I think someone is trying to blackmail you, Greg.

[Kilroy] But why involve you?

[Linh] It must be about the court case with the Green River Council. I'll bet it's that mayor.

[Kilroy] I warned you about suing the council. That was a stupid idea.

[Linh] That's easy for you to say. You didn't lose seven million dollars over that disaster in Clearwater. I hold you partly responsible for that loss, by the way. Anyway, why would I want your former lover killed? She was a key witness in my case.

[Kilroy] I'm not responsible for your financial woes. I only met Julia after you sent me to Clearwater to do your dirty work and get that approval out of her.

[Linh] I suspect that you're about to learn what those images are all about, Greg. Hopefully, it's just about money, but don't come running to me. That Clearwater screwup has cleaned me out. Now, I've got to go. Do you want to visit one of the girls?

[Kilroy] I'm too stressed for any of that.

[Linh] Is that all? I'm busy today, Greg. Let me know if you find out who's behind your blackmail.

[Door opening and closing]

[Linh] Idiot.

The recording was dynamite but, as Edwards had predicted, it was totally screwing with her head. If neither Linh nor Kilroy had murdered Julia Bennet, then who had? Perhaps it really was a break-and-enter gone wrong—unlucky for Bennet but useful for Ange's investigation. Her head was still spinning when their 3 p.m. meeting came around.

The meeting of Team Early Bird was a tour de force of teamwork and collaboration. Billy let the team know about their success in accessing both of Kilroy's and Linh's computers. 'Remember, the clock is ticking. We only have a week before Wormraider will erase itself. That was a brilliant idea of yours, Brian—also beautifully executed.'

'Thanks,' replied Edwards. 'I also left a little extra something on Kilroy's car. I figured it wouldn't hurt to track his whereabouts without relying on phone pings. With the stress he's now under, he might turn off his phone and crawl under a doona.'

'You've been watching him for some time, Brian. What's your assessment of Kilroy?' asked Ange.

'I've been listening to his drivel for several days now. He's obsessed with sex and politics—and his family to a lesser degree. Going by the conversation I sent you, he's spooked. But I don't think he had anything to do with Bennet's murder—or Linh, for that matter.'

Ange saw that Billy and Bree were staring at her with confused expressions on their faces. She replayed the conversation between Kilroy and Linh for their benefit.

Billy was the first to comment. 'I agree with Brian. We caught a lucky break, boss. I wasn't sure Linh would insert a USB stick in his computer like that. He's obviously quite tech savvy with all his Dark Web activities. I was more confident about Kilroy.'

'I'm glad Kilroy didn't avail himself of Linh's offer. That would have made me puke,' said Bree with a look of disgust.

'OK. We need to forget about Julia Bennet and focus our attention on whatever Harry Linh is up to. Brian, can you monitor Kilroy's movements and let us know if he does anything useful—or stupid?' asked Ange.

'How Kilroy hasn't joined the dots with Linh and the company he enjoys at The Pulse beggars belief. I guess turning a blind eye might be the trait of a successful politician,' observed Edwards.

Judy Ly joined the conversation. 'Speaking of which, I've got eyes on Madam Linh in Hanoi. I'll send a link now to the cloud drive I've set up to receive the video feed. Let me know if you think it's clear enough.' She paused for a minute. 'You should have it now.'

The team paused as anyone who was interested logged in. Billy spoke first. 'That's excellent, Judy. I can clearly see the faces of everyone coming out of the office. I just fast-forwarded through to our current time. That's a lot of people.'

'I know. We've only had the system live for six hours, and I've counted thirteen visits.'

'Andy, do you have any thoughts about your plan of attack once we know when any women are due to arrive—if they arrive?' said Ange. The conversation between Kilroy and Linh had rattled her convictions. She wasn't confident about anything anymore.

'We haven't gotten all that far. We've commandeered as much kit as we can get our hands on, and Matt also borrowed a long-range drone, supposedly to undertake some extra training during his week off. I've scoped out the International Terminal in Brisbane. If we assume that the women will be taken to a vehicle of some sort, most likely a van based on what we know, then all arriving passengers are funnelled down a long covered walkway that links the arrivals hall with the car park. We plan to get eyes on that walkway as soon as we can. If you thought Madam Linh's office in Hanoi is busy, imagine how many people file down that walkway every day.'

Ange turned the attention to the third wheel in the room. 'Bree, how are you going with your work on the Dark Web?'

'Unlike everyone else, I've gotten absolutely nowhere, other than to reaffirm my belief that there are a lot of sick puppies out there. It's frustrating. Sorry. I'll keep watching Linh's crypto wallet. This might help identify the number of women to expect, but there's no certainty he will have pre-sold his entire inventory.'

'Don't be sorry. It's all preparation. Your work is going to be crucial if we are to bring all this together.'

'What are your thoughts on that, boss? While we've been busy bringing home the bacon, I hope you've given this some thought in your spare time,' questioned Billy with a smile on his face.

'Yes,' added Edwards. 'I've been curious about your role on the team, Ange.'

'Goalkeeper,' offered Bree.

Ange was pleased to see that, despite the obvious tension and many obstacles in front of them, her team remained upbeat and kept their sense of humour. 'Funny, guys. My plan clings tenuously to Wormraider and getting access to Linh's website. If Bree gains access, she can provide us with some descriptions that might help narrow down who's coming through arrivals.'

'Won't we have pictures of the women?' asked Barnett.

Seeing as this was her patch, Bree jumped in to answer that question. 'The only time that I've accessed the site, I really only got to the front screen. All the women were shown as an avatar, a computer-generated likeness. If our theory holds and Linh administers the site, then surely there's a photo gallery sitting behind each avatar. His passwords should give us access to stuff like that.'

'Even if we can't get any photos, we know that the women are all aged in their mid-to-late teens, perhaps early twenties,' added Ly.

Ange thought back to where this had all started. 'Judy, remember when we interviewed Cua Kwm? She told us she was accompanied by an older woman who posed as her aunty, and she was led to a van where she sat watching videos until some other women joined.'

'That's my recollection, Ange,' replied Ly.

'And we also know that the other women were from Cambodia and Thailand. Bree, when you have a spare minute, can you investigate flights from Hanoi to Brisbane for next week? I guess there might be a lot of options. You should be able to narrow things down once we have a departure date and time out of Hanoi.'

Matt Wilkes joined in the fun, stating the obvious. 'There's a lot of ifs and mights in this conversation.'

'I know, but we've only just started. Have faith. If we can identify the actual women as they land and find out where they are being held, then we can cross-reference the video feeds from Hanoi, arrivals at the airport, and any screenshots that we harvest from Linh's computer—and bingo, case closed. Back yourself, guys. I do,' stated Ange, with more conviction than she genuinely felt.

'What do we do if your plan to access Linh's website doesn't work out?' asked Matt Wilkes.

'We'll need to reassess. The safety of the young women needs to take precedence, even if that comes at the expense of our case against Harry Linh. OK, guys. From now on, anyone can call a meeting at short notice. So, if there's nothing else, we all have work to do.'

Chapter 45

Sick Puppies

The case broke on Sunday night, although nobody knew it had until Monday morning once the crucial data had trickled into Billy's server. It was Bree who called a team meeting for midday.

Ange went over to the guesthouse and could sense the excitement in the air. She waited patiently until everyone had joined the meeting. 'Over to you, Bree.'

'Linh accessed his website last night. It's got a new name—BellBird. Which seems appropriate,' started Bree. 'He must have left the Shama website up as a strawman.'

'Why is BellBird an appropriate name?' asked Edwards.

Ange provided the answer to that question. 'Bellbirds make a beautiful sound, but they have a dark side and are brutal towards any other birds in their territory. Continue, Bree.'

'We have his password, but I haven't accessed the site. It would be best to do that when Linh isn't online himself. However, Wormraider has been feeding us some images and we think we've identified the women who'll be shipped to Australia.'

'Hold on, Bree. Something just occurred to me. Aren't you worried that Linh might detect your IP address? Like you think happened when you gained access to Shama the first time around?' asked Ange.

'Boss. Great question,' said Billy with a look of respect. 'I'm impressed. Bree will spoof Linh's IP address. Remember, Wormraider sends us these details with every packet of information.'

'Is there no end to your jargon, Billy? However, in your lexicon of IT lingo, spoof is a term that I can work out myself. You impersonate his IP credentials.

Correct?'

'Exactly. Very good,' said Billy, still smiling. 'Moving on, how about I share the images that we've collected so far?'

After a momentary pause, the face of a stunning young girl came onto everyone's screen. Billy paused for a moment before slowly flicking through five more similarly striking images. The reality of what Linh and company had in store for those beautiful young girls was equally stunning. Two of those had sold banners running diagonally across their picture.

Brian Edwards verbalised what was on everyone's mind. 'That brings home a dose of reality. That's horrific. They look so young and innocent.'

Bree wasn't finished with her news. 'That's not all. Linh has been spruiking his wares in a chat room called Puppies for Sale. How sick is that?' Bree paused over her rhetorical question before continuing. 'I think I have a handle on how the system works. The BellBird site operates like a timed online auction, just like eBay or a real estate auction. People first register their interest in a property, in this case a young woman, before being granted access to the equivalent of a data room containing a portfolio on each woman. I presume Linh vets each purchaser before granting access and there might be another level of security before any bids can be placed. Some can window-shop, but only verified buyers can place bids. There's even a Buy Now option, which must be the two transactions that we've already seen. But here's the kicker. Linh has just announced that the auction will end next Sunday night.'

'Do we know who the buyers are?' asked Ange.

'Not yet, but Linh must know them. He's granted access to a bunch of bidders, and more are coming in. I'm not sure I'll be able to assemble a complete list of bidders, given the way Wormraider cuts and dices snippets of information. It's too early to tell. We'll need unfettered access to his computer to be sure of all that.'

'OK. Our search warrant covers his premises in Sydney. I'll need to get the boss cracking on an additional warrant to cover any property they take the women to. That might be tricky.'

'Wouldn't we pick up the van the moment it leaves the airport?' asked Will Fox, the third and most reserved of the three federal officers.

'We'll need time to coordinate our activities. Plus, there might be another group of women being held.'

'We're not seeing that, boss—at least not at this point,' suggested Billy.

Brian Edwards showed his experience yet again. 'If we pick them up at the airport, we also risk that Linh will clean up his tracks. He seems clever. I'd be surprised if he hadn't planned for that contingency. The riskiest part of his operation must surely be getting the women through customs and immigration. I'm sure that he'll be ready to distance himself at a moment's notice.'

'I agree with Brian,' stated Ange forcibly. 'Sure, it's a moderate risk for those women. But if we don't do this properly, it's likely that we'll never shut down Linh's operation. Then we ultimately put even more women at risk. Bree, have you been able to confirm when the women might be coming into the country?'

'Unfortunately, I really only know when the auction will end. I'll keep looking, of course,' answered Bree.

Judy Ly spoke up. 'When Sammy and I went to visit Madam Linh here in Hanoi, she definitely mentioned Wednesday.'

'OK, then. Until we hear anything to the contrary, let's work towards Wednesday. It's the best, in fact, the only lead we have on a date, so we need everything in place by then. That only leaves us the rest of today and tomorrow. Bree, can you distribute the images of those young women to the team? Billy, now that we have some images to work off, can you run the Hanoi video feed through your super-duper image-recognition software? Will it work in this situation? What is that software package called?'

'Should do. That will need to run in the background and certainly won't be real time. It's called Pixelate. You've certainly made excellent use of it, boss,' replied Billy, referring to the pivotal role that Pixelate played in closing in on the GlitterStrip narcotics ring based on the Gold Coast.

'Excellent. I agree. Pixelate has been a godsend to us. Bree, once you gain access to the BellBird site, screenshot as much information as possible about each woman and shoot that around as well. Also, try to confirm if Wednesday is the day.'

'OK, Ange. I'll coordinate with Billy to pick a time when Linh isn't online and get all that done,' replied Bree.

'Brian. I think it's time to leave Greg Kilroy to his own devices. You have his phone and car under surveillance. Unless Kilroy does something unusual, focus your attention on Linh and The Pulse.'

'Agree, Ange. Got it. I'll also send around updates on Linh's comings and goings from The Pulse. I don't see any need to follow him around now that we have such strong digital surveillance,' replied Edwards.

Ange turned her last point of focus towards Team Brisbane. 'Andy, you guys probably have the most to do in the next thirty-six hours. Will you be ready?'

'No problem, Ange. We rarely get more than twenty-four hours' notice.'

'What do you want me to do, Ange?' asked Judy Ly, evidently feeling left out.

'You obviously need to stay in Hanoi in case we run into problems with the video feed. Other than that, in between our meetings, enjoy Hanoi and being with your cousins,' replied Ange. 'I'll get onto Sally Anders and see what we can arrange warrant wise. It might be tricky given that we don't know where the women will be taken once they leave the airport. Let's reconvene tomorrow at our usual time of 9 a.m. Brilliant work, guys. We're on the cusp of something big. I can feel it.'

Just to make sure overconfidence didn't spoil the party, Billy burst everyone's bubble. 'We thought that last time, boss. Remember?'

'You're no fun, Billy,' answered Ange in her most sarcastic tone of voice, before turning upbeat. 'Speak tomorrow if not before.'

Ange immediately rang Sally Anders to update her on the recent developments and their plan of action. 'My sense is that we need to synchronise our raids on Linh's offices and wherever the trafficked women are being held. It needs to be a complete surprise. Other than the women themselves, any hard evidence against Linh will likely evaporate if he gets wind of what we're up to. Plus, it would be good to get a handle on the other side of this sick marketplace. Linh's operation would be worth nothing without willing buyers. We need to nab them and send a strong and clear message to their kind.'

'Our warrant already covers The Pulse, but it's the location where the women are being held that's more difficult, given that we don't know where that is. I can't imagine any magistrate will be happy letting us go around raiding properties willy-nilly. You do realise that the situation you've described bears an uncanny resemblance to what happened just a few months ago?' posed Anders.

'I know. Worrying that we might screw things up is making me feel sick. I'm sure that we won't get another chance. How about you put a time limit on the warrant and nail down the wording on what we can and can't do? A week should do it. Do you think that might work?' asked a pensive Ange.

'Maybe. Depends on how good your brief is,' replied Anders.

'If we can't get a suitable search warrant, then the women need to be our priority, and we'll have to pick them up at the airport and let Linh cover his tracks.'

'I hear you, Ange. I'll do my best. It might be best to use the same magistrate. She seems like someone who might join our crusade. Get me that brief as soon as you can.'

Ange jumped to the task the moment that she'd ended her conversation with her boss. It took her until mid-afternoon to have properly set out her case and why they needed such broad powers. As she made her last pass of the document before dispatching it to Sally Anders in an email, she figured that the images of those beautiful and innocent-looking young women, being auctioned off like animals, should do the trick. The two with sold banners draped across their faces were confronting. She hoped so.

Billy rang later that evening with some surprising news. 'Boss, Harry Linh is one driven man. He's just organised another shipment of PEDs and some other weird stuff from China. What should we do about it?'

Ange thought this over for a moment. 'Nothing. Just keep collecting the data for future reference. It would be useful if we learned how he's getting the drugs into the country, but if we nab him for people trafficking, his drug business will also end. Those young women need to be our priority, and we don't need to be distracted by any fresh enquiry fronts.'

'Got it, boss,' replied Billy quickly. 'Agree. However, it would be interesting to know which line of business came first. Where there's smoke, there's fire—as you keep reminding me.'

Chapter 46

Flight Risks

With the pressure piling on, Team Early Bird went into overdrive. Bree accessed the BellBird site for the first time on Monday evening and found her way into Linh's inner sanctum. She screenshotted six of the sickest CVs imaginable and sent them around. The way the women were portrayed brought an instant response and seemed to firm up everyone's resolve to bring this gruesome marketplace to a halt.

Billy set up a feed of the video taken in Hanoi and fed it through Pixelate. He estimated the system lag to be no more than two hours, starting at zero in the morning and lengthening during the day as more and more faces needed analysing. He figured the software would catch up each night as the streets cleared. Naturally, Billy took advantage of the opportunity and asked for another more powerful computer. Ange just rolled her eyes and suggested that no computer would be fast enough for ambition as big as his.

The guys in Brisbane had the video feed from the Brisbane airport live by 9 a.m. Tuesday. This was an impressive feat within such a busy twenty-four-hour location as an international airport. Andy Barnett shared a link to the video feed through the WhatsApp group. The vision was crystal clear. Ange had expected nothing less from those guys.

The comings and goings of The Pulse were nothing startling. Kilroy was nowhere to be seen, and Linh made a single visit early Monday evening.

Ange waited pensively for word from Sally Anders regarding the warrant. She knew not to ring and bother her boss, but that waiting game proved excruciating. In the end, all Ange received was a rather innocuous text message.

Paperwork in hand. You're good to go, Ange. Break a leg.

All hell broke loose just as Ange was thinking about what to eat for dinner. Billy called her directly. 'Boss, we've just hit pay dirt. I picked up three of the women walking out of EZ Jobs. You'd better set up an urgent team meeting.'

Ange did as Billy had requested, and the team was online within fifteen minutes. Ange opened proceedings. 'Billy, tell us what you've got.'

'OK. We picked up three of the women that Bree harvested from the BellBird site coming out of EZ Jobs at 2:47 p.m. Let me play the video for you. It's only a minute long.'

Within seconds, everyone's screen was transported to the bustling streets of Hanoi. Six women emerged from the front door of EZ Jobs, appearing as three sets of pairs, each containing a younger woman and an older woman. The three younger women all pulled new-looking carry-on luggage. The suitcases being pulled by the older woman looked as if they'd been around the world a few times. All six women filed into a waiting van and drove away.

Bree chimed in once the video was complete. 'That looks to me like a tour group about to go on a trip. Seeing as they only have carry-on and wouldn't need to deal with checked baggage, I analysed flights leaving in the 6 to 7 p.m. bracket. It would make sense that they wouldn't want to loiter around the airport needlessly. There are quite a few flights leaving that evening that have connections to Brisbane, but the most efficient by far is the 6:30 flight through Singapore. It offers an excellent connection, and Singapore is one of the busiest airports in the world. Nobody would bat an eyelid, and the group would blend in easily.'

'That's the same flight I've booked for next Sunday,' added Judy Ly. 'It arrives in Brisbane from Singapore mid-morning by memory. None of the other flight options were half as good. There are a bunch of flights through China, but I guess they might be like me when assessing those options. There's far too much surveillance around Chinese airports for my liking, particularly if you're hoping to run under the radar.'

'It's 10:20 a.m. to be exact. Actually, if we assume that those women went straight to the airport, then based on what I'm seeing with my searches, 10:20 a.m. is the earliest that they could arrive in Brisbane,' added Bree.

'OK. This is good work, and I support that logic, Bree. We need to assume that this is happening tomorrow, most likely mid-to-late morning. Bree, that's only three women. Can you check if any flights from Thailand and Cambodia might connect with the Singapore-to-Brisbane leg? I guess it doesn't change anything, but it would be good to know what type of transport they might be using. Andy, will you guys be ready?'

'Absolutely. We'll do a second run over our game plan this evening, but we've got this covered, Ange,' replied Barnett, the confidence ringing in his voice of some comfort.

'Ange, I've just checked those flights. There are tons of options. There's a Manila-to-Singapore flight that almost matches up perfectly with the flight from Hanoi. The Phnom Penh flight isn't perfect, but it's workable.'

'OK. So, we could have three to six women inbound mid-morning. Andy, how are you going to track the ground transport?'

'I hope to install a GPS tracker if I get half a chance. Failing that, all three of us will be driving our own cars so that we can tag team the vehicle. We'll use encrypted UHF radios in case we drop out of mobile phone service. If we feel that the tail is getting uncomfortable, then we have our long-range drone that we'll get in the air.'

'Good stuff. Let's reconvene at 7 a.m. and check if there's been any developments overnight. Everyone try to get a decent night's sleep. The next few days will hopefully be very busy rescuing women and bringing down bad guys.'

Ange was up early the next morning and was already on her third coffee by the time their 7 a.m. meeting had rolled around. It was Billy and Bree who brought home the importance of the day ahead. 'The auction stepped up a notch last night. We have Linh logging into BellBird and removing the Buy Now options. It will be hard for him to claim innocent bystander status after that move.'

'How solid is all that?' asked Ange.

Brian Edwards chipped in. 'I can confirm that Linh arrived at 8:10 p.m. and left at 9:25 p.m.'

'The logs and images off Linh's computer started at 8:32 and he logged off at 8:56. That lines up with Brian's account of Linh's movements,' replied Billy.

'I presume you have evidence of Linh's movements, Brian,' probed Ange.

'A full sequence of date-and-time-stamped photos covering entry and exit from the side door at The Pulse. Call me an optimist, but I doubt Linh will wriggle away this time.'

'Let's not get ahead of ourselves. We don't have him in custody yet. Any competent lawyer will give him a fighting chance if we can't produce the actual women,' replied Ange, hosing down any exuberance that might bring about a mistake. 'Is the auction still scheduled to end Sunday, Bree?'

'No change. Midnight on Sunday,' was her immediate answer.

'That should give us plenty of time before any of the women get moved again. So, Team Brisbane. How are things looking in sunny Queensland?'

Much to Ange's relief, Andy was not falling into anything that even remotely resembled exuberance or overconfidence. 'We're good to go. It's going to be a tricky day, Ange. We need a lot of things to go our way. Billy, can you run our video feed through your software, maybe starting at 10 a.m.? We'll be on the ground watching, but we could always misread a face.'

'Will do. I already have it configured for the six women in question, but I'll just need to change the source of the video feed from Hanoi to Brisbane. I'll test it after we finish this meeting.'

'Excellent. I must get a lesson from you on how to use that piece of software sometime,' replied Barnett.

'I have every faith in you guys, Andy. I'll stay with Billy and Bree. Brian, you stick on The Pulse. Which reminds me, what has Kilroy been up to?'

'Model father and husband. Unless he's discovered my tracker and slipped out the back door, I can't see that he's been anywhere but home and his electoral office,' replied Brian.

'It might look that way in the real world, Brian, but our boy has been spending some *quality* time with his favourite porn sites. He has quite the collection. The man is a sex machine, especially when considering what's been going on in his life,' commented Billy.

'Well, off the back of that inspiring note—it's action stations. Good luck, Team Brisbane. It's pretty much over to you guys,' concluded Ange.

'No pressure, huh?' joked Barnett before turning serious. 'Whatever happens, Team Brisbane will do its very best.'

Chapter 47

Jocks Rule

Ange couldn't sit still. She paced nervously around the property, checking in with the guesthouse-cum-nerve-centre at increasingly regular intervals. Even though her team was well prepared, the dark shadow of the unexpected was ever present. That nemesis had spoiled far too many of Ange's best-laid plans. Naturally, atop her list of unforeseen misadventures was being shot—surely nothing would ever top that disaster. Ange could almost smell an unexpected bogeyman lurking just around the corner.

The fate of six women, and countless others to come, rested on the outcome of the next few days, days that would also be crucial for Ange's career. That burden, however, was hers to bear alone. Whenever she looked in on Billy and Bree, she took strength from their youthful energy and exuberance. It was obvious that they both loved their careers. Ange knew that she would sacrifice hers in a heartbeat in order to protect theirs.

Billy and Bree had made fantastic progress, and Linh seemed oblivious to their surveillance. Billy was quite excited by what they had found overnight. 'Boss, we caught a lucky break. Linh made the mistake of making some changes to a Word document saved on his computer. We only got one screenshot, but it looked pretty interesting.'

'It looks like a master list of registered bidders to me. It's mostly just usernames and dates, but some entries include additional information. There's even the odd phone number. It must be important, as the file was password-protected.' explained Bree.

'We have all that information from the key logs. It won't be hard to open the document when we have access to his computer,' added Billy.

'Can't you access it from here?' asked Ange.

'No, unfortunately. Wormraider only drip-feeds us with information. It's one-way traffic,' clarified Billy.

'What do you think the dates are all about?' probed Ange.

Bree answered with a grim-faced expression. 'My best explanation is the date that the bidder was registered. The list seems to be in chronological order. Before you ask, the earliest date is over four years ago.'

'That means hundreds of women have been purchased by these scumbags.'

'Sick, isn't it?' suggested Bree in a question that needed no answer.

'Billy, I've been thinking about these bidders. Let's assume that we save the women and get our hands on Linh before he can alert anyone. What do you think about adding a phishing cookie to each of the avatars? We know that they need to click on an avatar and then enter their credentials before they can access each woman's portfolio. Would that work over the Dark Web?'

'I can't see why not. The architecture of the site looks quite generic,' replied Billy, looking up and to the right, a sure sign that his brain was on high alert. 'In fact, I presume the Dark Web is awash with phishing scams. It would need to be a quick in and out phish—like a cookie of the type used by most normal websites. I reckon we could get a list of IP addresses at the very least, perhaps even an email address or two stored in a system file. Let's get through today and I'll do some work on that idea. We have until Sunday night to execute. I'll need access to his computer so I can modify the BellBird website. I love that idea, Bree.'

She left them debating the pros and cons of Bree's idea, proposing to come back later and in time to watch the Brisbane show unfold. As a manager of sorts, it was immensely rewarding to see her junior colleagues bouncing off each other as they charged ahead.

The fun didn't start until 10:50 a.m., when Andy Barnett rang Ange.

'Go ahead, Andy, I've got you on speaker.'

'I think the first of those women is coming our way. Can you guys verify? It's the one in the red shirt.'

Billy took a snapshot of the woman in question before flipping through the six photos from earlier. 'Correct, Andy. It's one of the women from Hanoi.'

'Roger that,' replied Barnett sharply, before ending the call.

'I'll reset Pixelate to start analysing from now on so that we don't have as much lag. We should have picked up that woman before Andy did,' stated Billy distractedly, as if he might have been talking to himself. This proved a master stroke, as Pixelate identified a second woman within minutes and while Andy's attention was focussed on the first target.

Ange rang Barnett. 'Andy, a second target has just arrived. She's wearing a white sweater.'

'Got it. We had four potential vans under surveillance. It looks like we've identified the right one. It's parked out of the way in a far corner of the car park. We'll have to be careful. I can't see how we can get a GPS tracker installed. Can you message me about any new arrivals? I won't be able to talk from now on.'

'Roger that,' replied Ange, in the swing of things and sticking with the lingo of covert operatives.

Over the next half-odd hour, three of the four remaining women came down the walkway. Ange texted the details of each fresh arrival to Barnett. After waiting some twenty minutes, Barnett rang Ange. She put the call on speaker.

'I'm in a place where I can talk. We have five women in the van. There should be one more if your intel is correct. Have we missed something?' asked Barnett.

Billy answered. 'Not a chance, Andy. As well as Pixelate, all three of us have been poring over the video feed. Maybe something has happened in Immigration?'

'OK. Let's sit tight. It's been the same each time. As each of the targets is dropped off, the chaperone leaves and catches a taxi. Unfortunately, we don't have enough eyes on-site to follow the chaperones off the airport.'

'That's the same MO that Cua Kwm explained when we interviewed her,' replied Ange. She was about to elaborate when Billy interrupted.

'The last woman has just arrived. She's heading your way now.'

'OK. We'll switch to UHF radio from here on, so we'll be off the air with you guys. We'll report in when we can. Wish us luck. We're doing OK so far,' said an upbeat Andy Barnett before signing off.

This plunged Ange into that horrible state of waiting but not knowing. Billy and Bree started nattering on about their phishing plan, leaving Ange to wander off and seek some comfort from Buddy.

It wasn't until well after 2 p.m. that Ange received a call from Barnett. She raced over to the guesthouse with the phone pressed against her ear, immediately placing the call on speaker as she walked through the door.

'We've got them. They're holed up on a property near Aratula. We've had the drone up. I'll send you some pictures when I get a chance,' explained Barnett.

Billy quickly pulled up a map which showed that Aratula was just east of Cunninghams Gap, a pass over the Great Dividing Range on the way to Warwick.

'Aratula is a lot closer to Brisbane than Hillburn. That was lucky for you guys,' observed Ange.

'The road they're on is a dead end, so only one way in and out. The bad news is that it's a dirt road and highly exposed. There's no way we could approach the property by vehicle without being spotted.'

'What are you planning to do now?' asked Ange, suddenly realising that she should have thought about this earlier.

'We'll take turns to keep eyes on the property. Matt has identified a location with a decent view of the place. I've called in Sam Jessop, the guy who helped us in Hillburn. He's bringing in some additional kit. We need to settle a plan on how to raid the property. Sam won't be here until early evening. Assuming we're successful, an extraction team will be needed to process the women and whoever else we pick up. I think it's time we come clean with our department. Ange, we've got our hands full here. Do you think your boss could sort that out?'

'If she can't, then I'll do it. That only seems fair,' replied Ange, not relishing that task if it fell her way.

'Thanks. Can we schedule a meeting at, say, 7:30 p.m.?' said Barnett.

'Well done, guys. Let's reconvene then. I'll send around a meeting invitation.'

Ange turned to face her two junior colleagues and the loud cheer that ensued even caught the attention of Buddy, who raced over to the guesthouse to join in the fun. It was an exhilarating moment. The three officers and one excited dog all sensed that they were on the cusp of success.

The drone image that arrived as an attachment to the Team Early Bird WhatsApp group was spectacularly clear. The configuration of the property was like Hillburn. A farmhouse and machinery shed formed a courtyard of sorts. A small relocatable building sat off to one side, presumably the jail in which the women were being held captive. The complex was shielded from the dusty dirt road by a copse of eucalypt trees, and a sparsely wooded hill ran up behind the property.

It seemed a highly exposed location which offered poor cover for the extraction team. Ange sent the image to Sally Anders, asking that she call back. Ange didn't need to wait long for that call.

'What am I looking at here, Ange?'

'For once, our day went perfectly, boss. All six women have been taken to the property shown in the image. It's near Aratula, just east of the Great Dividing Range on the road to Warwick. We're planning a meeting at 7:30 this evening. It would be good if you could attend.'

'Definitely. Do you have a plan, Ange?'

'Not yet—other than the benefits of extracting the women at the exact same time as we take down Linh. Billy and Bree are hatching a plan to hoover up the sickos who buy these women. It relies on keeping the auction going for as long as possible. We're hoping to take down both the buyer and the seller side of this gruesome marketplace.'

'What auction?' asked Anders.

Ange realised that a lot had happened since she'd last updated her boss, so she took the next ten minutes to bring her up to speed, answering questions as Anders probed their progress. Ange never ceased to be impressed by how quickly and incisively Sally Anders could cut to the core of any situation. 'You'll need an extraction team. Any thoughts?'

'Funny you should mention that, boss. Your name came up when Andy Barnett suggested that it was time to come clean with his department. I know that you've had reservations, but could you make that call? Perhaps ask them to supply the extraction team as well?' asked Ange, hoping like heck that her boss didn't sidestep her request.

'That will be my pleasure. I think it's time to fill them in on some facts of life. As you know, I kept a dossier on their piss-weak behaviour during the Ndrangheta matter. Leave that with me.'

Ange was relieved to see her boss step so readily up to the plate. 'Thanks, boss. I'll send you a meeting invitation for 7:30 p.m.'

'Well done, Detective. I'm impressed,' added Anders.

'I've done nothing. It's been the others who made all the breakthroughs,' replied Ange without hesitation.

'Sure,' commented Anders. 'That's what a good manager does, Ange. See you online at 7:30 p.m.' This was, as Ange mused, the pot calling the kettle black.

When that time arrived, Ange, Billy, and Bree were joined by Brian Edwards from his lookout opposite The Pulse. The team in Aratula was split in two. Andy Barnett, Matt Wilkes, and Sam Jessop were together in a hotel room, while Will Fox joined in voice-only mode. Barnett explained the situation. 'It's Will's turn to take watch at our hillside vigil. He's enjoying the wildlife.' The only comment from Fox was a thumbs-up emoji.

Sally Anders logged in to the meeting from a conference room surrounded by four serious-looking men. Ange recognised the room as being in Major Crimes' head office. Evidently, Anders saw the look of horror that spread across Ange's face. 'Don't panic, Ange. I saved the arses of these four guys from an angry politician a few years back. They know how the system works. We can trust them. I figured that we would need a team in Sydney to deal with Linh, so I pulled one together. I've briefed them as best I could.'

'You're the boss, boss,' replied Ange, the concern on her face dissipating. 'Do we all agree that the best course of action is to take down both locations simultaneously?' She waited through the murmurings of assent before continuing. 'Brian, you've been watching Linh for some time now. Is there a pattern to his movements?'

Edwards showed no hesitation in his answer. 'He's been like clockwork since the auction process started. He turns up each evening at around 7 p.m. and leaves sometime around 9 p.m.'

Billy chimed in to confirm the observation that Edwards had made on the ground. 'He's been online each night this week during the time slot that Brian mentioned. We're certain that Linh prefers to use the computer in his office rather than any mobile device.'

'I've glimpsed Linh through a window that fronts Hill Street several times. That's the side street, by the way,' added Edwards. 'I'm reasonably sure that his office is upstairs to the right of the side entry door. To be on the safe side, I've downloaded a copy of the plans that he lodged with council when he converted the building into a bar. I'll send the plans around now.'

'That works out well. We'd prefer to enter the Aratula property after dark. We'll be totally exposed once we leave the treeline,' explained Barnett.

'That reminds me, Brian. How many women do you think might be held captive at The Pulse? We will need to extract them once we have Linh in custody,' pressed Ange.

'I feel like there are three or four women there, but it's hard to tell from my vantage point with all the reflection off the windows,' replied Edwards.

'Leave that with us, Ange. I'll make arrangements to have them picked up. And don't worry, we won't be handing anyone over to Home Affairs until I have an ironclad assurance that the women will be processed under the victims of people trafficking legislation,' stated Sally Anders with conviction.

Ange then explained Billy and Bree's scheme to identify the buyers. 'Billy, you need to get to Sydney on the first plane tomorrow. It's important that you start work on Linh's computer as soon as his office is secured.'

The team debated the options for the next two hours. It was almost 10 p.m. before their plan of attack had been settled and Ange called a halt to the meeting.

Sleep, when it came, was fitful and restless. Poor Gus.

Chapter 48

Final Push

It was one of those days which presented multiple pathways. Regardless of Ange's ambitions, the outcome of the day ultimately sat in the lap of the gods. The only thing she knew for certain was that her team was first rate. Billy had caught the first flight to Sydney. Bree was staying put and eager to start her tracing duties. Ange rang Sally Anders first up to discuss something that had occurred to her during the early hours of the morning.

'Boss, we'll need a warrant to trace the IP addresses of any buyers we identify. What are your thoughts?'

'Given the terrible press our internet service providers have been copping of late, I don't see too much difficulty in getting that organised. How about I get us a general warrant that covers the main ISPs? I can extend the coverage down the track if needed.'

'Excellent. Billy should be arriving soon. Once he's unleashed his phishing cookies, we'll need to get cracking on tracing those buyers as soon as possible. There could be hundreds of people on that list. Can we get some more resources to help with that?'

'Let's get through today so we understand the full extent of the problem. We can review what resources we need at that point. But, yes, we will do what needs to be done, and I realise that we won't have a huge amount of time before the sickos cover their tracks.'

Judy Ly checked in, asking whether she should do anything to help. With her focus on what was about to happen in Sydney and Aratula, Ange had almost forgotten about Hanoi. 'Judy, I think you should stay in Hanoi for a while longer. It seems implausible that these women could have been shipped out of Vietnam without some help from local authorities. I know it's not really our problem, but it would be good to keep your camera live to see if any interesting figures reveal themselves. Are you OK with that?'

'Sure. I'm having a wonderful time in Hanoi. At the appropriate time, it would be helpful if Sally Anders could let my boss know about what I've been up to. They won't be thrilled that I sort of went behind their backs, but they'll also want to jump onboard if the prize is big enough. It would also be great if I could get some holiday leave back onto the books.'

'Will do. Judy. I think your role has been pivotal, so some credit is definitely due. However, let's not get ahead of ourselves. We have a big day ahead,' cautioned Ange.

As agreed at their meeting the previous evening, Brian Edwards had organised a fixed video feed from his lookout opposite The Pulse. During their rescue mission, Andy Barnett's crew would don body cameras, and he had set up a video feed that other team members could access. Ange had an interesting conversation with Bree about how they might set up for the day. 'Bree, now that Billy is in Sydney, it'll probably make sense to use his computer setup for the two video feeds. Do you agree?'

Bree looked at Ange as if she had lost her marbles. 'I don't have Billy's password.'

'You've already used his computer setup before. Why don't you just ask him for his password? He should have landed in Sydney by now,' pushed Ange.

'No way. I'm not going to ask Billy for his password. He wouldn't give it to me anyway,' replied Bree, before she pierced Ange with an insightful look. 'No wonder Billy is so worried about you and technology. I guess this happy-go-lucky attitude is standard for your generation.'

'My generation?' thought Ange, aghast that she would be considered some species of dinosaur. For goodness' sake, she wasn't even forty yet. Her parents had Ange and her siblings in their mid-twenties, and in her young mind, forty had been the cutoff point for being considered old. Now she was on the cusp of that milestone herself. How had that happened? An immediate recalibration was required. Fifty seemed a far more sensible cutoff point for the cliff edge that was middle age.

With that depressing thought, Ange fussed and fiddled through the day, checking her watch incessantly, waiting anxiously for darkness to fall and the games to begin. She checked in with the Aratula team just after lunch. 'How are things, Andy?'

'All good here, Ange. There are only two perps on-site. We haven't seen the women, but those two guys just delivered some trays of food to the donger. I'm not expecting this will be particularly challenging or difficult.'

'I'm pleased to hear that, Andy. Famous last words, huh? I'll check back in later this afternoon.'

'No need. We've got this, Ange. We'll be ready.'

After Brian Edwards gave her a similar response, Ange took Buddy for a long walk and, once she had calmed down, even managed a catnap. She took this as a sign of confidence in her team, rather than any middle-aged nana-nap.

Ange fixed an early dinner of tuna pesto pasta that she enjoyed with Bree on the balcony. They spoke little, as they were both silently contemplating the upcoming hours and their respective roles. Ange's primary responsibility was to fire the starter's gun, which might not seem significant, but the timing of her trigger finger would be crucial.

An eerie calmness descended on the guesthouse, arriving with those first tinges of a red sunset, caught on the bank of clouds that sat on the horizon and framed the ocean. Ange recalled a saying of the ages. "Red sky at night, sailors' delight. Red sky at dawn, sailors be warned." If this operation lasted until dawn, then that age old saying would undoubtedly hold true for detectives as well.

As Ange set up her laptop beside Bree's on the small kitchen table that had been Bree's work desk, she looked longingly over at Billy's array of screens. She had hoped that Bree had relented and secured access to Billy's multiverse. Bree caught Ange's look and simply rolled her eyes. With that issue settled for good, Ange logged herself into Andy Barnett's video feed, while Bree did the same for the feed coming in from The Pulse. As darkness fell, Ange couldn't resist the urge to send off a text to Sally Anders.

> *Are you guys all set?*

Not one to waste words, Anders sent a reply that was short and to the point.

On your mark, Ange.

Linh, or at least a man who looked like Linh through Bree's tiny laptop screen, entered the side door of The Pulse just after 7:40 p.m. A message to the team from Edwards confirmed this. As agreed at their meeting the previous evening, they hoped to catch Linh on his computer. Ange sat through the longest fifteen minutes of her life as she imagined Linh getting to his office, booting up his computer, and accessing the BellBird site. At 7:55 p.m., she fired her starter's gun with a short but loaded message.

Let's go, team.

She thought about adding 'good luck' or a fingers-crossed emoji, but didn't wish to tempt fate.

Now that the play was in motion, her eyes flitted between the two laptop screens. On Bree's laptop, she saw that two men had started an argument, just along the street from The Pulse near the side entrance. A large security guard came out of the door to break up the altercation. At precisely the same time, two more men moved sharply around the front corner of the building and slipped through the side door before it had closed. The timing and coordination of that move were breathtaking, giving Ange some comfort in the expertise of the Sydney team. The security guard never knew what hit him. Tasered, muzzled, and then handcuffed, he was trussed up on the ground in a second.

Ange turned her attention to her laptop and the action at Aratula. The jolting video coming from the rapidly moving body cams was hard to watch. Black fatigues and headgear made it impossible to tell who was who. Three of the team raided the farmhouse while the fourth checked out the vehicles and the machinery shed. Nobody wanted a repeat of Hillburn, where a lone straggler had crushed any element of surprise.

After a lot of shouting and demanding instructions, Ange saw two men wearing jeans and tee shirts being escorted out of the farmhouse at gunpoint. One of the team threw a set of keys towards another, who then walked across the courtyard and opened the door to the donger. Women immediately started shrieking, at which point the door was swiftly shut again. They should have thought this through. Who wouldn't start shrieking in such a situation? Andy Barnett rang Ange. 'Site secure, Ange. I guess you can hear the racket, even behind that closed door.'

'Stay put, Andy. You'll get a WhatsApp video call in a minute from someone who might help. Judy Ly, our woman in Hanoi, speaks Vietnamese. We know that at least three of those women speak that language.'

She immediately rang Judy Ly and was relieved when she picked up the call. Ange quickly explained the situation.

'Got it. Andy Barnett. I can see him in the Team Early Bird group. I'll hang up and call him straight away,' stated Ly.

Ange turned her focus back towards her laptop screen and watched Barnett take the call from Ly. He approached the donger and, with a nod of his head, waited while his colleague opened the door again. With his phone held out, Barnett stood in the open doorway. Ange could hear Ly speaking calmly but loudly in Vietnamese through Barnett's phone. The shrieking eventually abated, and the women appeared to listen to Ly. Ange was completely clueless about what was said, but all the women started crying. Despite not speaking their language, even Ange could appreciate the relief in their voices. Once the women had calmed down, they followed Barnett and his extended phone onto the gravel courtyard that sat between the three buildings.

Ange turned her focus back towards The Pulse just in time to see two men escorting Linh into a waiting car. As she saw an officer give Linh the ubiquitous hand-on-head move and usher him into the back seat, she knew it was all over. She and Bree embraced each other before turning back to the screen. They saw Billy scuttle in through the side door just as a nondescript white van pulled up, ready to extract any women being held captive upstairs. Ange switched her attention to Aratula, where she could see the extraction team spilling into the courtyard through Barnett's body cam.

There was still so much left to do. Now on autopilot, she progressively called Sally Anders, Barnett, and Edwards, letting them know that the operation was a success.

Despite the relieved expressions on the young women's faces, she'd thought she would feel better, perhaps even exhilarated. But the adrenaline that had been keeping her afloat for the past few days drained away, and suddenly she felt deflated, weary to her core.

'Well done, Bree. You've been amazing. I guess your job has only just begun,' explained Ange, tiredness obvious in her voice.

'Congratulations, Ange. Off you go. We've got this from here, at least for the rest of tonight.'

'Thanks. I need some sleep,' Ange replied flatly, before her sense of humour showed through. 'That's what people of my generation do after 9 p.m.'

Gus was watching TV when Ange walked into the house. 'We did it, Gus. I'm exhausted and can't believe how tired I am. I'm going to have a shower and crawl into bed.'

Gus came over and gave her a big hug. 'I'm so proud of you,' was all he needed to say.

Ange slept like a baby that night, the first time in ages. It was so, so nice.

Chapter 49

Mopping Up

The next few weeks were a blur of activity. For once, and in stark contrast to her last few investigations, the mop-up went as well as Ange could have hoped. Billy had moved himself and all his kit back to Sydney, and Bree was back to her hole-in-the-wall down at the Byron Bay station. Ange soon missed her junior colleagues, and the place seemed lonely without their energy and vitality.

Greg Kilroy resigned from politics 'to spend more time with his family'. Ange almost vomited when he fronted the press surrounded by his wife and children. She dearly wanted to out Kilroy for the slime he truly was, but Alan Campbell talked her down off that cliff.

'Ange, keep your information on Kilroy for another day. He's out of the picture for the time being, but he'll be back. Plenty of politicians before him have survived affairs and sex scandals. It would be good to have your dossier on Kilroy up our sleeves. Of course, if you feel that he was complicit with Linh in the trafficking of those young women, then that's a different matter,' counselled Campbell.

'Sadly,' conceded Ange, 'I can't see that Kilroy has done anything illegal. Immoral for sure, but not illegal. It kills me to leave him be.'

'I think that's a wise choice, Ange. Keep your powder dry. His true colours will shine through eventually, and then you can help make sure he gets his just deserts.'

'That's easy for you to say, Alan. I assume you're going to taste sweet revenge when you move on Daicos and his cattle rustling affairs. How is that any different?' countered Ange.

'It's not. Plus, I'm not planning to bring down Daicos,' replied Campbell offhandedly.

'What?' Ange exclaimed with genuine surprise. 'You mean all that work we did counts for nothing?'

'Not at all. If you'd asked me a month ago, I would have taken a very different stance on the matter. However, I've come to realise that his pub is a focal point where people meet, celebrate, commiserate, gossip, and all the other good stuff that comes from living in a small town. Plus, it adds some class and a bit of sparkle to the region. Edenview survives off the back of Daicos and his pub. I would be cutting off my nose to spite my face if that pub shut its doors. Anyway, I'm soon to be his landlord.'

'How does that happen?' asked Ange in mock surprise. She had learned never to be surprised by Campbell.

'Tony Daicos and I share a bank manager. I suggested to Daicos that he should sell his pub to me, rather than wait for his bank to call in his loan. It was a steal. I always wanted to own a pub,' replied Campbell wistfully. 'The kicker is that he borrowed heavily from Harry Linh for his equity stake. It explains why Daicos was so ready to help.'

'But why would Linh lend Daicos money in the first place?'

'He wouldn't say, no matter how hard I pressed him. I even threatened to spread the word that he's a cattle rustler. I'm sure you now realise how serious cattle rustling is around these parts. The only comment I got out of him was that Linh had no choice but to help him out, whatever that means. I guess Daicos has something on Harry Linh that would get both of them into even deeper water.'

'Perhaps Harry Linh or his cronies might come around one day to collect on the debt. I'd sure like to be a fly on the wall for that conversation. But hopefully that day will be a long way in the future. My boss, Sally Anders, has been taking the lead with charging Linh. I'd best tell her about Linh's relationship with Daicos. Sally is no shrinking violet.'

'Good. I presume dealing with Harry Linh will keep you busy. But be rest assured, Tony Daicos will cause you no further troubles,' stated Campbell with a steely tone in his voice.

'I don't like the sound of that. I hope any further revenge you're planning won't get either of us in hot water, Alan,' pressed Ange, her discussion with Terry Scott about how Campbell handled betrayal still ringing in her ears.

'You should know me better than that by now, Detective. Remember that idea we hatched about Billie's birthday bash? Well, seeing that I'm soon to be his landlord, Daicos has kindly offered to cater for that party as his personal gift to Billie. It's going to be huge—could cost north of seventy thousand. That was a very expensive cow that I lost.'

'That is very shrewd, Alan. It's a brilliant solution. I guess it's also tax-effective, huh? Free party and a cheap pub. You certainly didn't become a cattle baron by luck,' said Ange, admiring Campbell's pragmatism. 'But didn't you lose eight cows and a few calves?'

'I got all but one back. Thanks to the information your colleague gleaned from the surveillance camera looking over the drug farm, I learned that Linh was flushing my cows for eggs. The one that was butchered had stopped yielding anything. The calves hadn't been branded, so I used my expert eye to pick them out of the herd. After all, it's not like anyone is going to sue me.'

'How do you know all this?'

'I fronted the vet who was doing the flushing. This is a specialist procedure that not all veterinarians have the skills to carry out. Linh had contracted Fred Stewart to do his dirty work. He also does work for me—well, he did until I found out about his involvement. A professional vet like Stewart should have known to check with me when he saw that someone had altered my brand. Bloody hell. I'll be quietly spreading the word about that bugger. One day, he'll come asking for work and then he'll learn a lesson or two about loyalty and what it means to live in Green River.'

'Interesting. Alan, the last time we spoke, you mentioned that someone in your ranks had let you down. Were you referring to your vet?'

A darkness passed into Campbell's voice. 'No, unfortunately. Far worse. Dick Ainsley was one of my most senior people, and his betrayal has been hard to take. He'd worked for us for ages but was having an affair with one of Daicos's staff. Remember that woman who served us that night we all ate at the pub, Suzanne? Well, I sure wish I hadn't tipped her fifty.'

Ange immediately saw the daisy chain of events. 'So, Linh was only interested in the Green River shire because of Daicos and his pub, which is why he leaned on Kilroy to help locate the cannabis farm in Clearwater. Once Linh tried to emulate your success and become an instant Wagyu cattle baron, he leaned on Daicos, who then leaned on your philandering employee. There sure was a lot of leaning going on.'

'Exactly. And then you come along and tramp all over this snake's nest. Dick should have kept his under control. The Ainsleys lived in the second homestead on Emerald Downs, the one you pass on the main entrance in from the highway. He was perfectly placed to know when we had cattle in the front paddock. Billie and I were gutted when Brian told us what he'd found out. We watched their girls grow up. I even helped with their school fees.'

'What's happened to him?' probed Ange.

'His wife, Leanne, left him as soon as she found out about the affair. I obviously sent him packing. I don't know where he scuttled off to, and I don't care,' explained Campbell, his words tailing off as the depth of his disappointment showed.

'I can imagine how you feel. Being betrayed by someone you trusted is the worst. Believe me, that's the voice of experience talking,' agreed Ange, recalling how Peter Fredericks had screwed her over with his ambition.

'I'm glad there weren't any more surprises from that video feed. I would likely resign as mayor and move to the Gold Coast if any more disappointments came my way.'

'The Gold Coast? Then you'd get a proper lesson in backstabbing. Stay on Emerald Downs and then enjoy your holidays on the Gold Coast without looking too deeply. That's my best advice, and believe me, I've seen the best and the worst of what that place can offer.'

'Now, about Billie's birthday party. It's going to be huge. I expect you, Gus, and that dog of yours to attend. The invitations should be going out next week. If there's any other of your team who should attend, I would love to add them to the list.'

'You definitely need to meet my boss,' replied Ange. 'While I think of it, you may as well throw out those samples we scraped off the trailer that Fin commandeered. Remember, we had to race around collecting them just before a wild storm raced across the property?'

'I guess so. I doubt they would tell us anything that we don't already know. I have Daicos's balls firmly caught in a very tight vice. Billie has been on my case about getting *my shit out of her fridge,* as she put it. Which was a fair assessment given what's in those samples. I'll get around to it sometime,' replied Campbell, suggesting that he wasn't above keeping an insurance policy in place. 'I am pleased that Linh's court case evaporated. That was worrying me after Bennet was murdered. Do you know who did that?'

It was Ange's turn to sound bitter. 'No. That's killing me. It wasn't either Linh or Kilroy. I'll need to get to the bottom of that. Her death may have been an unfortunate outcome of an actual robbery, but it's too coincidental for my comfort. Did I tell you she tried to call me a few days before she was murdered?'

'No. That makes her death even more disturbing. I wonder why she wanted to speak with you—of all people.'

'I know. It's baffling. That missed call has been messing with my head. My investigation precipitated her fall from grace, so she must have hated me for that. Despite everything, I can't help feeling sorry for her.'

'I hear you, Ange. Choose your friends wisely. I guess Julia learned that lesson the hard way. You might not have been in her good books, but you've taken on hero status out here. Billie and Ellie have been plotting around you. You remember Fin's wife, don't you?'

'Of course. Ellie is hard to forget. A force of nature, that woman,' replied Ange, recalling their lively discussion over dinner at Daicos's pub. 'How am I involved?'

'I'll let them fill you in at Billie's party,' Campbell hinted.

'OK. I'm sufficiently intrigued. By the way, assuming the prosecution does a half-decent job, Harry Linh's two grazing properties are likely to come onto the market as proceeds of crime. Would you be looking to buy either of them?'

'I've already had a look. The property in Clearwater doesn't really get me anywhere. I'll keep my focus on properties next to Emerald Downs or Box Grove. The Singleton property is really a trophy asset. I'll leave that to some Sydney hedge fund executive.'

'You're always one step ahead, Alan,' mused Ange. 'Let me know if there's anything else I can do in the meantime.'

'I think you've done more than enough, Ange,' said Campbell simply, before they went their separate ways.

Unfortunately, as often happens in life, this comforting end to her project with Alan Campbell was soon undone.

Later that day, Ange saw that she'd missed a call from an unknown number. The caller had left a message, and Ange checked her voicemail to hear what the caller was chasing her about.

'Hello, Detective Watson. My name is Nina Pelly. I'm a friend of Julia Bennet. Could you call me back, please?'

Ange wasted no time in doing as the caller had wished. 'Hi, Ms Pelly, my name is Ange Watson. You left a message for me to call you back.'

'Thanks for calling, and please call me Nina. I wanted to discuss Julia's death with you. It's being treated as a break-and-enter tragedy, but I believe there's more to her death than the police are giving credit.'

Ange was on the verge of agreeing with Pelly but refrained from doing so. 'Why do you say that?'

'Because Julia confided in me about something only a few days before her death,' replied Pelly, before she broke down in tears.

Ange let Pelly calm down before pressing her to explain. 'Go on.'

'Julia was really upset over the government minister she'd been seeing, Greg Kilroy. He'd promised to leave his wife, but he was just stringing her along. Julia wanted to give him more time, but I said that she was being stupid and that he was a slime. I think that she really had fallen in love with him. Anyhow, during that conversation, Julia said that Kilroy wouldn't dare dump her because of the information she possessed, and it wasn't solely about Kilroy. I reckon that she'd run out of patience and threatened him.'

Brian Edwards was certain Kilroy had an ironclad alibi for the time when Bennet was killed. As satisfying as it might be to drag Kilroy into a murder investigation, Ange knew that she needed some hard evidence to pull any stunt like that. 'Did she elaborate on the information she had?' probed Ange.

'No. But she asked for my advice. I told her she absolutely must do the right thing and let someone know about what was going on. We talked about who she might reach out to if he did the dirty on her, and your name came up. Though Julia didn't like you, she believed you were the only person she knew who would do the right thing and not protect the government. She wanted to give Greg one last chance to leave his wife. That was the last time I saw her. I think I got Julia killed,' sobbed Pelly.

'That's not your fault, Nina. I missed a call from Julia, which must have been just before she died. I tried to call her back, but the call went straight to voicemail. We were likely to be dragged onto opposite sides of a court case, and I assumed it may have been about that. Then I heard that she'd been killed. It was quite a shock for me as well. You need to be careful. Have you told anyone else?'

'No. I wanted to check in case you'd spoken to Julia. It took me a while to track you down,' replied Pelly. 'I'm still in shock over what happened.'

'OK. Whatever you do, don't breathe a word about your last conversation with Julia. I'll keep an eye out and please ring me if you think of anything else. But don't go digging around Julia's death any more than you already have. Is that clear?' said Ange stridently.

'OK. I feel so terrible.'

'Whatever information Julia may have had will surely come to light. Thanks for contacting me,' said Ange.

'Julia was highly driven about her career, and this sometimes got in the way. She was a good friend to me. I'll miss her,' lamented Pelly, before she ended the call.

Ange sat back to think through the consequences of this news. Once again, her perception of Julia Bennet had been upended. She promptly called Sally Anders and updated her on the conversation.

'Boss, I think I'm partly responsible for Julia Bennet's death. I should have taken her call, even when I didn't recognise the number.'

'That's nonsense, Detective. Bennet might have believed she had some mystery info on Kilroy, but we probably already know it,' Anders observed.

'Maybe. It could have been something about the court case, or maybe she was alluding to the conspiracy between Linh, Kilroy, and Daicos. Perhaps she'd gotten wind of Linh's trafficking operation. I can't think what else it could be.'

'Exactly. And all those issues have now been resolved, Ange. We also know that neither of those guys killed her, and she was an attractive woman living on her own. She died from a knife wound, and knives have become the weapon of choice for petty criminals in this country. It seems highly plausible that she's just another unfortunate statistic. My sound advice is that you leave Bennet's death in the hands of the homicide squad.'

Ange remained unconvinced by this notion. 'I guess. But that's two unsolved murders on my watch now. In some ways, Julia Bennet's is even more baffling than Cua Kwm's.'

Sally Anders let out a resigned sigh. 'Whatever, Detective. As if anything I could say would change your mind. Now, I need your support in finalising our charges against Harry Linh. I've interviewed him several times, and he isn't giving me much joy. However, he made one very odd comment during our last discussion.'

'How odd?' asked Ange, thinking that nothing could be odder than an immigrant turned successful pharmacist, turned drug dealer, turned night club and MMA gym owner, turned people trafficker, turned Wagyu beef cattle breeder.

'I mentioned that trafficking young women might not rate highly on the pecking order of inmates and I hoped he had a thick hide. He replied that jail will be the least of his troubles.'

'What do you make of that?'

'I have no idea. I'm guessing he owes someone something. Perhaps his suppliers or someone in Vietnam? I've tried to push him to accept a plea bargain for information that might help us, but he said that it would only make matters worse. When I pressured him to elaborate, he completely clammed up. He hasn't said a useful word since, and I'm stuck talking drivel through his lawyers—who are good, by the way. We'll need to come at him from all angles, Ange.'

'Roger that,' confirmed Ange, enjoying using her latest piece of lingo. 'There certainly are plenty of angles to this case.'

By the time Billy and Bree had finished their tracing and tracking project, they'd outed eighteen registered bidders on the BellBird auction site.

'There are a lot more sickos out there, Ange. Word eventually got out, and the mongrels started covering their tracks. We've traced a few more who'd escaped to Thailand of all places, but the boss reckons we'll be able to get them extradited—eventually,' explained Bree over a coffee with Ange. 'What about all the women who've been trafficked in the past four years—before you became involved?'

'Billy isn't hopeful about tracing payments for anything older than a few months, but I guess he already told you that. Linh was clever enough to launder his crypto through a mixer and scatter it all over the place. That might all change if Interpol can catch up with Madam Linh.'

'Have any other women come forward?'

Ange's face took on a look of resignation. 'Judging by my interview with Cua Kwm, the women will be highly distrustful of police and wary about government officials. I can't say I blame them. I guess we'll have to wait and see, but I'm not hopeful.'

Linh's empire turned out to be paper thin. It collapsed soon after the forensic accountants started poking holes in his affairs. The Pulse had been bleeding money, propped up by Linh's nefarious activities. Worse still was his pastoral enterprise, proving yet again that Linh was no match for Alan Campbell. Linh's gym chain barely turned a profit, only surviving by secretly selling illegal performance-enhancing drugs and the like. Sadly, a couple of high-profile athletes had been identified as customers.

The closure of his cannabis farm and the takedown of Hillburn would have hit Linh hard. This precarious financial position explained why he was so keen to tackle the Green River Shire Council in court. It had always seemed like a risky decision to press on with that, but Ange now realised that Linh simply needed the money. People trafficking might well be the second-most-profitable form of organised crime, but Linh had an expensive machine that needed to keep turning over.

Linh's operation involving an army of mixed martial arts aficionados discreetly selling PEDs and other illicit substances through the Dark Web was quite profitable. However, it ultimately precipitated the downfall of his wobbly empire when the Clearwater cannabis dealer started skimming from his boss. Disaster, and black swans, often arrive from directions unforeseen.

Brian Edwards had furnished an interesting list of people who he'd caught paying a visit to that now infamous side door at The Pulse. Some local government officials, a newsreader, and two high-profile print journalists had been among Linh's patrons. Annoyingly, the journalists had all claimed that they were undertaking research for an expose. Nobody believed this for a moment. However, it was abundantly clear that Linh was using his VIP side door strategically. Sally Anders planned to take the same approach with the names identified on Brian's list.

With past inadequacies laid bare and aided by a not-so-subtle shove in the back from Sally Anders, the feds had become willing allies. Whether this sudden enthusiasm was to make amends or to jump on the bandwagon of success was irrelevant.

As things transpired, Ange's conspiracy theories about endemic corruption within the immigration department proved largely unfounded. With the help of

Billy's amazing video software, they identified two immigration officers who were in Linh's pocket. The scam was ludicrously simple. The two officers would ensure that they were on duty whenever a shipment of women was arriving. Immigration line-ups were chaotic at the best of times, so getting processed through the right booth was child's play.unfounded

Madam Linh disappeared, but Interpol was on her trail. Judy Ly had delivered her video evidence to Sally Anders, who had called in her favour with Interpol. They, like Ange, were convinced that officials were involved, so they were planning to involve the Vietnamese police at the appropriate time. It seemed in everybody's interest to plug both ends of the trafficking conduit, but only time would tell how serious the Vietnamese officialdom might be.

For her efforts, and much to her delight, Sally Anders had offered Judy Ly a job at Major Crimes. Ange was thrilled when Judy shared the news that they would soon be colleagues. The call turned out to be a sweet and sour moment.

'Congratulations, Judy,' said Ange with genuine enthusiasm. Though this news came as a pleasant surprise, she was a little miffed that Anders hadn't confided in her about the offer.

'I'm so excited, Ange. Thanks for putting the idea into Sally's head. I'll be working on juvenile crime. Hopefully, I can do more than push paper this time.'

'I can assure you that the boss is no paper-pusher. If that were the case, she would have moved me on ages ago,' laughed Ange.

'By the way, I stopped off in Singapore to visit Henry Chan on my way home. I never understood why he left so quickly.'

'I know,' added Ange. 'That whole thing about the Chinese Triads still bothers me.'

'About that. I have an explanation of sorts for you.' Judy paused, as if taking a deep breath. 'Apparently, Henry's brother-in-law is a complete tosser. Henry had sponsored him into Australia to attend university. According to Henry, he became too big for his boots and got involved with the Triads dealing narcotics. After he lost a pile of money when he tried his hand at wholesaling, the Triads leaned on Henry to pay off the debts racked up by his brother-in-law. Henry was well known to them after his time in vice. Anyhow, according to Henry, the Triads really are the kingpins of trafficking people out of Asia—and Australia, for that matter. Linh's operation was causing them concerns and keeping a lid on the prices they could charge.'

'So, the Triads forced Henry to be their man on the inside. Clever. Everyone thought that we'd struck a blow against the Triads when we took down Hillburn, when, in fact, we'd all been working for them to get rid of the opposition,' opined Ange.

'Henry reckons that Linh was too obvious and loose for their liking. If we believed that we'd cracked the whole trafficking industry apart, then maybe we might disband and leave the Triads alone for a while. Wallace and his cronies sure took that bait—hook, line, and sinker. Lucky for those women that you didn't.'

'But why did Linh exclusively use Chinese muscle in his trafficking division? He could have used anyone for that job,' asked Ange.

'Henry reckons that they were a smokescreen for misdirection by Linh. The bluffing and double bluffing that was going on still does my head in. Sadly, Henry was complicit in that deception.'

'And that almost worked. Well, it actually *did work* for a while,' reflected Ange. She sat in silence while she processed the implications of Ly's revelations. While it was a clever misdirection that Linh had tried to pull off, the double bluff of the Triads was infinitely more devious. It was ironic that Linh's Chinese muscle had led Ange to his people smuggling operation. She realised in a flash that her crucial breakthrough of tracing Dark Web activity had been part intuition and part dumb luck. She reminded herself for the umpteenth time: where there's smoke, there's usually fire. 'That's all very depressing. It seems like we haven't actually made any progress at all,' she concluded.

'I guess. However, we did rescue sixteen women, six at Hillburn and six in Aratula—not to mention those four poor women being held captive by Linh at The Pulse and being used for the enjoyment of Kilroy and others. We also shut down an active trafficking operation. We should be proud of that, at the very least,' replied Ly, doing her best to stay upbeat after Ange's frank admission.

'Yes, but the flow of victims in and out of the country will continue almost unabated. We barely dented the surface. All we did was beat the B team, which leaves the market wide open for the pros,' replied Ange, now thoroughly dejected. 'The public needs to know about this. I'll bet the average Joe has no idea how big a problem people trafficking is. I'll speak to the boss about it. She avoids press conferences like the plague, but someone needs to yell this story from the rooftops.'

Her relationship with Gus returned to relative normality. He neatly summed up the situation one evening over dinner. 'It's good to have *all of you* back, Ange.'

'I'm sorry that I was so distracted, Gus. It sometimes scares me how obsessed I can become about a case. This one was worse than most, as the fate of those women was so distressing. I couldn't help but think that I could have been one of those women, save for the great good fortune of being born in Australia and in such comfortable circumstances. It's easy to take all that for granted. The events of the past year have shown me that much of life is just plain dumb luck at its core.'

'For someone born in such comfort, as you put it, you certainly do your best to stay out of your comfort zone,' joked Gus before his expression turned serious. 'I really don't mind when you run off on your crusades—I love it, in fact. Just so long as you return. My lonely bachelor life up here on the hill was so, so boring before you threw yourself at me.'

'Very funny,' replied Ange in an exaggerated manner. Her expression and her voice softened as she walked around the table and embraced Gus in a big hug. 'Thanks, Gus. I'm very lucky that you didn't resist.'

'Oh, by the way. Have you been checking that surveillance camera we installed at Angourie?'

'No, I completely forgot about that camera. I had too many others buzzing in front of my eyes,' admitted Ange. 'Anything interesting?'

'Well, not really. Except that the daybed in the corner of our veranda has become a hookup spot for oversexed teenagers. I think I'll need to turn that camera off. I feel like a voyeuristic letch,' commented Gus before his expression became decidedly mischievous. 'However, I was reminded about our last weekend down there, so I hope you're not tired this evening.'

Buddy was another story altogether. He simply would not let Ange out of his sight, clinging like a limpet to her every move. It was comforting to have his company, and she enjoyed being able to stretch her hand down and find him ever ready for a pat or a scratch. He also spent an embarrassing amount of time sniffing her, as if she might have rolled in a dead cane toad and he liked what he smelt. Ange had once read an article about the extreme sense of smell enjoyed by dogs, and that they were being trialled for very early detection of some cancers. Ange's imagination went into overdrive for a day or two and she vowed to get herself checked out during her next GP visit. However, that thought, and most of the thousands of others that whipped through her consciousness each day, fell into obscurity as the realities of people trafficking and the politics of policing kept her busy.

Chapter 50

Football

It was almost four weeks after the takedown of Linh when pressure of a different type came to bear. Ange was surprised by the 6 p.m. news report that broke the story about Cynthia Phelps stepping down as police commissioner. Nathan Bradley, the police minister, found himself in the spotlight when he tried to downplay Phelps' resignation.

'Minister. Sue Elkington from The Times. What do you say to the rumours that the police service had become a political football?'

'My government makes no apology for our hard line on crime and our hands on approach to government. As police minister, it's my job to stay on top of what's going on in our great state of New South Wales,' stated Nathan Bradley forcibly, the stern expression on his face adding further gravitas to his proclamation about nothing.

'But aren't you concerned about the independence of our police service? What would happen if they were called to investigate a government minister, for example?' pressed Elkington.

'Not at all, Sue. That's a rather extreme situation that you've proposed. Cynthia, the former police commissioner, has resigned for personal reasons. There's nothing to see here other than a wonderful servant of the people taking a well-earned breather.'

'So, you're happy to go on the record that the probity and independence of the police service has not been compromised by your government,' pushed Elkington.

'Absolutely. I'm not sure what you're trying to drum up here, Sue. My government stands by its record. If the commissioner has made some errors of judgement, then that's her problem and she'll need to face up to those.'

'Ouch,' thought Ange from the comfort of her couch. 'I'll bet the commissioner is ruing the day she sucked up to that lot.'

Bradley barely drew breath before he switched the topic to the juvenile crime epidemic and made some bold statements about what his government was going to do about it. Ange smelt a rat and rang her boss.

'I just watched the press conference over the resignation of the police commissioner. You didn't play a part in that, did you, boss?' queried Ange.

'You really are a conspiracy theorist, aren't you, Detective?' replied Sally Anders, delivering an answer that neither confirmed nor denied Ange's veiled accusation.

'I'll take that as a yes, then,' concluded Ange with a chuckle.

'Which brings me to another matter,' said Anders, expertly deflecting the direction of conversation. 'The police minister and I are having a press conference next Friday to announce the outcomes of our investigation. I'm also planning to bring some attention to the people trafficking problem. This is all you're doing, Detective. I want you by my side and I won't take no for an answer—in case you were wondering.'

'Boss, you know how much I hate fronting the press. They haven't exactly been kind to me over the past couple of years. Come to think of it, I thought you avoided those things like the plague.'

'You deserve some recognition, Ange. Enjoy it, for once.'

The week leading up to the press conference was excruciating. Ange could barely remember any event less appealing. She slept badly, waking up each morning to a churning stomach. Even the ocean failed to ease her discomfort, and she could not decide whether she wanted Friday to come and go quickly, or never to come at all.

Naturally, Friday did come around, and Ange found herself in front of a massive press gallery, standing beside Sally Anders as the police minister did his thing. The butterflies fluttering in her stomach were insufferable.

'I'm here today with some exciting news and to reiterate our support of the amazing work that our wonderful and brave police service does in protecting our community. Rather than me take any glory, let me hand over to Senior Detective Sally Anders to fill you in,' announced a beaming Nathan Bradley.

Sally Anders took over the microphone and shared a full and graphic account of Ange's investigation, one that started with the discovery of Cua Kwm. 'All in all, we've rescued sixteen young women who'd been trafficked from Vietnam, Thailand, and Cambodia. We also put an end to a well-established trafficking operation. Except for the exceptional work of Detective Angela Watson, who is here by my side, those poor and unfortunate women would have been sold into slavery or prostitution. I'd like everyone here to acknowledge Detective Watson's achievement.'

With that, and in stark contrast to her previous encounters with the press, everyone present stood up and clapped Ange in a long and loud recognition of her efforts. Ange resisted a powerful urge to study her feet, embarrassed at being thrust into the spotlight in that way. She tried to smile and acknowledge her admirers, but it was an epic struggle of will not to crawl under a rug.

Evidently, Sally Anders could see Ange's discomfort and moved the conversation on. 'As a result of the spotlight that Detective Watson has thrown on this despicable trade in human life, the police minister has agreed to devote extra resources here in New South Wales towards stamping out this scourge on society. This is not a problem that can be viewed solely at a national level. Every state needs to play their part, and I'm pleased that New South Wales is stepping up.'

Anders took a moment to gather herself, her piercing expression demanding the full attention of anyone caught in her gaze. 'If there is anyone watching who's been a victim of people trafficking, or you suspect that you might have witnessed something untoward, please come forward. We need your support. You can either contact Detective Watson at Major Crimes or speak with your local police station and they will direct you her way. Now. Any questions?'

It was a brilliant piece of choreography. Ange could hardly resign now that she was the very public face of people trafficking in New South Wales. Equally, those who had been baying for her blood would think twice before coming back for another bite. As various members of the press gallery asked questions, some of which Anders answered and some she avoided, admiration for her boss snapped Ange out of her uncomfortable moment. The rest of the press conference was almost enjoyable.

Once hands had been shaken and platitudes given, the minister left, dragging the press gallery with him. Ange and her boss were already yesterday's news, and the two police officers wandered off to find somewhere nice for lunch. Ange was suddenly ravenous, and they soon found themselves seated in a Korean BBQ restaurant where they had eaten before.

Sally Anders waited until meals had been delivered to their table before she dropped the first of her bombshells. 'The minister has offered me the job of chief superintendent.'

'Wow. Congratulations, boss,' exclaimed Ange, before realising the implications of that news. 'That's Gary Bold's old job. Better watch out, the Ndrangheta might try to enlist you into their ranks. What a turnover. You'd even be in charge of Carruthers and Peter Fredericks. I like that idea. Have you accepted the job?'

'I have not yet accepted his bribe,' replied Anders with narrowed eyes. 'I'm *considering* his kind offer, more to make him sweat than anything else. Anyhow, there are a few things I need to settle before I give him my answer.'

'The way you played the police minister was impressive, boss. You know you'd make a fine commissioner?' suggested Ange in a rhetorical question.

Anders stopped eating and laughed out loud. 'Ange,' she mocked. 'Now you're just being spiteful because I made you the poster girl for people trafficking.'

'Don't laugh, boss. I meant it—in the nicest possible way, of course.' Ange laughed along with her own joke for a moment. 'And placing me on a pedestal like that was quite masterful.'

Anders smiled smugly. 'You liked that move, did you, Detective? I was proud of that idea, even if I say so myself. I'm glad you appreciated it.'

'You really should meet Alan Campbell one day. You two would get on like a house on fire. Actually, leave that with me,' Ange remarked, remembering the upcoming birthday party at Emerald Downs. 'Come on. Fess up. Are you planning to take the job, boss?'

'Probably, but only after I've extracted every pint of blood that the snivelling little twerp has running around in his body,' replied Anders with some conviction.

Ange laughed again. 'I thought you two were besties after that press conference.'

'Bradley will never escape the stranglehold that I have on him. I'm predicting a whole new era of policing in this state. Which brings me to one of my preconditions to accepting Bradley's offer. Assuming that I take the job, I'd like you to consider taking over my role as head of Major Crimes. Don't give me an answer now. I know that you're settled in Byron Bay. I just ask that you give my proposal some thought.'

The kimchi rice that had been working wonders calming her nervous stomach suddenly turned against her and exploded. 'Boss, I really appreciate your faith in me. But I'm not sure that I'm capable of doing your job. That press conference was excruciating. I almost threw up beforehand, and I've been a nervous wreck for the past week, ever since you told me about today. It's not like me. I normally handle pressure quite well.'

Sally Anders looked at her lead detective with compassion. 'Have you spoken to Kirby Hall about it?'

'No. I've just been too preoccupied,' answered Ange. Her nightmares were so vivid, so terrifying, that they inevitably led her thoughts back to her psychiatrist. Kirby's support had been a godsend.

'The type of trauma that you've experienced can manifest itself in all sorts of ways and when you least expect it. Believe me, I know. Promise me you'll make an appointment and visit Kirby—and sooner rather than later, Detective,' replied Anders, using Ange's official title to drive home the point.

'I promise, boss. I'll also give your proposal some thought. How about I get back to you after I've seen Kirby?'

'Excellent. Now, don't leave me hanging, Detective.'

'That's a poor choice of words around me, boss,' laughed Ange.

All things considered, as with most things in life, the day had not been the train wreck that Ange had anticipated in the early hours of the morning. Surprising, for sure—rewarding even—but certainly no train wreck.

Epilogue

Sue Elkington published a massive expose about people trafficking in the weekend edition of The Times. Sue had been conspicuous in her lack of questioning at the press conference. As she read the article, Ange came to realise that there had been no need. Clearly, Sue had an insider in the form of Sally Anders. Elkington's article was incredibly well researched, hard-hitting, and insightful. Even though Ange had been the genesis of that story, she learned a great deal about the flow of trafficked people in and out of Australia. Interestingly, and in no way true to form, Elkington stayed well clear of any accusations against the minister or his colleagues.

Ange rang her boss as soon as she had finished reading the article. 'Sue Elkington seems well informed,' commented Ange offhandedly. 'You wouldn't have helped her out, would you, boss?'

'It's an excellent article, don't you think?' said Sally Anders, another non-answer to Ange's loaded question. 'Sue Elkington is the only journalist in this city I trust to write such a story.'

'I gather that your deal with Elkington was to give her an inside running provided she left the police minister and his cronies to you. You're more politician than you think, boss.'

'You keep on with the insults, don't you, Detective,' replied Anders, a hint of mirth creeping into her tone of voice. 'Have you been to see Kirby yet? I'm still waiting for that answer, Ange, and Bradley is still waiting for mine. You should know me well enough to realise that I won't leave Major Crimes unless I know that the team is in capable hands.'

'I get it, boss. I'm driving up to Tweed Heads to see her Friday. She made me take some blood tests ahead of my appointment. I'm worried that she's going to put me on antidepressants, perhaps even cart me away on the spot.'

'I took them for a month or two after Max passed. Apparently, severe trauma can alter your body chemistry. The drugs that Kirby prescribed brought me back to equilibrium and I haven't needed to use them since—even with all the trauma that you've sent my way. Provided that you listen to what Kirby tells you, I wouldn't worry about a course or two of the correct medication. Let me know how it goes.'

'By the way, Julia Bennet's friend, Nina Pelly, messaged me. She saw the press conference. Between that and Sue's article, I think she's gained some closure. I don't know; it doesn't smell right.'

'You're jumping at shadows, Detective. Now get yourself properly checked out. I need you fit and well.'

Truth be known, Ange was just as keen as Sally Anders to find out what was going on. She was waking up in the early hours all sweaty, then her stomach would start churning, preventing her from getting back to sleep. Nothing seemed to work; even her sleepcasts didn't do the trick. Normally, she would fall asleep within minutes, as the calming monologue of her sleep coaches swept her away. Now she was getting to know their entire stories word for word.

Dr Kirby Hall seemed genuinely pleased to see Ange, which was a nice way to start an appointment with one's psychiatrist.

'Well, Ange, thanks for taking those blood tests. It's pretty clear what's going on with you.'

'Am I officially losing my marbles?' asked Ange, clearly the most obvious answer in her eyes.

'You're pregnant, Ange,' said Hall, all matter-of-fact-like. The look of shock that sprang onto Ange's face was like one of those innumerable scared cat videos on Instagram. 'Didn't you consider this a possibility?' queried Kirby Hall with a wide smile, a question that was more a statement considering Ange's reaction. 'I've made an appointment for an ultrasound. Let's head downstairs now and see what's going on.'

In that instant, Ange's perspective on life turned inside out and upside down. This was one of life's pathways that she'd passed over, a turnoff that she had somehow missed along the way. She barely said a word on their way downstairs and into a small consultation room. The sensation of having cold gel smeared all over her belly was an out-of-body experience. Nothing felt real anymore.

As the sonographer waved her magic wand over Ange's slippery belly, Ange could not make head nor tail of the images that flashed on the screen. A memory came of her peering into her uncle's fish-finder when she was a little girl, searching for quarry during summer holiday fishing trips. She almost expected the sonographer to proclaim that she'd found a gigantic school of baitfish.

'Ah, there we have it,' said the sonographer. She paused and looked directly at Ange. 'Do twins run in your family?'

Such was the double shock that Ange hadn't known whether to laugh for joy or cry in horror. This news, framed as an innocuous question, did nothing to help bring Ange back to reality. 'How long?' she mumbled, the only two coherent words that she could string together.

'I'd say seven to eight weeks,' deduced the sonographer.

Ange didn't need to count back in time to remember when she had fallen pregnant, and images of her weekend with Gus at the Angourie beach shack flooded her mind. The spectacular sex that they had enjoyed that night had broken a long and uncharacteristic drought. She had been so distracted with the intruder and all that had been going on around that weekend that she had missed a few of her daily contraceptive pills. It wasn't the first time that had happened. Ange had always believed it took months to fall pregnant after stopping contraception, especially after being on the pill for over two decades. So much for that old wives' tale.

The drive south back home was a blur. Her mind stayed outside her body and looking down from above. On autopilot, and without thinking, she turned east of the highway towards the Byron Bay Industrial Estate and Gus's factory outlet shop. As soon as she walked in the front door, Buddy came over to give her an extra-big sniff. In a flash of understanding, she realised what was going on with Buddy. He had known before she had.

Despite Ange's most determined attempts to control life's outcomes, Mother Nature remained firmly in charge. All things remained connected as the circle of life worked its magic, and Ange had stood no chance whatsoever against such forces. Gus's position on the matter remained to be seen.

She dragged her feet up the stairs to Gus's office on the mezzanine level. Dread took hold with each additional step. They'd only just started their relationship.

Now Gus had a partner, a dog, and apparently was about to become the father of twins. Pausing outside his office, she took a deep breath before pushing open his door.

Gus stood up and walked around his desk to give her a hug and a kiss. 'This is a pleasant surprise.' His face suddenly darkened with concern as he saw her strained expression. He'd known about her appointment with Kirby Hall and had taken charge of Buddy for the day. 'Are you OK?'

'Don't worry, I'm fine. Well, sort of. Gus...guess what?'

Coming Soon
Stitched Up
The final chapter of The Songbird Tragedies

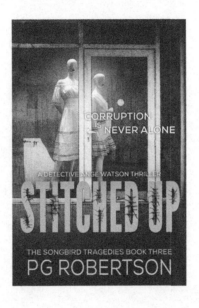

 Scan or click here to join the author's mailing list to stay alert to new releases and hear the latest news:
www.pg-robertson.com

 facebook.com/profile.php?id=100090607141784

 instagram.com/petergrobertson/

 amazon.com/stores/P-G-Robertson/author/B0BY4B55VP?ref=ap_rdr&store_ref=ap_rdr&isDramIntegrated=true&shoppingPortalEnabled=true

Now read the beginning of Stitched Up...

The woman had long since sized up her captors: big, loud, and overconfident—classic amateurs. Their bluster didn't fool her. She had been watching them for weeks, noticing their careless mistakes. They were easily distracted—boredom, fatigue, or hangovers always left them vulnerable. The reek of stale cigarette smoke and booze was a dead giveaway of their habitual late-night excess.

Back home, she'd have called men like these goondas, a term for the rough-edged enforcers who prowled the margins of society. But the comparison felt generous. True goondas were sharp, their skill forged in the furnace of necessity as they clambered over the multitudes. These men, by contrast, were lazy imitators, their tough-guy act undone by a comfortable life.

She had been biding her time, waiting for their complacency to open the door for her. The plan was simple—just slip away during their nightly routine. It was always the same: one captor would count the prisoners with a mechanical clicker, like a cricket umpire, while the other herded them onto a bus for transport to the dormitory-turned-prison. She'd chosen her hiding spot carefully and waited for days, biding her time for the perfect opportunity.

That moment came out of the blue, just after she'd been clicked off. It was the height of the rugby league season, and her two pretend goondas were massive fans. Australia's Penrith Panthers were playing the New Zealand Warriors, and the game was crucial, both teams jousting to sit atop the league table. Even though the woman knew none of this, she could sense the intensity of the occasion and the rivalry between the two men.

She heard their shouts, one of victory and one of despair. Something monumental was happening. She didn't hesitate. Her feet moved on instinct, slipping out of line and ducking behind a rusted metal dumpster, heart pounding as she crouched in its shadow. Even the other prisoners seemed transfixed by the commotion, none of them noticing her escape. For a moment, she dared not breathe.

The line shuffled forward, and soon the building was plunged into darkness. From her hiding spot, she heard the exit door clang shut; the sound reverberating through the empty building. She waited, straining her ears in the stillness, until she was certain no one remained. Only then did she unfold herself from the cramped hiding place, her muscles stiff and aching. The dim glow of emergency lights painted faint shadows across the walls, but the silence reassured her. She was alone.

Time was her enemy now. She rummaged through a nearby bin, finding a partially finished hooded jacket that would protect her from winter's chill. Tugging it on, she made her way to the fire exit. The cold air hit her like a slap as she stepped outside, stinging her cheeks and bringing tears to her eyes. She had no idea where she was or how far she'd need to run, but she knew one thing: she couldn't stay here.

Pulling the hood low over her face, she picked a direction and started walking. She had no map, no plan, and no allies. The only goal was distance—any distance at all. Whatever waited for her out there had to be better than what she'd left behind.

Catch up on the first volume in The Songbird Tragedies.

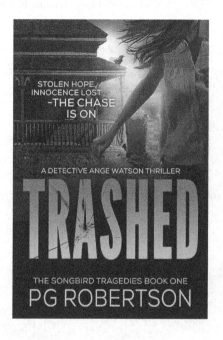

 Scan or click here to buy Trashed on Amazon: https://www.pg-robertson.com/trashed

 facebook.com/profile.php?id=100090607141784

 instagram.com/petergrobertson/

amazon.com/stores/P-G-Robertson/author/B0BY4B55VP?ref=ap_rdr&store_ref=ap_rdr&isDramIntegrated=true&shoppingPortalEnabled=true

Start at the very beginning with The Saltwater Crimes Trilogy.

Join Ange as she hunts a sophisticated criminal syndicate operating along Australia's rugged coastline.

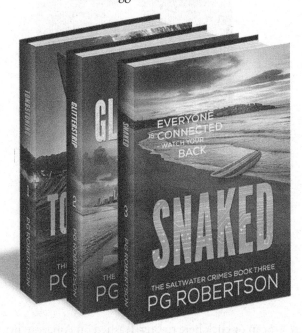

Scan or click here to buy The Saltwater Crimes boxset on Amazon:
https://www.pg-robertson.com/the-saltwater-crimes-boxset

Scan or click here to see the individual books in The Detective Ange Watson thrillers: **www.pg-robertson.com/books**

Author's Note

The characters in this book are entirely fictional. I have created them from good friends, work colleagues, acquaintances, strangers I've encountered, some people that I've met in the surf, and others that are purely imaginary. Likewise, except for any household names, the companies, and enterprises that underpin the plot are figments of my imagination and similarly fictional. My heroine, Detective Ange Watson, is a mixture of close friends—some who surf and some who do not. I trust you have grown to like Ange as much as I like my friends.

Places like Byron Bay, Texas QLD, Warwick, Tamworth, Sydney, and Brisbane are real. Namba Heads is a purely fictional town but is based on the iconic coastal villages in the Northern Rivers region of New South Wales, Australia. Clearwater and Hillburn are similarly fictional, but have their roots in the many small country towns found just west of The Great Dividing Range. I hope my writing has done justice to these spectacular places.

Even though the storyline is purely fictional, the idea behind the plot theme came from a trip to Vietnam with my family. We were trekking in the hills near the China-Vietnam border. Our guide was a delightful and enterprising young Hmong woman who told us about the perils faced by young woman growing up in that remote rural region. The impact of her astonishing stories stayed with me, making them a compelling subject to write about and the perfect crusade for Ange.

So Many to Thank

Thank you for reading Green River. I hope you enjoyed the journey and the slight change of scenery. Spending your precious time reading my books is incredibly gratifying for me. I hope you are looking forward to reading Stitched Up, the final chapter of The Songbird Tragedies.

Of utmost important, is the need to thank all those who gave me the encouragement to push on and write a second series. I probably should list you all individually, but the list is long and I risk missing someone important! Hopefully, I have already told you in person how much your support has meant to me. I cannot thank you all enough.

The Island Book Club always deserves a special mention. I will forever remember the scene of our inaugural book club meeting, sitting on the beach in our camp chairs one glorious afternoon, champagne in hand and laughter in our hearts.

I am also grateful for my 'media team', Sophie and Ben Hall, whose skills and comfort with new media amaze me. I must also thank my editor, Eliza Dee, and my cover designer, Karri Klawiter, for their dedication and forbearance in enduring my many and continued rookie errors.

Finally, if you have a spare minute, I would appreciate you posting a review of Green River on Amazon via your purchase history.

Glossary and Surfing Terminology

A brief description of some surfing terminology follows:

'Tombstoning' occurs when a surfer is held under the water by a wave following a heavy wipeout. Whilst the surfer is being dragged deep beneath the water, their surfboard is straining on the surface, connected as they are by a fully stretched leg rope. An obvious metaphor for a perilous situation, tombstoning is never a good sign and rarely fun for the surfer, although bystanders or fellow surfers will invariably find it all most amusing after the fact.

A **'left-hander'** is a wave that breaks to the surfer's left. That is, as the surfer catches the wave, he or she will turn to the left. Obviously, a **'right-hander'** breaks to the surfer's right.

A **'goofy-footer'** is someone who surfs with the right foot forward, and a **'natural'** is someone who leads with their left foot. The decision to choose one side or another is instinctual and set for life.

Surfing **'forehand'** indicates that a surfer is facing the wave face, **'backhand'** is the reverse. Most surfers find surfing forehand easier, particularly in steep demanding waves. Hence, a 'right-hander' favours a 'natural', and a 'left-hander' best suits their 'goofy-footed' cousins.

The **'line-up'** is the term used for the queuing area where the waves start breaking.

'Out the back' means the smooth clear water beyond any breaking waves. It offers a zone of calm where a surfer can sit up on their board to take a breather and enjoy their surroundings—well, until the next ride rolls in.

The **'peak'** of a wave is a term commonly used for beach breaks. It defines the apex of the wave face. Once perfectly positioned at the 'peak' of a wave, a surfer can choose to go left or right. The other descriptor for perfect beach breaks is 'A-frames', but these dreamy situations are disappointingly rare.

A **'rip'** is where seawater, carried in by the crashing waves, combines into a channel and rushes back out to sea. Dangerous for swimmers, they can be a godsend for surfers to help ease a long and tiring paddle.

Being **'inside'** means the surfer is the one closest to the breaking point of the wave, which is the surfer who is farthest inside on the line-up. On a headland or reef break, this would be closest to the rocks or reef, and inevitably the most ambitious take-off point. The surfer sitting farthest 'inside' technically has a right of way, a case of fortune favouring the brave. It does not always work that way, with **'drop-ins'** being the scourge of surfers around the world, usually spoiling the wave and often dangerous to all concerned.

Jostling for the premier position at the take-off zone is part strategy, part bravado, and part aggression. Called **'hassling'**, this can easily spiral out of control, and fights in and out of the surf are not uncommon in crowded surf breaks, and where localism is rife. **'Dropping in'** on an aggressive local will usually end badly. The old way to surf was to take turns. As the 'inside' surfer departed on their wave, the next would slide across and assume the vacated spot in the line-up, gaining rights to the next wave, and so on. This type of surf etiquette is now relegated to isolated or sparsely populated breaks.

A **'grommet'** is surfer slang for a young school-aged surfer, a term usually reserved for those with talent, their lightness, speed, and flexibility sometimes grating on the older surfers around them.

The **'rail'** on a surfboard is the outside edge, the shape and taper of which are critical in how a board performs.

'Longboards' and **'shortboards'** create quite different surfing styles and favour different wave formations. Longboards typically range from eight to eleven feet, or 2.5 to 3.3 metres. Shortboards are under seven feet, or 2.1 metres. The weight of a surfer will often dictate the type of board they choose, and the division between a longboard and a shortboard has blurred over time.

The number of fins on a board varies depending on the style of board. **'Single fins'** are mostly reserved for longboards or surfers wanting a traditional style. The original surfboards were all single fins. **'Twin fins'** are highly manoeuvrable, usually earmarked for small wave boards. A **'thruster'** sports three fins and is the most popular and versatile configuration for shortboards. **'Quads'** have four fins and sit somewhere between a twin fin and a thruster in terms of functionality.

A **'quiver'** is simply a collection of surfboards used by a surfer, as in a 'quiver of arrows' used by an archer.

Finally, a **'tube ride'** is when the surfer positions themselves within the curl of the wave, precariously covered over by the breaking lip, but remaining relatively untouched within the eye of the storm—so to speak. It's the most exhilarating of all surf manoeuvres, and waves that are 'tubing' are highly prized, yet relatively rare. Surf spots that regularly produce tube rides are usually very popular, difficult to travel to, or jealously guarded secrets.

Australian-isms

For the benefit of non-Australian readers, below is a short explanation of some idioms that I have used on occasion:

'Backhander'. Bribe or kickback, traditionally delivered in a fabled brown-paper bag and usually associated with corrupt officials.

'Bad egg'. Someone who is rotten to the core.

'Berko'. Going crazy mad, angry and out of control. The Tasmanian devil goes berko if cornered while eating their dinner.

'Billy'. Not to be confused with the amazing Constable Billy Bassett, a billy in the context of camping refers to a large metal bucket with a wire handle. Used to boil water on a campfire, a 'billy' is usually blackened, dented, and an essential item for any worthwhile camping trip.

'Buggered, stuffed, screwed, rooted'—you get the drift.

'Bushie'. Someone who lives in the country, most commonly on a rural farm/property/station, and well away from any major towns or cities. In general terms, one's degree of 'bushie-ness' is also directly proportional to the distance one lives from the coast.

'Curly request or question'. Refers to a difficult request or loaded question.

'Cadet'. Serving as a cadet is like work-experience for the armed services. Many of the more established secondary schools in Australia have an armed service cadet program for students.

'Camp oven.' A large cast-iron pot complete with a heavy cast-iron lid, otherwise referred to as a 'dutch oven'. Some campers are highly skilled at cooking with their camp ovens. Sadly, our method of camp oven cooking involves piling in a mixture of meat, vegetables, and stock, placing it on some hot coals, and then sitting back to enjoy a glass of wine.

'Chambers'. In Commonwealth countries, barristers are sole practitioners whose expertise relates to fighting court cases. A barrister's 'chambers' are essentially offices that provide a way for barristers to share overhead expenses without being part of the same 'firm' or directly sharing revenue. Barristers receive instructions from legal firms, which are comparable to American lawyers.

'Deckie'. A shortened name given to the deckhand working on a fishing trawler.

'Donger'. Slang for a small relocatable building ubiquitous in mining camps and on construction sites. Dongers are commonly used for temporary offices, sleeping accommodation, kitchens, ablution blocks, and the like.

'Feeling crook'. Feeling sick or unwell.

'Firey'. Slang for a firefighter.

'Gazumped'. When an Aussie says gazumped, they mean someone snatched something that was practically theirs, leaving them feeling cheated. The term originally comes from the real estate industry, where it describes the frustrating situation of having a deal seemingly finalised, only to find another buyer has swooped in behind your back and clinched the deal at a higher price. Being gazumped is not a good feeling.

'Hammer and tongs'. A reference to a blacksmith beating a lump of red-hot metal. It means approaching something with great vigour or vehemence.

'Hospital pass'. A rugby term which suggests that the recipient of a football pass is about to be crunched by a defender or two.

'Jackeroo'. The term used for a young man who is working on a sheep or cattle station as an apprentice of sorts. A jackaroo can also describe a spit-roasted kangaroo used for food, which I guess explains the day-to-day life of a Jackaroo, the person.

'Jillaroo'. The female equivalent of a Jackaroo.

'Kangaroo court'. An impromptu or unofficial court used to try someone without due process or evidence—a stitch-up, in other words.

'Larrikin'. Part rogue, part joker. The sort of person to enjoy a beer at the pub with, but not someone to risk with the family jewels. Larrikin is often used to describe the affable kookaburra, one of the coolest and most personable birds in Australia, also a ruthless killer of small birds and animals.

'Nong'. An idiot or fool, a term used endearingly and in jest toward a friend or loved one.

'A park'. A park can refer to either a park with grass and trees, or a single parking place for a car. Go figure!

'Public school'. Public schools in Australia and the US are open to all children and largely free, while private schools require payment of tuition fees. However, in a strange twist, English public schools are independent fee-paying schools, including elite institutions such as Eton College and Harrow.

'Rich tea biscuits'. A plain biscuit that is, as its name implies, a popular companion to a cup of tea. They are not just tasty, but importantly, hold their shape when 'dunked' into hot tea.

'Roached'. Has its roots from the word cockroach. Being roached normally refers to the situation where someone has scuttled behind your back to do no good.

'Roo'. Shortened nickname for a kangaroo.

'Ropable'. Angry and in a bad temper.

'Rort'. Another word for scam or con.

'Silk'. As senior counsel traditionally wore silk rather than the wool gowns worn by junior barristers, becoming a QC or KC is sometimes referred to as 'taking silk,' and the KCs themselves as silk barristers, or simply silks.

'Seachange & Greenchange'. Seachangers leave their lives in the city and move to the coast. Greenchangers move to the country.

'Smoko'. A remnant from the time when most everyone in the country smoked. It now refers to morning or afternoon tea.

'Spit the dummy'. A dummy, in Australian vernacular, is also known as a pacifier. When a baby is about to throw a tantrum, their face will turn sour before they spit out their dummy and go berko. It's a wonderfully descriptive phrase—part facial expression, part change of mood, part warning for the carnage about to be unleashed.

'Spruiker'. Someone who tries to sell their theories or hustle up business with their fast-talking. A person using a public address system outside a shopfront to attract customers is known as a 'spruiker'.

'Star Chamber'. The original Star Chamber was a court in 15th century

England. In Australia, it is often used to describe a secret hearing where the right to silence has been removed by legislation. Essentially, one must answer all questions and refrain from ever mentioning the proceedings. The very concept of a Star Chamber does not sit well with the average Australian.

'Stunned mullet'. Refers to someone who is in a form of temporary shock. An actual stunned mullet will be floating helplessly on the surface and unable to swim away.

'Watchhouse'. The name given to a small prison or holding cell in a police station where people under temporary arrest are kept.

'Whinger.' Someone who complains a lot, an approach to life that Australians have little time for. Sadly, whingers, in all their forms, seem to be on the ascendency.

'Willies up'. Slang for the jitters or a bout of extreme nervousness.

'Woop Woop'. A mythical town that sits beyond the black stump and a long way from anywhere. The town of Woop Woop is not mentioned in any Lonely Planet guides.

Made in United States
Orlando, FL
13 December 2024